BEFORE

HE

FINDS

HER

Also by Michael Kardos

The Three-Day Affair
One Last Good Time: Stories
The Art and Craft of Fiction: A Writer's Guide

BEFORE

HE

FINDS

HER

MICHAEL KARDOS

31652002888049

The Mysterious Press
New York

Published simultaneously in Canada
Printed in the United States of America

FIRST EDITION

ISBN 978-0-8021-2319-0
eISBN 978-0-8021-9161-8

The Mysterious Press
an imprint of Grove/Atlantic, Inc.
154 West 14th Street
New York, NY 10011

Distributed by Publishers Group West

www.groveatlantic.com

15 16 17   10 9 8 7 6 5 4 3 2 1

for Katie

It was the truths that made the people grotesques . . . It was his notion that the moment one of the people took one of the truths to himself, called it his truth, and tried to live his life by it, he became a grotesque and the truth he embraced became a falsehood.
—Sherwood Anderson, *Winesburg, Ohio*

It's the end of the world as we know it (and I feel fine).
—R.E.M.

PART ONE

1

My White Whale, Set Free

*September 22, 2006 * by Arthur Goodale * in Uncategorized*

Three weeks since my last entry, and I don't know if I'll be writing again any time soon. So please forgive me for today's lack of brevity.

Anyone who's followed this blog for any amount of time knows the premium I place on honesty and candor. So here's my disclosure: I'm writing today from a hospital bed in the critical care unit at Monmouth Regional Hospital. Last Sunday—all day, apparently—I was suffering from congestive heart failure. But who knew? Look, I'm a smoker and always have been. (Readers of this blog know all about my <u>failed attempts to quit</u>). For years, decades, I've awaited the numb left arm, tightening in the chest, those unambiguous precursors to a fast demise, or at least a stagger to the telephone before collapsing, maybe bringing down the living room curtains on top of me. Something dramatic. But mild back pain?

I had spent most of that day bent over the garden, pulling weeds and tying a few droopy tomato vines to their stakes in the hopes of keeping my plants productive until the first hard frost. Why wouldn't my back be aching? In the past, my cure was always three Advil and a couple of James Bond flicks on the TV while I lounged on the recliner. So that's how I treated my symptoms this time—with international intrigue and soothing British accents. And a couple of vodka martinis.

When Tuesday afternoon rolled around and the pain was no better, I called my doc. He said come in. I came in. Now I'm here in the hospital, where I'm told I might not leave.

Maybe if I had swallowed a couple of aspirin instead of those Advil, the attending cardiologist tells me. Maybe if I had driven straight to the hospital or dialed 911 instead of waiting two days. But why would I have done any of those things? That's not what you do when you're an old fool with a back sore from overdoing it in the vegetable garden. You don't dial 911. You watch television. You take a nap.

Who will pick my last tomatoes?

I'll stop being macabre. You deserve better than that. And there *are* some of you—both here in New Jersey and beyond. Last month this blog had 2,300 views, about 75 per day. I can hardly imagine 75 people being interested in my musings, but you're real, my readers, and apparently you're from all across the country and as far away as Vietnam and Australia. I'm constantly amazed. Such a contrast from my newspaper days, with its ceaseless and frantic scramble to increase paid circulation—that is, before we became a free paper in order to focus on ad revenue, and before we gave *that* scheme up and sold out to Kingswood Holdings, Inc.

So, my 75 loyal followers, please know that I'm deeply grateful to you for reading my postings these past three years and for sticking with me through my frequent meanderings and digressions. Despite my abiding respect for the strict conventions of newspaper writing, I've come to derive deep satisfaction and enjoyment from maintaining this blog, where word limits don't matter, where impartiality is besides the point, and where I may freely indulge in conjecture, parentheticals, and serial commas.

For obvious reasons, I hope this won't be my last post. But if it is, it is. I'm 81, a ripe age by any measure. I suppose that no age ever feels old enough, but with my daily cigarettes (a habit I picked up almost *seventy* years ago) and, with the exception of my own tomatoes, the takeout-menu-diet of a lifelong bachelor, I know I'm lucky to have made it this far. I don't regret never marrying or having children. If I had met the right woman and passed up the opportunity to spend my life with her, I'd feel different. Maybe it was the long hours on the job, or maybe it was my comically long nose. Regardless of the cause of my lived-alone life, the fortuitous effect is that my departure, when it happens, will be met with the sadness of quite a few, but the genuine grief of none.

Was I married to my work? This cliché might be true. If so, I ask that you don't pity the relationship. It was a strong marriage. I have loved being a newspaperman—publisher and editor and, above all, reporter. I can recall no better feeling than those moments when I was in thrall to a story that finally snapped together—the facts, and my particular way of telling them. Better than striking oil, I tell you.

What a shame that this time-honored industry is rapidly vanishing and becoming overrun by ideologues and illiterates. Our democracy requires better. But this is a problem for younger minds than mine to solve.

The title of today's post alludes, of course, to the unattainable object of Captain Ahab's obsession. This morning, a young male nurse entered my hospital room to check my vitals and the wounds in my chest and leg. (I had bypass graft surgery on Wednesday morning.) I asked this nurse what day it was, and he said, Friday, September 22. I told him that today was the fifteen-year anniversary of the Miller killings.

"The what?" he asked.

I was taken aback, though I shouldn't have been. The young man would have been a child when the murders took place. Still, Silver Bay is a peaceful town, even today, and the crime had been a major story in the news for weeks. I told him so.

"I guess maybe it sounds a little familiar," he said, having the sense to be kind to his loony, dying patients.

Faithful readers of this blog know that the Miller case is my white whale. In all the years I have lived in this town, there have been only five homicides. One man dialed 911 himself within hours and turned himself in. Three times, the men (they were all men) were booked within a couple of weeks and pled guilty to lighten their sentences. Ramsey Miller is the only accused who got away.

I lived—live—just one neighborhood away from where the Millers once did, and I was on the scene that morning only minutes after hearing the blaring of the first-response vehicles. I drove my car the few blocks to Blossom Drive and witnessed the aftermath of a terrible event, one that I've never fully been able to get past.

It shook us all. A couple of days after, I remember ordering my cup of coffee and plate of eggs at the Good Times Diner, same as every morning, and the waitress (Tracy Strickland, who always wore a "kiss my bass" pin on her waitress uniform) sat in the booth across from me, placed her elbows on the table, cupped her head in her hands, and wept. She was about Allison's age. I didn't pry. But you see, Silver Bay is a small community, and Allison Miller was the sort of woman you couldn't help admiring, and Meg was a girl just shy of three who deserved to grow up.

A couple of months earlier, while shopping in the Pathmark one afternoon, I happened to find myself in the same aisle as Allison and Meg. Allison, pushing a full shopping cart, was following her daughter, who was running in my direction and calling out the colors of the floor tiles. Finding herself beside me, Meg tugged the leg of my slacks, and commanded: "Pick me up!"

I hadn't held a small child for many years, maybe even de-cades—not since my niece and nephew were small.

"Up!" the girl repeated.

"You'd better do it," her mother said.

I lifted the girl—she was amazingly light—and for thirty seconds, maybe a minute, I held her, breathing in the smell of baby shampoo, while her mother hastily pulled items from the shelf and placed them into her cart. Meg seemed content to be held, watching her mother.

"Thank you, Arthur," Allison said, taking back her daughter and flashing a smile.

We had introduced ourselves not long before, while waiting together at the dentist's office. I hadn't expected Allison to remember my name or who I was, and now I didn't know what to say. Despite the countless interviews I've conducted, I've never been much good at small talk—especially with someone who was, even when harried in the supermarket, a knockout. So I nodded, maybe mumbled something. She coaxed her daughter back to sitting in the shopping cart and rounded the end of the aisle. I finished my shopping and paid. When I went outside, Allison was loading bags into her car. Meg was in the cart, kicking her legs. I considered strolling over and saying something neighborly. But it was late after-noon, and the sun was making this pretty image of the two of them—mother and daughter—and I decided not to ruin the tableau.

I never saw either of them again.

From time to time, when it seemed appropriate, I have posted pertinent public documents about the case, notable media coverage, and my own musings (here, here, here, and here, and less articulately in perhaps a dozen other posts). If you are a new reader of this blog (unfortunate timing, if so), here is a brief summary:

On Sunday afternoon and evening of September 22, 1991, the Miller family hosted an outdoor block party. As many as fifty people were in attendance over the course of several hours. The party ended around 9 p.m. Sometime later that night, after the guests were gone, an inebriated Ramsey brutally murdered his wife, Allison. (I won't rehash those details; the curious can read about it here.) The next day, authorities found her body in the backyard and began a search for Ramsey and their young daughter. Two witnesses placed Ramsey at the Silver Bay Boatyard the night before, around 10 p.m., and one of them saw him board his motorboat carrying a bundle the size and shape of a small child. Neither Ramsey nor Meg was ever seen again. The boat was never found. The prevailing theory—the correct one, in my view—is that Ramsey took the boat out to sea and threw his daughter overboard, either alive or already dead.

Because of the condition of Allison Miller's body when it was found, the time of death can only be estimated, and some experts disagree on which came first, the murder or the boat ride. The order matters when trying to create a chain of causality. Had Ramsey planned to commit both murders? Or did one horrible deed make the other, after it was committed, seem unavoidable?

(Writing this, I feel nauseated all over again. Apparently it's possible to feel ill on top of already being critically ill.)

I don't believe the case will ever be solved. Scratch that. As far as I'm concerned, the case was solved long ago: Ramsey committed two murders and fled. So what I mean is, I don't believe there will ever be sufficient answers that might get to the heart of what happened, and why. Nor do I believe that Ramsey's whereabouts, assuming he's still alive, will ever be known—especially now that Detective Esposito, who worked the case diligently and always had the good grace to return my phone calls, has retired to South Carolina, where the weather is better and the golf plentiful. He has earned his retirement, and I suspect he's making the most of it. Unlike the bitter and lonely protagonists of many detective novels, Danny always planned to spend his golden years on the fairways with his lovely wife, Susan. He knows better than to waste his time on a sad, frustrating, and hopelessly cold case.

It really is the strangest case.

If there was a motive, no one could ever uncover it. The family had no history of violence. Ramsey was, as far as anyone knew, a devoted husband and father. His run-ins with the law were long behind him. There isn't even a satisfactory explanation for the party that preceded the murders. Most news reports claim it was to celebrate Ramsey's 35th birthday, but that wasn't for another week. Others claim it was simply a block party—but the neighborhood never had one before, and the Millers apparently footed the whole bill. Was the party yet another part of Ramsey's elaborate plot? And then there's the mysterious fact of Ramsey's big rig, which he inexplicably sold the Friday before the murders. The truck was his livelihood. Why would he sell it?

Some in the community hold on to the hope that after Allison's murder, the little girl was kidnapped by her father and spared. That maybe she's still alive somewhere. I understand why people would choose to believe that, preferring to avoid thinking the unthinkable. But I've never believed in fantasies and refuse to start now. The man who just murdered his wife did not then motor out to sea to go stargazing with his young daughter before disappearing with her. It didn't happen that way.

The unthinkable is what happened.

Can I prove it? Not without the little girl's body, which is never going to be found. You can't dredge an ocean. But everything about this case has felt like dredging an ocean. Violent as it was, the crime was small-town. Ramsey Miller was no mastermind. Why did he do it? How did he vanish? The not-knowing has kept me awake for more nights than I care to recall. Only recently have I begun to admit to myself that the absence of proof is, in this case, a permanent condition—or at least a condition that will outlive me.

It helps to remind myself that supplying proof is the problem for a district attorney or maybe a newspaperman, and I haven't been a newspaperman for years. I'm simply a blogger and an old man who, approaching his own big sleep, feels done with all the hedging and the caveats and deigns to tell the plain truth.

So here it is: 15 years ago on this day there was a party, two murders, and a boat ride. Other than that, I know not one damn thing and never will.

My doctors are demanding that I rest, not type. I need to focus on my health, but they're asking me the sort of questions that lead me to conclude that "my health" is a euphemism for "my death." Which means that the time has come for me to close the laptop and bequeath my white whale to some younger, cleverer sea captain.

Bon Voyage,
Arthur Goodale

P.S. Please forgive me for disabling the "comments" feature on this particular post. Should these be my last written words, I'd prefer they not be followed by off-topic political sniping.

Posted by Old Man with Typewriter at 9/22/2006 2:23 PM | Comments are disabled.

2

September 22, 2006

Melanie Denison—for that was her name now—had ruined breakfast.

Otherwise, it was an ideal fall morning. There was no better time of year in Fredonia, West Virginia, everything still growing and sweet smelling, one last push before the first hard frost.

Her uncle Wayne stood by the window overlooking the back-yard garden, where tomatoes and peppers clung to worn stalks. "You know I love you," he said, turning to face her, "but what you're doing . . ."

Most mornings, one of them would say grace and then they would eat together as a family. Then Melanie would clean the dishes, Kendra would shower and dress for work, and Wayne would go outside to weed or cut the grass or spray dirt off the trailer's vinyl siding with his power washer—anything to be outdoors for a few minutes before driving to the Lube & More in Monroeville to work underneath cars for eight hours.

"You really don't have to worry," Melanie said. "I'm being careful."

"I don't doubt that, honey," he said. "But you have to see it's still dangerous."

Maybe. But the fact was, she was nearly eighteen. And the family's rules, in place for so long, were becoming harder than ever to abide.

You go straight to school. When school is done, you come straight home.

In high school, she could understand. But last Tuesday she'd stayed on campus at the community college to get lunch with some fellow freshmen. A couple of days later, she'd driven alone to the JC Penney in Reynoldsville to find jeans that fit her better. She actually had to convince herself that these weren't major transgressions.

"It's just that a *newspaper*, of all things," her aunt said.

Melanie didn't like keeping secrets from them. She had told them about joining the staff of the college paper as a way of testing the waters: see how they react, then decide what else they could know.

Well, they were flunking the test royally. Melanie set the glasses of juice on the table and asked her aunt, "What do you mean, 'of all things'?"

But she knew. She was a seasoned pro at imagining how her father might find her even after all these years.

Her aunt and uncle? Also pros.

"Does the paper have a website?" Uncle Wayne asked.

"I don't think so," Melanie said—though of course it did.

"Still," he said, "your picture could end up on the Internet."

It all sounded so paranoid, it was easy to forget that her aunt and uncle hadn't chosen to live like this, hidden away in a remote hamlet in West Virginia. But the U.S. Marshals had determined that this was best place for them all to "relocate," which meant to hide. Which was why, at seventeen, Melanie had never been to a city, had never stayed in a hotel or traveled farther than Glendale for its music and hot-air ballooning festival. She'd never ridden in an airplane or seen the ocean. Never met a famous person. She had hiked in the Allegheny Mountains but had never eaten sushi or a fresh bagel. She had twice seen tornados funneling in the distance but had never attended a dance or a football game.

Whenever she felt herself becoming too critical of her aunt and uncle, she would wait until she was alone in the house, open her uncle's desk drawer, and read through the horrible letters from the U.S. Marshal's office that he kept hidden there—letters she'd first come across innocently enough years earlier while rummaging for a pencil. The letters were horrible because they were uniformly brief, never more than a paragraph or two, and because they said nothing. Or, rather, they said the same thing again and again, which was the same as saying nothing. Ramsey Miller continued to elude the authorities; the authorities continued to fear for Melanie's safety. The letters were horrible, too, because they were crisp and clean and on nice paper (she pictured a tidy but bustling office where the employees joked with one another and talked about football games and their plans for the weekend), and they were horrible because of their consistently optimistic tone, despite there never being any real cause for optimism. She would return the letters to the manila file in the bottom desk drawer and remind herself not to depend on some hero in a police uniform ever coming to their rescue. Not after fifteen years. No, the only heroes were her aunt and uncle and the sacrifices they had made to keep her safe. But that didn't make it easy.

At least they were okay to be around. In winter, they played board games. They played cards. In spring, Melanie helped Wayne turn over the soil and plant the seedlings. Kendra bought cheap paperbacks from the CVS, and at sunup the two of them would carry their juice or coffee and whatever books they were reading out back, where they'd sit in adjacent chaise lounges, their privacy protected by the high hedges that surrounded their property, and by the woods beyond. Maybe once a month, as a treat, they ate at Lucky's Grill—always a weeknight at 4:30 p.m., when the place was mostly empty.

Her aunt homeschooled her through the eleventh grade, at which point Kendra admitted that she'd reached her limit as a teacher. So, frightened but excited by the idea of being away from 9 Notress Pass for seven hours each day, the next fall Melanie stepped onto the groaning yellow school bus each morning and afternoon, sitting either alone or next to Rudy, an autistic boy who pressed his nose against the window and said nothing. She didn't join any extracurricular activities. Didn't attend games. She went to school, ate alone in the cafeteria, and came home.

Still, that uneventful high school year had been a morsel of freedom, and now she found herself wanting more. After all, she couldn't stay shut inside the trailer forever, could she? If she were to die of natural causes at the age of ninety-five, having never seen or done a single thing, what kind of victory would that be?

Many of Melanie's high school classmates were bound for West Virginia University. They wore Mountaineer T-shirts and talked about how "we" were doing in various sports, as if they were already gone. Melanie made one weak attempt to convince her aunt and uncle that being one of 25,000 students would make her inconspicuous. She let herself fantasize a little about living in a dorm, going to football games, meeting boys. Making friends.

That TV show *Friends* had been on her whole life, it seemed, and she was always amazed by the smugness with which those six New Yorkers lazed in a coffee shop and took their banter-filled friendships and their freedom totally for granted. She let herself wonder if maybe college would be like that.

But college to her aunt and uncle meant student directories, ID cards, a wide-open campus where anyone could find her, follow her, do terrible things. In the end, they compromised. She could attend—part time—Mountain Community College, twenty miles up the road. She'd live at home and take a course or two at a time. Wayne would find her a used car and teach her to drive it. To help pay her way, she'd look for part-time work somewhere in Fredonia.

She accepted their best and only offer. If she couldn't be a Mountaineer, then she would be a Fighting Soybean.

"I don't understand your sudden interest in journalism, anyway," Wayne said, pulling himself away from the window. He uncapped a can of Folgers and spooned heaping tablespoons of grounds into the filter. He poured water into the machine and turned it on.

"It isn't sudden," she said. "I just think it's interesting."

"Well, sure it's *interesting*—but I still say it's a risk."

"Oh, everything's a risk, Uncle Wayne." She was suddenly queasy from the smell.

"That's right," Kendra said. "Everything is." She came over to Melanie and took her hand. "Baby, what's going on?"

"See? Exactly—I'm not a baby. And you both still think I am."

"You could never become a journalist," her uncle said. "You know that, right? Not until he's caught."

"He'll never get caught, and you know it." The words were out of her mouth before she could stop them.

"*Melanie.*" Kendra could always convey sympathy and admonishment in a single word.

"I'm sorry, Uncle Wayne." Melanie sighed. "It's just that I'm an adult. If I want to take a risk, it's really my decision." But that sounded ungrateful. "Come on, it isn't that big a risk when you think about it. And anyway, Ramsey Miller could be in Antarctica right now. He could be dead."

"He isn't dead, Mel."

"Yeah, but he could be."

Uncle Wayne shook his head. "I don't think so."

She was about to keep arguing over her father's hypothetical demise, ask how Wayne could be so positive he was still a threat, when suddenly her neck hairs tingled and she had her answer. She was sure of it.

There was a new letter. One that actually said something.

But she couldn't ask about it, since she wasn't supposed to know about the letters in the first place. And worst of all, as of about a year ago, Wayne no longer kept them in his desk.

The dripping coffee smelled so rancid that Melanie wanted to flee the house for air—except even the trees smelled sour to her these days. Feeling less confident, she said, "It's just a stupid college newspaper that probably nobody ever reads anyway. I don't see why you have to freak out." But she knew it was easy for her to talk a big game about taking risks when she had others devoting their own lives to her survival.

Her aunt and uncle glanced at each other. "Honey," Wayne said gently, "I love you dearly. But if you honestly think we're just freaking out for the heck of it, it only proves you need to think it through some more."

Underneath the table lay a rust-colored rug. She could make out the discolored blotch where as a flu-ridden child she'd vomited. She remembered that illness more than any other, lying on the sofa and watching game shows and soap operas for a week. Sipping ginger ale, nibbling on Saltines, throwing up into a trash can. Her aunt laying cool rags on her forehead, holding her, taking her temperature. Being there for her. Always being there.

Outside, the change of seasons caused migrating birds to sit invisibly in trees and caw at obscene decibels. Soon the leaves would change. But nothing ever changed inside these walls. Her aunt and uncle had furnished the hastily rented trailer with only two criteria: expediency and thrift—hence the Goodwill furniture, Walmart bookshelves, discount rug remnants. They assumed that their time here would be temporary. Once their initial panic had melted into a lasting, dull fear, they saw no reason (and had no money) to furnish the place a second time.

But it wasn't only the furnishings. The three of them—how they were around one another; the countless ways they'd arranged their lives so as not to be overtaken by their deepest dreads . . . a whole life could pass this way.

"It's always going to be like this, isn't it?" Melanie said. She wasn't feeling argumentative anymore. Rather, she was seeing the truth about her future, maybe for the first time. "No matter how old I am, or how old you are, or how long it's been. Nothing will ever change, will it?"

"When he's caught . . . ," Wayne began. At one time he must have said these words with conviction. Now they sounded perfunctory. Their life in Fredonia was all she knew and, more and more, all her aunt and uncle knew, too. The three of them hardly ever referred to the past at all, let alone to the "he" at the center of it. "When he's caught . . . ," Wayne began again. But he didn't seem able to finish the sentence, because it would have been pure fiction.

As if coming to the same realization, he frowned and poured himself a mug of black coffee. He set it on the kitchen table and steam rose into the air. Melanie willed herself not to gag.

"In other words, never," she said, her hand moving instinctively to her belly. She wanted to rub it, soothe it. The past couple of weeks, she'd been doing that in class, in bed, in the car. But she wasn't going to give up this secret—not yet—and so she lowered her hand again.

"When he's caught," her uncle said.

Midafternoon, Melanie was still feeling upset by the morning's argument with her aunt and uncle when, in her required math class, the instructor got to talking about fractals, mathematical designs that repeated at every scale. "Like how a head of broccoli has those florets," he explained, "each one containing self-similar smaller florets, which in turn contain even smaller ones." He was projecting images from his laptop onto the whiteboard behind him. "Or how the shoreline has the same basic windy shape whether you're standing on the beach and looking at a few yards of it, or if you're up in a satellite looking down at the whole coastline." He spoke slowly, with an air of strained mystery, as if he were a sorcerer and not a middle-aged community college instructor who wore the same blue blazer to each class session.

The fractals made for beautiful images, equations made visual and color-enhanced, and then an idea struck Melanie with such devastating force that her palms started to sweat.

"That's me," she muttered under her breath, staring at the projected image. "I'm a fractal."

"I beg your pardon?" The instructor stared at her. Melanie never spoke up in class, and the humming of the projector drowned out her voice. "Miss Denison, did you say something?"

She kept looking at the geometric shape, amazed because it was so obvious and true. She hid in her small house, hidden on a deserted road, itself hidden in a small town in a remote part of West Virginia. The same at every scale, her hiding, and so total it felt like a mathematical certainty.

"I'm sorry," she said to the instructor. She was calling attention to herself in the worst way—a way that wouldn't soon be forgotten. The weird, quiet girl was finally saying something. A few students chuckled nervously. "I just . . ." She looked around at the twenty or so other students and thought about this baby growing inside of her, how this smaller scale of herself would end up deeply hidden, too, layer under layer under layer.

This she couldn't allow.

"I have to . . ." She made fists of her clammy hands. She wouldn't have been able to finish her sentence even if she'd had the words. She stood and rushed out of the room, down the hallway, and into the bathroom, where she vomited into a toilet. She knelt on the floor until the queasiness subsided, went over to the sink, and splashed cold water on her face. She stood over the sink, rubbing her belly and taking controlled breaths, until she felt steady enough to drive back to Fredonia and wait for Phillip.

She sat on the concrete front steps of his rental house, feeling the breeze on her face and laundering time.

For the last couple of years, she had been reading old Nancy Drew and Hardy Boys mysteries in bed at night. She knew the books were for children, but she found them comforting to read at bedtime. The sleuths were always being bound and gagged, but they came out of every situation unharmed, and the criminal was always apprehended.

In one of the Hardy Boys books, a pawnshop accepted stolen money and then over-reported its sales. Money laundering, they called it. This is what I do, Melanie had immediately thought—only with time instead of money. The two hours of homework she told her aunt and uncle she was doing in her bedroom rarely took more than an hour. With the other hour, she paged through whichever copy of *People* happened to be stowed under her mattress. More recently, her job at the office supply store in town never demanded those extra hours that Wayne and Kendra believed she was putting in.

A trip to or from the college was the easiest way of all to launder time. From the start, she'd lied about her class schedule in order to give herself a full hour on either side of the day, two hours that belonged solely to her.

She didn't like deceiving her aunt and uncle, but they'd think it was a huge risk for her simply to be sitting here on this quiet street where no one ever walked (too hilly, no sidewalks) and where drivers, the few that passed by, had better things to do than take notice of her.

She wasn't the sort of person people noticed, anyway. A girl in Melanie's freshman composition class, Raquel something, was tall and blonde with huge blue eyes, and looked like she belonged on the red carpet. She carried herself with remarkably casual poise. *I'm happy to*, she'd say to their instructor whenever he asked her to pass out an assignment. *How was your weekend?* she'd ask whoever was sitting next to her. She chatted with people as if their presence made her day special.

Melanie didn't look like Raquel, and she didn't know how to act like Raquel.

And yet here Melanie was, and not Raquel.

It was 3:15. She didn't mind waiting, watching the cars pass. Her own home sat at the end of a long driveway on an unpaved road that cut through the woods. For a number of years, long before Melanie ever lived there, the road was nameless. Over time, a large, hand-painted No Trespassing sign that somebody had stuck into the ground where the road began suffered enough weather damage that those final three letters became too faded to read. First the neighbors, then others in town, and finally the U.S. Postal Service began referring to their road as Notress Pass.

Other than that sign and the story behind it, nothing was remotely notable about the road where she lived, which was the
whole point. There were a dozen homes, about half of them trailers. On any given day, fewer than ten cars might rumble by. Now,
sitting on Phillip's stoop, she imagined she was behind the wheel
of each car that passed, on her way to somewhere. It didn't need
to be somewhere amazing. Just somewhere else. She thought
about Dorothy, singing about wanting to go somewhere over the
rainbow. It'd been on TV again the other night, that stupid movie.
Why on earth would Dorothy want to go home at the end? She's
a hero, she has friends, everything is in beautiful color. What a
tragedy, returning to Kansas.

The high school let out at 2:30. Unless there was a faculty
meeting, Phillip was usually home by three. He wasn't expecting
her today, though, and it wasn't until 3:40 that he came walking
along up the hill, carrying a stuffed-full paper shopping bag. He
owned a thousand-year-old Mazda hatchback, but it had broken
down twice on his drive to West Virginia last year, and the brakes
made an awful metal-on-metal scrape. He preferred to leave it in
the carport, which meant lugging his groceries a half mile from
the store.

Seeing Melanie, he smiled and set the bag down on the ground.

"A sight for sore eyes," he said. "An absolute vision."

The temperature had spiked since this morning, the humidity
returning. Phillip still had on his coat and tie. His face glistened as
if he had the flu.

She got up from the stoop and went over to him.

"Don't," he said. "I'm disgusting."

She moved in for an embrace. Phillip's heart thudded against
her, and she imagined that she, and not the walk in the heat, had
caused it. They separated, and she picked up the grocery bag
while Phillip fished in his pocket for his keys and opened the door.

When they went inside, no cold blast of air greeted them—just some noisy overhead fans pushing around the oppressive air.

"What're you doing here?" he asked. "Your face is flushed—let me get you some water."

She was hot suddenly, and woozy. In Phillip's bedroom window was an old air-conditioning unit, but it only half worked and it blocked out the room's natural light. So she sat down on the sofa. The house was a one-bedroom shotgun shack, smaller than a single-wide, tidy, and decorated not so differently from her own home: everything bought cheaply or used.

He set the groceries on the kitchen table, filled up a glass of water, and handed it to her. She took a long swallow despite the taste and passed the cup back to him. He downed the rest.

"Your water tastes rusty," she said.

"Really?" He looked into the empty glass.

If only she had that girl Raquel's ability to put people at ease. But Melanie never had anyone to practice on. She knew it had to be frustrating for Phillip, trying to get close to someone who seemed capable of bluntness and secrecy and nothing in-between.

"I've been meaning to buy a filter," he said.

"Why don't you sit down." She patted the sofa beside her, but he was eyeing the grocery bag. "What's wrong?"

"Nothing," he said. "It's just . . . I don't want this stuff to spoil."

She knew what it was like when every dollar counted, each egg or ounce of milk something to take seriously. Her family had more money now that Kendra was freed up from tutoring Melanie and could work at the dollar store. But they'd never be a name-brand family. "Put everything away first. I'm sorry."

"Oh, don't be—just hang out for two seconds. Can I get you something else? Juice? Glass of wine?"

"No, nothing, thank you."

He stowed ground beef and yogurt and milk in the refrigerator —the other stuff he left in the bag—and sat on the sofa beside her.

"I've never seen you move so fast," she said.

"I don't like to keep my women waiting."

"How many do you have?"

He smiled. "Dozens."

"I have something serious to tell you."

"Oh." He sat up a little straighter. "Okay."

She couldn't just say it, could she, with no preamble? Melanie placed a hand on Phillip's knee and forced herself to look him in the eyes. "You're a really . . ." and to her horror, the word that sprang to mind came straight out of a Hardy Boys novel. *Swell.*

Swell?

She couldn't say that, of course, so she tried harder. ". . . a really great guy. What I mean is, I care about you."

He pulled his gaze away and bit his lip. He looked absolutely distressed. "You're breaking up with me."

"What?"

"That's what you're doing."

"It is?"

He looked at her again. "It isn't?"

Somewhere, Raquel was shaking her head in disgust. "Why would I break up with you?"

"*I* don't know," he said. "Listen, Melanie, are you or aren't you breaking up with me?"

"I'm not breaking up with you."

His body visibly relaxed. "Good. I'm really glad."

To launder time without arousing suspicion, you had to choose small increments. But this was going nowhere, and soon her aunt would come home from work, find her missing, and freak out. So okay, forget Raquel and her comforting chatter.

"When I was two and a half," Melanie blurted out, "my father killed my mother and would've killed me, too, but I got away but so did he."

For several seconds, the only sound was the pulsing of the ceiling fan. Phillip watched her face, as if gauging how to react.

"Is this a joke?" he finally said, but with gentleness in his voice. He knew it wasn't. She'd been secretive with him from the start, evasive to the point of bizarre. Why he'd put up with her this long, she had no idea.

"I've never told anyone before," she said, looking down at her lap.

He took her hand. "Oh, Melanie," he said. "Oh, dear God."

This wasn't the secret she'd come here to tell. But Phillip needed to know that the woman carrying his baby was putting them all at risk. And when he led her toward the bedroom, saying, "Let's cool down," she said yes. She had already laundered enough time this afternoon, and, especially after the morning's disagreement with her aunt and uncle, she knew she ought to be getting home. But looking at Phillip looking at her, she realized that she was sick and tired of laundering time, and that she was desperate, instead, to spend it.

When they went into his bedroom and he said, "Do you think you can tell me more? Can you tell me everything?" she said yes again. And when he said, "You know you can trust me, don't you?" she willed herself to say yes one more time—the brief hesitation not a matter of distrust but rather disbelief.

This is real, she told herself. *This is happening. I am doing this. I am not alone.*

3

September 19, 1991

Ramsey Miller had been awake for thirty-two hours when he stopped his truck for the hitchhiker.

Usually he preferred solitude. Maybe some local FM station (music, never talk radio—the beauty was in getting away from talk); maybe just the engine's hum and his own thoughts, while the forests and fields and mountains slid past. Not that he objected in principle to helping a stranger move from Point A to Point B. But strangers always felt the need to talk—about nothing or, worse, about *something*. Life lessons, road wisdom . . . whatever foolishness they were urgent for you to hear. As if they were doing you the favor. And when they weren't trying to impress you, they were stinking up the upholstery with cigarette ash or worse. After the first year of driving his big rig, Ramsey swore off hitchhikers entirely.

In the six years since, he'd made only two exceptions. First one hardly counted: no older than thirteen or fourteen, walking along the narrow shoulder of the eastbound side of I-80 at sunrise, middle of nowhere, PA, thumb in the air while sheets of rain pummeled her. From fifty yards off, she could've been a kid. Wasn't till she was in the cab and shivering that Ramsey decided she was *slightly* older than that.

"I'm going to New York," she said through chattering teeth, arms wrapped around herself.

No luggage, no umbrella. Soaked hair and clothes. After she was settled in with the heater blasting, Ramsey radioed ahead and deposited her at the nearest exit, where a couple of cops were waiting to get to the bottom of that particular tragedy.

The second hitchhiker was female, too, but older—probably older than Ramsey. Her hair was graying and chopped real short, but she wasn't bad looking—she was someone you might take up space with in a bar near closing time and think, *Sure, okay.* This was back a few years, when Allie was early in her pregnancy and the two of them got to arguing sometimes about nothing. The argument had occurred just as he was leaving for eleven days on the road.

About ninety minutes later—too soon for the road's gentle rhythms to ease his temper—he saw the woman thumbing a ride on the Jersey Turnpike, a handful of miles north of the Delaware Memorial Bridge.

He slowed to a stop, waited for her to come over, and said hop in. A couple of hours later, past the DC beltway, she was hopping out again. It was Saturday, and all they'd done was listen to part of a Top-40 countdown. She'd been an ideal passenger: quiet, nonsmoking. He took an exit to refuel and let her off, stopping at the edge of a flat of asphalt away from the fuel pumps and the other trucks. She got her backpack from the floor by her feet and said, "I sincerely appreciate the lift."

"You do, huh?" Ramsey said. "Then how about a kiss?"

"No, I don't think so," she said, hand on the door. It was locked.

Ramsey didn't especially want to kiss her, but the embers of his argument with Allie still burned, and he had the vague sense that he was owed something by somebody. "What are you, a dyke or something?"

"I'd like to get out now." The woman was glancing back and forth between Ramsey and her side window, her hand still on the door.

He waited long enough—six, seven seconds—before pressing the power unlock. "Yeah, okay."

He watched her leave the truck and walk quickly toward the safety of others, his self-loathing already cresting like a wave.

That ain't you anymore, he repeated to himself later that afternoon, seated at the end of a neon-lit bar just off the interstate that stank of piss and sawdust. He pounded shots of well whiskey and thought about how in the past he'd been responsible for all kinds of meanness. His heart had, at times, been black, and he knew he was a lucky SOB to have escaped his teenage years—and, let's be honest, his twenties—without crossing that invisible line you can't ever uncross. But all that was in the past. He'd worked so fucking hard to become a changed man. A family man, and soon to be a father.

That ain't you anymore.

Afternoon bled to evening. He drank hard and woke up puking his guts out in his truck in the Walmart lot, no memory of the half-mile walk from his seat at the bar. He wasted half the next day washing his bedding in some laundromat and scrubbing the fabric in his cab until the stench was gone and the stains faded, reaffirming with each wipe of the rag his vow never again to stop for hitchhikers.

Now, this third and last time, he was doing it for his own safety. Company policy and federal laws were already being violated—he was fudging the log book and was way over the eighty-two-hour limit—but these were no longer concerns. All that mattered was getting home by Friday afternoon.

He had been seriously revved all week, content only with his foot on the gas, and had logged as many miles in seven days as another trucker might in ten or eleven. Jersey to Memphis to Kansas City to Phoenix. He was due home, 2,500 miles away, in three days, but all his life he'd wanted to see how the real Grand Canyon matched up against the pictures he'd seen. So he took the extra day and drove north, trusting his juices to keep flowing at the same rate they had been, until he was home again safe and sound.

A miscalculation.

Now it was Thursday night. An hour earlier, the sun had dipped below the tree line behind him, and with 1,100 miles still to go, every part of him was sagging and slowing. It dawned on him that his body, being a body, needed sleep.

A few years back, he'd have gone pharmaceutical. Now he cycled through the lawful tricks—air conditioner full blast, heavy metal station roaring, face slaps, extra large Diet Coke, fast food fries—and they all helped push him through Missouri to the Illinois border. But that left fourteen hours, more or less. And while the truck's fuel tank might've been full, Ramsey himself was out of gas—besides which, his time spent at the Grand Canyon had left him feeling magnanimous. So when the truck's headlights fell on the man thumbing a ride on the shoulder of I-70, Ramsey put on the brakes.

"You're a kind soul," the man said over the engine's idle. He looked as if hitchhiking were his chosen profession: all-weather jacket, thick shock of gray hippie hair tied into a ponytail, huge backpack.

Ramsey waited while the man climbed aboard, stuffed his backpack by his feet, and strapped on the safety belt.

"This ain't your first ride in a rig," Ramsey said.

"Brother, you got that right." The man shuffled in the seat, trying to find a suitable position. "All I ask is that you deposit me a little further along this road than I was when you met me."

"Can do," Ramsey said. "But I got a favor to ask."

"Shoot."

"I'll be honest with you—I don't ever pick nobody up these days. But I'm dog tired, and I need help staying awake so I can get home."

"Sorry, friend—but I been clean for over a decade."

Ramsey shook his head. "I mean talking. Conversation—so I don't nod off."

"Well, that I can do." He adjusted the seatbelt. "Where's home at?"

"Jersey shore. North of Asbury Park."

"Bruce Springsteen."

"Yup."

The man nodded. "You regular tired, or coming down off speed?"

"I ain't coming down off nothing," Ramsey said. "But I wouldn't call it regular tired, neither."

They were far enough now from St. Louis that the sky was no longer tinted orange from all the lights. Traffic had thinned somewhat, and the outlines of woods lining the highway faded in the encroaching dark. Soon Ramsey could stop worrying about the deer. He knew to plow on through—a deer won't damage your cab too bad—but the road was dominated by fools who jerked their cars from lane to lane and slammed on their brakes to avoid twigs and jackrabbits and imaginary things, never noticing the semi in the next lane. So he was always glad when the deer hour ended and dusk darkened to actual night.

"How long you been on the road?" the man asked.

"Six days, 4,200 miles," Ramsey said.

The man let out a low whistle, either impressed or skeptical. "But no speed?"

"Sober as a judge."

"No wonder you're tired."

Ramsey sighed. "No wonder I am."

"You overdue for a break?"

"Like I said, gotta get home."

They watched the windshield a moment, and then the man said, "Looks like I just may be your fairy godmother."

"Now how's that?" Ramsey asked.

The man shimmied a little in his seat and pulled his wallet from the back of his blue jeans. "You aren't in the habit of giving lifts," the man said, "and I'm not in the habit of offering this particular piece of assistance." He removed something from his wallet and held it up for Ramsey to glance at. A driver's license.

"I can't read it in the dark."

"Well, it says Class A."

"I'll be damned," Ramsey said.

"Quit driving in eighty-six—flatbed for five years, dry van for ten. Name's Ed Hewitt."

"Glad to know you, Ed," Ramsey said.

They went another half mile before Ed asked, "Am I being too subtle?"

"Come again?"

"You're fading, man—I'm offering to drive for a spell so you can recharge."

Ramsey looked over at Ed. "You aren't serious."

"I most certainly am."

"I never heard of a hitcher driving the truck," Ramsey said. "That'd be a first."

"I imagine it would—but I been in lots of trucks, and you look more beat than fellows coming down hard. You sure you aren't . . ."

"I told you, I don't do that," Ramsey said. "Not since the kid was born."

Ed nodded. "Well, the way I see it, if we help each other out these next few hours, it'll raise the odds that we're both alive when the sun comes up."

The idea was absurd. Yet over these last few months, Ramsey had learned to trust the universe rather than his own limited understanding of it. And when fate drops a hippie with a Class A commercial driver's license into your cab, the best course of action might well be to switch seats and catch a few hours of overdue dreams—especially with so much to do these next couple of days.

So he slowed the truck again and stopped it in the shoulder, and once the two men had exchanged seats, Ramsey gave Ed a brief tutorial. But the guy didn't need one. He wasn't bullshitting. He worked the clutch like he'd never retired.

Maybe you are my fairy godmother, Ramsey thought as Ed accelerated to the speed of traffic. "She's gonna shimmy some—I'm carrying balloon freight."

"Got it."

"And it's windy out there."

"I know," said Ed. "I was walking in it."

"And remember, you get stopped for anything, it's bigger trouble than either of us needs."

"But no bigger than dying," Ed said, "which is what I see happening if we let you stay behind the wheel much longer."

"Fair enough," Ramsey said, reclining way, way back.

He dreamed again of flying. This time, a gentle summer breeze carried him high over the ocean like a lone gull dipping in and out of the clouds. Not since he was a kid had his dreams been so vivid and wondrous. He swooped down over walls of baitfish moving in unison and shimmering in the sunlight. Bluefish and bonita glided through the water alongside flashier, supersaturated fish that his dream transplanted from the Caribbean. He could smell the brine. Closer to the shoreline, jagged hills of orange and red coral jutted up from the ocean floor. If he were to dive under the surface, he knew he'd be able to breathe underwater. But he stayed in the air, where the sun warmed his skin.

When he opened his eyes again, he didn't know where he was. His truck, the highway. A millisecond of panic—*asleep behind the wheel!*—until he noticed that he wasn't behind the wheel. He looked over to his left, and the rest fell into place.

In front of him, the truck's headlights cut into dark empty lanes. The canopy of stars overhead revealed no sign of morning. The dashboard clock showed 5:12.

"You could've woke me any time," Ramsey said, rubbing his eyes.

"No need to interrupt a peaceful ride."

"Whereabouts are we?"

"We went through Columbus about forty minutes back."

"What'd you do at the weigh stations?"

"Pretended they didn't exist."

Ramsey massaged his neck, unstiffening it. "We're making good time."

"Not bad. Though I sure could use a pit stop about now."

"Next rest area, I'll buy you breakfast. You earned it."

"Can do."

Ramsey yawned and shut his eyes again, feeling the engine's hum, the road beneath him, the soft push of air past the windows. When they exited the highway a while later, the blackness around them had become infused with hints of blue and gray. The border between tree and sky was starting to become visible.

Today. Ramsey's heart rate quickened at the thought. *Today, it begins.*

After sleeping all those hours, the remainder of the drive was nothing. Ramsey reached the Toys"R"Us distribution center in Wayne, New Jersey, by 9:30. It was a frequent stop, and he trusted the dock supervisor to have him in and out. Sure enough the unload moved, easy paperwork, and by noon he was pulling into the Monmouth Truck Lot.

The office was a narrow trailer up on cinder blocks. Inside, the walls were wood paneled, the floor linoleum. Same as when he'd bought his truck five years earlier. Probably the same as twenty years before that. On the grassy lot itself, trailers and cabs sat like vast tombstones surrounded by swaths of reedy weeds. Nothing about the place hinted at a successful business, but Bob Parkins, the owner, knew more about trucks than anyone Ramsey had ever met. Ramsey had bought his sleeper cab and trailer here on a tip from his fleet manager after two years of driving a company truck. Hard to say whether the move from employee to dedicated owner-operator was worth it, but the tip on where to purchase had been sound. Ramsey came away with a dependable truck at a fair price. Since then, he returned whenever his rig needed servicing beyond what he himself could do.

A counter split the trailer down the middle. Behind it were a couple of desks with papers piled everywhere, Bob's filing system. In a corner of the trailer, on the customer side, was an upended milk crate, and on it sat a coffeemaker, a stack of Styrofoam cups, and a container of powdered creamer.

"Help you?"

The guy behind the counter was some kid with a faded blue collared shirt and stupid-looking spiky hair.

"Where's Bob at?" Ramsey asked.

"Took the afternoon off," the kid said.

"You gotta be . . . " He felt the heat climb and took a breath. "Bob said he'd be in till three today. I talked to him from the road, coupla days ago. I made sure."

The kid shrugged. "Weather got good, and he hasn't had a day off in forever. He went fishing."

"What do you mean, 'weather got good'?"

The kid nodded toward the window. "You know—sunny. Warm."

There was a time before Ramsey started driving when he considered buying a fishing boat and chartering it out. The risks ended up being too great—bad weather, red tides, polluted water, expensive insurance—but you didn't need to be sea smart to know that today was no fishing day. "Wind's blowing hard out of the northeast. There's gotta be four- to six-foot seas out there."

The kid shrugged again. "I wouldn't know about it."

"You don't fish?"

"Nah, never did."

"Your old man never took you?"

"My old man's a piece of shit."

Ramsey sized the kid up some more. Shirt too large in the shoulders and neck. Probably a hand-me-down from the piece-of-shit himself.

"So Bob ain't coming back today?" Ramsey said it more to himself than to the kid. He was counting on Bob being here, making everything nice and easy.

"That's what taking the afternoon off means."

"You being smart with me?" When the kid's eyes narrowed, Ramsey backed off. The kid's name was Frank, according to the tag on his chest. He couldn't be older than twenty or twenty-one, and he had a lousy old man and a crappy haircut and God only knew what else. "Forget it. Listen, Frank. Bob sold me my truck five years ago. I need to sell it."

Frank looked out the window again. "The Kenworth?"

"The very one."

"What year is it?"

"Seventy-four."

"How many miles?"

"Million two."

"You bought it with how many?"

"About five hundred thousand."

He nodded. "Runs good?"

"Real good."

"You trading in for a newer one?"

"Nope."

"Then why do you want to sell?"

"That's my business."

The kid looked unsure whether to be courteous or a brat. He wasn't a bad-looking kid if you ignored the oversized shirt and that spiky haircut of his. But girls his age probably liked his hair that way. And he had an okay job, which was more than Ramsey had at his age.

"Bob'll be in tomorrow at seven," Frank said. "He can—"

"No, I need to sell it now."

"I can't just buy your truck, man."

"Name's Ramsey, son."

"Bob'll want to run diagnostics on it, test drive it—"

"I want fifteen thousand for the whole thing. Cab and trailer."

The kid looked confused. Ramsey suspected it wasn't a new look. "If it runs like you say, it's worth three times that."

"I don't want three times that."

"Well, like I said, Bob'll be in first thing tomorrow."

"Tomorrow's no good."

The kid looked at Ramsey like he was drowning. He hadn't learned yet that sometimes you just needed to do a thing. Like how Ramsey had left that fellow, Ed, at the rest stop earlier that morning. Ramsey was grateful to him for driving all those miles, but it was important to be alone for the last leg of his last drive in his truck. That's how he always imagined it. So when the two of them went into the rest stop for breakfast, Ramsey handed Ed a twenty and said to order something for the two of them. *I forgot something in my truck*, he said, and that was that.

"Tell you what," Ramsey said now. "Is Ralph over in the shop?"

"He and Andy, yeah."

"Give Ralphie a call. He knows me. He knows I shoot straight."

"He ain't sales."

"I *know* he ain't sales—just get him on the phone for me."

Frank looked relieved, having something to do. He pressed some buttons on the phone. Seconds later: ". . . and he says he's got to sell it *today*." He held the receiver to his ear, then said, "Yeah, okay," and handed the receiver to Ramsey.

"What the hell you doing?" Ralph said over the phone.

"I'm selling you my truck is what I'm doing," Ramsey said.

"You gotta let me look it over," he said. "Leave it here, come back tomorrow. We'll get you hooked up. Bob'll give you a fair price."

"It's got to be now, Ralph. Fifteen thousand in cash. You know I take care of my truck. You know it's a steal."

"Ain't my call—boss is *fishing*, man."

"Oh, he ain't catching nothing. Do him a favor. You know I'm on the up-and-up."

Ralph wheezed into the phone and said, "Put Frankie back on the phone."

Ramsey handed back the receiver.

38

"You sure about that?" the kid said. "But you ain't—" He grimaced. "All right, man, I'm just saying. Yeah, okay." He hung up the phone. "Looks like you got yourself a deal."

"That's good to hear," Ramsey said. "I appreciate you calling up Ralph like that." He nodded in the direction of the shop. "He lay into you a little bit there?"

"If shit goes down, it's on him, not me."

"Trust me," Ramsey said, "the truck's good." He glanced out the window. "Wind's gonna calm down over the weekend. That's when you want to be out in the ocean, not today. Saturday will be ideal. Sunday, too."

"Like I said, I don't fish."

"No, I suppose you don't," Ramsey said. "Well, find some other way to enjoy your weekend. You got a girl?"

The kid actually smiled. He had alarmingly bad teeth. "Yeah."

"Treat her right. Show her a good time."

"I always do." He leered some.

"Nah, I don't mean that. I mean buy her something nice, take her out, cause you never know."

"Never know what?"

Ramsey didn't want to start freaking the kid out. He needed that truck sold. "I'm just talking. Title's in the cab—I'll go get it."

"Yeah, okay." Kid still looked a little puzzled. "I'll start on the paperwork. There's a lot of it."

Ramsey checked the clock on the wall. "Think you can have me out of here in a half hour?"

"You're selling your truck," Frank said. "You got someplace more important to be?"

"Yeah, I do," Ramsey said. "I got band practice."

He returned to his truck for the title and a last look around. Before coming to the Monmouth Truck Lot, he'd cleaned the trailer, scrubbing his own existence away. Ramsey always kept the cab neat—but there was the bedding, tape collection, towels, sleeping bag, old fleeces, survival kit, road atlas, fire extinguisher, alarm clock, laundry detergent, rolls of toilet paper, paper towels. The cab was like the smallest apartment he'd ever lived in, and by far the most comfortable. He'd spent well over a thousand nights in it. So it wasn't a truck he was selling, but a second home. Or maybe a first home.

Too many truckers were slobs, their cabs ankle deep in dirty clothes, fast food wrappers, soda cans, cigarette butts, old tubs of chew, spit cans, piss bottles, porno mags, balled-up paper towels full of snot or cum, petrified French fries . . . you name it. *That's your home, man,* he'd reminded a rookie driver some years back who'd been generous with his pill supply. *You gotta smell that when you drive and when you sleep.* Ramsey was hardly some blowhard always handing out free advice, but he had an instinct for when a kid could land either way, and he considered it his duty to tip him in the right direction if he thought it might make a difference.

And the truth was, a cab was a decent place if you let it be. More than decent. That's what Ramsey had discovered early on, then taken for granted but rediscovered these past few months. Rolling along some hot highway on the way from who-cares to doesn't-matter, the temperature just right, the music just right, you have your own kingdom.

But that was over now. He opened the storage compartment between the seats, where he kept the few items of special importance: couple of photos of Allie and Meg, a notebook where he sometimes jotted down stuff that occurred to him on the road, a song lyric, whatever. A few mementos collected over the years: small cow skull whittled by a dude in Amarillo; necklace of green Mardi Gras beads; smooth blue stone that he found one silent, foggy dawn on a beach in Trinidad, California; pinecone from

Colorado, where on a whim one windy summer afternoon he pulled to the side of the road at the wide point of a pass cutting through the Rockies and ate his lunch at a picnic table. All of it, he put into the black trash bag.

He picked up his copy of *The Orbital Axis*, its cover creased and spine worn, and nearly decided to keep it before changing his mind. From moving apartment to apartment over the years, he'd gotten into the habit of keeping a thing only as long as it was useful. The book had led him to sell the truck. Well, here he was, selling it. He added the book to the black trash bag, which he spun around a few times and knotted at the top.

The cab looked and smelled fresh, but it wasn't his kingdom any longer. Before hooking up with Allie, he'd moved apartments all the time, eviction coming about as frequently as a head cold. He'd forgotten all about that sad feeling of leaving a place, knowing you'll never smell that particular smell ever again. Even a place you don't like. Even if you only lived there for three or four months before getting chased away by some prick landlord. It had to do with mortality. Leave a place, and you've finished a chapter, moved closer to the end.

Now, keys in pocket, title of ownership in one hand, trash bag in the other, he gave the truck one last look and shut the door.

He didn't need to come by fifteen thousand dollars this way. He wasn't poor. There was money in savings, enough or close to it. But symbolic actions mattered. Filling out a withdrawal slip at the bank didn't mean squat, whereas selling your truck showed commitment. Finality. He'd promised Allie back in June that he wouldn't sell, and he'd kept his word. He kept working right through today. She'd been right, as she almost always was. Working was the best thing. He lifted the trash bag higher and tossed it onto a pile of other trash bags inside the green dumpster behind the sales office.

But now he was done with work. Time to cash out. And this, he knew, walking into the sales office again carrying the title of ownership, was the proper way to do it.

The kid was no wiz at simple math and kept hitting the wrong buttons on his calculator. Nearly an hour passed before Ramsey's business with Frank was done. But okay, the title was signed over, the keys placed on the counter. In Frank's shirt pocket were two hundred-dollar bills, courtesy of Ramsey.

(Two hundred bucks? What for?)

(For helping me out today, Frank.)

(Jesus.)

(Like I said, do something nice for your girl.)

In Ramsey's front pants pocket were the other 147 hundred-dollar bills and five twenties. One of the twenties was for the taxi ride back to Boater's World, where his car was parked. For years, the store manager let him park his truck there when he wasn't on the road, and his car there when he was. After driving the truck, the Volkswagen always felt to Ramsey like a toy.

At 1:45 p.m. he arrived at the Methodist church and walked through the side door labeled "Kid Care." He wished his daughter's day care wasn't at a church. But Allie had done the research and said this place had the best reputation.

"I'm here for Meg Miller," he said to the woman sitting in a black swivel chair. "Didn't see no one in the Ladybug Room." He knew this woman by sight and found her distasteful.

That was why—the scowl. On her desk were stacks of paper, a typewriter, and a huge white mug with lipstick smears on the brim. She held up an index finger as if the form she was reading were vitally important before looking up. "Mrs. Miller said you wouldn't be here until three."

"Well, I'm here at two."

The woman sighed. "They're in the Little Gym. Do you know where that is?"

He didn't.

She braced her palms against the desk to help herself stand up.

"Let me ask you something," Ramsey said, following her into the hallway. "Is Meg the best kid you ever had here?"

Along the walls, between classrooms, were hooks with names above them. On the hooks hung jackets and knapsacks.

"She's a well-behaved child."

"And sweet, too," he said.

"Yes," the woman conceded, "she is."

"Goddamn right she is." Ramsey smiled, watching the woman flinch.

Meg: three months shy of three years. Preferred running to walking. Hair, wavy with funny-as-hell cowlicks when she woke up in the morning. Best laugh in the whole fucking world. Loved the color orange. Amazing with numbers and letters, except for the tricky patch between U and X.

She spotted Ramsey in the entrance to the gym and came running, all teeth and flailing arms, shouting, "It's Daddy!" over and over. She was never shy around him, even when he came home from a long haul. He knew to give Allie credit for all the photographs of them—of him—stuck on the refrigerator, in albums, the daily reminders of Daddy while he was away, no different from what military spouses did. There was no bigger dread than your kid not knowing who you were.

Ramsey stepped into the gym. "Hey, baby," he said. He'd seen other dads glance around self-consciously when their kids delivered a blast of full-on affection. Men were always glancing around. That was their problem.

When Meg reached him, he rocketed her into the air and swung her around a couple of times. He kissed her cheek, she honked his nose, he carried her outside to the parking lot, and they were on their way.

Or they would've been if he could secure the car seat's straps around Meg's shoulders. When he took too long, she started to fuss. He tried to remember the words to some kid's song, any song at all. "Oh, I love trash," he sang. "Anything trashy or smashy or grungy—"

"I want Daddy to sing Barney!" she shouted, still squirming, the one arm that'd been secured now free again. The tears were real.

Not liking Barney and not knowing what he (she? it?) sang, he ignored the request. "Come on, Meg." he said. "Baby, let me just—"

Not a chance.

By the time she was secured in the seat—crying, miserable—Ramsey's whole face was sweating. He started the car and turned up the radio, which helped. Thank you, John Cougar Mellencamp. He told Meg they were going to the playground, and her face brightened at once, and he cursed himself for not thinking to mention that *before* trying to put her in the car seat.

The afternoon's itinerary was simple: playground, home, band practice. All week, Ramsey had looked forward to this hour alone with the kid. Back when Meg was a baby and couldn't sit up or play with toys or do hardly anything, time spent alone with her slowed practically to a stop. But now she did everything: ran, threw a football (usually into the shrubs, but still), climbed on him like a monkey. And whenever he returned from being away, she was ready with new words and fresh techniques for getting him to obey her.

In the park was a shallow pond where kids threw balled-up bread to the turtles. He had forgotten to bring bread, but Meg was happy dropping woodchips and pebbles into the water. Then she ran over to the playground and tried the slides. Ramsey sat on the green metal bench at one of the picnic tables bordering the play area and watched. On this sunny afternoon, he found himself wanting time to slow just as it was picking up speed. His daughter was the result of Allie and himself, but she was neither of them. She was becoming herself, entirely.

When he looked at his watch, more than a half hour had passed. "Okay, Meg," he said, "time to go."

"No, Daddy!" she called, and raced toward the twisty yellow slide.

Another man was coming his way with two kids, boy and a girl, both a little older than Meg. The man's hands were stuffed into the pockets of his khaki pants. He had on a loosened tie and sports coat. Seeing Ramsey, the man saluted. Nothing in the world was more depressing than other men at a playground, with their sad salutes and their "Mr. Mom" remarks and that look on their faces of having been snookered—like they'd thought they were headed to a Jets game with their buddies but somehow ended up here.

"We're about to leave," Ramsey said to this other man. "You have yourself a good weekend."

The man shot Ramsey with an imaginary pistol and called over to his boy, Tino, to leave the baseball cap ON like he'd been told a thousand times.

"They're all deaf at this age," the man said to Ramsey, heading over to where his kid had flung his cap to the ground.

Ramsey was working on a plan to leave the playground without tears when Meg ran over to him, took his hand, and said, "Want to go home." There was no figuring her out.

They were halfway to the car when, out of nowhere, she looked up at him and said, "Meg feed the turtles."

"We did, baby," Ramsey said. "We already—"

"Meg feed turtles now!" She yanked her hand away and repeated the demand, hysteria entering her voice.

So they walked over to the bridge and threw more woodchips into the water, until Meg said, "Want to see Mommy." She walked cheerfully to the car and, amazingly, climbed into the seat without a fuss.

When they arrived home, Eric's pickup and Paul's El Camino were both facing the wrong way on the street. The pickup's body was caked in dried mud. The El Camino was rusted and dented, with a black trash bag duct-taped into place where a rear window should have been. Ramsey imagined the neighbors looking out their front windows and shaking their heads.

He and Allie had moved to the Sandy Oaks neighborhood from across town back when they decided that Allie would go off the pill. The people living here worked in offices with secretaries of their own. If asked, they'd call themselves "comfortable," which was horseshit. In the scheme of things, they were rich. *He* was rich. Anyone who didn't go to bed fretting about money and wake up fretting about it all over again? Rich. And damn lucky to be living someplace where you were never woken up at 3 a.m. to drunken obscenities shouted down the street, to police sirens, to glass shattering in the road.

More than three years since they'd moved in, and whenever he drove up to his home he still felt, for an instant, as if he were visiting someone else—someone wealthy and temperate and respectable. Then he reminded himself that he had all those qualities now, more or less, and had worked damn hard for them.

"Down, Daddy!"

Meg insisted on walking to the door rather than be carried. On the way, she petted a hedge, got down on her hands and knees to examine an ant, and asked Ramsey repeatedly where the sorties (stories? shores?) were. The closer they got to the house, the more Ramsey could hear the low tones of the bass guitar. He felt it in his chest, vibrations like the engine in his truck before putting it into gear and driving off someplace. But he wasn't going anywhere, not anymore.

"Can you feel that?" he asked.

Meg knocked on the red front door. "Home."

"That's right, sweetie pie." He stroked her hair. "We're home."

4

September 22, 2006

Uncle Wayne and Aunt Kendra had never hidden from Melanie the fact that they were raising her because her mother and father could not. When she was five, they explained that her mother had died and her father had gone far away but that they, Kendra and Wayne, loved her very much and thought of her as their own daughter. This was one of her earliest memories, and what she remembered most clearly about it was that to stop her from crying, they had all climbed into bed and watched *The Little Mermaid*, her favorite movie, on videotape, and shared a large bowl of buttery popcorn.

When she was ten, they explained that a very dangerous man had ended her mother's life and unfortunately had not yet been caught. He was still dangerous, which was why their lives had to be so private. Two years later, they explained that her father had been that man—something that by then Melanie had already suspected.

She sat beside Phillip now on his neatly made bed, the air conditioner straining to cool the room, and told him the essence of what she'd learned over the years: how her name used to be Meg Miller, and how when she was a little girl her father had thrown a big party and then, later that night, strangled her mother and dumped her body into the backyard fire pit. She told him about how she herself was believed to be dead, too, and how Wayne and Kendra were able to get her away, and how the U.S. Marshals, working with local law enforcement in two states, had successfully hidden her but utterly failed to apprehend her father.

"But he knows you're alive," Phillip finally said after several seconds of saying nothing.

"Of course," Melanie said.

"Then why is it a secret?"

"If everyone else thinks I'm already dead," she explained, "then we never have to worry about reporters or TV people or anyone trying to find me. No one can ever help my father, even accidentally." Phillip was rubbing her hand with his thumb. "Anyway, it wasn't my decision, and it had to get made really fast. And no one ever thought it would take this long to find him."

"Are you still afraid of your father?" he asked.

"I'm terrified of him," she said. "He's a madman."

"Can I ask why you're telling me about it now?"

She decided not to mention the fractals. But come on—had he not noticed her larger breasts, her clearer skin? Did he not find it strange that suddenly she was saying *No, thanks* whenever he offered her a glass of wine? Why was she telling him now? Because it isn't just me anymore, she wanted to say. But she needed to know how he would take the news of her strange past before going further. "I've wanted to tell you for a while," she said, "but I didn't want to scare you away. Is this going to scare you away?"

His arm was around her now. "Of course it won't," he said. "But . . . " He frowned.

"What?"

"It's just that all of this happened so long ago. And you have a new identity, and obviously look a lot different from when you were a little kid." He shrugged. "What makes you think your father's still looking for you, anyway?"

She could have told him about the letters, hard evidence that Ramsey Miller was still out there causing trouble. She could have mentioned the feeling she would get sometimes that someone was out there watching her. She would catch something in her periphery, turn her head, and see nothing. But the chill would linger. Even out in her own yard, in bright daylight, sometimes she'd gaze into the hedges and swear she saw movement. But this was bogeyman stuff, more than likely, so she decided to answer Phillip's question another way.

"When my father dragged my mother into the fire, they think she was still alive. He choked her and left her to burn." She watched his eyes, hoping he would understand. "What I mean is, I don't get to be optimistic."

Phillip said nothing for a moment. Maybe he was imagining the murder scene, the charred flesh. "I wonder if it's time for someone other than your aunt and uncle to look out for you," he said. "They can't do it forever—and I'm not afraid."

"You're not, huh?"

"Not really. Nope." He chanced a smile. "Which is weird, because I'm actually afraid of a lot of stuff."

"Yeah? Like what?"

"Oh, you name it. Flying. Heights."

"That's the same thing."

"Not to me," he said. "Also, tornadoes."

"You don't live in a trailer," she said. "We had a couple of close calls when I was a kid."

"And I'm afraid of having to use CPR on somebody at school and then doing it wrong. And being crushed in an avalanche."

"Is that everything?"

She thought he might say yes. Instead: "Rabies."

"Like getting bitten by a bat?"

"Sure—a raccoon, a bat . . ."

"But you're not afraid of a murderer?"

"No—just everything else." He shrugged. "Maybe it's because you mean more to me than bats or airplanes or whatever." His smile was more confident. "You look very pretty right now."

He kissed her mouth, her throat. She placed a hand on his arm. "Seriously, Phillip—I have to know if this is all too much for you."

"Seriously, Melanie—it isn't."

"Don't answer so fast," she said. "I want you to really think about it."

"*It isn't.*" He looked into her eyes. "I can handle anything."

She bit her lip. "How about one more surprise. Can you handle that?"

The box of condoms said 96% effective. But 96 percent effective, it turned out, was a world away from 100 percent, and now she was in her tenth week. Before telling Phillip, the only two people who knew were herself and the doctor at the college health center, who had confirmed those drug-store pregnancy tests with yet another test, then handed her several pamphlets ("Your Guide to a Healthy Pregnancy"; "Breastfeeding with Success"; "Labor, Delivery, and Postpartum Care"), all of which she skimmed late that first night before stowing them in the back of her closet behind a box of old clothes.

She'd been careful and responsible, yet the result was no different from that girl in high school last year whom Melanie had actually overheard saying, *We thought God would keep me from getting pregnant.* And her options—either an abortion or the prospect of introducing a baby into her hidden, fearful home—were too awful to think about. So for a few weeks, she didn't. She went to class. She went to work. She read her Hardy Boys and Nancy Drew mysteries. The pamphlets stayed stowed.

Which was why she felt glad, in a way, that her instructor had shown the class those fractals this afternoon. They made her see that she didn't want to stay hidden at every scale any longer, and didn't want her child to be hidden at all. And those two desires intertwined. If not for the child, there'd be no reason to stop being who she'd always been—the fearful, hidden girl.

When she actually said the words "I'm pregnant" to Phillip, at first the color drained from his face, his own version of morning sickness. "I intend to have the baby and raise it," she said. "Just so you know."

He said all the right things. He'd be there for her. He'd support her. He went so far as to say that he was "excited about this," which she didn't believe but appreciated hearing. Before long, his face regained its color. And gradually the two conversations—her past, their present—melded into one.

She knew he found their relationship odd. How could he not? They almost never went out in public other than for coffee or soda at the gas station or, a couple of times, for a very early dinner at the McDonald's on the highway. She let him assume it was their age difference that made them reclusive, the fact that he was a teacher at the high school where she'd just graduated.

As she'd become more comfortable around him, she began to imply that there was more to the story. She'd wanted to tell him about it but saw Phillip's invitation for her to reveal herself, to trust him, as coming from an earnest young man who viewed the universe as fundamentally benign. It wasn't him she distrusted but rather his optimism.

But things were different now, and he had a right to know everything. So everything is what she told him. And as she shared her secrets with this person of her choosing, each disclosure lightened her, made her feel less alone. It was like nothing she'd ever felt before. Phillip held her long after she was done talking.

By then it was early evening. She knew she should call her aunt and uncle. She didn't want them to worry. But there would be no reasoning with them. She imagined telling them the truth: *I'm at my boyfriend's house. He's twenty-three.* They'd demand she come home right away. And she could actually see herself obeying them, allowing herself to be yanked right back to the house on Notress Pass.

So maybe she did want them to worry, a little. Maybe that's what they needed to finally begin to understand that she wasn't a kid anymore. All she knew for sure was that she needed to prolong this moment with Phillip through dinner and beyond, and whether that was despite the potential repercussions with her aunt and uncle or because she wanted there to be repercussions, she wasn't sure.

She stayed. She didn't call home, and she slept in Phillip's warm bed, and early Saturday morning, with the birds noisy outside but the room still dark, she awoke beside him feeling a little surprised that he wasn't already long gone, having driven his Mazda as far as it would go or thumbed a ride back to Connecticut. Content, she fell back to sleep. When she woke up again it was to the sound of Phillip in the kitchen putting away last night's dishes, whistling a few notes of something soft and tuneless—and these ordinary sounds filled her with gratitude and wonder. This was the permanent rupture, she could feel it, separating every day in her past from every day in her future.

The air conditioner blocked her view through the window, but she didn't hear rain. No rain meant that their plan for today was on—a plan, made hastily before falling asleep last night, that to Melanie had seemed monumentally reckless. Yet she'd agreed to it.

The carnival at the Baptist church opened at eleven. There would be games and rides and food sold out of carts. The two of them would go there and spend the afternoon together like regular people.

So many bodies, and she was moving toward them. The excitement she felt last night at the thought of going to the carnival with Phillip had faded over breakfast, faded more on the walk over. She'd been able to compress her fear into the smallest nugget. But stepping onto the church grounds, her body stiffened. It would be easy to release his hand, turn around, walk away. Rush home and apologize to Kendra and Wayne for being an ungrateful niece.

She willed herself on.

As they walked toward the center of the grounds, stepping around muddy patches, Melanie kept an eye out for anyone she might recognize. What if someone spoke to her? She walked head down, avoiding eye contact and talking only in quiet, clipped sentences that were lost among the carnival sounds. "Pardon me?" Phillip kept asking. Finally, he stopped walking and put his hands on her shoulders. "Melanie—no one cares that we're here."

She chose to believe him and tried to enjoy herself, taking in the scene: kids riding the Zipper and shrieking; clusters of people huddled at the game booths; smoke from the food carts rising into the sky; couples everywhere strolling arm in arm or hand in hand. She took Phillip's hand again and let herself be guided through the grounds.

When she first smelled the smoked meat, corn dogs, caramel popcorn, she awaited the nausea, but it was just the opposite

—she found herself wanting all of it, right now. And the creaking of the rides' moving parts, the shouting coming from the game booths, the hum of generators beneath a curtain of calliope music, it hit her all at once, a sharp hunger. *Look at what I've missed,* she thought. Then she shook it off. She hadn't missed everything. She was here, right now, living this.

She stopped walking on the trampled grass and looked around, slapping one finger into her palm, then two fingers, then three.

"What are you counting?" Phillip asked.

"I'm making a mental list of the things I've never done before."

"What've you got so far?"

"Funnel cake," she said.

He whistled. "What else?"

"Ferris wheel."

"Is that a good idea?"

"How do you mean?" When he placed his hand gently on her belly, she said, "Oh, look how slowly it's turning." They watched until the ride stopped, and a couple of young children—seven or eight years old—stepped out of a car. At its highest point, the cars swayed gently in the breeze. "I can definitely do that," she said.

"Well, count me out."

"Why? I thought we could . . ." She grinned. "Oh, right. Heights. I forgot."

"It's a common fear," he pointed out.

She patted his hand. "You're a delicate flower. Oh, and I've never played one of those games where you try to win stuff."

So they tried to win stuff: ring-toss, then a booth where Phillip's plastic racehorse, moved forward with a squirt gun, finished a close second. The winner, a boy of eleven or twelve who himself looked like a horse, with a broad nose and hair down to his neck, pumped his fist into the air and reached out to the game attendant for his prize, a stuffed-animal horse, which the boy looked proud to receive until it occurred to him that he was a twelve-year-old boy holding a stuffed animal. He handed the horse to a smaller girl beside him, who hugged it to her chest.

Melanie was watching the girl pet her new horse, combing back its mane, when she heard: "Mr. Connor! Miss Denison!"

Melanie dropped Phillip's hand and spun around. Her twelfth-grade English teacher, Mrs. Henderson, beamed at them. "Why, just look at you!" She was flanked by her two daughters.

"Hello, ma'am," Melanie said.

"You know, Bethany was just asking me if I'd run into any of my students here, and I said to her, well, we'll just have to wait and see. Isn't that what I said?"

"Yes," said her older daughter, who was six.

"No, *I* said it," said her three-year-old sister.

"You *didn't*," Bethany said.

"And now here you are," Mrs. Henderson said, "looking beautiful as always. So what have you been doing with yourself?"

"I'm taking classes at Mountain Community," Melanie said. Saying it made her realize how proud she was of this small achievement.

"Oh, I'm glad to hear that," Mrs. Henderson said. "I thought you'd decided against college."

"My parents and I talked it over." She always referred to Kendra and Wayne as her parents. "Aunt" and "Uncle" would invite questions.

"Parents do know best sometimes," she said, and raised an eyebrow. "Now on to more pressing matters: Phillip, why didn't you tell me that you and Melanie were an item?"

"We like keeping our business to ourselves," he said.

It wasn't particularly scandalous, the two of them. He was never her teacher. Their age difference was only six years—five, come December. He'd graduated from the University of Connecticut and come down here as part of the Teach for America program. Had she seen him in the high school hallways? Sure. But they didn't formally meet until after she'd already graduated, and she was working in the office supply store and he'd come in one day as a customer.

"Oh, how silly!" Mrs. Henderson said. "Secrets don't stay secrets for long in Fredonia. Well, you picked yourself a good one. Melanie didn't have much to say in class, but she's as smart as— Caitlin, please don't do that. *Caitlin*. You'll get muddy." She took her younger daughter's hand and helped her to stand up again before refocusing her attention on Melanie and Phillip. "Young love is a wonderful thing!" she announced, and then fake-whispered to Melanie: "You watch out for his big city ways."

Melanie forced a smile.

"We were about to head over to the Ferris wheel," Phillip said.

"Of course. You two have yourself a good time." She winked at Phillip. "See you bright and early on Monday, young man."

He smiled back. When they'd walked away, he said, "That woman is an idiot."

"She was always nice to me."

"Let me ask you something—did you learn anything from her?"

A good point. Melanie was better educated in the progression of Caitlin's toilet training than in *Hamlet* or *To Kill a Mockingbird*. "Well . . ."

"And she treats me like a child. You know she's only twenty-six?"

That seemed impossible. "So tell me," she said, "what exactly are those big city ways I've been warned about?"

He stopped walking. "Come over again tonight, and I'll show you."

Her face got warm. "I'm going to ride the Ferris wheel now."

It was almost 1 p.m., cooler than yesterday, a lovely day to be out. As she waited in line, she plucked a dandelion out of the grass and tucked it behind her ear. The ride attendant put her alone in a pale-green car, lowered the lap bar until it was snug, and said, "Bon voyage." A few seconds later, she was rising into the air and swaying softly. The ride didn't go very high, but at the top was a view of the streets of her town, the houses and lawns and cars. Below were the fairgrounds, clumps of people waiting for rides and food. She went up and around, down, up again. The car moved slowly, and the sensation in her belly wasn't unpleasant. She lost sight of Phillip. Scanning the ground for him, she noticed a group of young kids waving at whichever car was at the top of the loop. Next time she reached the top, she waved back, and then, scanning the crowd again for Phillip she noticed an older man watching her. His gaze stayed on her as she came down to the bottom of the ride, and as she climbed again he raised a large camera to his face and held it there.

"Hey!" she shouted, but he was already walking quickly away, melting into the crowd.

When her car descended again—how many loops would this ride make?—she shouted to the ride attendant, "I need to get off the ride!" but he either didn't hear or didn't care, and there she went up again, and down again. "Please!" she shouted the next time, her eyes filling with tears. She considered leaping off, but this was a crazy thought, and anyway she was stuck underneath the lap bar. When the attendant had lowered the bar, his fingers had grazed her thighs. Was it an accident? A cheap feel? In the span of seconds, the whole place had turned sinister.

On the next loop she spotted Phillip again—he had moved off to the side, near where she'd be exiting—and she shouted, "Stop the ride!" just as it began to slow. The attendant started letting people out of the cars beneath her, but the process was maddening: one car, then another, then another. Finally, hers. She ran down the ramp and nearly collided into Phillip.

"Did you see that man?" she asked.

"Who?"

She grabbed Phillip's arm and tugged him in the direction the man had gone. "He was watching me. He took my picture. We have to find him." As they ran, she described him: thin, older, gray facial hair, faded blue jeans. They move in and around the crowd, which had swelled from just a few minutes earlier. There were too many people. They'd never find him. He was already gone.

Then, remarkably, there he was: over by the game where you threw Wiffle balls into colored cups to win prizes. His camera was out again.

"Why did you take my picture?" Melanie asked, breathless.

The man turned to face her. "I did?" He studied her face. "Oh—the Ferris wheel." He stuck out his hand. "Manny Simpson, *Mason City Democrat*."

"You work for the newspaper?"

"Of course." He nodded to his camera. "I'm taking pictures for tomorrow's paper."

She was momentarily relieved. Who had she thought this man was? She'd been reading too many Hardy Boys novels. But her relief lasted only a moment. "You can't put my picture in the paper."

"You looked lovely up there—so happy. And with that flower in your hair . . ."

She reached up to where she had put the dandelion behind her ear, but it must have fallen out during her rush across the carnival grounds. "You can't use it."

"She doesn't like being photographed," Phillip said.

"I'm taking hundreds of photos, and the paper will probably only use two or three, so it's highly unlikely—"

"You can't, though," Melanie said. "You have to promise."

"All right. I'll make a note of it. No lovely girl on the Ferris wheel." He smiled and turned away.

Still feeling uneasy, and no longer hungry, Melanie said to Phillip, "I want to leave."

"Are you sure?"

She didn't want to disappoint him. This was supposed to be their day out. Their day together. "I'm sure," she said.

They walked away from the carnival, back toward Phillip's house, neither of them talking. Finally, he said, "What about my own camera. I'm just curious. Would you ever let me take a picture of you?"

She thought about it. "No."

"Don't you trust me?"

"It isn't a matter of trust."

"I don't understand."

"If I didn't want you to photograph me naked, would you understand that? Even if you never planned to share the photo with anyone else?"

"Sure," he said.

"Then just think of me as naked all the time." She didn't like her own response—too flippant for the occasion—and she stopped walking. "Okay, I don't like having to say this, but I will. I need you to protect me. Not like a policeman or a parent. I'm not a helpless child. But I'm also not some typical college freshman. I spend every minute of every day looking over my shoulder. It isn't a joke."

"I get that," he said, rubbing her arm. "It's just that it was all so long ago—"

His touch felt good, but she needed him to understand. "You've been dealing with this for less than a day. I've been dealing with it for fifteen years." The sun had moved out from behind some clouds and was heating up the ground. Before long, the day would probably be as oppressive as yesterday. They started walking again. "Forget it," she said. "We can talk about it some other time."

"All right." He put his arm around her. "But I can handle it. I really can."

These were reassuring words that raised her spirits until about three seconds after he'd said them, when a squirrel dropped out of the tree under which they were passing. It had either misjudged a jump or slipped, and came whooshing out of the branches and plopped down onto the road just a few feet in front of them.

Melanie heard: *Slap, slap, slap, slap, slap, slap.*

The squirrel froze, momentarily stunned, before finding its bearings and darting away from the road toward the curb and scurrying up the nearest tree.

Melanie looked left. Phillip was no longer beside her. She turned around. He was at least twenty feet back, looking sheepish in his flip-flops, which had broadcasted his hasty retreat.

"What the hell was that about?" she asked.

"It startled me."

"You ran away from a squirrel?"

He walked back to her. "It could have been rabid."

She started walking quickly ahead without him, this man whose quirky fears were suddenly not remotely endearing. Maybe she'd been drawn to him because he was so different from her aunt and uncle. But if they were smothering her, this was no antidote. An antidote like this would get her killed.

"I need to go home," she said. "I need to not see you right now."

"Melanie—"

"Let's just walk."

The carnival sounds faded. Soon there were only their footfalls and the cars going by, and the birds and, yes, squirrels mocking them from the trees. When they reached Phillip's house, they went inside and Melanie collected her backpack and returned to the front door.

"I'm sorry," Phillip said.

She wouldn't look at him, wouldn't talk to him. She wasn't intentionally giving him the silent treatment, but she felt nauseous and sweaty and exhausted. She descended the concrete steps and returned to her car.

There was only one way to deal with the storm she was walking into. By the time she'd made it back to Notress Pass and driven up the pebbly driveway and put the car into park, her aunt and uncle were already rushing out of the trailer.

"I'm fine," Melanie said, shutting the car door behind her. "I spent the night with the man I've been seeing. But things between us didn't work out. I'm very tired and need to rest. We can talk about anything you want, I promise—but later. I'm very, very sorry for worrying you, and I love you both very much." She walked between them, her face hot with humiliation, and was quickly past, up the stairs, into the trailer, into her bedroom, shutting the door and locking it behind her.

Her aunt and uncle, to their tremendous credit, didn't come knocking.

An hour later, she'd emerged from her bedroom and was lying on the living room sofa, feet resting on her aunt's lap. Her uncle sat in a chair opposite them. "I thought there might be a future with him," Melanie said, "but I was wrong. That's really all there is to it. I'm sorry to have worried you—I know that was awful of me."

She'd expected plenty of yelling when she returned home. Wayne and Kendra weren't people who yelled, but Melanie had never stayed out all night. There was no rule forbidding it, because such a transgression was unthinkable.

Yet there had been no yelling, no tirades when she came out of her room—only concerned embraces and as much patience as she could possibly hope for. They were wonderful from time to time, she had to admit.

"Who is this man?" her uncle asked.

Melanie shook her head. "It doesn't matter. It's over."

"When did you meet him?" her aunt asked.

"Did he hurt you?" her uncle asked.

"No, nothing like that. He's a decent guy. It just didn't work out."

Her aunt and uncle exchanged glances. "You told him, didn't you?" Wayne said. Melanie briefly considered lying, but her hesitation told them everything.

"So what happened?" Kendra asked. "He couldn't handle it?"

"Something like that," Melanie said.

Her aunt, eyes wet, reached out and took Melanie's hand. "That's why you have us. We'll protect you—always, always, always."

5

September 20, 1991

Before that amazing and utterly accidental late-morning moment seven years back when Allison Anne Pembroke stepped out of the elevator and into the third floor of Monmouth Regional Hospital, Ramsey's entire life had added up to nothing, $0 + 0 + 0 = 0$, the equation of a loser whose existence was as aimless as it was pointless. Flash forward a year, and the two of them were still together, and not just together but a whole new equation with a sum far greater than anything he'd ever imagined himself contributing to. In quiet moments he'd fall into the habit of asking himself the obvious.

What if we hadn't met? What then?

He'd imagine the alternatives when falling asleep at night, and on interstates, and while fueling up. The scenes he imagined always led to the same conclusion: He'd be dead. Beer bottle to the head, knife to the gut, maybe a high-speed chase. Or he would've woken up one gray day and said *enough already* and used his belt to rig up a nice noose. Or something less dramatic—illness, since Lord knows he didn't take care of himself when he was on his own. Surely he'd have died as he had lived: angry and alone, underwhelmed and underwhelming, unwilling to give of himself to another or see the beauty in anything or anybody. He'd have left the world a little worse off than he had found it. That would have been his legacy. His tombstone would have read, *Here lies another shithead.*

Before meeting Allie, he had never been in love or close to it. When he would stop to dwell on the matter as a teenager and young man, this lack of love gnawed at him, so he tried to convince himself that he didn't give a shit. He had honed this particular skill, not giving a shit, over many years, which served him well much of the time but also made him take risks he knew he shouldn't. The cars he stole, for instance. You ought to feel a thrill, revving somebody else's engine and peeling away from the curb. Going through their glove box, looking under the visors. But there was no thrill in it. What he stole, he stole to pay rent and buy food. The fights he got into brought him no satisfaction, either—not when a fight almost always meant a night in some drunk tank that reeked of every human excretion. And it wasn't as if his fights were ever about anything noble. Nobody was defending anyone's honor. Typically it was about nothing at all. You get drunk, you get mad, shit happens. It was sad, this life of his, like a mushroom pushing out of the ground after a hard rain, random and poisonous. He actually tried out this metaphor on his friend Eric while lying in the hospital seven years back, hopped up on painkillers. Eric was trying to cheer him up with dirty jokes, but Eric was too religious for the jokes to be dirty enough, and there was no cheering up Ramsey that day, anyway. He had mangled his leg out of his own stupidity, he'd just been canned from the only good job he'd ever had, and he'd been given a summons for taking a drunken swing at a cop.

A mushroom? Eric had said. *What you are is a fool.*

He was absolutely right. And yet a day later, Allie stepped out of the elevator and into Ramsey's life.

He didn't deserve her—especially not then, when anything redeeming about him was hidden under a thick shell of defensiveness, evasion, and straight-up aggression cultivated over many years. But they got together, he and Allie, and they stayed together. She taught him what love meant, how it was the truth that made all other truths possible. She came along at the exact right moment and saved his life in every way that a life could be saved. So for her, he did that singular thing that human beings almost never did no matter how much they might want to, and never, ever for another person.

For her, he changed.

The door swung open as he was reaching with the key. The surprises revealed themselves gradually. The late-afternoon light always made her face lovely, for instance, but today her beauty staggered him.

And when he stepped into the house, he was struck by its tidiness. The housekeeper came on Wednesdays, letting herself in and out, but by Friday, especially when Allie was alone all week with the kid, the place would revert to its natural state. Not today.

He followed Meg inside. "The house looks great," he told Allie. "So do you." It immediately occurred to him he should have reversed the order of compliments.

"You didn't tell me they were coming over," Allie said.

"I didn't? The guys? Sure, I did."

"No."

Of course they needed to rehearse, with the gig on Sunday. But maybe he hadn't told her. When she bent down to kiss Meg on the head, saying, "Hi, sweetie," Ramsey saw that underneath Allie's Monmouth College sweatshirt was a lacy red bra. The panties would match, he was sure of it. Allie used to keep two sets of underclothes, one for when Ramsey was on the road and another for when he was home. He only ever saw the shapeless, faded garments in the laundry hamper, until after the baby was born, at which point dutifully separated laundry became an extravagance, and the only pertinent question became whether something was clean enough.

These small surprises—tidy house, sexy underwear—were like Easter eggs for him to find. A lit candle somewhere filled the house with the smell of fall. A Sam Cooke CD was playing, though the sounds coming from the garage drowned it out.

Meg ran through the house toward the kitchen. Watching their daughter together somehow reset their reunion. "It's good to see you," Allie said. She placed a hand on his arm and kissed his lips. "Thanks for getting her today."

"Happy to," he said. Allie could have gotten Meg from day care herself—she often came home from work early on Fridays—but before leaving town last week Ramsey had said he would do it. He had developed, over the years, this technique for proving his own decency to himself—making small promises that he could fulfill. This time the promise had come from the basic need to spend a little time alone with Meg before the weekend's bustle of activity.

Six, seven years ago he would come home from a week away, and within minutes he and Allie would fall into bed. But Allie was still trying, the Easter eggs proved it, and Ramsey knew he ought to try, too. His face needed a shave, his hair a trim. He didn't like wearing sunglasses, and over the years his squinting had etched permanent gouges in his face. He should've exercised more. He was thin, always had been, but that wasn't the same as being fit. Not like when he was younger and could drink a twelve-pack and spend the whole next day in the sun doing some rich guy's yard work.

In the kitchen, Meg was peeling magnetic letters off the refrigerator and dropping them on to the floor. "I was thinking we could get pizza for the guys," Ramsey said. "From the good place."

"How long do you think rehearsal will go?"

"Don't know—but I'll make sure we turn everything down at eight." Meg's bedtime.

"Because I was hoping you and I could have some time tonight."

Already the plastic letters were everywhere. Now Meg was over by the toy barn. When she threw a plastic pig across the room, Allie said, "Sweetie, don't throw the animals," and Meg pursed her lips and slammed a cow onto the ground.

"Are you little mad?" Ramsey asked her, and cursed himself for forgetting to use this surefire trick back at the park.

"*Big* mad," she answered, already smiling, her anger allayed by their inside joke.

Ramsey winked at Meg and said to Allie, "The thing is, this isn't some ordinary jam session. We got a gig coming up."

"You do?" Feigned astonishment. "Why, I had no idea."

Okay, he deserved that. He'd been yammering on about the gig for weeks. But Allie only knew the half of it. There hadn't been time during these last few days of reflection and near-constant driving to tell her that the plan had expanded. And they had to be finished rehearsing by ten tonight because of the town's noise ordinance. When they'd first moved to Sandy Oaks, a cop had broken up a weeknight jam at 8:30 p.m. Someone in the neighborhood had called the cops on them anonymously, rather than just knocking on the door like a normal human being and asking Ramsey if they could turn it down a notch or two. Welcome to the neighborhood.

"I want us to be great, is all," he said, getting a six-pack from the refrigerator and setting it on the counter.

Laid out on the kitchen table were 3 x 5 index cards, with more cards in a plastic box. Allie had a computer in her office at work, but she preferred the index cards, which she carried with her when she traveled from doctor's office to doctor's office, wearing tight business skirts and being outgoing and drumming up demand for whatever new drug her company decided that these doctors' patients' bones or blood or organs couldn't do without. Fridays, she confirmed the next week's appointments. It wasn't lost on Ramsey that at different points in their lives, they both worked as drug pushers—he as a sixteen-year-old pot dealer, she as a grown woman shilling expensive pharmaceuticals for a megacorporation. But he kept this observation to himself.

Allie handed Meg her *Little Mermaid* cup of water. "You guys will be playing for family," she said to Ramsey. "They'll be proud no matter how you sound."

"Yeah, about that." Just then, the bass amp got a lot louder. The last thing they needed was a cop breaking up their rehearsal before it got started.

"About what?" Allie asked.

But Ramsey was heading upstairs to the guest room for his guitar case. "About *what*?" she called after him. Seconds later, he was back. He kissed Allie's neck, bent down and kissed the top of Meg's head.

"I'll tell you later," he said. When Allie's eyes narrowed, he added, "Don't worry—it's good. Like a surprise. Killer bra, by the way."

He grabbed the six-pack with his free hand and headed to the garage. As soon as he'd opened the door separating the laundry room from the garage, a beer can was arcing toward him, and he had to drop the six-pack on the ground (it was either that or the guitar) to catch it. Ramsey opened the can, took a swallow, and looked around.

"I had a dream last night," he said, closing the door behind him. "I could fly, and breathe underwater." He set the guitar case on the ground and snapped it open. "I could do anything. I think that dream was about this gig." He looked up at the guys. "It's going to be like that on Sunday. Like flying. And breathing underwater."

"Amen," said Eric.

"Preach to us, brother Ramsey!" called Paul from behind his drum kit. Eric, sensing sacrilege, shot his younger brother a look.

Ramsey wiped down the fretboard with a rag and lifted the guitar out of its case.

"You have no idea," he said, "how good it is to see you assholes."

Ramsey gladly parked his car outside, in the driveway, to make room for the drumset, microphone stands, speakers on tripods, a jumble of patch cords and speaker cables snaking across the ground. The four-channel P.A. sat on a scratched-up coffee table that Ramsey had claimed from someone else's curb back when he needed to furnish his first apartment on the cheap. Tacked to the drywall were a half dozen rock-star posters and twice as many classic album covers. In the corner of the garage stood a spare refrigerator/freezer, left by the house's former owner.

They had a name, Ramsey and Paul and Eric and Wayne. They called themselves Rusted Wheels, but they weren't a real band. Real bands played out. The point of Rusted Wheels was always exactly this—to jam in Ramsey's garage. They met up every couple of weeks, depending on Ramsey's driving schedule, and in all that time, since before Allie was pregnant, there had never been talk of playing in public. There had never been a need. Playing a gig, they all knew—or at least suspected—meant hauling gear and negotiating payment with dickhead bar owners and hustling for people to show up, and that all seemed a lot like work, which was the opposite of why they came together to play.

How many teenagers jammed in similar garages? Plenty—but teenagers appreciated nothing. You had to be over thirty and overburdened. You needed battle scars to prove you'd earned the right to a few hours of amplified jams and words sung with feeling and reverb.

"Wayne called me earlier," Paul said. "He can't make it tonight."

Case in point: Wayne was under thirty. When you're young and still have all your hair, apparently the rules of band practice don't apply.

"He's not coming at all?" Eric asked.

Paul gave a *Hey, not my problem* shrug.

"What's he got that's so important?" Ramsey asked.

"He's performing brain surgery." Paul drank from his beer. "He didn't say, I didn't ask. Probably a date." He belched. "You remember those, don't you?"

"I just want to do these songs right on Sunday," Ramsey said. "I want us to be good."

"I got sad news for you, pal." Eric grinned. "We ain't good."

"Well, it ain't Sunday yet, either." But Eric was right. Only Wayne had any real talent. Paul was especially weak on the drums. His tempos defied all logic. But he had problems of his own—handicapped son, wife who'd gone inpatient a couple of times for depression. He worked as an EMT, so it wasn't as if he could veg out on the job. He was a good man who needed Rusted Wheels at least as much as any of them.

Ramsey removed several sheets of paper from the back pocket of his jeans. He had composed the set list in his head while driving through New Mexico and written up four copies at a truck stop in Amarillo.

"This is a lot of music," Paul said, scanning the list.

There were eighteen songs, many of them already part of the Rusted Wheels repertoire, plus three or four that they'd tried in the past and found too hard. "Some neighbors might be coming," Ramsey said. "I want it to be a real show."

They'd slogged through a third of the list when, at 7:30, Allie came into the garage carrying pizza boxes. At eight Ramsey made them play quieter, but at nine they were still going strong. At a couple of minutes before ten, they settled on an ending to "Magic Carpet Ride," called it quits, and made plans to meet up again the following afternoon.

By then the garage felt superheated, three bodies working hard. Eric was slick with sweat. Paul had stripped down to his undershirt. Ramsey felt the urge to say something before they dispersed. "I can't thank you men enough. This gig, your dedication. Your friendship." He forced himself to look at Eric and Paul, rather than down at the concrete floor or across the garage at the ladders hanging on the wall. "It means more to me than you could know." And with no one knowing what to say next, Ramsey decided to cut them all a break. "Okay, fuckheads, see you tomorrow."

Eric snapped open a can of Diet Coke. "So spill it, partner. What's going on?"

"How do you mean?"

"Come on—the marathon rehearsal, your rousing speech . . ."

Paul had left. Ramsey was changing his guitar strings. The instrument was damn fine, better than he deserved—a Telecaster with a sunburst finish, Allie's gift to him for his thirtieth birthday. That guitar replaced the piece-of-shit knockoff-of-a-knockoff that followed him from lousy apartment to lousy apartment over the years.

New strings brought out the Telecaster's full depth, but Ramsey knew better than to change them right before the gig. They'd go flat every two seconds, and he wasn't a good enough musician to make corrections on the fly. He wasn't good enough to tune his new strings while holding a conversation, either, so he laid the guitar back in its case. "I want to tell you a true story," he said, "about something I did three days ago."

Eric's eyes widened. After all these years, he was still protective of Ramsey. He still felt responsible. "I hope it's nothing bad."

"No, you idiot. I went and saw the Grand Canyon." Ramsey tossed a few empties into an open trash can. The beer was really for Paul and Wayne. Eric was in A.A., and Ramsey drank exactly one beer each rehearsal to prove to himself that he could stop after one. "Ever seen it?"

"The Grand Canyon? Of course."

"I don't mean in pictures."

"Then no, I haven't seen it. Been too busy."

"Well, I been busy, too. But I was in Phoenix on Tuesday and my load-in got done early, and I said to myself it was time to see something I always wanted to see. Something I always heard you've never seen till you see it in person. So I drove through the desert, and when I got there I parked my truck and I saw it."

It felt familiar, telling Eric about something he did or some-place he went, though with a crucial difference. Early on in their friendship, Ramsey's stories were usually confessions: The time he got drunk and beat up some prick outside the Pink Pony. The time he got canned for insubordination. He would confess, and Eric would listen and offer a few words to remind Ramsey that we weren't simply the sum total of our mean-spirited actions.

"So how was it?" Eric asked.

Off and on these past couple of days, heading east, Ramsey considered how he might describe the indescribable. "It was big.

74

And silent." He frowned. "Damn. I can't do it. There's no words, you know?" There was only a feeling born of an expanse so wide that standing on the rim was like leaning over the surface of an empty planet. At the same time, he liked knowing it wasn't some other planet but just dumb old America. And he liked knowing that he was experiencing the same stunned hush, the same loss for words, that other men had experienced for as long as there had been people to stand there and look. No, he couldn't describe to Eric what he could barely describe to himself, about feeling small and unimportant, but in the best sense. *You don't matter as much as you think you do*, the canyon told him, *so lighten up*. To get that feeling, to grasp the wisdom written on the immense canyon walls, you had to be there yourself. Otherwise, you sounded like the sort of hitchhiker Ramsey despised, blathering on and saying nothing.

"I got high that day," he said. So maybe this was a confession after all, he realized.

"Weed?" Eric asked.

"Amazing weed."

"Maybe not the best idea," Eric said.

"Maybe no, maybe yes," Ramsey said. "What happened was, I got this idea into my head to climb down into the canyon a ways. There was a trail. It looked sort of steep, but what the hell."

"Sure. Worst that happens is you fall a few thousand feet to your death."

"Exactly. So about a half hour down the trail I can smell it. A minute later, I come across a couple of kids, guy and a girl, on a big flat rock soaking up the sun."

"Hanky panky?"

Eric was thirty-nine, only five years older than Ramsey, but sometimes he sounded like a whole other generation. "No, they weren't screwing or nothing. They were just sitting there, smoking and talking and looking out at everything. It was already a lot hotter there than up on the rim. It felt like July all of a sudden. They had a jug of water and they offered me some, and then they offered me the joint they were smoking, and I surprised myself by taking both. These kids, they were smart. In college. We talked." Ramsey tried to recall the conversation. With a good conversation, though, where you're just having it and connecting with other people, do you ever remember *how* it got good? "You got to understand the degree of beauty there," he said. "It was late afternoon, and the sky was this dark shade of blue you don't ever see in New Jersey. The light kept changing. Every few minutes it was like a whole new landscape. A sight like that makes you open up. I told them things I haven't even told *you*, and you're my best friend."

"Shut up," Eric said, and looked away.

"Well, you are. It shouldn't embarrass you to hear it."

"I ain't embarrassed." But Eric was still looking over at the Jimi Hendrix poster.

"Yeah, you are. See, there's your problem. You're a hell of a guy but you'll never admit it."

Eric looked back at Ramsey. "So what'd you tell them at the Grand Canyon?"

Ramsey smiled. "I told them the truth."

"Care to elaborate?"

It occurred to Ramsey that maybe Allie had confided in Eric. She was the only person he'd ever told about the orbital axis. If she told Eric, it would be a betrayal, but a minor one, done out of her love and concern. She knew that Eric held sway with Ramsey, and for good reason. Were it not for him, Ramsey would still be some angry shitbag drifting from job to job, some legal, some not—except, now he'd be a thirty-four-year-old shitbag, which was a lot less forgivable than being an eighteen- or a twenty-year-old one.

"It means," Ramsey said, "that I told them they better take in all this beauty while they can, cause it won't be here forever."

"You told them the Grand Canyon won't be here forever?"

"Nothing will. Not me or you or this garage or the Grand Canyon, neither."

"Ramsey Miller, philosopher."

"Bust my balls if you want, but those kids taught me something. I offered them a few dollars for the weed I'd smoked, but they wouldn't take it. The guy, after college he plans to join the Peace Corps. He said the key to life is magnanimity. Can you beat that? His word. It means generous."

"I know what it means."

Ramsey doubted this but let it go. "He says if you have magnanimity, it comes back to you twofold. Sure enough, we'd just started back up the trail. It was steep and not an easy climb—you know that means something, coming from me—and the girl he's with, she steps funny on a rock and twists her ankle, bad. I'll tell you, once the sun goes down it gets real cold in the desert. This time of year, it goes below freezing. So they'd of been in real trouble. They didn't have provisions or nothing. Just that one jug of water, and we'd already finished most of it off."

"But they had you."

Ramsey smiled, remembering. "Me and the boy took our time, making sure every step was in the right place. We got his friend up to the rim, safe and sound."

"The Lord had a plan for you that day."

That wasn't Ramsey's point at all, but he stopped himself from correcting his friend. "Afterward, when I was driving, I kept thinking about those two. I shouldn't call them kids, because they weren't kids. But I kept thinking about them, and about magnanimity. And that's when I realized we're doing this gig all wrong.

It shouldn't be just for us—our families and whatnot. We need to invite everyone."

"Who's 'everyone'?"

"Everyone in the neighborhood."

"You hate everyone in the neighborhood," Eric said.

"That's my point—we need to come together. Listen, I know there's people who don't think much of me, and for a long time I didn't care. Or I did, but it was easier to pretend I didn't. But that ain't how I want it anymore."

"And you think a party will fix everything?"

"Ain't a matter of fixing things—it's about doing what's right. I want people coming to my house, eating my food and drinking my beer and listening to Rusted Wheels. I want their kids trampling my lawn."

Eric glanced at the door separating the garage from the rest of the house. "Ramsey, I have to ask. How much does Allie know about this plan of yours?"

"Haven't had time to fill her in yet on all the details."

"You might want to get around to that. I doubt her ideal Sunday includes hosting all your snooty neighbors."

"*I'm* hosting," Ramsey said. "She can sit back and drink margaritas. Point is, this is no time for selfishness or hard feelings or any of that bullshit."

"What do you mean, 'no time'?" Eric asked.

Yeah, Ramsey thought. Allie told him. Definitely.

On a freezing January afternoon, Ramsey had sat her down and explained the orbital axis to his wife, what it meant, and she made him swear to keep it between them. Frankly, he didn't care who knew, but he gave her his word and kept it, because he loved her, honored her, and obeyed her, just as he'd promised six years earlier. Anyway, she had a point. There were some things that people would rather stay ignorant about.

Take those kids in the Grand Canyon. During their truth session, before the shadows got too deep and they all started back up the trail, Ramsey had swept his arms across the magnificent vista and said, *You know, God's going-out-of-business sale is coming sooner than you think.* He chose to say it that way for their benefit—clever, a little humorous to lighten the impact—but when the kids started trading glances, he backed off right away, laughing at himself and blaming the weed. He told them about a time when he had been high and decided it would be a good idea to climb the utility pole by his apartment, and then it started to thunder and lightning, and he got so scared that he froze way up there like a cat in a tree, and the power company had to come and rescue him in one of their bucket trucks. It hadn't been a funny experience at the time, and he'd been drunk, not high, but he told it the way he did because he admired and respected these two kids and wanted them to like him. That was before they all began their ascent and the girl sprained her ankle and Ramsey got to show them what kind of man he could be, what kind of man he was.

"My friend, there's no time for bullshit," Ramsey said to Eric now, "because that's not how a magnanimous person behaves."

In the family room, Allie was facing the TV—a drama, from the serious, argumentative voices. "Eric's leaving," Ramsey said as he led his friend to the front door.

"Good night, Allie," Eric said to the back of Allie's head.

"Mhmm," she replied without turning around.

"She feels my judgment," Eric said once he and Ramsey were alone outside. His voice was just above a whisper. "I shouldn't be judging anyone. That's the Lord's job, not mine."

Ramsey always felt uncomfortable when Eric talked as if he were in church or at an A.A. meeting. "Nah," he said. "She's just really into her show."

Once Eric was gone, Ramsey went inside and sat at the kitchen table, bit into a slice of leftover pizza, and began writing his to-do list. The pizza was cool and hard, but he *tasted* it. It was that way with everything now: land and sky drenched in color. The band's music reverberating in his gut with richer resonance. The felt-tip pen dragged across paper and a car whooshed by out front. In the family room, the music on the TV swelled toward a dramatic crescendo. In the laundry room, the dryer thudded rhythmically: *b-b-duh, b-b-duh*. The dryer caused the recessed kitchen lights to pulse as if transmitting a code he was this close to cracking. He was paying attention, noticing everything. Some people—scientists, maybe, or detectives—must live this way constantly, attuned to every crumb of sensory data. He might have imagined the experience exhausting, but it was the opposite. He felt the world offering up its treasures. The least he could do was receive them.

He should go to Allie. He would. But first, the list. Thirty-four years old, and he'd never thrown a party before. How much food do you buy? How much beer? Where do you find a pony for pony rides?

He looked up. Allie came over and stood behind him, a hand on each of his shoulders. She pressed down with her thumbs. She'd been loosening his shoulders this way for seven years, ever since he returned from his first week on the road. *My shoulders are killing me, Allie,* he'd said, and she came to him and knew exactly what to do. She worked her thumbs now, pressing hard. Ramsey let out a sigh.

"You schedule a band practice for the minute you come home," she said. "Now you're hiding in here."

"I'm making a to-do list."

"Unless I'm on that list," she said, still rubbing, "I'm not interested." Dark outside, but the curtains were open, and in the window's reflection Ramsey saw the two of them. The tableau looked intimate, yet all the details were in shadow. "It's a joke, Ramsey. We can still joke, can't we?"

"How do you mean?"

"Come on."

"What?"

She let out a breath, almost like a laugh. "You've been gone twenty-six of the last thirty days."

"I have a job."

The rubbing stopped, though her hands continued to rest on his shoulders. "You haven't had a schedule like that for years. I can only conclude that you can't stand being here, with us."

"No, Al—you know that's not true."

"And Eric—what the hell is *his* problem?"

"What do you mean?"

"He's creeping me out lately. The way he looks at me—he's acting weird. You're all acting weird." She sighed. "Even when you're here, it's like you're not here."

"I'm here now," Ramsey said. "I really am."

"Then let's go to bed."

"Soon," Ramsey said. "The thing is, I'm inviting some extra people to the gig, and I want to be sure there's enough activities and food—"

"What extra people? Who are you inviting?"

He shrugged. "The neighbors."

"*Which* neighbors?"

"Well—all of them."

Her hands on his shoulders curled into fists. "Because of your orbital axis."

"It isn't mine, Allie."

She sighed. "Can I ask why you plan to invite the neighbors?"

"I want to bring people together."

"You want that? Come to bed."

"Soon," he said.

"You'll come to *our* bed soon? Is that what you're telling me?"

When he didn't answer right away, she said, "Goddammit," and walked away from him, toward the sink. Ramsey turned around to look at her directly. She had on her plaid pajamas. From behind, she could have been any age, anyone. A stranger. She poured a glass of water, drank it down.

Ramsey brushed his teeth in the upstairs hall bathroom while one of the songs from tonight's rehearsal ran through his head. He couldn't help agreeing with Mick Jagger. Satisfaction was fucking elusive.

The house was quiet. He imagined Allie in their bedroom, on the other side of the closed door, waiting for him, reading by the light of her bedside table.

Unless she'd given up on him. That was a possibility, too.

He rinsed, wiped his face. Checked himself in the mirror. There was no good mirror in the truck, and after a long haul his own face always surprised him a little. His hair had gray in it now. The lines in his face were deepening. He looked every bit of his thirty-four years. He wanted to go to Allie, longed to. It wasn't that he preferred the trundle bed in the guest room. But the trundle was hard, like the mattress in his truck, and that was the only place he slept soundly anymore. In fact, he slept better parked at a truck stop—even with the drunken shouting, middle-of-the-night Jake brakes, and lot lizards knocking door-to-door—than he did in his quiet bedroom with Allie.

He was no fool, though. Tonight he needed to be with her. Allie had looked beautiful earlier, sun-kissed in the doorway. The small, gradual surprises this afternoon were all enticements for him to share their bed tonight. As husband and wife. As lovers. It had been too long. He knew this.

He got as far as their bedroom door and hesitated.

Magruder.

He tried to push the name from his mind. It was impractical, thinking about that man now, with Allie. Best to put it away once and for all. *Your wife is in there waiting for you,* he thought. *Go to her.* If he could be magnanimous to his neighbors, to strangers, then surely he could be that and more to his wife.

Husband and wife. Lovers. He took a breath, held it, breathed out.

I love you, Allie. I married you and I would marry you again and I will marry you a thousand times over, from now to as long as we both shall live.

He gently pushed open the bedroom door. The overhead light was dimmed, the candle on her bedside table lit. Seeing him, Allie smiled.

"Well, hello there," she said, and closed her book.

6

September 24, 2006

The rules at 9 Notress Pass arose as they became necessary. An early rule: Do not reveal your home address. Later, when Internet access became available, there was never any discussion about getting it. Wayne and Kendra knew nothing of IP addresses. They simply didn't want their name and address in a database unless there was no choice. Sometimes, like with the electric company, there was no choice. But any time there was, they chose no: no cable TV, no Internet, no newspaper delivery.

No library card.

That was the first time Melanie remembered breaking one of the family's rules. Every so often, Kendra brought her to the library, where for an hour they'd sit together quietly and read before going to McDonald's for lunch. Sometimes Melanie would read a book, other times one of the celebrity magazines. Sometimes she'd pretend to read but really she'd be watching others in the library—mothers reading to small children, the librarians gossiping behind the book-return counter. McDonald's was an even better place to watch people. Truckers on their way to Charleston (Columbus? Chicago?) smothered their food with ketchup and mustard, and chubby kids cried for soda refills, and teenagers a little older than Melanie punched the cash registers and barked commands to one another to keep everything running smoothly.

One afternoon when she was fifteen, Melanie convinced her aunt to drop her at the library before running her errands, rather than leaving her at home or taking her along.

At the library, Melanie examined the "newly received" shelf, looking at the covers of novels until one caught her eye. It had a picture of a girl about Melanie's own age standing on a balcony and looking out over a city. The city wasn't in America—she could tell from the way the buildings looked: very old, colorful, and built into a hillside. The novel was titled *The Cobbler's Sister*, and from the inside flap, Melanie learned that the city was Salamanca, Spain.

She was sitting by the window, reading the opening pages, which had wonderfully descriptive sentences that wound around like the narrow streets of Salamanca, when a number of younger kids stomped into the library. The middle school must have just let out. The kids' pent-up energy, released all at once, made reading impossible, so Melanie closed the book and began to page through a magazine. Practically the whole issue was devoted to the wedding between Jessica Simpson and Nick Lachey. Ordinarily, she'd be enthralled. An eleven-carat diamond headband was attached to the bride's veil. But that day, she wished she could keep reading the novel. Her aunt would be returning soon. So she went up to the counter, determined to get her own library card. Taped to the counter was a note:

To obtain a library card you must present either a driver's
license or a piece of mail addressed to you showing that you
reside in the town of Fredonia. No exceptions. Thank you.

The only mail that she could remember coming to her house,
rather than the P.O. box, was the phone bill. Maybe she could
steal the envelope from the kitchen trash the next time it came.
But when would she next be left alone here at the library? It could
be weeks, maybe longer.

"May I help you?" asked one of the librarians.

If there were a house nearby, she'd have dug through strangers' trash to find an envelope and said to the librarian, *Yes, this is
me.* But there were no houses on this block, just a barbershop and
a dollar store and a Baptist church.

"No, ma'am," she said, and returned to her seat by the window, furious. She tried to free her mind of Salamanca, its 800-year-
old cathedrals, its olive trees. Jessica Simpson and Nick Lachey
had been serenaded by a twenty-five-member gospel choir. The
reception hall had been decorated with 30,000 roses.

By the time her aunt picked her up, Melanie vowed that the
next time she was allowed to visit the library alone, she would
leave with her own library card and as many novels as she could
cram into her backpack without her aunt noticing.

Eight months later, she did just that.

The books she borrowed, she read late into the night and hid in
her closet or under the bed. The library was a way to escape
Notress Pass, and the books they contained allowed her to escape
it further.

Tonight, however, Melanie had come to the library not to borrow books but rather for its Wi-Fi. Behind the building, in the dim
shadows cast by an orange streetlight some hundred yards in the

distance, she crouched against the library's brick exterior wall, holding the laptop computer that Phillip had lent her two months earlier. PROPERTY OF FREDONIA REGIONAL HIGH SCHOOL read the label stuck to its side.

There was so much to see and learn online, and not just about celebrities. If the library books were her glimpse at the larger world, the Wi-Fi Internet connection was freedom writ large. Whenever she snuck out her bedroom window and walked here at night, she sat on the ground and read as fast as possible, no agenda, just clicking links and typing words and phrases into search engines and exploring the wider world though the computer screen. Once her initial thirst was quenched, she visited a few particular websites: the online edition of the *Silver Bay News*. The *Star-Ledger*. The *Asbury Park Press*. There were others, too, but those were the papers that had published the fullest coverage of her mother's death and the failed hunt for her father. Her aunt and uncle had only ever told Melanie the barest facts of the crime. Beyond that, they never spoke about the place where Melanie had lived for the first thirty-three months of her life. From the newspaper archives, she began to fill in the gaps.

How strange it always was to see that name—Meg Miller—in print, to read about her own alleged demise. *Death by drowning.* Reading those words always made her throat constrict and chest tighten as if she really were being held underwater. Then again, everything in those articles made her lightheaded and nauseous, a feeling not unlike morning sickness.

One reporter in particular wrote about the crime over a period of years for the *Silver Bay News*, with articles appearing on the first anniversary, the fifth, the tenth. One night, Melanie had searched online for the reporter's name—Arthur Goodale—and learned that he'd retired from the paper but kept up a news blog. Sometimes he would write about the "Miller killings," and these posts always struck her as surprising and sort of wonderful. To know that somebody still thought from time to time about her mother, and about her, too, made her feel less alone. She hoped that he might write about her mother this week, with another anniversary coming and going—the fifteenth.

She didn't expect to read that Arthur Goodale was dying.

His heart had given out, and now he might never leave his hospital bed or write another word. This connection to her past, tenuous as it was, would soon be severed. She herself had no memories at all of Silver Bay. She tried over the years to see her mother's face, the walls of her nursery, the kitchen where she must have sat in a high chair and eaten meals. Anything. But not a single image remained.

She shut the laptop computer, stood, brushed the dirt off her blue jeans, and began to walk toward the woods, toward home. Why hadn't she told her aunt and uncle this afternoon that she was pregnant? Was it embarrassment, believing that she and Phillip would . . . what, get married? Live happily ever after? And live where? In Fredonia? In Connecticut, near his family? She had let herself believe that Phillip Connor might be the key to a fresh start, but she should have seen that for the fantasy it was. She never should have let herself get carried away. It was depressing and dangerous.

Anyway, none of that mattered. Phillip probably thought she was crazy by now, and her aunt and uncle would find out about the baby soon enough.

The night sky was brighter than usual, the moon nearly full. She crossed a couple of streets and entered a larger section of woods that would have her home in fifteen minutes. Had she driven to the library, the car's engine would almost certainly have woken Kendra, who was a light sleeper, and these excursions were too important to jeopardize. Plus, Melanie liked the woods at night. She'd never been afraid of them, and consequently she knew them well. Or maybe it was because she knew them well that she wasn't afraid.

Yet tonight she wasn't enjoying the walk. Despite herself, she kept thinking about Phillip, leaving him at his front door looking hurt and confused. Had she broken up with him? Even she didn't know. So he ran away from a squirrel. So what? And then she started thinking about that poor journalist in New Jersey dying alone, eighty-one years old and totally off base about the case that had haunted him for years.

"Surprise!" she said aloud. "Meg Miller is alive!"

A twig snapped.

Someone was in the woods with her.

She looked around and saw no one. Her imagination? Other than the occasional deer, the only animals out here were small—squirrels, possum—and they kept to themselves.

She found the woods comforting, she reminded herself, not spooky. Whatever hormones had turned her favorite smells putrid were playing games with her brain's fear center. Or something. Her pace quickened, and she tried to move quieter, and then she started thinking about killers and rapists on the loose, behind every tree.

Her breathing quickened. *I'm losing the woods*, she thought. *They were mine, and now they won't be anymore.*

Before her semester began, her aunt and uncle had given her a cell phone with prepaid minutes, but she'd used up all the minutes long ago, talking to Phillip. Still—if she'd had minutes left, would she have called him now? She hoped not. These were her woods. She willed herself to slow down, relax—*no one is here; no one is here.* Yet by the time she saw the abandoned tractor, the landmark telling her she was just a few hundred yards from Notress Pass, her sweat had turned cold and her pulse throbbed in her neck. The air was still. The only sounds were her quiet footfalls and her heavy breaths. As she passed the tractor, she could swear she saw a shadow glide across it, and she let out a gasp and started sprinting. She squeezed through the tight gap in the hedges, discovered long ago, onto her own property. Her aunt and uncle must not see her leaving or returning, or else there would go her freedom. Still, she half hoped that one of them would spot her darting across the lawn. At this moment she yearned for their safety, yearned for them to take away her freedom. It didn't matter that the woods had been hers. They were gone now. She climbed through her bedroom window, closed and locked it, and slipped soundlessly into bed, not even removing her shoes.

She fell asleep but was awakened by images of hundreds of snapping turtles crawling over one another to get at her—a recurring nightmare since childhood. She awoke several more times, sweating, then freezing, then sweating again. During one of the sweating spells, she removed her shoes and clothes. During the next freezing spell, she found her pajamas in the dark and put them on.

The next time she awakened was to the hard wrap of knuckles on her bedroom door.

"Yeah?" she groaned.

"Get up." Her uncle's voice, uncharacteristically stern.

The room was getting light. She looked at the clock: 7 a.m. Her alarm would go off in fifteen minutes. So why the urgency? She sat up in bed a moment, trying to shake off sleep, and left her room wearing her pajamas and slippers. Her aunt was seated at the kitchen table. Her uncle stood beside her, leaning over the morning paper.

"Come over here," he said without looking up.

She knew without having to look. But she looked anyway.

"He promised not to use it," Melanie said. "I made him promise."

The photographer must have had a powerful zoom lens. She could see individual freckles, each petal on the dandelion.

"People can't be trusted, Melanie," her aunt said.

There were three photographs in a row. Hers was in the middle. To her left, two small children with wide grins, attacking a tall cone of cotton candy. To her right, an older man wearing a gold-and-blue West Virginia T-shirt, giving the camera a thumbs-up. Behind him, the Zipper ride in motion, a blur of purple and green.

A single caption described all three pictures: *Local Fredonia residents enjoying the First Baptist Church's Carnival for Christ.*

Her uncle shut the paper and began to pace the small kitchen.

"I never gave him my name," Melanie said. Still. There was her photo, large and clear, placing her right in Fredonia. And the *Mason City Democrat* published an online version. Did her aunt and uncle know? Probably not, but *she* knew. Her image was now online. Permanently.

"So is this your definition of being careful?" Uncle Wayne put his hands up to his head and massaged his temples. He sighed. "I want you to come to work with me. Learn the trade."

"What—you mean fixing cars?"

"It's been good for this family. You're left alone to do your work—"

"Uncle Wayne, I'm in college."

"Well, your aunt and I don't think you should be. It's causing a lot of problems."

"College has nothing to do with it."

He glanced over at his wife. "We'll talk about it tonight, Mel. You have class today, don't you?"

"Yes."

"Then go to class. But I want you to consider something. You're seventeen and still alive. That isn't luck."

"I know, Uncle Wayne," she said.

Her uncle made the coffee. She endured the smell and poured the juice. They sat together at the table.

Thank you, Lord, for providing us with this food that will nourish and sustain us, said Aunt Kendra.

Amen, they all said.

After Wayne left for work, Kendra walked out of the kitchen and, a minute later, returned again carrying a manila folder.

"You're right, you know," she said to Melanie, who remained at the table. "You aren't a kid any longer." She placed the folder on the table in front of Melanie. "I'm going to take a shower. I think you should take a look at these." She squeezed Melanie once on the shoulder and walked toward the bedroom.

When Melanie heard the water come on, she opened the folder. The newest letter was right on top of the small stack, dated just a little over a month earlier.

It was worse than she'd imagined.

United States Department of Justice

U.S. Marshals Service
Investigative Operations Division

VIA NEXT-DAY EXPRESS MAIL

August 18, 2006

Wayne Denison
P.O. Box 31
Fredonia, WV 26844

Mr. Denison:

Pursuant to our phone conversation of this afternoon: Ramsey Miller is confirmed to have been in Morgantown, West Virginia, on the afternoon of August 14.

His fingerprints were taken off the handle of a switchblade after an incident near the University of West Virginia campus. By the time police arrived, Mr. Miller had fled the scene, and his whereabouts at this time are once again unknown. The fingerprint match, which came through this morning, was conclusive.

Be assured that we have no reason to believe that Mr. Miller knows of your location. Still, Morgantown's proximity to Fredonia is obviously troubling. We are in touch with law enforcement in Fredonia as well as with W.V. Highway Patrol and the Marshal in Charleston, but we are also asking your family to be especially alert and vigilant. Vary your routines, including your routes to and from your home. Report anything unusual to local law enforcement and do not hesitate to contact my office at any time.

We will be in touch as soon as we know more.

Sincerely,

Avery Lewis
U.S. Marshal
U.S. Courthouse
50 Walnut Street
Newark, NJ 07102
201-555-1108

She reread the letter, which must have arrived the same week that Melanie had started classes at Mountain Community College. Yet her aunt and uncle had said nothing, nor had they done anything to stop her from starting school. So she'd been wrong about them. They could actually show remarkable restraint.

She scanned the rest of the letters, which were stacked in reverse chronological order. There were eight total, most of which she'd read before.

> . . . to your recent inquiry as to the present status of the case that pertains to your ward of court: We continue to receive tips as to the whereabouts of Ramsey Miller. We are actively pursuing these tips and will inform you right away of . . .

> . . . will be retiring from the U.S. Marshals Service at the end of this calendar year. Going forward, U.S. Marshal Avery Lewis will be the lead investigator . . .

> . . . but has again eluded local law enforcement. Fingerprint evidence corroborates the eyewitness account, which placed Mr. Miller outside his former home early in the morning. Unfortunately, the eyewitness did not report the information for several hours because . . .

> . . . hope to have positive news for you before long. In the meantime, I trust that you are all adjusting to your new environment. If you ever . . .

Eight letters in fifteen years. Together, they told a sad story of botched opportunities and administrative detachment, and it seemed pretty clear that within the walls of the U.S. courthouse in Newark, New Jersey, the successful capture of Ramsey Miller had never been anyone's top priority.

"We do the best we can, Mel," her aunt said when she came back into the kitchen dressed for work, her hair blown dry. By then Melanie had returned the letters to the folder and was staring across the kitchen at the clock above the sink. "I hope you know that." Kendra took the folder back and left the kitchen with it.

When she came through the kitchen again to leave for work, Melanie said, "I'm sorry."

"Oh, don't be sorry, honey." Her aunt came over and knelt down to Melanie's level. "Just be careful."

Melanie didn't get up until her aunt had left the house. Then she began to straighten up the kitchen. She was about to throw away the newspaper, but instead folded it into quarters so that her photograph remained visible. She returned to her bedroom and looked at it some more. Her mother had died at twenty-eight. In the photo that many of the papers ran when covering the murder, her mother might only have been a few years older than Melanie was now. She was standing on a beach, wearing a gray sweatshirt and squinting a little in the sunlight. Behind her was the ocean. One hand was on her head, trying to keep her hair from blowing every-where. Only one in a hundred women, maybe one in a thousand, could look that glamorous trying simply to keep her hair from knotting up.

From this and other photographs of her mother that she'd found online, Melanie concluded that although she resembled her mother, the resemblance was limited to component parts—angular chins, brown eyes, small noses—rather than cumulative effect. Her mother's beauty, alas, had not been passed down, though on the best of days, with the humidity low and her acne in remission, Melanie sometimes felt a little pretty.

She got dressed, and removed her textbooks and notebooks from her backpack and stowed them in the closet. Then, rethinking, she retrieved one of the notebooks—a journalist should always have paper handy—and put it into her backpack again, along with the newspaper and some clothes: bras, underwear, a couple of shirts and skirts, and another pair of jeans. She got her toothbrush, toothpaste, razor, and hairbrush from the bathroom and put them in, and carried the backpack, purse, and laptop computer from her bedroom into the kitchen. She returned to her bedroom for another pair of shoes.

After getting her driver's license, she'd briefly driven a loner from Uncle Wayne's garage, a boat-sized Chevy Caprice, until her uncle had bought her a Ford Escort with nearly 200,000 miles on it. But the radio wasn't bad and Wayne made sure the engine and tires were in perfect working order. Before leaving town, Melanie would stop at the gas station to buy a road atlas and to top off the tank and get a hot cup of tea for the long drive north, to the one place where she was forbidden.

I'm breaking every rule.

The thought should have brought her no thrill. It did, though. It brought a small thrill. Though she'd never driven farther than the college, she always enjoyed being behind the wheel, her body settled into the seat, her mind drifting, imagining.

This was no field trip, though. No adventure. She reminded herself that she was about to visit a terrible place where her father committed murder and her mother burned.

But Arthur Goodale was alive—for now—and she needed to see him while there was still time to find out everything he knew about her mother's murder. And then she would do what everyone else had failed to—find her father before he found her. Then she and her baby would live without fear.

Before going to the car, she tore a blank page from the notebook and found a pen in her bag.

She wrote:

Dear Aunt Kendra and Uncle Wayne,
I'll be back in a few days. Please, please don't worry. I promise I'm
okay.
Love,

She hesitated. Melanie? Meg? Finally, she decided on "M." She left the note on the kitchen table, beside the salt and pepper shakers.

Then she was on her way.

7

September 21, 1991

In a day, the world would end dramatically. But right now it was just another dreary Saturday morning in New Jersey, the sky a misty and monochrome gray as Ramsey walked from his car to the Kinko's.

At 6:30 a.m. the copy shop was empty except for a young man behind the counter sitting cross-legged on a table and eating a banana. One more large bite before coming over to Ramsey, who set his coffee cup on the counter, removed the hand-drawn invitation from his pocket, and unfolded it.

"I need a hundred fifty of these," Ramsey said, sliding it across the countertop. "But typed up all nice."

The young man was already thick in the jowls and starting to sag. He looked at the paper and said nothing until he'd swallowed the gob of banana. "I can set you up on one of the computers over there." He nodded toward the far wall.

"No, I don't use those," Ramsey said.

"It's simple."

"Simple enough for you to do it for me?" The three twenties were already out of Ramsey's wallet and on the counter.

Sixty bucks sounded all right with Danny Chester, Customer Associate, and twenty minutes later Ramsey was leaving with 150 invitations—large, eye-catching typeface on bright blue paper. Danny had thrown in an image of a kid's teeter-totter in the top right corner, maybe hoping for a tip.

Task one was complete with ninety percent of America still in bed.

Main Street Music didn't open until ten, leaving Ramsey with time to stop by the Shark Fin Marina, not far from his present location. Before long he was approaching the marshes on his left and the Shark Fin Inlet on his right. Despite two decades having passed, everything looked the same, and he wondered now why he'd never thought to pay a visit here before, considering it was a rare place from his youth that held warm memories.

He drove toward the boatyard—the road unpaved gravel, still— where at this time of year about half the boats were in the water and half were dry-docked. The smell of burning diesel always reminded him of the boatyard, but it hadn't occurred to him before now how much the rows of dry-docked boats resembled trucks at a yard or a loading dock, and how his love of these boats—many of them thirty-five or forty feet or more—might have fed his attraction to the big rig, which was like a yacht on wheels, its cab a marvel of efficient interior space, pushed along by a massive diesel engine.

Ramsey parked his car in one of the visitor spaces by the docks and inhaled the sweet, rotting smell of the inlet. The water this morning looked glassy, with just a single charter boat creeping at no-wake speed toward the bridge that led out to the ocean. This time of year the water remained warm but the wind could whip.

With summer gone, only a few boats were needed to satisfy the demands of the most ardent fisherman. Ramsey was too far away to read the boat's name. A seagull hovered over the stern, but the boat wasn't weighed down yet with fish. The gull swooped up and, cawing, veered off toward the ocean.

Ramsey walked over pebbles to the boatyard, trying to identify any of the half dozen men he passed. Some of them looked younger than he was. When an older man with a clipboard stepped out of the office, Ramsey approached him and asked whether his father's old boss, Bruno, still worked there.

"Bruno Crawford?" The man sniffed up a bunch of snot and grimaced. "Afraid he died eight, ten years back."

Ramsey nodded. "I used to come here as a kid. My old man worked here, and Bruno was always good to him."

"Bruno was before my time, but I only ever heard good things." He held out his hand. "Donny Mazza. I manage the yard."

"Ramsey Miller."

"Glad to know you, Ramsey. You a boater?"

"Not really," he said. "I keep a thirteen-foot Boston Whaler on a floating dock in Silver Bay."

"That's just the boat you want for tooling around the bay."

"It is," Ramsey said. "Wish I had more time to take it out."

"Don't we all?" Donny looked around at the boats, the water. "The boat owner's curse—we're all too busy." He smiled at Ramsey. "Now what can I do you for?"

"I was in the area, is all," Ramsey said, "and thought I'd drop by and kick around a few old memories."

"Been a long time?"

Ramsey did the math. "Twenty-four years."

"Well, it's good to have you back," Donny said. "Tell you what. You relax, take in those memories, and let me know if you need anything. We got a full pot of coffee in the office."

"Nah, I don't plan to linger," Ramsey said. "I was hoping Bruno might still be around—I'm having a party tomorrow and wanted to invite him."

"I'm awfully sorry to be the one to rain on that parade," Donny said. "Dino's still here, though."

"Who?"

"Little fellow with the one bad eye? He goes back longer than anyone. Not sure if he goes back twenty-four years."

A few names came to mind: Bert. Chuck. He tried to recall Dino and conjured up a small, trim man in the same greasy clothes they all wore, but maybe that was only his imagination working. "Say, Donny, you don't by any chance want to come to a block party tomorrow in Silver Bay? There'll be plenty of food, and my band's gonna play a set or two. You'd like it."

"Wish I could—but tomorrow I'm working all day."

"Then come by after."

"Can't." The shift in Donny's smile was almost imperceptible. When he said, "Thanks, though," his voice dropped a few decibels.

Crazy fuck. That's what Donny Mazza was thinking.

"I ain't crazy," Ramsey said.

"Never said you were, friend." The smile looked false now, frozen.

"Yeah, but you thought it." Ramsey felt his heart rate quicken, the blood rush to his hands and feet. He demanded—commanded—that he stop this, pronto. He wasn't twenty anymore, and he wasn't drunk, and this was no hole-in-the-wall bar. He took a breath. Softened his face. "I'm playing around." He didn't dare lay a friendly hand on the other man's shoulder. It would be taken the wrong way. Instead, he forced a smile of his own. "You're a good sport."

He shouldn't have come. The past was nothing but a fish straight out of the ocean—slippery, and never as pretty as you think. Without another word, he returned to his car, every step of the way feeling the shame of Donny Mazza's stare.

He rumbled back along the gravel road, retreating hastily from his past to the safety of his to-do list.

He walked every street in the Sandy Oaks development, placing an invitation into each mailbox, and tried to figure out why he'd been willing to beat the hell out of some dipshit boatyard manager who did nothing to deserve it. How was it, he wondered, that he was still a breath away from that sort of madness? After all these years, had he really changed so little?

Then again, he hadn't gone through with it. He'd walked away. Surely that said something. But not much. And he wondered what miniscule difference—a slight change in inflection, a single extra utterance—might have led to a different outcome. As a kid he'd heard his father at the boatyard once talking with another man about how the United States and the Soviet Union had nearly blown up the earth over missiles in Cuba. The war never happened, but it just as easily could have. That's what stayed with Ramsey for years afterward: The fact that the world had survived didn't mean that anyone had behaved well or wouldn't push everything over the brink the next time around.

He could save time by driving from mailbox to mailbox, but he wanted to press his feet to the asphalt in this neighborhood of families. By now Allie knew many of their fellow owners of half-acre plots of soft sod and border shrubs and close proximity to the better primary school. To Ramsey, the people were basically interchangeable; they certainly didn't give two shits about him. But like he said to Eric, the point of this party was to treat them like lifelong chums.

Even David Magruder, whose mailbox was crooked and loose on its stand. Ramsey had never spoken to the man but knew what he looked like from TV—long face, balding, big teeth. Yet he exuded utter confidence when he told you what was "on tap for the weekend." A TV weatherman must be the only job in the world with no penalty for being wrong half the time.

Ramsey briefly considered skipping this house. But no. If Ramsey was serious about being magnanimous, then he *must* invite Magruder. He slid an invitation into the mailbox.

Three more streets. Then he'd turn to the other tasks on his list—sound equipment rental, ball pit rental, materials to buy for the stage, kegs to reserve, fire pit to dig, food to buy and prepare . . . the list was long, and he looked forward to doing all of it.

Seventeen hours later, he was still checking off items, though he'd accomplished a hell of a lot for one day. Even figured out the pony situation. (As simple as looking in the yellow pages under Party/Children.) The woman promised a healthy and gentle Rocky Mountain pony as well as a trained Great Dane to lead the pony around.

The afternoon's rehearsal went smoother with Wayne there. His excuse for having gone AWOL the night before was lame—"girl trouble." Even after three years of living in Jersey, there were still flare-ups with this girl Kendra back in West Virginia who'd stayed stuck on him. *Cut the cord and find yourself a Jersey girl!* Ramsey had wanted to say on any number of occasions. But he knew that love was a messy thing, and he wasn't going to get on the kid's case today—not after Wayne had convinced his manager at the music store not only to rent Ramsey a P.A. but to run it during the gig.

Wayne was basically a decent kid trying to figure shit out, same as anyone. It hadn't taken him long, a couple of years earlier, for him to barf out his story the day Ramsey came into the music store for strings: raised in foster care in West Virginia, ditched the on-again/off-again girlfriend (or tried to, anyway), and left home at seventeen on a Greyhound bus the moment he'd scraped together two hundred bucks, nothing but a knapsack of clothes, his acoustic, and a vague notion that seeing the ocean might be a good thing.

"Actually, it was my foster dad's guitar," Wayne had said. "I figured he owed me."

Ramsey smiled. "I take it your family wasn't *The Waltons*."

He thought maybe the kid wouldn't get the reference, but Wayne shook his head and said, "Man, you wouldn't believe me if I told you."

Ramsey wasn't about to get into a pissing contest over who had the crappiest boyhood, so he let it go.

In the couple of years since, Ramsey sometimes broached the topic of Wayne learning a trade and making a real living. The kid always brushed him off, which was fine—he was young with no obligations—but Ramsey couldn't help trying to steer him in the right direction, like Eric had done for Ramsey. One thing Ramsey had come to believe, you had to pay it forward. Otherwise, the planet was fucked. Of course, a young man alone in the world wasn't going to seek out guidance. Not the right sort of guidance, anyhow. So you had to reach out, show him you gave a damn by overpaying him to clean your truck or change the oil and filters, and while he's there with the hood up, you teach him a thing or two about the engine.

Asking him to join the band, though—that was no simple generosity. Not with Wayne's fancy chords and clean solos. Truth was, Wayne was too good for Rusted Wheels, but evidently the camaraderie, or at least the free beer, meant enough for him to keep showing up most of the time.

Their rehearsal today ended around five, and despite all he still had to do, Ramsey took Allie and Meg out to their favorite restaurant overlooking the bay. Meg behaved herself, scribbling on the paper place mat with crayons given to her by their waitress and chattering to herself. Allie and Ramsey watched Meg, watched the bay, and spoke little, but the restaurant was festive enough from other people's conversations that their silence didn't announce itself.

Now, at 1:30 a.m., Ramsey carried the trays of hamburger patties out to the garage refrigerator. He drove to the 24-hour Exxon station for another twenty-pound bag of ice.

He wouldn't try to sleep tonight.

Last night hadn't gone well. Allie clicked off her light and they kissed and he tried to imagine that it was long ago with the jagged scar still fresh on his thigh. Allie had just moved into his apartment over the laundromat with the dryer-exhaust smell and the squeaking bed that made them laugh. But none of it would stay fixed in his mind.

They fumbled awhile in the dark, he and Allie, until he slid her hand away and said, *Babe, I'm sorry*. He explained that his back hurt from all those hours on the road. He went to the kitchen for a heat pack, and when he returned he told Allie he was going to try the trundle bed for a while, see if the hard mattress might help.

When he returned home tonight from the gas station with the bag of ice, rather than go upstairs he wiped down the kitchen counters and scrubbed the downstairs bathroom, because that was the one the guests would be using. At 4 a.m. he sat in the living room with his guitar and a pair of headphones, closed his eyes, and started to run through some of the songs in the set. He soon abandoned those for his all-time favorites. Zeppelin, the Stones, the Allman Brothers, Skynyrd, Hendrix, the Who, the Doors, the Dead. It was nothing less than the soundtrack to his whole life he was strumming, everything electric and tinged with blue.

He felt his breathing slow and his muscles relax, similar to how his body responded to being on the road these past few months. When he was behind the wheel, all the human struggles—wives and husbands, rich and poor—faded away, leaving only the soothing sounds of a well-tuned engine and wide tires rolling over a hot highway.

He'd always enjoyed driving, but since learning about the orbital axis his life in that truck had come to feel important, like he and the truck were a drop of the earth's blood moving along a wide vein to deliver vital nutrients. Didn't matter if it was pallets of Campbell's soup or Huffy bikes or Gap jeans. He and the rig, he sensed, were part of a system larger than himself, much larger than the company he worked for. Used to work for. These past couple of months, he found himself requesting longer hauls from the fleet manager. He hadn't been a true over-the-road driver since buying his own truck. The company treated him well, and for years he had it good—fairly regular stops, no-touch freight, usually stayed east of the Mississippi. Nearly always home for his mandatory thirty-four-off.

But when he started requesting longer hauls and more territory, the fleet manager was more than happy to oblige—isn't often an experienced driver requests *less* predictable routes—and sometime in the past few weeks Ramsey had started getting creative with the log book. Started driving for sixteen, seventeen hours, watching the road the way an NFL quarterback watches the field—hyperalert and able to see everything before it happens. Wet roads and wind gusts and weavers and tailgaters and narrow lanes and deer and none of it raised his pulse. And all this without a single illegal substance. The brief naps in his berth felt like the most restful sleep of his life.

No question, the orbital axis was having an effect on him. As the days and weeks passed and July became August and then

September, Ramsey had begun to feel an electrical charge in the air all the time, as if a thunderstorm were always imminent, even under a blue sky. And yet he knew that this charge wasn't electricity at all, but rather the tug of galactic forces beginning to nudge everything into place, including him.

He was glad he hadn't sold the truck back in June. That'd been his first instinct.

"What would you do instead?" Allie asked when he ran the idea by her.

"Why would I need to do anything?" he replied. With no reason to make money anymore, he could stay at home. He could jam with Rusted Wheels and hang out with the kid. And his presence in town would keep Magruder away, without anyone ever having to bring it up or admit to a damn thing. Ramsey could pretend like he never knew—he would give her that gift—and he and Allie could face the end together, man and wife.

But she wanted him to keep working. And—there was no denying this—the road was tugging at him, hard.

Now, as he played the guitar through headphones in his silent house, he allowed himself to consider his own childhood, all those regrets, and yet he could chart exactly how his rough start had led to Allie, and how their love had led him to a respectable job, to their home in a good neighborhood, and, of course, to Meg. He imagined their daughter all grown up. He saw her as a school principal, doling out punishments to kids like Ramsey. He couldn't help smiling at the thought.

It was sad, of course, that the future he imagined would never come to pass, but not overly sad. The orbital axis gave him perspective. Made him see that we were all just small animals on a small planet in a huge universe, not cold but impersonal. Matter-of-fact. A planet forms and then it dies, end of story. And the closer the end came, the more Ramsey felt resigned to it, the way in a movie, when the screen goes black and you know the credits are about to roll, you become resigned to the ending even if it isn't the ending you might have chosen.

At 6:15 a.m., a time when fishermen and truckers readied their vessels, Ramsey removed his headphones, laid the guitar on the sofa, and went upstairs. First he entered Meg's bedroom, a risky maneuver because if she woke up now, with the birds already chirping outside, she would be up for the day. He stood over her crib. Recently, she'd started sleeping with a thin pillow. But she never wanted any stuffed animals in there or even a blanket, preferring instead to face each night alone. She was asleep on her stomach, her face toward the wall, and Ramsey watched her body's gentle rise and fall. He could easily watch her for the next hour, but he pulled himself away, slipping back into the hallway and toward the master bedroom.

He'd told Allie that he would be up late, not to wait up, but it looked as if she had waited—for a while, anyway: The candle on the bedside table was burned down to the base. The TV remote lay on the bed not far from her hand. Twenty-eight years old, and she still slept on her belly, same as the kid, a fist curled under her chin.

Standing over her—she was so, so pretty—he wanted to wake her, to lie wordlessly beside her at the beginning of their last day together. But the curtains were open, and the light would wake her soon enough. How incredible, he thought, moving toward the window and looking out above the rooftops across the way, that this morning looked exactly like every other. There was no way to see those eight other planets dragging themselves mindlessly into position. But they were. He could already feel it, the inevitability.

He considered frying up some eggs and serving Allie breakfast in bed. He did that sometimes on her birthday and on their anniversary. She was going to die tonight. They all were. That was an unfortunate given, a scientific certainty, but in the meantime he could bring her eggs. Then he changed his mind. Let her sleep. Anyway, his remaining tasks wouldn't take care of themselves: propane to buy at the grocery store, and horseshoes. He still needed to pick up the kegs from the liquor store. And Eric would be here soon to help him build the backyard stage.

The list seemed to grow even as it shrank, but he'd get it all done. The party would be a success, and the band would play better than it ever had, and because of Ramsey Miller the overall goodwill on the planet would have been increased by some small but measurable amount. And when the gig was done—the last chord played, the amps silenced—he would clutch his family tight, and knowing he'd led a fuller life than he ever could have imagined, he would welcome the earth's own spectacular finale.

8

September 25, 2006

For ten glorious miles, the road trip was as Melanie imagined: windows down, adrenaline pumping, radio remarkably static-free as she wound around hills and through forest, crisp morning air mixing with the smell of mint tea steaming in the cup holder. If there was a better feeling than being behind the wheel, chugging along an open road on a sunny morning, she couldn't imagine what it would be. For ten miles her troubles were forgotten even as she was driving toward them.

But as she approached the county line, she rounded a sharp curve and became the next in an eternal line of cars with their brake lights on. A full minute at a dead stop. Then she began creeping along so slowly that she might as well have been walking to New Jersey. When the radio station began to crackle, she shut it off, and in the stillness there was time to consider where she was going and why, and to think about how easy it would be to turn the car around, to find Phillip and tell him that, yes, squirrels were damn scary creatures, and let's just hunker down in your bedroom and never leave.

But what would that solve? She'd still be living in hiding, in fear.

Yes, but you'd still be living, she thought.

Trouble ain't nothin to fear—it'll find you there, it'll find you here.

A lyric from one of the songs her uncle played on his acoustic guitar. Maybe once or twice a year, he fetched it from the back of his bedroom closet and wiped off the strings with a rag and messed around with a few songs. When he did, it was always music from a long time ago. Bands Melanie knew by name, but not bands she knew. They were from before her aunt and uncle's time, too, but Wayne explained to Melanie that he was an old soul. Melanie figured she must be an old soul, too, because she liked the songs he played, and the way he played them—as if he went someplace deep into the songs and was inviting Melanie and Kendra to go there with him. For a man who played so rarely, he was really good—anyone could see that. There was this guy who played the guitar on the quad sometimes at college, and his fingers strained to make the chords and his voice strained to sing the melody. Her uncle's hands were always relaxed, and his voice found the melody the way water finds the low ground. And although he sang other people's words, the words themselves mattered less than the feeling behind them. But he had to be in the right mood. And even then, after twenty or thirty minutes of song, the guitar went back into its case, which went back into the closet for another long hibernation.

After nearly an hour on the road, the two eastbound lanes merged into one. An enormous pine tree had fallen across the road and taken down a power line with it. One at a time, cars from both directions crept onto the grass along the eastbound shoulder and squeezed by the mess.

Some three hours later, she approached Baltimore. By then she'd eaten all the snacks she had with her, the tea was long gone, she was desperate to pee, and her driving leg was throbbing. Her reward, after a quick restroom break and more fuel for herself and the car, was several hours of white-knuckled driving on I-95. She couldn't get over how wide the highway was and how many vehicles traveled on it, and how fast everyone was going, and how recklessly: cars darting between lanes, eighteen-wheelers cutting her off, motorcycles roaring past, weaving as if they weren't particularly interested in remaining alive. There were a million radio stations to choose from, but she couldn't imagine listening to music while navigating this sort of highway. She clutched the wheel, kept her foot on the gas and her eyes on the road ahead, reminding herself not to become distracted by all the billboards and all the cars entering and exiting the highway, by the approaching Philadelphia skyline, by the stretches of oil refineries and power plants, all soot and smokestacks that looked as if they belonged in a movie about the end of the world.

The Rand McNally road atlas took her as far as Monmouth County, New Jersey, Exit 105 on the Garden State Parkway. By the time she rolled down the window to pay the toll collector, she felt exhausted from the trip. After a few miles of car dealerships and strip malls and impatient drivers, the speed limit dropped—to thirty-five, then twenty-five—and traffic thinned. Sidewalks and trees lined the road.

When she passed the WELCOME TO SILVER BAY sign, she half expected the town to look familiar, though of course it didn't. Shore Dry Cleaning was on her left. Luigi's Pizza was on her right. Had she ever eaten there? Was it even around back then? She passed a couple of brick office buildings, a number of homes, then a two-block stretch of shops and restaurants before coming upon a yellow hotel on her left called the Sandpiper. One hotel seemed as good as another, so she parked her car in the lot and went inside.

"I need a room to sleep in, please," she said to the man behind the counter. He was older, at least sixty.

"Two queens or a king?" he asked.

His question sounded surreal, until she figured out he meant the beds.

"Oh, it's just me," she said, and immediately regretted saying this. Kind faces could be deceiving. People did horrible things. She considered telling him that someone might be joining her later.

"I'll need to see a credit card for incidentals," he said. When she frowned at him, he added, "In case you order a movie, or make any long-distance calls."

She had planned to sign the guest registry under a false name, like the people were always doing in Hardy Boys novels. Nobody in Silver Bay would know the name Melanie Denison, but she didn't want there to be any way to trace her having come here.

"No, that won't be necessary," she said. "I'll be paying with cash."

"I understand," the man said, "but it's our policy."

She bit her lip and dug into her wallet for her debit card and handed it to the man, who swiped it and told her that her room was down the hallway on the first floor. He handed her a plastic room key and her debit card—but not before taking a good long look at it.

"Enjoy your stay, Ms. Denison. There's a pool out back." He shrugged. "It's a little grimy." His face brightened again. "If you need anything, be sure to ask."

She already had a question. "Where can I get a map of town?"

He knelt down and reappeared with a photocopy of a hand-drawn map. He pointed to the star and said, "We're right here." He tapped his finger against the solid blotch running along the right side of the map, labeled ATLANTIC OCEAN. "If you ever get lost," he said, "just head east."

From the diner two blocks away, she ordered a cheeseburger and French fries to go. She ate in her room with the TV on, changing channels. The Yankees and the Devil Rays were scoreless in the first inning. *Casablanca* was just beginning. The Skipper hit Gilligan with his hat. This was how you stir-fried pork. A man in a suit told three other men in suits that the antiwar rallies on Wednesday would lead to real change. Race cars roared around a track. The number of channels boggled the mind.

The sky outside her window began to lose its daytime blue. The sun would set soon, and she was tempted to stay in her room and see exactly how many channels there were. Maybe even watch a movie on HBO. But there was one thing she had to do before the day was out. And according to her map it would be easy to find: zero turns.

After a couple of miles of driving east along the edges of suburban neighborhoods, the landscape became watery. She crossed several small bridges over marshes, then was back on solid land for another mile or so until the houses became older and larger, and the road abruptly ended. In front of her, a boardwalk ran north to south.

She got out of her car, stepped onto the boardwalk, and was struck as if by a physical force by the ocean's enormity, by the sun's fierce reflection off the water that rose and dipped everywhere, white peaks spilling over themselves all the way to the horizon. No photograph or TV show she'd seen had ever gotten it right. To call the ocean "blue" or "green," to name a single color, was like defining a living, breathing human being with a single adjective. To call the air "salty" was to ignore all the other smells, the muskier, living ones that, remarkably, didn't bother her at all—whether it was fish or seaweed or critters dying in their shells.

A few people, maybe a dozen, were walking along the board-walk, looking straight ahead, and Melanie wondered how they could not all be staring east. How could their knees not be weak?

She walked north along the boardwalk a few dozen yards until a gap allowed her to descend to the sand. There, some reptilian part of her brain knew what to do: She kicked off her shoes and socks, cuffed her pants to mid-calf, and walked across the cool sand toward the water. Back at the hotel the air was calm, but here a strong breeze whipped and snapped her hair, which she brushed away from her face with her hand. She wondered if this could be the same spot where the photograph of her mother was taken.

Away from the boardwalk, she was alone. The only sounds were the waves, the wind, and the gulls.

Where water met sand, the ground became rockier and full of black shells and seaweed. She stepped more carefully, bent down, and cupped water in her hands. Tasted the salt, swooshed it around her mouth before spitting it out. When another wave pushed water past her and up over her ankles, she held her ground and her feet got sucked into the wet sand. The sensation was sur-prising, even a little frightening. And although the shoreline might have looked the same at every scale, she didn't feel like a fractal any longer, having removed herself from the old pattern. The waves, the gulls, the salt air all went a long way toward erasing any lingering doubt about having come here.

Behind her, the sun dropped over a thin band of clouds, turn-ing the sky astonishing shades of pink and red and orange. She couldn't care less. Sunsets put on their gaudy show everywhere. Not this, though: waves smashing onto the shore, and beyond it the water rising and falling and colliding into itself, and still farther the wide, endless stretch to that thin, perfect line where sky and earth meet.

Her lack of planning was its own strategy. Planning ahead would mean imagining all the potential pitfalls—just the sort of thing that could have her packing her car and returning to Fredonia. So the next day, instead of calling ahead to the hospital, fretting over whether Arthur Goodale was allowed visitors (or, she hesitated to think, whether or not he was even alive), she simply showed up at Monmouth Regional Hospital and hoped for the best.

She dressed like she imagined a journalist would: skirt, blouse, more makeup than she felt comfortable wearing. Hair pinned up. She ditched the backpack and carried a spiral notebook, its first three pages containing the questions she'd written last night and this morning. She stuck a pencil behind her ear.

Her hands were clammy, but she felt refreshed from a surprisingly good night's sleep and energized by the fact that she had actually done it, had traveled here on her own to New Jersey, to this hospital. The place was vast and sprawling, nothing like the clinic back home. Yet somewhere within these walls, Arthur Goodale was waiting to talk with her. He just didn't know it yet.

She parked the car and followed the signs for the main entrance. Inside, she scanned the signs on the wall for the critical care unit, then rode the elevator to the second floor. Two women in white coats stood behind a high desk labeled NURSES STATION. Seeing Melanie, one of them smiled. Melanie approached the desk. "I'm here to see Arthur Goodale," she said to the smiling nurse. "Is he still here?"

The nurse asked, "Are you family?"

"Me? No."

"May I ask your relationship with Mr. Goodale?"

"Actually, we've never met." When the nurse squinted at her, she added, "I'm a reporter."

"With . . ."

"The *Star-Ledger*." The biggest paper in the area.

"We try to restrict visitors in the unit to family and close friends." She exchanged a glance with the other nurse. "I'll have to ask the patient if he's willing to see you. Assuming he's awake. May I ask your name?"

"Alice Adams," she said. "Would you please tell him it's about the Ramsey Miller case?" She hadn't said her father's name aloud more than a dozen times in her life.

"One moment." The nurse walked down the hall and entered a room on the left. Seconds later, she was back in the hallway— remarkably, waving Melanie over. "He's all yours."

The door was already open, so Melanie stepped into the room and was struck by Arthur Goodale's compromised state: shirtless, thin blanket pulled halfway up his chest. Several monitoring devices ran underneath the blanket. His left hand was connected to an IV. His face had several days of white stubble, the hair on his head was white and wispy, uncombed, and his pale blue eyes were set within a dense web of wrinkled skin, with dark bags underneath. Were their situations reversed, she wouldn't be accepting visitors.

"I'll admit, you've piqued my interest." The strength of Goodale's voice surprised her. "Who are you again?"

"Alice Adams."

"I'd shake your hand, but I'm attached to too many machines," he said. "A horror show, getting old. Though I'm told it beats the alternative. Please, hand me my glasses." They were on the bedside table. She did as asked, and he fumbled a bit sliding the glasses into place. "Much better." He smiled. "Take a seat."

Melanie moved the room's lone chair away from the wall and sat.

"So how can I help you?" he asked.

"I've read your blog," she said.

Apparently, this was the right thing to say, because his eyes lit up a little. "Is that so?"

"I only started recently, but I went back and read everything about the Miller case. And everything you wrote about it in the *Silver Bay News*."

"Going back how far?"

"Everything."

He attempted a whistle, but it was all breath and no tone. "It's a fascinating case."

Fascinating wasn't the word she'd choose. "It's terrible, what happened."

"It was. But I think it's finally becoming ancient history. I had a nurse in here the other day—a local—who knew nothing about it." He cleared his throat. "So what's your interest in the case?"

How, she wondered, had this already become his interview? "I work for the *Star-Ledger*."

"Crime beat?"

"Sir?"

He blinked a couple of times. "How long have you been writing for the paper?"

"About a year."

He scratched the stubble on his cheek. "You're not from New Jersey."

"No, sir—I grew up in a small town in North Carolina." She opened her notebook. "Mr. Goodale—"

"You can call me Arthur."

No way could she do that. She wasn't brought up that way. Now she'd have to call him nothing. "From what I can tell, you know more about the case than anyone."

"Well, the police obviously know more than I do."

"Do you think?"

"The police? I should hope so."

"Even now that the lead detective has retired?"

"Well, the file's still there."

She nodded. She dreaded going anywhere near the police station, but knew she probably couldn't avoid it if she wanted all the facts. "I plan to look at that," she said.

"At what—the file?" Goodale's eyes narrowed. "The investigation is technically still open."

His point escaped her. "So . . ."

"So with an open case, the police won't let you see a thing." He gazed out the window. The view was of a brick wall, another wing of the hospital. He looked back toward Melanie. "You can imagine that a hospital is a fairly depressing and extremely boring place to be. And I've never been a TV watcher." He sighed. "So I hate to do this, because it's refreshing to have a visitor, and a pretty one at that—but you're either the worst journalist I've ever met or you're lying to me about being one."

"Pardon me?"

"You're very polite—and I can tell that's genuine. Ingrained. Your parents raised you right, and I mean no condescension in that." He licked his lips. "But what is this? If you're simply interested in the Miller case, you've come to the right place. I'm happy to chat about it—I hardly ever get to, anymore. But you don't have to pretend to be a journalist."

"I'm not pretending, sir."

He smiled. "Ronny Andrews is an old friend of mine. I know the kind of reporters he hires and the sort of assignments he— you don't know who that is, do you?" Another smile. She was starting to seriously dislike that smile. "Ronny Andrews edits the news desk at the *Ledger*. He'd be your boss."

This was all a game to him.

"May I ask why you don't think I'm—"

"A pencil behind the ear? Come on. And you display no knowledge whatsoever about how journalists get their information." He paused. "Also, you look fifteen years old."

"I'm way older than that."

"Anyone who says 'way older' isn't way older."

"Well, I am." *What am I doing?* She ordered herself to quit arguing with the one person who could help her, who also happened to be in critical care.

"Then how about this: You haven't asked me how I'm feeling."

"Sir?"

"Even a reporter who's all business would ask me that. And we've already determined that you're ingratiatingly polite." She made a mental note to look that word up. "So I can only conclude that for whatever reason, you're pretending to be reporter when in fact you're something else."

Plan A was to pose as a reporter for the *Star-Ledger*. Plan B didn't exist. "How are you feeling today?" she asked.

"Tired and uncomfortable. But thanks for asking." His smile had softened, or maybe she just chose to see it that way.

"You're welcome, Mr. Goodale," she said.

"Call me Arthur."

She forced this much-older man's first name from her throat. "*Arthur* . . . I want to know everything there is to know about the Miller case."

"Now *that* I believe," he said. "It's what I want, too. I've wanted it for fifteen years. But I'm a journalist who spent much of his adult life in this town. What's your reason?"

His voice, his eyes—they betrayed the rest of his body, this hospital room. He wasn't a frail man. *He knows who I am*, she thought for an instant—though of course he couldn't.

"You're a really good interviewer," she said.

"Thank you, Alice. That's flattering. And I'm thrilled that you've read my blog. I really am. But I'm frankly not thrilled at all with the way you come in here and start telling me lies. So how about we start again. Who are you? And what's your real interest in this case?"

She respected his investigatory instincts, but he was driving her mad. For her, this was life and death. For him, it was an entertaining break from soap operas and his view of the brick wall.

She summoned all her courage. "Mr. Goodale, would you really like to know who I am?" she asked, lowering her voice to add drama.

"I truly would." His voice had lost its tinge of superiority, become plainer—the voice of an unassuming journalist seeking a source's trust.

"Can you keep a secret?" she asked.

"Yes, Alice," he said. "I really can."

She held his gaze as long as she dared. "Well, so can I."

She stood, turned her back on him, and walked toward the door. She was halfway into the hallway when he uttered a single word that meant nothing to her.

She stepped back into the room. "Sorry?"

"Magruder," he repeated. When she didn't respond, he said, "David Magruder."

Alice frowned. "The TV guy?" She pictured the square jaw and cleft chin, the thick salt-and-pepper hair, the dramatic interviews with storm survivors, criminals, antiwar activists—and quite often of late the spouses and children of soldiers who were overseas.

"Fifteen years ago," Arthur said, "he was only a local weatherman. Listen, this is probably nothing, but—" He sighed. "Did you mean it when you said you can keep a secret? Or was that just a clever exit line?"

She remained just inside the doorway. "Both, I guess."

"Fair enough," he said. "Shut that door, please. Don't go. I don't want you to go." She shut the door. "Now take a seat again. Please." She sat and waited. Finally, he said, "I'm going to tell you something that I haven't written about."

"I thought that was the point of your blog," she said. "You can write whatever you want."

"No, not everything. I'm not going to slander a man like David Magruder, even on the blog. That'd be asking for a lawsuit."

"I'm not a real journalist," she admitted, sensing that a bit of truth might go a long way.

"You aren't going to stick a needle into me," he said. "That's enough for me."

"What if I spill your secret?"

"You won't." He shrugged. "Or you will—what do I care? I'll probably be dead in a week."

She smiled at his attempt at gallows humor, opened her notebook, and removed the pencil from behind her ear.

It wasn't much, what he told her. Before David Magruder started on his path to fame and fortune (a path, Arthur made a point of saying, that included cosmetic surgery and a hair transplant), he was a weatherman on the local TV news. He happened to live just down the street from the Millers. And of the few dozen people who attended the block party, he was one of them.

"Sounds like he was just being a neighbor," Melanie said. Yet she had trouble imagining David Magruder as being anyone's neighbor, or having come from anywhere other than the TV, already fully formed and photogenic and wearing perfectly fitted suits.

"Exactly," Arthur said. "But that's what makes it strange. Magruder wasn't a neighborly man. I knew him then—not well, but well enough to tell you that he was already too big for this town. In his eyes, anyway. So I've never understood why he attended a party thrown by some trucker he probably didn't even know."

Maybe it was relevant, Melanie thought, or maybe Magruder had simply found himself with a little free time that day. Maybe he liked hamburgers. "Is that everything?" she asked.

Arthur shook his head. "In the days after the crime, the police questioned everyone who attended the party. Which is what you'd expect. But Magruder—he was questioned more than once."

"How do you know?"

"Alice, I've lived here my whole life. I have friends on the force."

She couldn't imagine anyone being friends with a policeman, but she took him at his word. "What did they ask him?"

"I don't know," he said. "But the police must have thought—for a while, anyway—that he knew something or saw something, or maybe had information that might help them find Ramsey." Something started buzzing, and Arthur became distracted for a moment before realizing that the sound was coming from the hallway and not one of the machines in his room. "I really don't know. But my attempt to speak with him about the crime is what ended our acquaintanceship, and he's refused to speak with me ever since."

"What do you think he might have known?"

Arthur still seemed distracted, glancing around the room, up at the blank TV mounted to the wall, then back at Melanie. Finally, the buzzing in the hallway stopped and he visibly relaxed.

"If you came here looking for answers, I'm afraid I don't have any. Everything you read on my blog and in my articles? That's it. It's all I know, except for what I just told you. I know it doesn't amount to much. But if you're set on investigating what happened on the night of September 22, 1991, there are worse places to start than with David Magruder."

"Except that he won't talk to a journalist about it."

"Then it's a good thing you aren't one." Yes, his smile was definitely irritating, but she would try to get used to it. "I think I can help you, Alice. But if you find out anything, you have to tell me, okay? It's really boring in here." He frowned. "And this case. It's important to me."

She nodded. "It's important to me, too."

9

Melanie took a deep breath, let it out, and entered the dim marble lobby, which was empty except for a security guard in the far corner, sitting behind a desk. As she approached, the man glanced up at her. She told him she had a 3:00 appointment with David Magruder.

"ID, please." He barely looked up from the newspaper spread across the desk. When she didn't respond, he said, "Driver's license? Passport?"

Yesterday, she'd given a false name to Magruder's assistant. "I don't have my license with me," she said. "I took the train in from New Jersey."

He looked up from the paper. "What's your name?"

"Alice Adams." The more she said this name, the faker it sounded. "Mr. Magruder is expecting me. His assistant never said anything about—"

"Hold on." He picked up the phone receiver and dialed a few buttons. "Yeah, a young woman—Ms. Adams—says she has an appointment with Mr. Magruder." A long moment passed before he said, "Okay. I'll send her up." He hung up the phone. "Sign here. Eighteenth floor. I need to look in your bag."

On the eighteenth floor, the elevator doors opened directly into a reception area with carpeted hallways extending in both directions. Hanging on the wall behind the reception desk were enlarged photographs of David Magruder and the name of his current TV show, *Magruder Reveals*. Melanie had watched it a couple of times. Everyone was always shouting and crying and reconciling, and the music in the background told you how to feel.

A stunning woman with long black hair and a black dress sat behind a small wooden desk. She was quietly telling someone on the other end of the telephone line that "some people are just bastards, and you can't let the bastards stand in your way. You just need to . . . Hold on." She lowered the phone. "Yes?"

"I'm Alice Adams," Melanie said. "I have a three o'clock appointment with Mr. Magruder."

The woman looked Melanie up and down and uncapped her hand from the phone receiver. "I'll call you back," she said, hung up, and dialed an extension. "Mr. Magruder," she said, her voice sultry and full of promises, "I have an Alice Adams here who says she's waiting to see you." She picked a speck of nonexistent lint off her shoulder. "All right, I'll tell her. Thank you." She hung up the phone and said nothing for five seconds, ten. She was studying her fingernails.

"Is Mr. Magruder—"

"Yeah, I know. He's coming." She looked up from her nails. "Where are you from, anyway?"

"North Carolina," Melanie said.

"Yeah, your accent is crazy thick," the woman said in her crazy thick New York accent, and then, thankfully, the man Melanie recognized from TV and the photos overhead came rushing around the corner.

Arthur Goodale had told her to forget about posing as a pro. *You're a college student working on a project, spotlighting Magruder and his amazing career. You're completely enamored with him.* She'd laid it on thick with his assistant, embarrassingly so, but the approach had worked.

"Alice?" Magruder came up to her now, arm extended, beaming at her as if she were the celebrity. "I'm David. I'm so glad to meet you." His handshake was firm, his palm dry, just as she knew it would be. "Come on," he said, "let's go back to my office where we can chat." She began following him. "Did you have an easy trip?"

She decided not to mention her battle with the NJ Transit ticket machine, or being overwhelmed by Penn Station and the crush of people with their briefcases and their scowls, or, emerging onto 34th Street, being stunned by the searing daylight and mammoth buildings and wide sidewalks and the crowds everywhere she looked, moving fast, fast.

"Yes, sir," she said, and smiled.

"Good. Jeremy told me you're majoring in broadcast journalism. Hard road, changing landscape—but if you keep your eyes and ears open and your nose clean, then you'll . . ." They passed a few offices where on the other side of the glass young men and women sat at cubicles and stared at their computer monitors. Everyone was on the phone.

David Magruder had on a dark blue suit with subtle pinstripes and freshly polished black shoes. On TV, he was a good-looking middle-aged man with terrific hair and a pleasing voice. In person she wouldn't call him handsome, exactly. The parts were all there: cleft chin, blue eyes, that perfect head of hair, but the parts didn't quite fit together. It was as if he'd been ordered a la carte.

He had stopped in front of a double door with a TAPING IN PROGRESS sign attached to it. "They're doing promo spots right now," he said. "Otherwise, I'd give you the full tour. Come on, let's go to my office."

At the end of the hallway, he opened the door and waved her in. His office looked about the size of Melanie's home on Notress Pass. One corner was nothing but floor-to-ceiling windows, overlooking a large portion of Manhattan. Magruder strolled over and scanned the skyline as if it had been erected this morning just for him.

"I do well," he said. "But nothing was ever handed to me."

When he was done looking out his window, he turned around, smiled at Melanie, and told her to take a seat. The sofa was leather, soft, and probably cost more than all of her family's furniture put together. Above the sofa were photographs of Magruder shaking hands with President Bush, and another with him shaking hands with President Clinton. Both settings looked like the Oval Office. That seemed to be the recurring theme—Magruder with incredibly famous people, most of whom even Melanie recognized: Madonna, Tom Cruise, Michael Jordan. Angelina Jolie. Hillary Clinton. Magruder flashed the same smile in all of them: friendly, slightly crooked, with his teeth showing a little. A smile divorced from an actual expression.

He sat down on a leather chair at the head of the coffee table, which looked like a slab of petrified wood. He crossed his legs. The crease in his pants was sharp enough to cut steak.

"We produce a show a week, which airs on Wednesday night. Thursday we're off, and then on Friday morning we start all over again."

"That sounds really intense," Melanie said.

"Maybe. Though I have to tell you, Alice, after years of daily TV and having to chase every unfolding story and be everywhere at once, it feels like a walk in the park. I can plan my shows ahead of time, get the interviews I want."

Now that Melanie had a better look, she noticed that Magruder's face had the same orange cast as some of the girls at college who hit the tanning salon too often. Not sure what to say next, she took Arthur's advice and paid a compliment. "Your office is amazing," she said.

"Thank you. This whole floor is mine," he said. "The network wanted me to rent space in their building, but I said fuck no. Pardon the bravado, but it's the truth. I refused to have them looking over my shoulder." He shrugged. "What're they gonna do, Alice? Last week, I got a twelve-share with those marines, guy and a gal who got nailed by an IED and fell in love in rehab. We broadcast part of the wedding, their first dance . . . did you happen to catch it?"

"I'm sorry," she said, "but I missed it."

"Well, you'd have been weeping. Trust me, it was very beautiful." He smiled again, but the smile quickly vanished into an expression of genuine concern. "I have no manners."

"Sir?"

"Would you like coffee? Tea?"

"No, thank you."

"I'd offer something stronger, but I probably shouldn't, ha ha. But if you want it, it's here. But we probably shouldn't."

"If you have any water."

"Sure, we can rustle that up." He picked up the receiver of the phone on the coffee table and dialed an extension. "Please bring Ms. Adams a glass of water. No, nothing for me." He hung up. "You're southern."

"North Carolina," Melanie said.

He nodded. "It's a sexy accent, and it suits you—you're quite lovely—but you'll want to lose it or you'll be relegated to the small markets. This isn't a come-on, by the way, just some free advice. Back when I was doing weather, I used to sound like a real hick. Point is, I lost the accent. Point is, I beat out *60 Minutes* last week. Ratings talk. Everything else walks." He slapped his lap twice, as if encouraging a small, obedient dog to jump up and be petted. "So—your class. Tell me about it."

"It's called Introduction to Mass Media," she said.

"What school?"

Last night she'd gone online to prepare for this question. "Gaston College."

"Never heard of it." Exactly why she'd chosen it. "Go on."

"Well, one of our assignments is to interview someone in TV or radio. I thought I'd have to find someone back home, but when I found myself in New Jersey for a cousin's wedding and realized I'd be this close to New York . . . anyway, I'm like your biggest fan."

Arthur Goodale had insisted she say that.

"So instead of interviewing some local yokel, you came to me. That's ambitious. I like that. And I always try to make time for the next generation of media moguls." His smile was reassuring. "So what do you want to know?"

She unzipped her backpack, removed her notebook and pen, and scanned the list of handwritten questions. She decided to begin with a question about past shows he worked on, but almost at once he stopped her. "You can learn all that on Wikipedia. Lesson number one: Don't waste your interview's time. What is it you really want to know?"

She looked at the list again. He'd just invalidated eleven of her fifteen questions. If only she were subtle and clever and able to improvise, able to chat. All she could do was skip to question twelve on the list. "You're single with no children, isn't that right?"

"It is," he said, a little uncomfortably. "But again, that's something—"

"Why do you still live in Silver Bay?"

He frowned. "I don't talk about my home life." He must have realized that sounded curt, because he added, "I'm sure you understand why a public figure might want to keep his private life private."

This was a serious blow—her plan, such as there was one, was to get him talking about Silver Bay and then, acting naïve, bring up the crime. How do you develop a rapport?

"My school assignment," she said, "is to get to know my subject. His life as well as his work. That's why I asked about Silver Bay."

"Trust me," he said, "my work is a lot more interesting than my life." He shifted in his seat.

Five, maybe seven seconds of silence. Her armpits felt sweaty. Feeling out of options, she shut the notebook and braced herself. "When you lived in the Sandy Oaks neighborhood," she said, "how well did you know Allison and Ramsey Miller?"

"I beg your pardon?" He leaned back in his seat and got a good look at her. "Were you not just listening to me?"

"In nineteen ninety-one—"

"What the hell kind of a question is that? I'm not discussing that."

"I only wondered if you knew them. Because you lived in—"

"I know where I lived, sweetheart." No smile now. "I don't talk about that. You don't ask about that. Do we have an understanding?"

Her heart pounded. "Yes, sir."

"I didn't know either of them. Not even a little. Okay?"

"Okay," she said. He was lying, though. Why would he lie?

"Damn right, okay."

Just then, a young woman barged in carrying a tray. "Here you go," she sing-songed. On the tray sat a single glass of ice water.

Melanie and Magruder watched as she set the glass in front of Melanie, on a ceramic coaster. She smiled. "Anything else?"

"No," Magruder said.

"I didn't know if you wanted lemon or not," she said, "so—"

"We're fine," Magruder said.

"All right," the woman said, her smile faltering and then reaffirming itself. Then she left.

"I'm really sorry," Melanie said when the woman was gone, doing her best to sound apologetic and reasonable. She meant it, too. She didn't want to be burning this bridge already, when there was no other in sight. "I promise, I didn't mean to upset you."

"You? You can't upset me." She looked down at the table, accepting his condescension. He took a breath, laid his hands down on his lap atop those perfect creases. "Why don't you try telling me the truth. Why are you really here? Who are you?" When she didn't immediately answer, he asked, "What college did you say you're going to?"

"Gaston College."

"We'll see about that. Because *this* . . ." He motioned to her clothes. "The college students I know would've dressed up for an interview." At Arthur's advice, she had dressed like a "typical student": simple blouse, worn blue jeans. Sneakers. Hair in a ponytail held together with a black elastic. Subtle lipstick and a touch of eyeliner—an amount that Phillip always mistook for no makeup at all. "If I find out you're with the *Enquirer* or some other—"

"I promise, I'm a college student," she said.

"You promise." He laughed. "No, you're a liar. I can spot a liar every time." He glanced around his office at all those photographs, as if refueling. Then he massaged his temples. When he spoke again, his voice was softer. "All right, Alice. I'll tell you what

I know." He leaned in closer. "I know two things: I know you're going to leave through the door you came in. And I know it's going to happen right now."

"Sir?"

"You heard me."

Her vision began to get swimmy, and she fought to control herself. "Mr. Magruder—"

He reclined in his seat and folded his arms. "I'm waiting for my two things to come true, dear."

"I can ask other questions." She looked down at her notebook, the useless list. "What is it like to inform so many millions—"

"Let me make it plainer." His voice had hardened. "Get the fuck out of my office."

She stood up, placed her notebook back into her backpack. She felt Magruder's stare as she walked to the door. She felt it all the way down the hall to the elevator—which took an eternity to arrive.

"Don't keep pressing the button," the receptionist said. "It doesn't make it come any faster."

After hurrying past the security guard and leaving the lobby, she walked a full two blocks before realizing she was going in the wrong direction, then backtracked the twenty blocks to Penn Station. Her feet throbbed, and she felt lightheaded and nauseous from not eating—she'd been too nervous to eat for most of the day—and all she wanted was to lose herself in the train terminal at rush hour, where thousands of people would cocoon her in anonymity.

When she got there, she saw from the list of departures that the next Coast Line wasn't for 30 minutes, and braving the coffee smell, she stood in line to buy three donuts and a bottle of orange juice. She moved away from the counter so that she would no longer smell the coffee, sat against the terminal wall, and bit into the first donut. It was the most incredible thing she'd ever tasted. All around her, throngs weaved past one another. If everybody who lived in Fredonia was put inside this railroad station, it probably wouldn't be this crowded, but at the moment she felt reassured by all those people, to be just one among them, an anonymous grain of sand on the beach.

She filled her stomach and was ignored by everyone. She'd botched the interview badly, probably left West Virginia for nothing—but at least she was in Penn Station, this subterranean place of human voices and music and track announcements. It was wonderful and safe. A paradise. A womb. She could stay here forever.

She drank some juice, wiped her lips with a napkin. As she was deciding which donut to eat next, a tall man in a yellowed tank top and camouflage pants ran past. He was middle age at least, his hair ratty and gray, but he had ropy arms. He'd barely passed her when a heavy uniformed policeman caught up and tackled him to the hard floor. Then an even more massive officer jumped on top of the man, who was already down, and his face mashed into the ground. This second officer lay across him, covering him with his body, while the first officer yanked the man's arms behind him and snapped handcuffs around his wrists. By this time the man was howling wordlessly, like an animal badly hurt, and the first officer was telling him to shut up, shut up right now, as people nearby stopped what they were doing and edged closer, and a few started taking pictures with their cell phones, and one man in a business suit said to another man in a business suit, "Fucking New York," and when Melanie saw the small pool of blood on the ground near the man's head, the donut she'd just eaten felt like a stone in her gut.

Afraid to stand because her legs might not support her, she squeezed her eyes shut, covered her ears, and started reciting the names of Nancy Drew characters as if it were a litany: *Carson, Nancy's father. Eloise, Nancy's aunt. George, the tomboy; Bess, George's plump cousin; Ned Nickerson, Nancy's boyfriend; Hannah, the housekeeper. . . .*

PART TWO

10

1965

His was a love story, though the love came later. First came all the climbing.

As a young boy, on nights when his father and mother put too much beer or vodka into themselves and got to screaming and hurling picture frames containing happier times, Ramsey would scurry up the black oak behind the apartment building, perch in a nook, and sway with the highest branches. Eighty feet up, his breathing eased. He'd sit up there for two or three hours before becoming so drowsy that he feared falling in his sleep or so butt-sore that he had no choice but to climb down again and face the loud and unkind earth.

Yet the earth wasn't always unkind. Saturday afternoons, his mother sometimes took him ice-skating. He kept to the perimeter, hand on rail, but enjoyed the friction of his blades on the ice.

He liked watching his mother, an expert skater. A single warm-up loop and she was drifting toward the center, where she might slide backward, spin, even leap into the air. While the strange truck smoothed the ice, Ramsey and his mother would put quarters into a vending machine near the skate-rental counter, and a paper cup would drop down and begin to fill. They passed the salty chicken broth back and forth. It gave them the warmth they needed for another hour on the ice.

And sometimes he went with his father to the Shark Fin boatyard, where Ramsey would watch his old man climb inside churning engine rooms as large as bedrooms. His father might explain a thing or two about whatever he was working on. Sometimes he took advantage of Ramsey's smaller size and asked him to squeeze into a space. More often, he let Ramsey explore the docks and climb aboard the dry-docked yachts. The other men in the boatyard trusted Ramsey not to drown or fall or break anything. They always took the time to shake his hand, not because they cared about him but because they respected his father. Ramsey liked these men's faces, red and deeply lined from the wind and sun, and he liked their generous laughs and the black coffee they drank out of Styrofoam cups, and how their clothes were always stained with grease from a hard day's work. He liked knowing that his father was one of these men.

When the workday was over, the two of them would share a Dr Pepper at the end of the dock overlooking the bay. Standing there, the sun warming the backs of their necks, his father would look out at the charter boats returning with their day's catch, a cloud of seagulls hovering over the decks.

I got my mind set on a thirty-eight-foot Sea Ray, he'd say. Or: *I got my mind set on a forty-six-foot Viking*. Or maybe that day his mind would be set on some other yacht, as if he had all the money in the world to spend and all the time in the world to contemplate his purchase.

It would be years before Ramsey started to sort out just how much of his parents' troubles came from life's usual slop of suffering—money troubles, boredom, graceless aging—and how much was due to the particularly poor alchemy of two people with hard tempers and short fuses. More and more, anything could set their ferocity into motion: something quoted from a newspaper, someone's car in the wrong parking space, a comment, a glance, or nothing at all. Ramsey would sit rigidly on the sofa or on his bedroom floor and wait for it to start. He could always sense it in the atmosphere, the way animals know a storm is coming. And when one parent's remark begat a louder response, and when the profanity started, and certainly by the time the first coaster or mug or TV remote got slammed down onto a coffee table or hurled against a wall, Ramsey would be long gone, already halfway up his tree. His parents never stopped him or called his name. When he came home again, they never asked him where he'd been. Then again, the flecks of dirt and crumbles of tree bark on his clothes and in his hair surely gave him away.

One fall night a week before his ninth birthday, Ramsey was hiding in his tree and imagining, as he often did, how it might be to live alone in a log cabin in the mountains, maybe by some lake, where at night all you heard were crickets and coyotes, and where there were a zillion stars overhead. He'd been learning constellations at school and was naming them to himself when a patrol car pulled silently up to the apartment building, its flashing lights blotting out the stars and brightening the branches around him like a multicolored strobe. He felt cold, sitting up there without moving, but seeing the patrol car made him start to sweat. One of his parents, he figured, had finally gone and killed the other. Neither had resorted to physical violence before, unless you counted the sliver of glass lodged in the meaty part of his mother's hand, just below the thumb, from when she'd slammed down and shattered a mug. But their rage had grown worse in recent months, and now anything seemed possible.

But no: His parents were still shouting at each other. The wind that night came from the west, carrying their voices all the way up the tree.

The officer knocked. The shouting halted.

A short while later, the officer emerged from the apartment, shook his head once as if clearing it of muck, walked to his car, and sat in it for several minutes with the headlights off. Like the officer, Ramsey sat and waited for the fighting to resume. When the officer finally drove away, Ramsey counted to five hundred before climbing down again.

"You probably saw what happened here tonight," his father said to him, sitting at the foot of Ramsey's bed an hour later. It was a school night. Ramsey already dreaded having to wake up in a few hours. He watched the fish decals stuck to the walls. During the day they looked happy, but at night, lit by the dim lamp on his dresser, they were shadowy and sinister. But because they'd always been there, he never thought of asking that they be taken down.

"The police came," Ramsey said.

"They came because some nosy neighbor felt he had to get involved." His father found one of Ramsey's feet under the covers and began rubbing it in both of his hands. "But it's true, your mother and I are no good at keeping our mouths shut. We're going to try fixing that."

Ever since Ramsey could remember, his father's coarse thumb on the soles of his feet calmed him. It never tickled. "I don't like it when you fight," Ramsey said.

"Of course you don't. I don't like it, either. That's why your mother and I are going to fix it."

"You promise?" In daylight he never would have dared ask his father to promise anything. But the dark bedroom made it hard to see his father's face and therefore easier to push.

The rubbing stopped. "Listen to me, son. You don't know yet what it's like to be in love. How sometimes it makes you crazy."

"You're in love with Mom?"

His father laughed. "Indeed, I am. Most of the time, anyway."

He'd never tell his father this, but Ramsey was in love, too. With Rachel Beaner. But there was no possibility that what he felt, looking over at Rachel in the next row of desks, had anything in common with what his father might have felt, looking at his mother. And besides, Ramsey knew that if he and Rachel ever married, he'd love her *all* of the time. And he'd never raise his voice to her, not ever.

"Then why won't you promise?"

"Jesus, Ram . . ." From the kitchen came sounds of dishes being rinsed, then clanking together as they were placed in the drying rack. More than once, his father and mother had fought over not owning a dishwasher. Ramsey couldn't remember, now, which side either of them was on. Or maybe they'd switched sides. "Yeah, okay, kid," his father said. "I promise."

They shook on it in the dark. And for six days, his father kept his promise. His mother maintained her own civility, too, despite not having promised anything. And on the seventh night, a Sunday, the night before Ramsey's birthday, his father and mother went out for a drive, and only his father came home.

The rain had fallen steadily that day—not violently, but nice—and Ramsey's mother and father had sat together on the sofa, reading parts of the paper aloud, something they hadn't done for some time. His mother's feet were up on his father's lap. Ramsey lay on the rust-colored carpet reading the comics and listening to the rain on the roof.

After supper, his parents went out on a few errands, his father's wink—so fast, Ramsey had nearly missed it—leading Ramsey to believe that birthday presents were involved. They left him at home in front of the TV with a glass of soda and a bowl of pretzels. His mother said something to the effect of "We'll be back in an hour"—but who knew, exactly? By then, Ramsey was fully engrossed in *Lassie*. When the rain began to fall heavier on the roof, he got off the sofa and turned up the volume. Sunday was a good night for TV. He watched *Walt Disney's Wonderful World of Color*, then *Branded*. By then he should've been in bed. *Bonanza* was on next and when no one returned by the end, he watched *Candid Camera* and then *What's My Line?*, which his parents sometimes talked about but never let him stay up for. By then he knew something was wrong, and when the building's superintendent led in two policemen, and Ben Cramer's father went over to the TV and shut it off, Ramsey—whose arms by now were shaking and legs were shaking and mouth was dry despite all the soda—looked up and, not knowing what to say, said, "Hey, I was watching that!"

"Tell me," Ramsey said.

Outside. Recess. The day after the funeral.

"You sure you want to hear this?" Larry Ackerman's father was a cop, which meant that Larry heard the sort of rumors that could be trusted. His parents had no clue that the air-conditioning vent in their bedroom broadcasted all their conversations.

"*Tell me.*"

Larry glanced over at Ben Cramer as if he were Ramsey's keeper. Maybe for the moment, he was. Ramsey had stayed with Ben's family in the days leading up to the funeral, and had only returned to the apartment yesterday. Today was his first day back at school, and Ben's parents must have asked him to stick close—that, or Ben was as loyal a friend as a nine-year-old could ever hope to have.

Ben nodded.

"All right," Larry said, softly, and sat down on the freshly mown grass. The other two sat so they made a tight circle. They were at the edge of school property, fifty yards from the playground and all the other kids and lunch monitors. *I have information you'll want to hear*, Larry had said, first thing that morning in the hallway. But they were in different classes in the fourth grade, and Ramsey had to wait for three long hours.

Sitting here now, near the chain-link fence separating school property from a narrow creek that ran through much of town, Ramsey knew that to Larry this was all a game, like trading ghost stories. But if Larry knew the truth, then Ramsey wanted to hear it. All he knew for a fact was that his mother was dead. Yesterday he'd stood over her casket and looked at her face. Everyone had said, *You don't have to*, but he did have to. Neither his father nor anyone else had said one word to explain what had happened, other than *car accident*. Ramsey knew not to ask his father for details—like how his mother could have been killed when his father didn't seem to have a scratch on him.

"Your father and mother were fighting," Larry said now.

"He didn't kill her." Ramsey had considered and rejected the possibility so many times in the last week that the words came automatically. Anyway, if that was what had happened, then his father would be in jail right now, not back at the apartment.

"Let me finish," Larry said. His voice softened again to ghost-story decibels. "They were fighting in the car, and your father got really mad and made your mom get out."

"Out where?"

"Out of the car. He kicked her out in the rain and drove away. And then—" Larry looked back toward the school. A handful of kids were playing kickball, and he watched as a girl kicked a slow roller toward the pitcher and ran to first base. The pitcher threw the ball at the girl but missed, and she was safe.

"And then what?" Ramsey asked.

For the first time, it must have occurred to Larry that this wasn't a ghost story he was repeating. He watched the kickball field a moment longer before looking down at the grass. "She got hit."

"What do you mean?" Ben asked.

"It was dark and raining," Larry said. "The truck driver didn't see her."

"A *truck?*" Ramsey said. He knew he'd never be able to stop imagining the thud of his mother's body against the truck, the sight of her in the air, turning, the sound of her hitting the ground. His mother.

"A pickup," Larry said. "The driver was going around a curve, and it was really dark and the rain was heavy. He wasn't speeding or nothing." The next thing he said, he must have overheard word-for-word through the air vent. "A damn tragedy, is what it is." Even his register dropped so he sounded like his father. He looked up at Ramsey and reverted to his own voice. "She's in heaven now."

"That's true," Ben added.

Ramsey tried so hard to believe them that tears came to his eyes, but he knew his friends were fools. He had long observed how other kids spoke about their dead grandparents and great-grandparents as if being dead meant dancing with angels and eating supper with God. But the truth was, when you're dead, you're dead. His father had said so a long time ago, after a stray dog they'd kept for a couple of weeks had died of distemper. It wasn't pretty, but it made sense. When a dog was dead, it was dead, and the same was true for people.

"Why do you suppose your father did that?" Ben asked. "Why would he kick her out like that?"

"I don't know," Ramsey said, looking out past the fence and the creek and into the thicket of woods. Who knew why anyone did anything? But then the answer came to him. "I think he was trying to keep a promise."

A week after the funeral, his father returned to work at the Shark Fin boatyard. That Saturday, Ramsey went along. It could have been any other Saturday, except that when the workday was done and they stood at the end of the dock, Ramsey felt the urge to talk about his mother. He wasn't sure what he wanted either of them to say. He would have liked his father to say something comforting for Ramsey's sake even if neither of them believed it. Like how his mother was in heaven. At least a dozen times, Ramsey almost asked the question—*is Mom in heaven now?*—and each time he caught himself. When he finally got a sound to leave his lips, it was more of a squeak than a word.

"How's that?" his father asked.

"So is your mind set on a forty-two-foot Sea Ray?" Ramsey asked.

His father shook his head. "No, son. It sure isn't."

Ramsey knew he was right not to ask if his mother was in heaven. He kept looking out at the boats and the gulls and the water. At one point he felt the gentle weight of his father's hand on the back of his neck, and he told himself that this was enough.

Maybe his father was thinking about yachts, redemption, or nothing at all—but he wasn't thinking about his work, given the injuries he started sustaining. First there came the minor accidents—mashed fingers, concussion, twisted ankle—and then the major one. A sailboat boom swung around and walloped his father in the back, throwing him off the dry-docked boat and down onto the concrete.

This was less than six months after Ramsey's mother died, and it seemed to be the injury his old man had been waiting for. Now he spent his days kicked back in the recliner, watching TV, the remote control resting on his ever-expending belly. At some point in the afternoon he would replace the remote with a vodka on the rocks. A woman named Gina, who rang the register at the 7-Eleven where his father bought his smokes, started coming over to the apartment. She came with snacks from work and sometimes went grocery shopping for them. Ramsey couldn't understand where the money came from, with his old man not working. He didn't know about disability payments. All he knew was that when Gina worked the morning shift, she'd come over at 2:30 and she and Ramsey's father would start their drinking and their shouting, a return to the fighting his parents used to engage in. If Gina worked the evening shift, it all started earlier.

Twelve years old. He came home from school to an apartment that had been either burglarized or tornado-ravaged from the inside.

"Dad?"

Drawers pulled from shelves and overturned, cabinets emptied, stacks of unopened mail swept off the kitchen table. Books littered the floor. Every object in the house, it seemed, was strewn and tossed and disregarded.

"Dad?" He considered running to the phone to dial 911 or banging on a neighbor's door for help. But then his father emerged from the bedroom, limping as always from his bad back, muttering to himself, a look of anger and horror on his flushed face. His eyes glassy. Drunk, drunk, drunk.

"What's going on?" Ramsey asked.

"Have you seen my wedding ring?" his father asked.

He hadn't.

"It's got to be here." His father knelt down on the floor in front of the sofa, an action that resulted in his cursing at whatever pain flared or sliced through him. He rummaged through a desk drawer that'd already been rummaged through.

"Where's Gina?" Ramsey asked, because he knew that something was making his father act this way.

His father looked up from the carpet. "Gina has left us, son! She is, and I quote, *moving on and improving herself.*" He ran his hands under the sofa, then under the cushions. All he found were crumbs. He turned around so that his back was against the sofa. "Fucking whore," he muttered, burying his face in his hands.

Ramsey had no idea what to do, so he just sat there and watched his old man come apart. After a minute or so, his father moved his hands away from his face. His eyes were redder than ever. "I loved your mother," he pled to his son. "I loved her so much."

Ramsey nodded. "Okay."

"You don't understand. You're only a kid. There's no way I can explain it to you. I just loved her."

"What did she look like?" Ramsey asked.

"What?" his father said. "What are you talking about?"

"Mom—what did she look like?"

"Don't ask me a question like that," his father said. "You remember."

"I don't," Ramsey said. "I want to, but I don't. What did she look like?"

"I said don't ask me that."

"Sorry."

His father tried to take a deep breath, but it caught somewhere in his gut and became a whimper. He looked around at the trashed apartment. "What the hell am I gonna do?" he said. "Will you just answer me that?"

"I . . ."

"Shut up before you embarrass yourself, Ramsey," his father said.

The black oak looked dead for months, its remaining leaves brown and crusty, before some guys got around to taking a chain saw to it. One late October morning, when the leaves of all the other trees were in full color, a cherry picker raised one of the men up, and he started chain-sawing through the lower, thicker limbs, then the higher, thinner ones, all of Ramsey's hiding spots dropping to the ground one after another. Though he couldn't remember the last time he'd hidden in the tree, he still thought of it as his. He sat on a chair in the kitchen and watched through the window as the men shed layers of clothes over the long morning, calling out to one another, working the cherry picker, branches falling every minute or two, until only the trunk was left standing like a totem pole that someone had forgotten to carve. Then they cut that down, too. By noon the men had chopped the branches into pieces, fed them into a wood chipper, sectioned the trunks and loaded the pieces on to their truck, and were gone, leaving only a low stump and the cherry picker's muddy tracks mashed into the grass.

Ramsey was fourteen. He wore his hair longish and shaggy and had developed a habit of squinting even in shade. He was a short, lean kid with a voice pitched too high for menace. When the men left, he went outside to where the tree had stood only a few hours earlier. The stump was covered in sawdust. He brushed the dust away to reveal the tree's age: so many rings, so much survival. He looked around, hoping to see a new hiding place in case he ever needed one. The roof? The storage garage? Or maybe the tree coming down was a sign. He considered this possibility all afternoon and tested it that night. When his old man came into the kitchen for a refill, Ramsey headed him off, removing a beer can from the refrigerator and opening it. He began to pour the contents down the sink.

"Hey, stop that!" his father shouted. "What the hell you doing?"

Ramsey considered calling his father by his first name—*I'll do whatever I want, Frank*, or *This ain't your concern, Frank*—but decided it was better, older, not to pay his father any notice at all. When the last trickle was in the drain, Ramsey dropped the empty can into the trash and calmly explained to his father that he would no longer allow alcohol in their home.

"You got to be joking," his father said.

"Do I look like I'm joking?"

"You look like a kid who's upset because your fucking tree came down." He whistled once. "God almighty, what a baby."

"Hey—"

"Don't *hey* me. You should be thanking me for getting the rental office off their asses before that tree crushed us in our sleep."

His father, hands on hips, met Ramsey's gaze, and Ramsey felt the tears well up. "You should've asked me first." He meant to sound tough, but he heard the quaver in his own voice.

"Oh, yeah?" His father stared him down. "And who the hell are you?"

His father was a master at mutating a fight so that the fight itself became the issue. He'd had years to perfect the art, but Ramsey was only an amateur and no words came.

"I think you'd better answer me, son."

"You shut up!" Ramsey finally shouted, and socked his father in the nose.

In the past, his father had occasionally shoved Ramsey into the wall or the refrigerator but never struck him with a fist. And

Ramsey had never done anything remotely like this to his old man or anyone else. The punch connected because it contained the element of surprise: It surprised them both. And all the blood was another surprise, which made up for the fact that what he'd said to his father was so damn stupid. *You shut up?* He knew he'd have to change the story when he told it later to Ben. That was where he decided to go, Ben's house, until things cooled down.

He knew better than to take time to pack a change of clothes, a toothbrush, or a coat. He left the house with his father standing in the kitchen, dripping blood onto the linoleum.

Who the hell am I? Ramsey said aloud, walking through neighborhoods and past shops that were closed for the night. *I'm your goddamn son, that's who.*

He wanted to hate his father but wasn't up to it. It was sad, seeing him there in the kitchen, looking hurt in every way, without even Gina there to help. Still, Ramsey felt himself waking up on that walk across town, and was glad for it. That punch had opened something in him that he didn't think he'd be closing any time soon. He imagined and reimagined the scene back at the apartment—his father's insolence, the blood. He shivered from the cold and the excitement. Cars whooshed by on Second Avenue in both directions, but otherwise it was a cool, quiet night with the smell in the air of burning leaves. Ramsey's left hand, his punching hand, tingled but didn't hurt at all. Just the opposite. It felt warm and ready. It practically glowed in the dark. He made a fist, unclenched it, and made it again, having absolutely no inkling that his solo walk across town on this night, so crisp and shimmering with promise, was to be the highlight of his next ten years.

I'm the one who settles the score, he said in a movie star's deep drawl.

I'm your worst nightmare.

11

POLICE ARREST RECORD
RAMSEY JEFFREY MILLER

JURISDICTION DESC: MONMOUTH COUNTY CLERK
OFFENDER ID: 33204
DOB: 09/29/1956
RACE: WHITE
SEX: MALE
HEIGHT (FT): 5' 8"
WEIGHT (LBS): 148
HAIR COLOR: BROWN
EYE COLOR: BROWN
ALIASES: NOT KNOWN

CHARGE #1
CHARGE ID: 555009321

STATUTE: 2C:17-3 STATUTE DESC: CRIMINAL MISCHIEF
CHARGE: CRIMINAL MISCHIEF, 4TH DEGREE –
DISORDERLY PERSONS
    VANDALISM
CHARGE CLASS: CLASS 1 MISDEMEANOR
CHARGE DATE: 07/16/75
AGE WHEN ARRESTED: 19
DISPOSITION: GUILTY
SENTENCE: FINE, COMMUNITY SERVICE
NOTES: SUBJECT FOUND VISIBLY IMPAIRED IN PARKING
LOT OF BIG AL LIQUORS. PARKING LOT LIGHTS WERE
SMASHED. HE ADMITTED TO DRINKING "TOO MANY
TO COUNT" AT HOME AND BECOMING ANGRY WHEN
THE STORE'S NIGHT MANAGER REFUSED TO SELL HIM
ALCOHOL BECAUSE HE WAS VISIBLY INTOXICATED. HE
ADMITTED TO SMASHING THE LIGHTS WITH ROCKS
AND ATTEMPTED TO DEMONSTRATE BUT ALL THE
LIGHTS WERE ALREADY SMASHED. WHEN ASKED HIS
NAME THE SUBJECT SAID NEIL ARMSTRONG.
IDENTIFICATION CARRIED BY THE SUBJECT PROVED
OTHERWISE.

CHARGE #2
CHARGE ID: 555010301
STATUTE: 2C:17-3 STATUTE DESC: CRIMINAL MISCHIEF
CHARGE: CRIMINAL MISCHIEF, 4TH DEGREE –
DISORDERLY PERSONS
    VANDALISM
CHARGE CLASS: CLASS 1 MISDEMEANOR
CHARGE DATE: 02/11/76
AGE WHEN ARRESTED: 20
DISPOSITION: GUILTY

SENTENCE: FINE, PROBATION
NOTES: SUSPECT INVOLVED IN AN ALTERCATION AT
STUFF YER FACE RESTAURANT WHERE HE WAS
EMPLOYED AS KITCHEN STAFF. MANAGER CALLED THE
POLICE AND ACCUSED THE SUSPECT, FOLLOWING A
REPRIMAND FOR FAILING TO WASH DISHES
APPROPRIATELY, OF PLACING THE MANAGER'S HAT,
LEATHER GLOVES, AND HAIR PIECE INTO THE DEEP
FRYER. WHEN CONFRONTED BY POLICE THAT
AFTERNOON AT HIS HOME, SUSPECT CONFIRMED THE
MANAGER'S STORY.

CHARGE #3
CHARGE ID: 555019986
STATUTE: 2C:12-1 STATUTE DESC: ASSAULT
CHARGE CLASS: CLASS 1 MISDEMEANOR
CHARGE DATE: 9/4/76
AGE WHEN ARRESTED: 20
DISPOSITION: GUILTY
SENTENCE: FINE, PROBATION
NOTES: SUSPECT INVOLVED IN AN ALTERCATION
WITH A NEIGHBOR IN HIS APARTMENT BUILDING
AFTER NEIGHBOR ASKED SUSPECT TO TURN DOWN
THE MUSIC IN HIS APARTMENT. A THIRD NEIGHBOR
CALLED THE POLICE AFTER THE FIGHT BEGAN. BOTH
MEN ADMITTED TO HAVING CONSUMED ALCOHOL.
BOTH WERE TREATED ON THE SCENE BY PARAMEDICS
FOR MINOR CUTS AND BRUISES AND REFUSED
FURTHER MEDICAL ASSISTANCE.

CHARGE #4
CHARGE ID: 555018100

STATUTE: 2C:17-3 STATUTE DESC: CRIMINAL MISCHIEF
CHARGE: CRIMINAL MISCHIEF, 3RD DEGREE –
DISORDERLY PERSONS,
     POSESSION (MARIJUANA, 50G OR LESS) – RESISTING
     ARREST (NO WEAPON)
CHARGE CLASS: CLASS 1 MISDEMEANOR
CHARGE DATE: 06/04/78
AGE WHEN ARRESTED: 22
DISPOSITION: GUILTY
SENTENCE: FINE, JAIL, PROBATION
NOTES: SUSPECT REFUSED TO LEAVE THE PREMISES
OF A HOUSE WHERE HE WAS EMPLOYED TO MOW AND
EDGE THE LAWN. SUSPECT SPOTTED BY HOMEOWNER
IN WOODS BEHIND HOUSE. HOMEOWNER
APPROACHED SUSPECT AND NOTICED HE WAS
SMOKING A MARIJUANA CIGARETTE. WHEN HE TOLD
SUSPECT TO LEAVE THE PREMISES, SUSPECT REFUSED.
WHEN POLICE ARRIVED ON THE SCENE, SUSPECT SAID
THAT HE HAD BROKEN UP WITH HIS GIRLFRIEND THE
PRIOR EVENING AND "THOUGHT HE WOULD CHILL
OUT HERE." WHEN OFFICER ATTEMPTED TO ARREST
SUSPECT, SUSPECT CLIMBED NEARBY TREE.
ADDITIONAL OFFICERS AND A FIRE TRUCK CAME TO
THE SCENE AND THREATENED THE SUSPECT WITH A
HIGH-POWERED WATER HOSE. SUSPECT CLIMBED
DOWN WITHOUT FURTHER INCIDENT.

CHARGE #5
CHARGE ID: 555019867
STATUTE: 2C:12-1 STATUTE DESC: ASSAULT
CHARGE: ASSAULT
CHARGE CLASS: CLASS 1 MISDEMEANOR

CHARGE DATE: 10/2/79
AGE WHEN ARRESTED: 23
DISPOSITION: GUILTY
SENTENCE: FINE, PROBATION
NOTES: POLICE WERE CALLED TO THE CORNER
TAVERN BECAUSE OF AN ALTERCATION. BOTH
SUSPECTS WERE TREATED ON THE SCENE AND
ARRESTED WITHOUT INCIDENT.

CHARGE #6
CHARGE ID: 555117394
STATUTES: 2C:12-1 STATUTE DESC: ASSAULT
 2C:17-3 STATUTE DESC: CRIMINAL MISCHIEF
CHARGES: ASSAULT, CRIMINAL MISCHIEF 2ND DEGREE
CHARGE CLASS: CLASS 1 MISDEMEANOR
CHARGE DATE: 08/15/81
AGE WHEN ARRESTED: 25
DISPOSITION: GUILTY
SENTENCE: FINE, JAIL, PROBATION
NOTES: SUSPECT WAS DELIVERED A PACKAGE FROM
UPS. HE THEN FOLLOWED THE UPS DRIVER TO HIS
TRUCK AND WITH A KEY CREATED AN APPROX 4 FOOT
GOUGE ALONG THE SIDE OF THE TRUCK. WHEN
ASKED TO STOP, SUSPECT TOLD THE UPS DRIVER
THAT IF HE SAID ANOTHER WORD HIS TRUCK
WOULDN'T BE THE ONLY THING CUT. WHEN POLICE
ARRIVED, SUSPECT SAID HE DID IT BECAUSE WHEN
THE FRONT DOOR WAS OPEN, THE UPS DRIVER MADE
A REPEATED MOTION WITH HIS TONGUE IN THE
DIRECTION OF SUSPECT'S GIRLFRIEND THAT SUSPECT
FOUND OFFENSIVE AND INAPPROPRIATE. WHEN
QUESTIONED, THE UPS DRIVER SAID HE DID NOT DO

THIS, AND THAT ANY LIP SMACKING WAS DUE TO
EXTREMELY CHAPPED LIPS. (HE PRODUCED A TUBE OF
BLISTEX FROM HIS PANTS POCKET.) THE GIRLFRIEND
WHEN QUESTIONED STATED THAT THE SUSPECT
"WAS ALWAYS ACTING LIKE AN IDIOT" AND THAT SHE
HAD TAKEN NO NOTICE OF THE UPS DRIVER.

CHARGE #7
   CHARGE ID: 555332344
   STATUTE: 2C:12-1 STATUTE DESC: ASSAULT
   CHARGE: ASSAULT
   CHARGE CLASS: CLASS 1 MISDEMEANOR
   CHARGE DATE: 08/08/83
   AGE WHEN ARRESTED: 27
   DISPOSITION: GUILTY
   SENTENCE: FINE, JAIL, PROBATION
   NOTES: AFTER BEING EVICTED FROM APARTMENT
FOR FAILURE TO PAY RENT, THE SUSPECT
CONFRONTED LANDORD IN THE PARKING LOT AND
SHOVED HIM AGAINST THE BUILDING'S BRICK
EXTERIOR, CAUSING BRUISING TO THE LANDLORD'S
SIDE AND SHOULDER. LANDLORD PHONED POLICE
AND SUSPECT WAS LOCATED LATER THAT DAY IN
MUGSHOTS BAR AND WAS ARRESTED WITHOUT
INCIDENT.

Absent from the police arrest record: Ramsey's first disorderly
persons arrest, later expunged, for which he spent the night of his
sixteenth birthday in the drunk tank. And of course all those actions that weren't crimes but that were nonetheless reckless and
unwise: rude comments to teachers, fights in the hallway, a host

of foolish behavior that led to detention, suspensions, and threats of expulsion.

Nor does his arrest record mention the Porsche, keys left on the seat, that he swiped one night from the parking lot of the Trattoria, took for a joyride, smashed, and abandoned. Or the weed he sold to a few discreet classmates and later to those same individuals once they'd graduated. Or the time he drove a truck of stolen electronics from one warehouse to another, or the time he kept watch outside a house while some other guys broke in through the back door and took whatever they could cram into a couple of canvas bags.

And there was the time—the only time—that he accepted money from one guy to beat up another guy. He was never told, nor did he want to know, what beef the one guy had with the other. He knew only that he was risking a felony but that it would be the easiest 300 bucks he'd ever earn, since the fight didn't have to be fair. This was fall 1983, not long after he'd spent three days in county jail for shoving his asshole landlord. If caught now, he'd be looking at a lot longer than three days. So he was careful. After learning the guy's routine, he waited outside his building one weekday morning at sunrise. The man descended his front stoop and yawned audibly before heading into the alleyway to the parking lot. One unsuspecting shove from behind and into the brick wall, a few hard punches, a few harder kicks once he was down on the sidewalk, and it was over.

That final kick to the jaw, though. It felt a little too much like scratching a deep itch, and it scared him. He replayed the beating in his mind once he was back home—his new home, across from the plasma donation center, the shittiest apartment God ever created. He lay in bed with the lights off and shades drawn and studied the cracks in the ceiling. Before that day, the only time he'd beaten someone while sober was that single lucky punch that had busted his old man's nose a decade earlier. Since then, Ramsey hadn't grown all that many inches, but he'd gotten much stronger. And the feeling of his hard shoe torquing toward that man's face . . . it was nothing at all like the spontaneous bar fights of his past, fueled by beer and momentary rage. This was a darker, smoother feeling, one he could imagine needing to revisit. He felt disgusted with himself, nothing new, but for the first time he felt afraid of himself, too.

With no food in the apartment, hunger eventually drove him outside. But when he passed the sub shop on the corner he kept walking, because walking felt better than eating. He briefly considered walking all the way to the police station and turning himself in, but his feet pulled him eastward, toward the ocean. It was mid-September, a dry day with the sky a deep blue interrupted only by the white half-moon. A generation or two earlier, you might have still called this town a resort, but not anymore. Now it was just a town that happened to sit next to an ocean.

The road ended where the beach began. At first, still a block away, he saw water brilliantly alit with sunlight, the beginning of three thousand miles of shining sea. But as his eyes adjusted and he crossed Ocean Avenue, he was hit with the truth: plastic containers, crushed cans, overturned shopping carts and postal bins and waves of junk shoved ashore by the incoming tide. Worse this year than the last, worse than ever, and it wasn't lost on Ramsey that he felt drawn to the place where all that trash ended up. Every damn year, he thought, was one earth's revolution closer to the end of his life, and so far his life had amounted to a heap of garbage. There was no point to any of it. He was broke, friendless, estranged from the old man, unable to hold down a job, and his only reason for staying in this town was that moving would cost money. That, and the half dozen steady marijuana customers who gave him a fighting chance at paying whatever landlord had been too lazy to do something as simple as a proper credit check.

One of Ramsey's customers had only one arm and wore a permanent smirk. He had the bad luck of being born a year earlier than Ramsey and got sent to Vietnam. Now he worked pest control, spraying other people's homes with poison. Even that guy could keep it together. Ramsey stood on the boardwalk, looking down at the ruined beach and added self-pity to his list of faults. He turned around and got irked by the guy who seemed to be looking at him.

He crossed Ocean Avenue again and approached the base of the telephone pole so the other man had to crane his neck and look straight down. "How's that job?" Ramsey called up to the man, who looked too thick in the middle for a guy in that line of work.

"You yanking my chain?" The man looked at least a decade older than Ramsey, though that might've been because of his face, which was weathered from the sun like the faces of the men his father had once worked with.

"Fuck you," Ramsey said. "I'm just asking."

"Then here's your answer: It's a better job than you'll ever have."

"Tell me something I don't know," Ramsey said.

"Oh, so now you want my pity?"

"Man, I don't want your nothing. But if I ever wanted it, believe me I'd just take it and it would be mine."

The man watched Ramsey for a second. "I don't know what that means," he said.

Neither did Ramsey.

To his amazement, they both laughed. Ramsey couldn't remember the last time he let himself do that.

"Listen, man," Ramsey said, working to rid his voice of aggression. "I'm asking is that good work, being up in those poles like that?"

"You need a job? Is that what you're saying?"

"Yeah."

"Then stop by the GSE office on 36. Ask for Dennis. Tell him Eric Pace sent you."

"Why?" Ramsey asked.

"*Why?* You just said you're out of work."

"No—I mean, why would you do that for me?"

Eric shook his head. "Man, I thought you didn't want my pity. Make up your mind."

"Yeah, okay," Ramsey said. "Maybe I'll go over there in the morning."

"Or don't—it's all the same to me." The man went back to screwing or unscrewing a metal box near the top of the pole.

"Hey!" Ramsey called up. Eric stopped working and looked down again. "You never said if it's a good job or not."

Eric paused to consider the question. "It can be. It all depends."

"Depends on what?"

"On whether you can climb."

Four weeks later, and Ramsey was an eager grunt at the start of a four-year apprenticeship to become a journeyman lineman. Training expenses and supplies would come out of his paycheck, but the pay was good and for the first time he'd have medical benefits. He knew he'd been handed a gift he didn't deserve, and he told himself not to fuck it up. During the classroom part of his training—daylong sessions on electrical theory and equipment and safety—he did his best not to squirm or fall asleep. He applied for his CDL permit, and the company started training him to drive a truck. At night, he studied hard so he would pass the motor vehicle exam on his first try.

Eric Pace, the guy he'd met up on the pole, volunteered to be Ramsey's first mentor. Other than being a Jesus nut—A.A. had done it to him some years earlier—Eric was a regular guy with uncommon generosity. It drove Ramsey a little mad that his training would literally be "from the ground up," and that out on the job site, his day-to-day was entirely earthbound: work site setup and breakdown, loading and unloading trucks, digging trenches for lines and holes for power poles. But he told himself to be patient for once.

He wasn't someone who ordinarily quit things cold turkey, especially things he was good at like drinking and asshole-being, but because it all meant a lot to him—the job, his friendship with Eric—he found it not so hard, really, to keep those baser tendencies in check. And on the third Friday of his training, two very good things happened: He passed his CDL exam and he picked up his first paycheck. Obviously, it was time to celebrate. He decided on Chuck's Main Street Tavern, because it was only a few blocks from his apartment and a DUI would be a real screw right now.

When 2 a.m. rolled around and Chuck kicked out the last stragglers, Ramsey stepped out onto the sidewalk feeling happy, which almost never happened leaving a bar, and invincible, which always did. The storefronts on his street were all closed, the windows dark in most of the apartments above them. A few Christmas lights drooped under windows, a few wreaths hung on doorways. And though the night felt too warm and sticky for early December, the weather didn't stop Ramsey, as he ambled along the sidewalk, from singing a booming, belch-punctuated rendition of "Jingle Bells."

Across the street from his apartment building, he sized up a power pole that he'd never really noticed before—simple three-phase subtransmission pole (forty-five-footer, from the looks of it) with a streetlight attached and an extra line to the nearest building.

He thought: *Yes. Yes, I will.*

Because it was bullshit, when he really considered it, how after three weeks he hadn't even been allowed near the *practice* poles behind the main office. He removed his coat and laid it on the ground at the base of the pole. He didn't have his spikes on him, of course (spikes that the company made him buy to the tune of ninety-five dollars), but by squeezing his legs around the pole, he was able to start creeping upward. In fact, climbing a utility pole, even without the spikes, wasn't very hard at all—though he was pretty toasted, and by the time he was halfway up the pole he was sweating and sucking wind. His heart thudded. His hands felt raw and were cut with splinters. But he kept climb-ing—squeezing his legs, pulling with his arms—because he was on a mission. He belonged to that special class of climbers, those who felt more free up here than on the ground. It was total bullshit that he was only allowed to dig ditches and wash the fucking trucks.

He knew from his training and from common sense that you could get fried too close to the power lines, but the lines were still five or six feet above his head, which seemed far away until light-ning slashed the sky and the lines above his head hissed in re-sponse. Seconds later another slash, closer this time (since when was there lightning in December?), and in his surprise Ramsey slipped an inch or two and felt a sharp pain in the meaty part of his left hand, where a large splinter of wood must have gotten lodged. Shit, he thought. He looked up again at the wires, then down again, and got a little queasy. Bed-spins. He hated bed-spins even when he was in bed.

He eased the pressure between his legs so his weight would carry him down the pole a few inches, but his left hand was nearly useless, and he almost fell. His legs squeezed the pole again. More lightning crackled, and the power lines started humming and hissing again, and thunder rolled across the sky, and these facts came to mind: Linemen on the poles always wore rubber gloves and insulating gear. Apprentice linemen were forbidden from working on live-wire poles until after an entire *year* of training.

The insanity of what he was doing came into sharper focus.

"Help!" he called. "Help! Anyone!"

He was calling out to God and to the cats that roamed his street, because there sure didn't seem to be any people around. Everyone was probably watching him from behind their darkened windows. He should just climb down. But the ground was spinning hard now, and his hand . . . *shit*. He didn't like what the nosy neighbors were probably thinking about him right now, but he'd forgive every last one of them if only somebody would pick up the damn phone and call for help.

The wind howled, and every flash of lightning made him brace for a taste of those 765,000 volts. His legs trembled, and the sweat on his body had turned cold. Then the rain started in—hard— because of course it did.

When flashing lights finally rounded the corner and came his way, for the first time in his life Ramsey felt grateful for the sight of a patrol car. But when the officer approached the pole and shouted up to him about a bucket truck that'd arrive in short order *courtesy of the electric company*, Ramsey shouted, "Fuck that!" and tried once more to scramble down on his own power. Damn, the hand hurt. But pain was only pain, and he gritted his teeth and lowered himself a foot, two, three. The hissing above him lessened, and he focused all his attention on this one thing, getting himself to the ground before the truck came.

Now his left leg was bleeding. What the hell? It only stung a little—what had he even cut it on? Probably a nail sticking out of the pole. The leg hurt less than his hand. But damn. Blood was definitely dripping down the one side. His pant leg was sticky. The worst part was, he couldn't lower himself anymore. The cut leg didn't allow it. If he were ten, twelve feet in the air, he'd have let go and taken his chances with a fall. But he was still close to thirty feet up.

"I cut my leg!" he shouted down to the officer. "I think it's bad." His whole body was shaking.

"Can you hang on? The truck will be here any second."

"How about a fucking ladder?"

"Just hang on." While they waited, the officer tried to keep Ramsey calm. "I'm Officer Ogden," he said. "You're going to be okay. We'll just wait a—"

"*Bob* Ogden?" Ramsey said.

"Yes, sir," the officer replied.

Bob Ogden was a year younger than Ramsey. They'd gone through school together, and now he was a cop with a cop's uniform and a cop's car, and Ramsey was trapped like a shivering cat in a tree, too stupid to know its own ass from third base.

Ramsey said, "You were a pussy in high school."

"How about we just wait for the truck," Officer Ogden said.

It was the only time Ramsey would ever stand in the bucket.

When he was finally on solid ground again, his legs were shaking so hard that he could barely stay upright. But that didn't stop him, the second that Bob Ogden came over, from taking a swing at the officer. Ramsey ended up in the road, splayed on his back, with Officer Ogden standing over him and shaking his head—because he, being sober, already knew what was still hazy to Ramsey: that by morning, Ramsey would be facing a court date, no job, and a line of staples in his thigh.

The next day, thunderstorms gave way to a hard, steady rain. Ramsey's roommate slept. On the muted TV, race cars looped stupidly around some track. Beneath the heavy disinfectant smell in the room, Ramsey detected traces of a thousand diseases. Hospitals always made him feel sick. Yet the doctors reminded him that it could've been much worse (electrocution, broken spine), and he knew he was damn lucky to be lying there, medicated on a soft bed. The pills, the pills, thank God for the pills, which insulated him from the sharpest pain and the bleakness that would otherwise be devouring him. His former self would've already been scheming ways to steal some of those pills for later use or profit. His current self was simply grateful that they were in his system.

Climbing was all he ever did well, and now they'd taken that away from him. The "they" in his thoughts were hazy and constantly changing: his supervisor at the electric company, Officer Ogden, his father, Gina, his teachers, karma, his own stupidity. He'd never climb again. His leg was a disaster, and apparently so was his constitution. He'd been terrified up there. Lightning and thunder had never bothered him when he was a boy in a tree. It thunders, you climb down. No big deal. You don't clutch on for dear life and make a spectacle of yourself. Jesus.

There wasn't even anyone to pity him. Eric had visited briefly, called him a fool, laid a hand on his shoulder, and left for work. His roommate, a teenager who'd been beaten to a pulp, was useless as a distraction, what with his jaw wired shut.

Late afternoon, a big female nurse with a man's haircut shoved him out of bed and made him walk down the hallway. *Up, up, let's go, just to the water fountain, just to the EXIT sign, just to the elevator and back, just to the far wall, just, just, just.* The two of them left Ramsey's room, and he limped past the nurse's station. When they got near the elevator, it opened. Its sole occupant stepped out, carrying a vase of flowers.

This was his future wife.

She was startlingly pretty, alarmingly so—with the sort of face you only ever saw when part of what you saw came from your own imagination: You're in a bar when you've had a few but before you've had too many, when the jukebox is playing the right song and the lighting is dim and cigarette-fogged. You know that what you see isn't real, that everything will change in daylight.

Well, it was daytime, and the only music came from some idiot doctor down the hall whistling to himself. Yet her green eyes were real, her smooth skin was real, every last thing.

When she smiled, Ramsey knew. That fast. He'd fallen for pretty faces before—who hasn't?—but one thing those pills did was filter out the noise and let you perceive the essence of things. He could practically see the light within her—not purity, exactly, or innocence, but an essential goodness that her lived experience hadn't quashed.

"What took you so long?" Ramsey asked.

She played along, looking at her watch. "I'm only three minutes late—I didn't think you'd mind."

She had on a white top and blue skirt, well tailored. Business attire, he supposed. Professional but snug-fitting. He was glad he had on the sweatpants that Eric brought him, rather than the paper gown. Glad he'd brushed his teeth. Glad he happened to look his best when he was a little scraggly with a day or two of razor stubble—something he'd been told by some girl once and chose to believe now.

What Ramsey did next was positively absurd, nothing he'd ever do in a bar at 1 a.m., let alone in a hospital corridor beside his overbearing nurse. He said, "I'm just glad you made it," and doffed—doffed!—an imaginary hat. She'd obviously come to visit a sick friend or relative, making the next thing out of his mouth utterly inappropriate. "And how thoughtful of you to bring me those."

She looked at the flowers, then back at Ramsey. "Just be sure to change the water every day," she said. A small card was attached to the bouquet. She plucked it off and handed him the vase.

"Wait . . . what?"

"These aren't cheap, either," she said. "There are gardenias and lilies . . ." She squinted. "What am I saying? You're a man, you don't care. Trust me, though—they aren't cheap." She looked over at the nurse. "Will you make sure he changes the water every day? Otherwise, he won't do it."

It was nice to see his nurse speechless. She nodded.

"Excellent!" she said to the nurse. To Ramsey she said, "Well, take care now," and pressed the elevator button. The doors opened, and she was gone.

The next day, she was back.

He'd spent hours thinking about her, the pills that worked miracles on a leg doing nothing to dull the ache of knowing he'd failed to get her name before those elevator doors closed. In the dark overnight hours, the error had grown enormous and irrevocable.

But here she was again, his only visitor since yesterday afternoon, when a policeman came by with a court summons. Three light-knuckled knocks on the door, the same knock of faux respect perfected by the attending physicians before they entered with whatever grim news they couldn't wait to dump on you. But it was neither cop nor doctor. Today she had on blue jeans and a long-sleeve T-shirt. Less makeup. She looked even lovelier. It was a word—lovely—he'd never considered in his life, yet it was the only word that fit.

He felt embarrassed. In the hallway, standing face to face, he could pretend he wasn't an invalid. Now he lay in bed, same clothes on as yesterday, a frail patient with his mute roommate looking on. He hadn't showered since the day before coming to the hospital. He propped himself into a sitting position, stifling a grimace of pain, and made a show of examining the new bouquet she'd brought, which was significantly larger than yesterday's.

"Those are nice," he said. "I like the . . ."

"You have no idea what any of these are."

Taped to the vase was a cream-colored card with neat cursive writing:

> *To Ramsey Miller.*
> *Feel better soon!*
> *Your friend, Allie*

"So me and you are friends now?"

"Don't believe everything you read," she said, smiling.

He nodded. "That one there's a purple rose."

"The purple part's right—it's an iris."

"Huh. Looks like a rose."

"Not really."

"How do you know my name?" he asked.

"The nurse's station," she said.

He looked up at her. "Are you rich or something? These flowers cost a lot."

"They seemed to make you happy yesterday. That's what flowers do—so I figured, what the hell?" She noticed yesterday's bouquet sitting on the table beside his bed. "They look good there."

"Who were they for?"

She shrugged. "I don't know. Someone. Don't worry, she got her delivery later."

"You just lost me."

"Well, I brought up another vase later." She squinted, as if trying to figure out what she was missing, and smiled. "Of course— why would you know? I run the flower shop downstairs."

"Ah." Ramsey motioned to his two bouquets. "So you aren't exactly paying for these."

"Are you kidding? On my salary?"

"Won't you get in trouble?"

She smiled. "I manage a small flower shop for a very large chain. I think there's like a thousand stores. No one cares if a few flowers get donated to a worthy cause." He must have flinched, because she said, "What's wrong?"

He couldn't bear to tell her that *a worthy cause* was the best compliment he'd ever been paid. So he said, "It's just . . . I got to be honest. I'm gonna be here another few days. And I'm sort of getting used to the sight of fresh flowers."

Her outfit yesterday, he learned later that day when she ate her bagged lunch in his room, was because of a job interview. She was a college senior, business major, with an eye on the pharmaceutical industry—specifically the corridor of companies between Princeton and New Brunswick: Merck, Johnson & Johnson, all the biggies.

She sat in the chair beside his bed, one leg underneath her, sipping from a sweating cup of Diet Coke.

"You can't imagine," she said. "They hire you right out of college, no experience, and you can pay back your student loans so fast." When she named the starting salary, Ramsey was pretty sure she had it wrong.

"What would you actually do?" he asked.

"Drug rep."

"Yeah, okay, but what would you *do*?"

She shrugged. "Meet with doctors and their office staff, talk about the drugs your company makes, give them free samples and other swag." He didn't want to admit that he'd never heard the word *swag*. She must've read confusion in his face, because she added, "You know—coffee mugs, pens, stuff like that."

Ramsey nodded. "And that makes them buy your drugs?"

"I guess," she said.

"So what about the flower shop?"

"That's just getting me through college. The pay is terrible, but it's super easy. And there usually isn't much to do, so while I'm there I can study."

"And hang out with creepy older men."

"You aren't that much older."

"I thought you might say I wasn't creepy."

She raised an eyebrow. "Well, are you?"

He actually had to think about it. "No."

She watched the TV a minute. Downhill skiing. No one crashed. "So what happened to your leg?"

Telling her about the leg meant telling her about his job at the utility company, and how proud he'd been to pass his CDL exam on the first try, and how the best and freest days of his life were gone, gone, gone before he'd even had a chance to climb a single pole for real.

"You'll find another job," she said, as if the whole mess of his life could be capped like a pen. "An even better one."

"I will, huh?"

"Of course. You're a take-charge kind of person. Like me."

He laughed. "Did you not hear everything I just told you?"

"Sure, but that was the story of your past. It ended with you here, in the hospital, talking to me. Now it's your present."

"You're saying that today is the first day of the rest of my life?"

Her face reddened. "I know that sounds cheesy, but it's true."

He wanted to believe that he could emerge from the hospital as if from a cocoon, transformed from anything he'd ever known or been. And of the many reasons why he began to fall so quickly in love with Allie, one of them was because he yearned to become worthy of her too-generous assessment of him. And in that way, she was already correct—in falling for her, he was taking charge of his life.

"Hey, do me a favor?" Ramsey asked, and looked over at his roommate. "Bring that guy some flowers tomorrow. I'll pay for it—the kid hasn't had a single visitor." His roommate looked over and waved, then looked back at the TV.

"Okay," she said, and whispered: "Can he really not talk at all?"

"Nope," Ramsey said.

"Bummer. Yeah, I'll bring him something." She stood up. "Well, I know where to find you."

The next day, the roommate got his flowers. Ramsey's came with helium balloons.

The day after that, both roommates were discharged. It was Allie's day off, but she'd already given Ramsey her telephone number.

The roommate was being kicked out first, so Ramsey said, "See you, man," and strolled around the hospital for a while so the kid could pack his things and leave in peace. That was what the nurses wanted, anyway—for Ramsey to walk walk walk. So he went the length of the hallway, then the hallway above and the one below. When he returned, his leg was throbbing a little. His roommate had left a slip of paper on Ramsey's pillow.

Topaz Trucking, it read in neat letters. Below it, a phone number.

Bobby Landry is my uncle. He's a training manager there. (I noticed your bad leg isn't your driving leg.) Is your CDL Class A? That would help.
Take care,
Vic
P.S. Don't tell Bobby where you met me.
P.P.S. Don't blow it with the flower girl.

To his own astonishment, Ramsey didn't blow it. The vow he made to change his life was no transitory side effect of the good meds. It was real and lasting, and every bit as solemn as the vow that Eric had made years earlier to quit drinking and thank Jesus for every last thing. In fact, first on Ramsey's own agenda was to deal with his booze situation. He was reasonably sure he wasn't an alcoholic, but he knew he had to cut way back. Eric still put a dollar into a shoe box every day that went by without him taking a drink. Ramsey tried a ritual that suited him better: one drink whenever he drank, and no more. If that didn't work, he'd try something else.

He dialed up Topaz Trucking, met with the mute kid's uncle, and a week later enrolled in the company's training program.

At home, he followed his doctors' orders to the letter, stretching the leg and cleaning the wound meticulously. And while he was in the spirit of cleaning, he bought a new vacuum and a mop and some Windex. He bought a napkin holder for the kitchen table. He bought a kitchen table for the napkin holder.

He also began making lists. He listed things to do each morning: forty sit-ups; fifteen push-ups; walk to the ocean and back, followed by fifteen minutes of leg stretches; wash any dishes/pots/pans in the sink; read the front page of the newspaper; learn a new word from the dictionary.

He listed current skills and skills he'd like to acquire. He listed short-term goals (pay all bills on time; stay sober for three months; learn some more chords on the crappy electric guitar that was gathering dust in his closet), and he listed things he felt grateful for (living this long; meeting Eric; having health insurance when he got injured; meeting Allie).

Meeting Allie. Of course she was the reason he did any of this, why he awoke each morning with energy and optimism rather than festering in his dark bedroom all day and letting his leg harden into a permanent, painful handicap. Each day brought the possibility that he'd see her. She might come over after her shift with takeout, and maybe she'd stretch out on his sofa and study for one of her classes. Or maybe they'd watch something dumb on TV. Or maybe they'd go into his bedroom, and she'd be gentle with his injured leg and less gentle everywhere else.

Like Ramsey, she was alone in the world. When she was a freshman at Monmouth College on a soccer scholarship, she told her evangelical parents about dating one of her teammates, and that was pretty much that. Within the year, her mother and father had sold their home in Freehold and moved to the Florida panhandle, where the weather was warmer and the people more God-fearing. Allie was told, explicitly, that she wasn't welcome in their new home.

"The funny thing," she said, telling Ramsey the story in his apartment one night, "is that Amanda and I were only together that one semester. Turns out, I like guys."

"Glad to hear it," he said. "But that was it with your parents? You never patched things up?"

"We talked a few times on the phone. My father agreed to let me back into their lives if I agreed to fly down there on my own dime and stand in front of their congregation and admit to my sin and pledge that I'd stay pure until marriage."

Ramsey smirked. "I hate to break the news to you, babe, but you ain't so pure."

She hit him with a sofa cushion. "If I needed their money, I might've said whatever stupid thing they wanted me to. But they were broke, and I was paying all my own bills. So I didn't see the point."

"People sure are different," he said to her.

"Yeah, they were always intense, but it got a lot worse over the years."

"No," Ramsey said. "I mean . . ." He was thinking about the difference between Allie and himself: how his own response to his family's dissolution was to become a degenerate, while hers was to play varsity soccer, earn a 3.5 GPA, and manage a flower shop. He shook his head. "Never mind."

She started spending the night—once, then twice, then a few nights a week. They'd just about gotten into a regular routine when Ramsey's training period ended. It figured that he'd be hitting the road just when he finally had a reason to stay in town. Yet when he factored out the utility company, which had canned him for good the day after his late-night climb, he wasn't qualified for anything that paid more than minimum. And working for Topaz Trucking was a great deal. The company was paying for his training, and there was a guaranteed job at the end with a salary even better than he had been making not climbing telephone poles. And for the second time in his life, Ramsey had a job he could actually stand—one with a future, too, provided he didn't do anything stupid again, like slicing up his driving leg.

As a rookie, he went over-the-road, meaning anywhere and everywhere. But unlike a lot of truckers gone for three, four weeks at a time, he had it pretty easy. Home every two weeks for four days.

Those were good days.

He was home for Allie's college graduation and cooked dinner from a recipe in the Sunday paper. He was leaving the next morning. After the dishes were washed and the two of them were on his sofa with *Led Zeppelin IV* playing on the stereo, he took Allie's hand and said—casually, but with his heart pounding—"So if we got married, would you be okay with that?"

Fifteen days later they landed at McCarran International Airport and were in Vegas fewer than six hours before a grinning minister at the Xanadu Drive-Thru Wedding Chapel declared them man and wife. Flower bouquet, boutonnière, five-by-seven photo, marriage license: eighty-seven dollars, plus tax. Back in their motel room, they propped the photo up on the dresser, and Ramsey couldn't stop looking at it. He'd never seen that expression on his own face before. One of the words he'd learned recently from the dictionary was *effervescence*, and that was close, but the more accurate word was a lot simpler. *Joy.*

12

By 1991, six years later, Allie was a senior sales rep whose boss was grooming her for management, and Ramsey was doing damn fine, too. He'd built up enough goodwill at Topaz that they started keeping him east of the Mississippi, usually seven days away rather than fourteen. He and Allie remained man and wife, remained in love, the love having become more nuanced, perhaps—less desperate, but more dependable, a love as essential to each of them as their blood and bone, inseparable from the life they had created together, the child they had created.

Which was why Ramsey's phone call with Eric on the morning of June 10 completely blindsided him.

The argument that morning between Ramsey and Allie had been over Meg's day care. Meg was two and a half, and her December birthday made her one of the oldest in the Ladybug group. Allie thought she should move up to the Grasshoppers, where she'd be one of the youngest. Let her learn from the older kids, Allie said. Let her be challenged. Ramsey thought: She comes home happy every day. Why rock the boat? Besides, she was challenged enough, navigating a dozen other kids and two teachers every day. She'd be challenged her whole life, same as everyone. Why rush it?

They didn't shout at each other, Ramsey and Allie. That was never their way. And this fight that Ramsey and Allie were having, it was about nothing. Meg would be fine in either group. Ramsey knew this. But he also knew that Allie was being short-tempered with him lately, as if any view he held was the wrong one. From time to time she brought work-stress home, especially at the end of the quarter when there were reports to complete, but her stress had always shown itself as an unspecified moodiness, a cloud that settled over the house for a couple of days before lifting again. This was different. Her impatience seemed directed specifically toward him.

So when she said for the fifth or maybe the thousandth time that she wanted Meg to be *challenged*, that it was important she be *challenged*, Ramsey said, "For Christ's sake, Allie, it's fucking day care, not NFL training camp."

He didn't intend to sound mean or rude—okay, rude maybe—but people hear what they want to hear. And her dismissive reply—"Oh, fuck you, Ramsey"—felt worse than if she'd hit him. In all their years together, neither of them had ever said that to the other, even kidding around. And because he was hurt and stunned, he left angry later that morning on a weeklong haul without so much as a good-bye. Last time he'd done that was three years earlier, and it had ended with him frightening that poor hitchhiker in his cab and then nearly drinking himself to death.

Driving the familiar roads that began most of his trips, he felt awful about the fight and how he'd left. She had looked especially attractive this morning. The outfit she had on, and her hair, curled with the iron she used . . . whatever it was, Ramsey would have preferred to part for the week with a proper good-bye in the bedroom, rather than fighting about day care in the kitchen. And now he was alone in his truck, heading away, and Allie was alone in the house, and although they'd talk on the phone tonight or maybe tomorrow, the hurt wouldn't fully resolve until he returned, which was too long.

He didn't like driving agitated, never had, so he blasted the radio. It helped some—music always chilled him out, kept him from stewing in his juices. Near the Jersey/Pennsylvania border a couple of hours later, a song came on by one of the new Seattle bands. He could take or leave what he'd heard so far from these bands whose music sounded like heavy metal on downers. That was why he had on the classic rock station, songs he knew and loved, but somehow this one track had made it into the rotation. It wasn't classic, not yet, but something about it grabbed him. The lyrics were half indiscernible, half impenetrable. Nirvana, the DJ said the band was called. The song sounded nothing like any nirvana Ramsey might imagine, but that was okay. The energy and the anguish were real.

Ramsey took the next exit to find a gas station with a pay phone and call Eric, who was spending his hard-earned, week-long vacation renovating his kitchen—ripping out linoleum, putting in tile, installing new cabinetry. When Eric answered, Ramsey informed him that he'd just heard a new song that they must learn right away, and if he *hadn't* heard it yet, then he'd better put down the trowel or tile or grout or whatever and get his ass over to the radio, pronto, and request—

"Hold it a minute," Eric said. "I need to tell you something." But then he didn't say anything else.

"You still there?" Ramsey asked.

"Yeah, I'm here. I hate to . . ." He paused again. "Ah, shit—but you have a right to know."

Ramsey wasn't sure why all his muscles had suddenly tensed. Then it occurred to him that until that moment, he had never heard Eric utter a single vulgar word.

"What is it?" Ramsey asked.

"I went to pick up my amp from your house earlier." Of course. With his fast exit this morning, Ramsey had forgotten to tell Allie that Eric would be dropping by. "So I was driving down your street. And I saw something."

"Well, don't draw it out, man. What'd you see?"

"Yeah, okay." He heard Eric take a breath. "It was Allie, standing in the driveway with a guy. I'm pretty sure it was David Magruder—you know who he is?"

"The weatherman? Yeah, he lives down the street from us."

"He does? Oh. Okay. It was him, then, for sure. Well, the thing is, they were standing in your driveway, by the front door. And . . . Ramsey, he had his arms around her."

"No," Ramsey said. "You got it wrong. They don't even know each other." But did they? How would Ramsey know? With him gone half the time, he couldn't be sure. Except, Allie would have mentioned Magruder at some point. Unless she didn't want Ramsey to know.

"It was him," Eric said. "I know what he looks like."

"Then there's an explanation." Ramsey's mind worked to come up with one. Sprained ankle, one leaning on the other? "Trust me, I'm sure—"

"And they were kissing," Eric said quickly.

The phone receiver became a heavy weight in Ramsey's hand. He lowered his voice. "Like a real kiss?"

Eric's silence made everything worse. He could tell that his friend was thinking hard about his words, something that friends shouldn't have to do. "You don't want the answer to that," he said.

"I fucking do," Ramsey said.

Eric cleared his throat. "What can I tell you, man? They were kissing. He had his hand . . ."

"Where?"

"Doesn't matter. On her rear end, okay?" Another throat-clear. "I didn't want to tell you. I was praying on it when you called."

"Did they see you?"

"No, I doubt it. I was driving toward the house, and when I saw what I saw, I just kept going. It all happened fast, a couple of seconds. Anyway, they were still kissing when I drove past. They weren't looking anywhere else."

"Man."

"Listen, I'm real sorry. I didn't want to tell you. But I figure that God must have put me in my truck and made me bear witness so I could be the one to break the news. So I had to tell you, you know?"

All around Ramsey, cars were fueling up. A man in overalls returned to his pickup from the gas-station store carrying a cup of coffee. A hundred yards away, vehicles rushed across the highway overpass in a steady hum. An absolutely ordinary Monday morning on the road in the middle of nowhere, U.S.A.

"Sure, man," Ramsey said, barely aware of Eric's words anymore, or his own. "Sure you did."

His call with Eric must have ended, and Ramsey must have climbed back into his truck, shut the door, and started the ignition, but he couldn't remember doing any of it. Couldn't remember leaving the gas station or pulling back onto the highway or shutting off the radio, but he must have done those things as well.

He continued west toward Pittsburgh. Without music, his thoughts drifted and focused, drifted and focused. He replayed the morning—something extra in the way Allie had put herself together, the way (he now remembered) she wouldn't quite meet his eye—and he replayed all the times lately when she'd been short-tempered with him or exasperated and he couldn't figure out why, almost as if she wanted to be mad at him. His thoughts drifted further back to times when they would be pushing Meg along in her stroller and Allie would exchange nods or smiles with neighbors who walked or drove past, many of them men. He visualized Magruder's house—split-level, gray, just a few hundred yards from their own—and how Allie never once mentioned that she knew him. That seemed more damning than anything. Other neighbors, she mentioned: the retired couple who lived across the street, the boy at the end of the block who was bald from chemo, the veterinarian with the Great Dane puppies that Meg played with. But Magruder? Not one fucking word.

A truth began to emerge like a person walking toward him through thick fog—invisible, invisible, then startlingly clear.

She'd done this once before, cheated on Ramsey, though she refused to see it that way. When they first started spending time together, she was still seeing some college boy. She never mentioned him until the day she told Ramsey that it was over.

What's his name? Ramsey had asked.

It doesn't matter what his name is, she said. *What matters is that I ended it. I chose you.*

He'd believed her. It hurt, though, knowing she'd continued seeing this college boy while things with Ramsey were heating up. (Not "seeing him," Ramsey told himself now. No sugarcoating, big guy: "fucking him.") He'd been alarmed at the time, how she had it in her to lead two lives without him ever having a clue. But by then he was already in love with her. And like she said, what mattered was that she'd ended it with the other guy. Anyway, the two of them were having this conversation in a fairly expensive restaurant, celebrating three months of whatever it was they were. And the fact was, she *had* chosen him. That was what mattered, he told himself at the time.

He wondered, now, how long it'd been going on with Magruder, how long the life he thought he was leading wasn't his life at all. Weeks? Months? Or much longer? And he wondered if over the last few years there had been *other* other men. He tried to remember all the men on his block, every last leering accountant and dentist, every shithead with a business suit and a neatly mulched yard. But they all blended together. And soon enough, those other men stopped mattering—they were merely interchangeable parts—and he began to see Allie more clearly than he'd ever seen her before.

He must have been driving, but the universe was collapsing in on itself, obliterating time and distance, and now he was a boy in a tree and now his mother was turning in the air and now his father was bleeding in the kitchen and now he was smelling piss in a drunk tank and now he was lying in bed in one dark apartment and now in another and now, and now, and amid this barrage of memories, all the rage he had worked tirelessly over the years to rid himself of came rushing back as if through a busted levee. He was driving toward Pittsburgh, past farms and over hills and through valleys, but what he saw was Allie as she'd first appeared from inside the hospital elevator, blue skirt, vase of flowers in her hand, and then he saw her standing outside his house kissing David Magruder, and then their hands were all over each other, and she and Magruder were in bed, clothes on the floor, and he was inside of her, thrusting, and she was looking into his eyes.

Ramsey didn't touch the truck's radio dial. He wanted the silence, the thoughts to keep coming, wanted to experience in its fullness the fact that the single truth he had lived by every day since first meeting Allie in that hospital corridor, the truth that made all truths possible, was a lie. And the worst part was, he should have known it. Should have seen that his life these last seven years had been too good to be true—the wife, the kid, the house, the two-car garage, the job, the band, and on and on. But now, alone in his cab with no distractions, he saw the past seven years for what they were: a big sham. *That* was the only truth. He should have known.

The land rose as he bypassed Wheeling and crossed the Ohio River. He passed a weigh station without stopping, and then the land flattened again to ten million acres of corn stalks and soybean crop. He saw none of it. As his big rig rolled at a steady seventy-five miles per hour toward Columbus, his anger continued to build and crash down on him in waves—strong, then stronger still—again and again and again, a rage so distilled and devastating, it was almost like bliss.

He pulled into the Buckeye Travel Center around 5:30 p.m. for diesel and a leak. Got out of his truck and blinked several times in the late-afternoon haze. Once more he became aware of his surroundings. After fueling up, he entered the facility and went through the shop toward the fast food. Ordered a sub and looked around for a place to sit. Half the dining area was roped off for construction. He didn't want to return to his cab yet, though. The travel center was already doing him some good, forcing him to move in a world of other people. He knew he easily could've driven off the road, earlier—from inattentiveness or from a decisive yank on the steering wheel. Jump an overpass and create one of those video-game fireballs.

When a man left his table near the windows, Ramsey claimed it. At the adjacent table, a man wearing a Pennzoil cap sat hunched over a book spread open on the table. The pages were all marked up. Bible, Ramsey figured. Many truckers passed their time that way—all well and good until they found one another, and suddenly you're stuck listening to a group of impassioned truckers quoting—probably misquoting—chapter and verse and tossing their discoveries around as if the truck stop were their personal church.

When the man turned the page, Ramsey saw it wasn't the Bible, not unless there was a new version with charts and graphs. The young man wore a button-down shirt and brown pants. He was sort of short and thin like Ramsey, but not muscular. Clean-shaven but with terrible acne. His glasses were wire-rim, the lenses round and professorial. The Pennzoil cap might have been a red herring—he was probably a student, not a trucker. Ramsey unwrapped his sub, and as he chewed he kept glancing over. Eventually, he took a sip of soda and said, "So you in school or something?"

The man looked up from his reading. "Me?" He shook his head. "No, I drive for Safari."

"They got a good reputation."

"Can't complain," the man said.

"The way your book is marked up," Ramsey said, "I had you pegged for a Bible thumper. Then I saw the graphs and whatnot."

"Student wasn't a bad guess." He licked his lips. "I went two semesters at Humboldt County College. Was gonna be an oceanographer. I always had a knack for science." Although the man looked younger than Ramsey, his smile was already full of nostalgia. "But life gets in the way sometimes."

"Brother, I hear you there," Ramsey said.

The man shrugged. "What I found, you don't have to be in school to be a student." He patted his book twice for evidence.

"So what's that, an oceanography book?" Ramsey surprised himself, engaging with this other man, shooting the shit today of all days. But he'd been so deep inside himself, it came as a relief to talk to someone who didn't know him from Adam.

"There's oceanography in here," the man said, pulling his chair a little closer to Ramsey, "but a lot more than that." He licked his lips again. "See, there are these two scientists—one's an astronomer and the other's a geologist. They're two of the leading scientists in their fields, and . . . well, you know how when the moon is full, the tides get extra big?"

"Of course," Ramsey said, and went on to tell the man about having grown up at the shore—how on moon tides, boats in Shark Fin Inlet were always getting grounded on sand bars.

"So you know that the moon affects the earth's gravitational pull—it's literally sucking the water up and pushing it back down again." The man touched the bridge of his glasses. "And when a planet—Jupiter or Mars or any of them—when it lines up with the earth and the moon, the tides get even bigger. That's called a planetary conjunction. Doesn't happen too often. But it's nothing compared to what's going to happen on September 22 of this year, when they *all* line up."

"All nine planets?"

"Plus the moon." His eyes widened. "That's called a superconjunction. It's never happened before—not like this, anyhow."

"So the tides should get pretty wild," Ramsey said.

"The tides?" That smile again. "Brother, you won't be thinking about the tides." He licked his lips some more.

Ramsey looked down at the book. "And it's all in there?"

"Everything you want to know—or maybe everything you don't want to know. But I choose knowledge over ignorance."

"Mind if I take a look?"

The man gave Ramsey a once-over and looked down at his book. "Tell you what. I was planning on showering before getting back on the road. You want, you can have it till I'm ready."

"To be honest," Ramsey said, "I wasn't much enjoying my drive today. I don't mind putting it off a while longer."

The man shut the book and handed it over. The cover was entirely black except for the title, which was printed in large yellow capital letters—*THE ORBITAL AXIS*—and the two authors with Ph.D. after their names.

"Have at it," the man said, and went off to the showers.

It was a day for hearing hard truths. And this scholar/trucker/whoever-he-was—he was right: The tides weren't the half of it. The book wasn't long, under two hundred pages, but each paragraph was jammed with ideas, with long sentences in a small typeface. From the introduction alone, Ramsey knew that he wouldn't be able to understand most of the science, and the charts were largely impenetrable, but the broader picture nonetheless soon began to emerge: There had never been a superconjunction as pure and complete as the one coming in September, and it was going to affect more than just the oceans. The tectonic plates, Mother Nature's concrete slabs lying beneath the continents, were going to buckle and snap and cause unprecedented numbers of earthquakes and tidal waves. But most important, the gravitational effect of all those lined-up planets would be cataclysmic. As in, for a brief period—several hours, maybe as long as half a day—there would barely be any gravity. As in, kiss your ass good-bye.

There was far more to *The Orbital Axis* than Ramsey could absorb in thirty minutes. So when a half hour came and went, then thirty-five minutes, and the man hadn't returned from his shower, Ramsey took his absence as a sign. He got up from the table with the book and returned to his truck. He didn't feel much like driving and went only as far as the next rest area, where he used the bathroom and brushed his teeth. Back in the cab, he stripped down to his boxer shorts, and though it wasn't even 8 p.m. he got into bed. He examined the book as if it were an exotic rock or seashell, turning it over in his hands, touching the surfaces. He opened the book and thumbed through it. Pages were dog-eared, much was underlined, and there were scribbles in the margins. He turned back to the introduction and began to read, unhurried this time, doing his best to understand, trying to free his mind of everything but the words and the sentences in front of him, working to be the best unschooled student that he could be.

Whenever his mind started drifting back to Allie, to the affair that could easily gut him like a fish, he forced his attention back to the book, the book. And the more he read—there went 11 p.m, there went midnight—the more relieved he felt by the notion that he, Ramsey Miller, wouldn't have to do one damn thing about his awful predicament. On the night of September 22, in a little under three months, God would take his own tools out of the garage, sharpen them up, and set everything right.

Only, not God. The cosmos. The universe itself.

The apologies came a day later. So easy. She apologized for her words, he for leaving in a huff. They talked twice more that week, quick conversations from rest stops, and over the course of several days, his anger evaporated into the ether, just as the trees and rivers and beasts would all do in three months' time. After the trip's last drop-off, he deadheaded back to the Boaters World lot feeling purified, exchanged the truck for his Volkswagen, and drove home. Kissed his wife, his daughter.

"How was your week?" he asked Allie that night over dinner.

Her week was fine.

"Eventful?" he asked.

No, she said, not especially. How was his week?

"Remarkable," he said, and took a bite of chicken. Sipped his beer. "I'll tell you about it after Meg goes to bed." And he did. He sat her down and told her about meeting up with the other trucker and reading his book and what it all added up to. He didn't tell her that the book was still in his truck, didn't want her reading it, taking on the role of debunker. He wasn't looking for a debate or a confrontation. He told her because she was his wife. And despite what she'd done to him, to them, she had the right to know that her time on this planet was more limited than she might think. She could do whatever she wanted with the information. As for him, he was thinking of selling his truck. Why did he need it anymore? he asked her. What was the purpose of working to earn money? Also (and this he didn't mention), Ramsey's presence at home should be enough to keep Magruder's hands off his wife.

Maybe for the same reason, Allie told him he ought to keep working. Then she suggested he see a shrink.

"I ain't crazy, honey," Ramsey said, and yawned. "What I am is dog tired." He'd logged 800 miles that day.

So they went to bed with the matter unresolved, and to Ramsey's surprise the resolution happened of its own accord. Hours of sleeplessness, despite his exhaustion, led to brief spells of frantic, sweaty dreams of cars and houses, trees, entire forests hurling upward toward the sky. By sunrise, the road was already pulling him back, the tug so strong it startled him. Since Meg's birth, he was usually home for sixty hours between hauls, but he found himself making up some story about an urgent delivery, an important customer, and he was packing hastily and kissing his family and racing back to Boaters World. Shifting that diesel engine into gear was like surfacing from the bottom of a pool after holding your breath ten seconds too long.

He drove more and more, missing Allie and Meg with every mile—but he'd been a trucker enough years now that he'd long since massaged that familiar ache into a softer longing. Anyway, it felt good to long for them, because longing was the opposite of rage.

Before long, he was rarely driving fewer than seventeen hours in a twenty-four-hour period. The law called what he was doing an "egregious violation," but nothing about it felt egregious. He cut back his coffee intake to almost nothing. He'd always slept best in his cab, but his sleep now—each night nothing more than an extended nap—was the most restful and dreamless of his life. He was rarely back in Jersey for more than a day, day and a half, before leaving the house again for Boaters World and his pre-trip inspection. And rarely out of arm's reach was the beat-up copy of *The Orbital Axis*, his reassurance that he wouldn't have to deal with Allie's affair—because he didn't trust himself to deal with it well.

He read the book cover to cover several more times, adding his own notes in the margins, his own underlining. Without trying, he memorized passages. He developed a habit of looking up at the sky, especially on remote stretches late at night when everything was dark and star-filled. And as the days turned into weeks and June became July and then August, Ramsey could swear he felt an electrical charge in the air all the time, as if a thunderstorm were always imminent, even when there were no clouds. And yet he knew that the charge wasn't electrical at all, but rather the tug of galactic forces beginning to nudge everything into place, including him.

In Phoenix on the morning of September 17, he was about ready to start home again with his load of bicycles bound for Toys"R"Us when he saw, hanging in the warehouse bathroom, a framed photograph of the Grand Canyon. Like every photo he'd ever seen of it since being a boy, it didn't even look like Earth.

"How far am I from the Grand Canyon?" he asked the dock supervisor when she handed him the forms to sign.

She squinted at him as if she couldn't fathom a single reason to visit that pile of rocks. "Maybe three hours?"

It would set him back at least half a day, and he was already on a tight schedule. But it was now or never, and three hours didn't seem so far to drive. New Jersey didn't seem so far.

Hell, on the energy currently pumping through his veins, he could easily drive to Mars and back.

PART THREE

13

September 28, 2006

Melanie sat beside Arthur Goodale in his bed in the critical care unit of Monmouth Regional Hospital and waited for his laughter to subside. It was a deep laugh that revealed a mouth full of yellow smoker's teeth and finished with a cough that sent him grasping for the cup of water bedside.

Melanie had just told him, reluctantly, about her disastrous meeting the previous afternoon with David Magruder.

"You, my young friend," he said, when the coughing had subsided, "are a truly awful interviewer."

"It was bad," Melanie said. She didn't like being amusing to him.

"Bad?" Another laugh. "Your *second question* was about Ramsey Miller?"

"He said he didn't want to be bothered with the routine stuff."

"Sure, but . . ." He shook his head. "Listen, moxie is one thing, but oh, boy. Your interviewing technique . . ."

"I get it," she said. "I'm horrible at this, and I blew our only chance."

"Now, wait a minute—who said it was our only chance?" He looked out the window. Still nothing but a brick wall. "No, it probably was." He sighed. "Well, your options were limited from the start. You could probably try tracking down Eric Pace."

"I think I know that name," she said. Probably from one of the news articles she'd read online.

"He was a close friend of Ramsey's," Arthur said. Melanie must have given him a terrified look, because he smiled. "Relax— I interviewed him years ago. He's totally harmless." She found this hard to believe, but she needed to be willing to talk with any-one who might know something useful. "Not that he ever gave me anything useful, either. But you never know."

"How can I find him?"

"He used to work for Garden State Electric, in their equipment warehouse. It shouldn't be too hard to find out if he's still in the area."

She nodded. She would do it. She would steel herself and meet the totally harmless Eric Pace, who just happened to have been friends with a murderer. "Who should I be this time?" She wasn't feeling ready for the return of Eager Young Coed.

He smiled. "I'd go with the *Star Ledger* cover."

"I thought I'm not a believable journalist."

"Oh, you aren't. Not to me, anyway, but I am a journalist. He won't know the difference. Just remember to *ease into* the conversation."

She thanked Arthur for his help, but when she went to stand up to leave he reached for her arm. "Come on, Alice—what's your interest in all this?"

And why not just tell him? Funny, she'd expected the pressure in her chest to tighten here in the town where the crime had occurred. Yet Ramsey Miller had last been spotted in Morgantown, not here. And in fact, away from West Virginia and the daily reminders that her whole life was constructed around a single secret, she found it easier to imagine that her secret didn't matter or even exist. She was staying in a hotel. She had seen the ocean. She had traveled alone to New York City, had been one anonymous soul among millions. How could she be of any consequence to anybody? But she knew better.

"Sorry," she said, "but I can't."

"You can't, huh? So you want my help, but you won't be honest with me?" His expression was parental. He wanted her to feel guilty. "Do you know what I think, Alice? I think you're selfish."

"No, I'm really not," Melanie said, heading for the door. "I'm not even doing this for me."

Sometimes you catch a break. The woman behind the counter at GSE made one phone call and told her that Eric Pace supervised the utility warehouse across town. She wrote the number and address on a slip of paper. When she called the number from a gas station pay phone, Eric said she should come by at 4 p.m.

It was one o'clock now. So she returned to her car and drove toward the star she'd drawn on her map, the place that'd been pulling and repelling her since coming to town.

232 Blossom Drive was a white, two-story wooden house with a steep roof and columns in the front. On the front stoop, several flowerpots framed the red door. The flowers were in bloom, bright blues and yellows.

It all looked extremely ordinary, yet sitting in the car, pulled up to the curb across the street from the house, she felt her hands shaking. For several minutes she didn't get out of the car. She watched the house and imagined, and the imagining nearly made her drive away. But she made herself step out of the car and onto this quiet street with mature trees and well-tended lawns. She couldn't just stand there and stare, however, so she walked along the street—there were no sidewalks—until it ended in a T. One of the houses on this other street had belonged to David Magruder, but she didn't know which. They were all nice houses, much larger than the trailer she lived in. Some of the houses had basketball hoops in the driveways. A couple of them had bicycles or tricycles out front. She walked back along Blossom Drive, this time on the even side of the street, and when she reached 232, she stopped again. It was one of the few houses with a privacy fence bordering the backyard. You couldn't see out. You couldn't see in.

She walked up the side yard to the fence, where there was a gate. By moving the gate a little she was able to peek through a gap by the hinges and see—a backyard. More lawn. More shrubs. A few large oak trees near the back fence. A cluster of smaller, scragglier trees. In a spot away from the trees, a chaise lounge. A soccer ball. It didn't make sense. How could this place—

"Can I help you?"

A woman in faded blue jeans with a bandana in her hair and a baby on her hip was standing near the house and looking at her.

"Sorry." Melanie immediately backed away from the fence. "No, ma'am. I didn't mean to pry."

The woman watched her—not angrily, just curious and maybe a little concerned.

"I'm sorry," Melanie repeated, quickly walking to her car. She started the engine and drove toward the T, where she made a U-turn and left the neighborhood.

"Been a long time since anyone asked me about my friend Ramsey," said Eric Pace, after Melanie had identified herself as

Alice Adams, crime beat reporter for the *Star Ledger*. He was an obese man sitting in an armless wooden chair, behind a metal desk. On the desk were several wire bins filled with forms.

"You still think of him as your friend?" After slinking away from the house on Blossom Drive, Melanie had treated herself to a bacon cheeseburger from the diner, cable TV, and an hour-long nap. She'd driven to the utility company feeling restored and eager to talk with Eric, but uneasy, too, about meeting the man who knew her father as someone other than the subject of a lurid news story.

"I still think of him," he said, "and that counts for something." He was in his fifties, maybe older, wearing a collared shirt with the company's name on the breast. Tired eyes. Except for an oval-shaped patch of raw skin on one cheek, his face was so pale it looked translucent. It was hard to imagine he had once worked outdoors. "So has there really been a development in the case?"

"We got a tip the police are renewing their search for Ramsey Miller." She didn't like lying to the man, but otherwise there'd be no plausible reason for her to have sought him out.

"Well, no cops have been here to see me. Not for years. So what do you think—some new evidence turn up?"

"I think someone might have seen him somewhere and reported it."

His index finger scratched the pink patch on his face. "Saw him where?"

She reminded herself of Arthur's advice to ease into things. "I'm only speculating. I really don't know." She took a breath. "So how are you, sir?"

He seemed to study her a moment. "Me? Look around." Flickering fluorescent lights, vast warehouse, rows of equipment stacked on pallets, no windows anywhere, the only sound a distant forklift. "My ex passed on five years ago," he said. "My brother, a year after that. My sons are grown and gone. They couldn't get away fast enough." He coughed. "They have their own lives. I leave them alone. I come here, and I think about drinking, and when I leave I go to my A.A. meetings, and on Sundays I pray in church. That's how I am."

She was relieved, at least, that he was talking to her about his life. Unlike David Magruder, Eric didn't seem like he was going to toss her out on the street. "You and Ramsey Miller worked together."

"I wish he could've stayed with it," he said. "Before my knees gave out, I used to get a great deal of satisfaction from being a lineman. It was interesting work. Challenging. It was good for me, and good for Ramsey, too, for the short time he did it."

"What was good about it?" she asked.

He squinted as if trying to see the answer somewhere far across the warehouse. "I liked knowing I was bringing light into people's homes. And I liked training the apprentices." He looked around. "Now I sit on my butt and check boxes on forms, make guys sign their name on pickup and delivery. Sign here, here. Initial here." He took a long breath. "It's bull, Alice—but if you live long enough you're gonna get sick, and the union benefits are worth their weight in gold." Although there wasn't another soul around, he lowered his voice. "When the ex got sick, I remarried her just so she'd have the benefits."

"You and your ex-wife stayed close?"

Eric smiled. "She hated me. You can't blame her. When we got married, I was a lousy drunk. When we split, I was a lousier one. But we stayed in touch because of the boys."

Melanie wasn't sure how they'd gotten to talking about Eric's wife. This was what happened when you eased into a conversation.

"How long did Ramsey Miller work here?"

"For the power company? Just a few weeks."

"Why'd he stop?"

Eric paused before answering, as if choosing his words carefully. "He hurt his leg on a climb."

He seemed to have no more to say on the subject, so Melanie asked, "Do you have any guess as to why he threw the party at his house on the night of the murder?"

"You stay on point, don't you?" His smile was friendly enough, but tired. Who could blame him? This place would sap the energy out of anyone. "No guesswork needed," he said. "But I'm not gonna tell you."

"Why not?"

"I won't make him sound crazier than the press has already made him out to be."

"Mr. Pace, he *was* crazy."

Eric shook his head. "He lost his way. He believed something with all his might, and when it didn't come to pass . . . well, we all know what happened. But he loved his wife and daughter."

"No, he didn't." Realizing that she sounded personally affronted, she added, "How could he have?"

"Ramsey Miller battled to be a good man. He just lost the battle. And I get it. I lost more than my share."

"You never killed anyone."

Eric looked into her eyes, and she felt reprimanded for her flip comment. "I found the lord Jesus Christ and put my faith in him before it was too late."

"Are you saying that religion would have stopped him from doing what he did?"

"I'm saying he insisted on walking alone, and nobody can do that. But it's too easy, calling him a monster, or crazy. He was neither."

"What did he believe with all his might?"

Eric shifted in his chair. "Forget I said that. Ramsey was hardly the first man to worship a false prophet."

"Sir?"

He scratched his face again. "He spent too much time alone. His job as a trucker demanded it, but it wasn't good for him. He got to thinking in ways that worked against him. I tried to help, but I should've tried harder."

"What could you have done?"

"Now there's the sixty-four-thousand-dollar question. All I know for sure is that I should've been my brother's keeper, like the good book says. Only I wasn't. All that time in church and I failed the most basic test. On the night when my friend was crying out for help, I wasn't listening." He bit his lip. "I sat in that God-forsaken bar, and then he . . ." His breath had a wheeze to it. "Well, that's my cross to bear."

"What bar?" Her eyes were adjusting to the dim lighting, but the warehouse smelled of mildew and rust. What a horrible place to spend every day.

"It really doesn't matter," he said.

"It does to me. Please."

He watched her a moment. "When we all left Ramsey's house that night, the guys and I went for a drink. Me and Paul and Wayne. At the old Jackrabbits—"

"Wayne?"

"Wayne and Ramsey played guitar. I played bass. My brother played drums."

She knew she shouldn't be so surprised—her uncle had been friends with her father, and he played guitar. But Uncle Wayne never talked about that night, and she knew better than to ask.

"The bar was less than a mile from the house," Eric was saying. "It wasn't very late, and I don't drink. It would've been easy for me to check up on them. We even discussed it, the guys and me. But

Wayne and Paul were already three sheets to the wind, and I was dog tired, and Paul started saying that the best thing we could do was give Ramsey and Allie time to cool off. I let myself be convinced. We paid our tabs and went home. But I was sober, and I should've known better. I should've checked on them."

"You aren't to blame, Mr. Pace." As soon as it was out of her mouth, she realized it probably wasn't a very journalistic thing to say.

More face scratching. "That's kind of you," he said. "But the fact is, Ramsey was having a time of it, and I knew it, and I was his friend. I should've gone. If I had gone back to that house, I think maybe I could've stopped it."

Melanie felt suddenly woozy. What if Eric—or Uncle Wayne or Paul—*had* dropped by? Might that have changed everything? Would her mother be alive today? Would her father be someone who'd merely gone through a rough period in his life, rather than becoming a murderer on the run, or—worse—on the hunt?

"For a long time after," he was saying, "I was certain that the whole reason I became an alcoholic was so that years later, on one particular September night, I'd be guaranteed to be stone sober and would be my brother's keeper and save a couple of lives." He sighed. "I'm a humbler servant these days. I'm less certain about what the Lord wants out of me, and I'm less certain He wants me introducing other people to His word. May I ask if you're a believer?"

"Mr. Pace, I don't think my beliefs are relevant." She wondered if it was really Eric's knees that had relegated him to the warehouse, or if maybe he had been preaching a little too fervently to the apprentices.

He smiled. "No, I suppose not. But I do know that the Lord forgives us for our sins, and if He can do that, then we should be able to forgive ourselves. So that's what I've been trying to do all these years. Forgive myself."

Melanie nodded. Although the two of them were alone in this warehouse with the workday ending, she couldn't help feeling safe around Eric, and sympathetic toward him. She knew how it felt to be stuck inside a place for years on end, wondering *what if, what if*.

"Where do you think Ramsey Miller might be now?" she asked.

Eric closed his eyes for a couple of seconds, and Melanie found herself looking at the irritation on his cheek and wondering if the rawness made him scratch or if the scratching had caused the rawness. When he opened his eyes again, he said, "For a long time I would dream about him coming to me. I dreamed I convinced him to turn himself in and accept man's punishment and God's judgment." He shrugged. "He could be anywhere. He could be dead."

"Do you really think?"

"No, not really. Ramsey's a survivor." His smile widened to reveal a missing tooth. "The man's too stubborn to die."

She arrived back at the Sandpiper Hotel with a sandwich and a Coke, feeling ready for a meal, more cable TV, and an early night's sleep. Thirty minutes in that twilight of a warehouse had worn her down. No wonder Eric had accepted her invitation to talk. And unless he was lying, he believed he knew why her father had thrown his party. It couldn't just be a birthday celebration, could it? But what then? Tomorrow, she'd see whether Arthur thought it might be important, or just some habitual teaser that led nowhere.

Walking toward the hotel lobby, she gave only passing notice to the black Lincoln Town Car parked in the fire lane. When she heard the name "Ms. Adams?" being called out the car window, the name she'd invented didn't register at first.

Then the driver's door opened and a man stepped out. "Excuse me." Melanie stopped walking. "Are you Alice Adams?"

The man was dressed in dark blue jeans and a gray blazer. Black shoes with a fresh polish. He was very tall and his hair looked mussed in a purposeful way.

"Yes, sir," she said.

The man nodded, as if he knew all along. "David Magruder wants you at his home."

14

It took all the nerve she could summon to get into that car. She had no clue how Magruder had found out where she was staying or why he might seek her out after the way he'd chased her away the day before. *Remember why you've come all this way,* she kept telling herself, looking out the tinted window as the car rolled away from the hotel. *You're here for answers. You're here to be brave.*

They drove toward the ocean, went over several marshes, then turned onto a winding road where on either side the homes became larger. After some more driving she saw the bay through the trees and knew they had to be close. She'd never seen anything like it—homes that could be museums, each landscaped with its own small forest, it seemed, hand-tapered so that every branch of every tree hung just so. Some of the houses were obstructed from the road by hedges or trees or fences, so that you only caught them in glimpses—and in addition to being awestruck by these estates, Melanie couldn't help feeling bewildered by these people for whom privacy was merely an aesthetic choice.

Magruder's house was almost completely hidden, first by a row of hedges and, behind it, a wrought-iron fence. From the road, only the roof of the house was visible, set far back on the property. The driver pressed a button on his remote device clipped to the sun visor, and twin gates slowly opened.

"Here we are," he said—his first words the entire trip—and pulled into the pebbled driveway.

Inside the gate, the driveway curved around a grove of trees and then cut like a moat through several acres of lawn toward the stone house. When the car approached the house, she could see clear through one of the downstairs rooms to the dock out back, a sailboat tied up there, the wide expanse of the bay.

Somehow the driver was out of the car and opening her door before she could even grab the handle. Once she'd exited the car, he shut the door behind her and dialed his cell phone.

"We're out front, David," the man said, and put the phone into the inside pocket of his blazer.

She looked up at the driver and said, "Thank you," as if this had been her idea all along.

"Don't mention it," he said.

Before they reached the front steps, the door opened and David Magruder stepped outside wearing black pants and a maroon cashmere sweater with the sleeves pushed up. He was all smiles, a replication of his greeting the day before. "Welcome, welcome," he said, rubbing his hands together. "Thanks for getting her, Bill."

The man nodded. "My pleasure," he said, and returned to the car.

When the two were inside the house, Magruder said, "You look very pretty today." Maybe he meant it to be nice, or ice-breaking, but considering how he had behaved in his office the day before, the compliment came off as super creepy. And either he didn't know it, which made him dense, or he did know it, which was worse. Regardless, she was feeling extremely aware of the fact that the two of them were alone in the house.

"This is a big house," she said.

He laughed. "I suppose it's a little much for a bachelor pad." The room they were in—the one she saw from outside—could comfortably seat thirty. "But you can't beat the view."

No, you couldn't. Beyond the house, beyond the dock and the sailboat, Silver Bay shimmered. Across the water, maybe a half mile away, another line of mansions mirrored those on this side of the water. Toward the north, the bay opened up so wide she couldn't see the other side.

"Listen," he said, "I want to apologize for yesterday. The way I treated you was . . . well, it's unforgiveable. There were problems with the show we were working on. My anger had nothing to do with you."

Almost certainly a lie, but at least they were talking.

"It's all right, Mr. Magruder," she said.

"You're in my home. Please—I'm begging you to call me David."

She nodded. "All right, David."

"Good. And it's definitely not all right," he said.

What's going on? she wanted to ask. *Why am I here?* But she'd learned her lesson about getting to the point too fast. "Is that the ocean over there?"

"That's New York Harbor," he said. "From the roof deck you can see the Manhattan skyline." He took her hand. The gesture was too intimate, and she almost pulled away but relented. "Come on—I want to show you my office."

His office was out back. The yard was private and absolutely serene, the only noise coming from the engine of a distant motorboat. They passed the pool, with its own pool house (*It's really a guesthouse*, he explained. *I didn't ask for it, but it came with the property*) and they passed the garage (*I was going to have Bill pick you up in the Ferrari, but then I thought you might be more comfortable in the Town Car*) and they passed a clover-shaped pond (*Would you believe the osprey have been swooping down and stealing my koi!*), and finally they entered a smaller structure, built beside the dock, that made her feel as if she were on a yacht, everything wooden and polished and uncluttered. There was a sitting room and office adjacent to a full kitchen and what looked like a fully stocked bar. On the walls hung various medals, plaques, and framed letters both typed and handwritten.

"In the main house," he said, "the walls are full of original artwork. George Rodrigue, William Baziotes . . . would you believe I recently acquired a Warhol? But *here*"—he motioned to the wall— "is where I keep what really matters. Gifts from soldiers, students, husbands, wives . . . ordinary folks whose lives I've helped in some way over the years. They mean a lot more to me than my Emmys."

He was showing off, but only when he opened a half-empty bottle of Scotch and poured himself a not-small glass did it occur to her that he might also be drunk, or at least on his way. Other than on TV, she'd never seen a drunk person before. Wayne and Kendra rarely drank alcohol. Being drunk was less obvious than she would have thought—or maybe Magruder was a subtler drunk than most.

"What's your poison?" he asked, and smiled.

"No, thank you—I'm okay," she said.

"I know you're okay," he said, "but I want you to be comfortable."

He couldn't keep still. A tap of the foot. A slight bite of the lip when he thought she wasn't watching. It reminded her of Phillip, screwing up the courage to kiss her that first time.

"Did you know that presidents vacationed here, once?" he asked. "In Silver Bay, I mean. Woodrow Wilson, Teddy Roosevelt. And movie stars: Jayne Mansfield, Buster Keaton. A train used to run right up to the bay. The boardwalk—have you seen it?"

She said that she had.

"It's nothing, now," he said. "But at one time it was jam-packed with the rich and famous. You wouldn't know it, but there's history in these five square miles." Another sip from his drink. "It's a lot quieter now, but that's how I like it. Silver Bay is my antidote to the New York office. I don't know if I could face the insanity every day without a serene place to come home to." He smiled. "And that, by the way, is my answer to you from yesterday—why I still live in Silver Bay." Another sip. "You should sit at the desk for a minute." The wooden desk had nothing on it and was right up against a floor-to-ceiling window overlooking the bay. She sat down and placed her hands on the desk's cool, smooth surface. "So what do you think?"

When seated, she couldn't see the dock—only the water. "It's like being on a ship," she said, though she'd never been on a ship.

"That's because it's how I designed it. See across the water? That pinkish house?"

It was one of the largest on the bay. "Yes."

"That's my ex-wife's house. I know—it's all very Gatsby. But she bought it after the divorce, and I wasn't going to be the one to move."

Melanie had no idea what he was talking about. And before she could stop herself, she made a mental apology to Arthur and asked, "Why am I here?"

"Why, indeed." David looked out over the water. "You're here because I treated you badly yesterday and wanted to make up for it."

"That's nice of you," she said. "But you don't have to ingratiate—"

"Also, I was hoping you might answer something for me."

Ah. "I can try."

"I'm really glad to hear you say that," he said, finishing the drink and setting the glass down on the desktop. Looking out at the water, he said almost offhandedly, "Who are you?"

"What do you mean?" She kept her breathing steady. "You already know. I'm Alice Adams."

He sighed. "You're a lovely young woman—beautiful, in fact—but you'll notice that I haven't called you Alice since you've arrived. That's because there is no Alice Adams enrolled at Gaston College. Which makes sense, given that your name is Melanie Denison." Hearing her name said aloud gave her body a physical jolt. "Except, there's no Melanie Denison enrolled at Gaston College, either. So I was hoping you'd be willing to explain that for me."

"No," she said, all of her muscles tightening. "I'm not willing to."

He took a long breath and looked at her. "You need to understand that I do this for a living. Even if the Sandpiper Hotel hadn't given us your real name, we'd have found it out. I have a very capable staff. Compared to the kind of investigatory research we do every day, this is nothing." When she didn't respond, he said, "Look, Melanie, if you're working for one of the rags, that's your business. I'll even keep it a secret." She continued to stare out the window. "I'm not angry about yesterday, anymore. Honest." He gave her a smile that was probably meant to seem reassuring, but she couldn't help thinking that the person he was reassuring was himself. "In fact"—he reached out and took her hand—"I'd like to become better acquainted."

If she were better at this—if she were Nancy Drew—she would pull her hand away and fearlessly continue her line of questioning from the day before. She'd get what she came for. Instead, she quietly said, "I should go. This isn't a good idea."

Magruder's eyes widened. At first, she thought he had become angry, but no. There was fear in his eyes, or something like it. He couldn't stop looking at her. At last, he said, "Let down your hair."

"I beg your pardon?"

"Your hair. I'll have Bill return you to your hotel in just a minute. I swear it. But do this for me first."

She felt very alone in this man's bachelor pad. "Mr. Magruder, I don't know what you think I'm here for, but—"

"I'm not making a pass at you. But please." His voice was suddenly desperate. "Put your hair down, and I'll answer whatever questions you came to New York to ask me."

And with that promise, she found herself removing the clip from her hair. She hadn't cut it in a while—it was about the longest it'd ever been. Tied up all day, it would look scraggly, so she ran her fingers through it a few times before facing him head on.

He squinted a little in the early evening light, and the way he studied her face felt both clinical and tender. And just as it occurred to her why he might have made his request, and why he was now looking at her so intently, his eyes watered and he said, "Oh, my God." He opened his mouth as if to say more—once, then again—before going to pour himself another drink, larger this time.

He dropped into one of the leather chairs, took a swallow, and set the glass down. "I didn't actually think . . . I mean, it crossed my mind, but . . ." He closed his eyes. And when he opened them again and confirmed that Melanie wasn't a mirage but an actual young woman in his office, he smiled and said, "You aren't the spitting image of your mother, but you come damn close."

15

They sat together on the sofa, watching the sun dip behind his ex-wife's neighbors' homes across the bay. Melanie held a glass of water while David Magruder went through most of a bottle of champagne. "You sure you don't want any?" he said. "I mean, if Meg Miller being alive isn't cause for celebration, I don't know what is."

The man could put away a lot of alcohol. He was clearly practiced at it.

"Water is fine," she said, the ice cubes knocking together in her glass surely giving her fear away. He knew. Him. A journalist. An untrustworthy journalist. A volatile journalist with money and power. It couldn't be worse.

"What about food—are you hungry? We could rustle something up in the main house."

Her stomach was growling. For the baby, she had to get on a better eating schedule. But how do you eat when you're nauseous all the time? "Maybe if you have some crackers or something."

"Crackers?" He laughed. "Sure, we can rustle up some crackers." But he didn't get up. He still seemed stunned. "Look at you—Meg Miller. God damn." He shook his head. "Meg Miller, alive and well."

"I go by Melanie," she said.

"Sure, okay. Melanie." He smiled at her. Now that he knew her secret, he couldn't stop smiling. "Where've you been all this time?"

She shrugged. "Hiding."

"You lost me."

"From my father. So he can't find me."

His smile disappeared. "You've been hiding since nineteen ninety-one?"

"That's right."

"Oh, Jesus."

"And I know your job is to expose stuff, but you have to keep this secret. You have to. Please. The only reason I'm alive today is that everyone thinks I'm not."

"Your accent—do you really live in North Carolina?"

She shook her head. "Please. I'm not going to tell you, and I'm begging you not to try to find out. I need your help." She had sought David out because of the unlikely possibility that he'd have something useful to say about the night of the murder. But when she thought about how easily he had investigated her without her knowing, a new idea started to take shape. "I need you to help me find my father."

"Darling, your father had a fifteen-year head start. The police have gotten nowhere. I'm not sure what you think I can do."

"You said you do this for a living."

"I'm a TV journalist, not a bounty hunter."

"But you can try, can't you?"

The yard had darkened a shade, and he squinted out the window, as if Ramsey Miller might be standing on the dock, waving at them.

"I can try."

He insisted on taking her back to her hotel, but she insisted on being the one behind the wheel.

"I've been drinking for enough years to know when I can and can't drive," he said.

"Either I drive or I'm calling a cab."

He shrugged. "It's a nice night—we'll take one of the convertibles."

"How many cars do you own?" she asked.

"Six," he said. Then: "Seven. I forgot about the new one. Can you drive a manual transmission?"

"No," she said.

"Then so much for the Alfa Romeo." He grinned. "Come on, we'll take the Corvette."

They went out to the massive garage, where seven shiny cars were parked in a line. The yellow Corvette was in the center. After David pulled the car's top down, they got in, and she backed out of the garage, scared to death of hitting something, and went around the circular driveway to the road.

She turned left and accelerated, the engine revving beautifully, and headed back to town, passing the large estates, and then the road curved around so that it ran along the bay, which looked smooth as glass underneath a sky that was fading from purple to black. She hadn't ever ridden in a convertible before, let alone driven one, and she decided on the spot that of all the things missing from her life, this one ranked high.

"You remember your way around?" David asked from the passenger seat.

"Only from the past few days. I have no memories of this town," she said. "I wish I did. I wish I could remember my mother. I try all the time."

At the light, she turned away from the bay and headed west on Main Street.

"Let me tell you something. She's worth remembering."

"So you weren't strangers."

"No," he said. "We were close. I loved your mother."

"What do you mean?"

"What do I mean? I mean we were good friends. She was a wonderful person. I think I'm actually pretty drunk."

"Were you ever more than friends?" Melanie was glad that it was dark and she had a reason to keep her eyes straight ahead.

"No," he said. "Never. Turn right here."

"Why?"

"Just do it—I want to show you something."

The turn sent her in the direction of her parents' old neighborhood. She'd seen enough of that for one day. But then he had her make another turn, and another, onto a road that was new to her.

"Pull into that parking lot," he said. There were no other cars. "Drive to the end there and park. You need to see this."

David got out, and she followed. Though it was dark out now, she could see that they were in a park, a pretty spot with mature trees and a playground ahead and a pond off to the left. At the edge of the playground were a few picnic tables. David climbed up and sat on one of the tables.

"So is it familiar?" he asked.

"No. Should it be?"

"This is where you used to play."

"Really?" She tried to imagine herself as a toddler, sliding down those same slides. Swinging on those same swings. She climbed up on the table and sat beside David.

"There used to be a taller slide over there with several twists. It was your favorite. And that rubbery surface is new. Back then there were woodchips, I'm pretty sure. Same swings, I think. Though sometimes you just liked chasing the birds."

"Why do you know this park so well?" she asked.

"I used to meet your mother here when she came with you," he said. "With your father away so often, I think she appreciated the adult company." Melanie knew from the articles she'd read that her father was a trucker. "We would talk."

"What would you talk about?"

"Oh, I don't remember now. Our jobs, our lives, politics, the weather . . . whatever was on our minds, I guess. You'd throw crusts of bread to the turtles in that pond." He smiled. "That was the only way to lure you away from the playground and back to the car—the promise of feeding the turtles."

I used to play here. I used to feed the turtles. This was my home.

Melanie climbed off the table and went over to the swings. There were bucket swings for babies and another set for older kids. She sat in one of the larger swings, lifted her legs, and glided back and forth a few times before lowering her shoes and dragging to a stop.

"Thanks for taking me here," she said, going back over to him. "Sometimes I feel like I don't have a past. So . . . thanks."

"You're welcome," he said. He reached out and clasped her shoulder, then moved his hand away. The gesture brought unexpected tears to her eyes. She turned to face the pond.

They stayed like that a minute—him sitting on the table, her standing beside it—their eyes adjusting to the dark. A gentle breeze moved the leaves in the nearby trees.

"Back at the house," Melanie said, looking at him again, "you told me I could ask you whatever I wanted."

"Okay—I might have said that."

"You did."

He nodded. "All right."

"After the murder, why did the police talk with you several times?"

"Who told you that?"

Melanie held firm. "You said you'd answer my questions."

A bullfrog honked from the pond. "You're being tough," he said. "That's a good journalistic instinct. I used to be a tough journalist, you know. Pretty legit. I have those instincts. But I like having money, too. Sometimes it's a trade-off. God damn, I make a lot of money." He shook his head. "I'm just so glad you're alive. You have no idea how mind-blowing this is."

She returned the smile. "The police . . ."

"Right. Okay. My mistake was that I was honest to them up front about being friends with your mother. And also . . ." He shrugged. "I had a shit alibi for the time of the murder."

"What was it?"

"It was that I didn't have one."

"You mean they thought—"

"No, they didn't think anything. This wasn't a whodunit, you know? But the police like tidiness—people verifying other people's stories. And God forbid if anyone is ever alone. I was married then—bad idea, by the way. I highly recommend never doing that. But I was married and my wife was in New York that night. Anyway, these local yokel cops were looking for the same thing you're looking for now: something that might help them find your father. Well, I didn't know anything. I barely knew the man. But you know how it is. I'm a public figure, and there are people in this world who make a lot of money running with nonexistent stories about public figures. Which is why I don't ever talk about that time in my life, or about knowing your mother. I was very fond of her, and what happened was horrible, and I don't like being reminded of it."

"You didn't say 'fond.' You said you loved her."

The bullfrogs were louder now, and the crickets. It reminded her a little of West Virginia, the woods teeming with life.

"She was a beautiful, complicated woman," he said.

"And you loved her."

"Yes," he said. "I loved her very much."

David Magruder had interviewed movie stars and astronauts and every living president. Yet it felt less strange than she would have imagined, driving a drunk celebrity around in his fancy convertible.

"I wish I'd brought a six-pack," he said from the passenger seat, his eyes closed. Though her hotel was only a couple of miles from the park, by the time she arrived David was fast asleep.

She pulled the car into a parking space and shut off the engine. She nudged his arm, rousing him.

"You need to call your driver," she said.

"He isn't on twenty-four-hour call, Melanie."

"Then a cab."

"I'm a grown man," he said, and yawned.

"Well, there's no way you're driving yourself home," she said.

"Of course I am." He sounded wounded. "I've been my driving—" He tried again. "I've been driving since dinosaurs roamed the earth."

Her room had two beds, but no way. "There's a sofa in the hotel lobby," she said. "You can sleep there for a couple of hours."

He looked at her and smiled. "Your concern for me is wildly endearing. Tell you what—leave me here. The seat reclines way back. I'll just rest awhile."

"I guess," she said.

"She guesses!" He grinned drunkenly. And when she handed over the keys, he leaned forward and kissed her cheek. "Absolutely amazing," he said, reclined his seat, and shut his eyes.

"You'll probably want to put the top up," she said softly. When he didn't answer, she said, "Good night, David," and shut her door, leaving him there to sleep in the Sandpiper parking lot. She did it reluctantly, suspecting that the minute she entered the hotel, the Corvette's fancy engine would roar to life. Which was exactly what happened.

16

September 22, 1991

After standing over his sleeping wife for a serene minute, Ramsey left their bedroom and went downstairs. His hands needed something to do, so he put on his coat and work gloves, went outside, and began carrying the sheets of plywood and two-by-fours from the garage to the backyard. It was still more night than morning outside, and cold—but the work encouraged a sweat. When he'd finished moving all the wood, he went inside again to wait for Eric.

The tap came only a couple of minutes later. The two men shook hands. Ramsey would've offered Eric coffee, but his friend was already carrying a cup from 7-Eleven, so they cut through the house and went out back.

" 'Preciate your help," Ramsey said. "I know it's cold out here."

"Cold nothing. We're a band, aren't we?" Eric said. "Band needs a stage."

One good thing about the cold, everyone's windows would be shut. Ramsey didn't want the neighbors moaning about the pounding of nails on a Sunday morning. Not that this would take long. The plans were so simple, Ramsey barely needed to explain them to Eric: six pallets supported by thirty-six-inch sections of two-by-fours, which the hardware store had precut yesterday. They'd finish in time for Eric to get to church.

Ramsey offered up his work gloves, but Eric declined and blew into his cupped hands. The ground was wet, so they knelt down on one sheet of plywood while working on another. Each man started on a pallet, working apart, not talking for a spell, the rhythmic hammering like a drumbeat to a song you can't quite remember. Just as Ramsey expected, a project like this was what he needed. It was good to build something. After a few minutes, Eric broke the rhythm, saying, "So Wayne tells me you're cracking up."

Ramsey looked up from his work. "What's that now?"

Eric set down his hammer. "The end of the world, Ramsey?" He said it disappointed, the head shake implied. His father had used the same tone when Ramsey was young and his rap sheet still in its infancy. *Shoplifting, Ramsey? Vandalism, Ramsey?*

Ramsey had never intended to tell Eric, whose clay brain religion had baked hard, but now he knew anyway. Which explained why he'd agreed so readily to get up in the dark and come over here. He'd decided to be a one-man intervention.

"I know it to be true." Ramsey shrugged. "That's all there is to it, my friend."

"Ramsey—"

"I *know* it." He said it final like, and made a point of returning to the two-by-four he was hammering into place. The morning was getting lighter, beginning to feel like today and not yesterday.

"So you know the world is ending, but you don't bother mentioning it to me?"

"Didn't see the point," Ramsey said.

"You told Wayne."

"Yeah, I told Wayne, but I hadn't planned to." Outside the music store yesterday afternoon, after arranging the P.A. rental, Wayne was smoking a cigarette and moaning to Ramsey about how he'd barely gone surfing all summer. So Ramsey told him he'd better get to it on Sunday morning, and he told him why— not too much detail, just the *Reader's Digest* version.

"So why'd you tell Wayne and not me?"

Ramsey stopped working again. "I'll bet you never knew that Wayne grew up in some shitty orphanage till he was ten. Or that when he was eleven, his foster dad broke his arm for fighting at school. Cracked it right over the kitchen table."

Eric said nothing for a few seconds. "I'm sorry to hear that, but what's your point?"

"My point is, Wayne's had it rough. And he hasn't had one damn person in his whole life to look up to, and for some crazy reason he looks up to me. He confides in me. So I was returning the favor."

"Well, you shoulda confided in me, too."

"Oh, come on, man, don't look all hurt—I knew you'd think I'd gone loony. Or worse, you'd believe me and start to freak out about your standing with Jesus."

"Strange, how I don't remember reading about this in the newspaper."

"Make fun if you want," Ramsey said, "but it's no joke."

"So what's your source?"

Ramsey remembered everything about that late-afternoon: the roped-off seating, the other trucker, the way time had seemed to stop. "Saw it in writing a couple months back. In a science book." Eric still had that parental look on his face. "I read it cover to cover. Trust me—it adds up."

"You're no scientist," Eric said.

In a tree near the back fence, a couple of squirrels sounded like an old couple bickering. When they quieted down, Ramsey said, "Let me ask you something. Do you believe in God?"

"What?"

"Come on—do you or don't you?"

"You know I do," Eric said.

"But you ain't a priest or a prophet or nothing, are you?"

"It's different." He set his hammer down and drank some coffee. "My belief is about putting trust in Jesus Christ. It's about having faith in the Holy Spirit."

Ramsey tried to imagine a time before Eric's conversion, when he was just another drunk, one more fuck-up in over his head.

"So on a scale of one to ten," Ramsey said, "how much do you believe in Jesus and God and all that?"

"Don't ask me that," Eric said. "It's crass, putting it on a scale."

"So you won't do it?"

Eric sighed. "Whatever, Ramsey. Ten. All right? I believe it a ten."

Ramsey lowered his voice. "You can knock that number down a peg or two if you want." He smiled. "No one's listening but me and the squirrels, and we won't tell."

"I don't need to lower my number." Eric glanced up at the sky. "And there's always someone listening."

"Ah, so you're only saying 'ten' out of fear. That's messed up."

"You got it wrong."

"Then you're hedging, so just in case Jesus is real you don't end up on his bad side."

"Ramsey, it's a ten, okay? You asked me, and I gave you my answer. I have complete faith in our Lord and Savior Jesus Christ."

"All right, all right," Ramsey said, hands raised in defense. "You don't need to get all nutty about it. So your faith is a ten. And so

230

is mine. You wouldn't know it, because I always said the concept of God was a bunch of—" Seeing Eric's eyes narrow, he softened his words. "I've never been a believer."

"That I know," Eric said.

They started working again, and Ramsey knew what was coming and waited for it. He'd forgive Eric, because his friend was an addict. Eric used to be addicted to booze, and now he was addicted to God.

"Maybe this is the right time for you to reconsider your own relationship with Jesus," Eric said after a long-enough pause that not saying it must have felt like ignoring the world's worst itch.

Ramsey smiled. He knew people. "Nah, it's too late for me." He said it to lighten the mood, self-deprecate a little. But when it came to Eric and God, there was no mood lightening. "What I'm saying is, I already know all about faith. In fact, I have more of it in my little finger than most people have in their whole body, even religious kooks."

"*Hey . . .*"

"I only mean that without faith I'd be dead by now."

Eric said, "I've always respected how you pulled yourself up, with God's help."

"God nothing, man—*you* pulled me up. And Allie did, too. That's what I'm talking about: For twenty-seven years I never had faith about one damn thing in my life, and then out of the blue I decide to put my faith in some douchebag stranger hanging from a utility pole who's giving me lip—I decide *that* guy's gonna save me . . . and he does! You. You fucking did." Eric cringed from the double blow of a compliment and an obscenity, but Ramsey could think of no other way to make his point. "And when I'm in dire straits again, some college girl enters my hospital corridor, and I take one look at her and somehow I know with complete certainty that lightning's gonna strike me a second time and now *she's* gonna save me. And she does. But it's more than that. She keeps on saving me every day since, twenty-four/seven/three sixty-five—just like I knew she would."

"Does all this by any chance have to do with—" Eric took a breath. "With what I *saw* a few months back?"

Since their phone call back in June, Ramsey and Eric hadn't ever talked about what had taken place in the Millers' driveway.

"We were never supposed to meet," Ramsey said. "The damn flowers weren't for me. But okay, we meet and I say to myself— *put your faith in her.* And believe me, I've had enough hours alone in my truck to consider the matter from every angle. And now the end is almost here."

"So you say."

"Listen—up till now, in my whole entire life I've only ever known two things for sure: that I needed to put my faith in you and in Allie. Almost every other decision I ever made was a bad one, but not those. And that's because it wasn't ever a decision. It was a feeling— I just knew. And now here's this third thing that I know even stronger than the other two put together. Ten times stronger." He shook his head. "I can't explain it, but I don't need to."

"I still say we'd have heard about it on the news."

"Not if the government doesn't want to alarm everybody and there's nothing they can do about it. Then they'd keep quiet so there's no mass panic. It's like if a thousand nuclear warheads were about to obliterate the U.S. They'd keep it to themselves. Nobody ever fucking tells the truth."

"Ramsey—"

"No, I get it. You think I'm wrong. But the fact is, my faith is better than yours, because there's science to back it up."

"So where exactly is this science book? You keeping it to yourself, or can I have a look?"

"I don't have it any longer," Ramsey said.

That parental look again.

"For what it's worth," Ramsey said, "I never once asked you what makes you so sure about Jesus and Mary and all the rest."

"You want to see my book?"

"No."

Eric looked at the plywood scattered around them. "I'm willing to put up a grand says you're wrong."

Ramsey smiled. "Nice bet. If I'm right, you don't need to pay up."

"I only ever make smart bets."

"Except on me, you mean," Ramsey said.

"Yeah, you were always my long shot." Eric tried a smile of his own but it didn't stick. "Listen, man, we're gonna play this gig, and then we'll all go to sleep tonight and wake up tomorrow and it'll just be another Monday. And when that happens . . . it's not going to *disappoint* you somehow, is it?"

But how does one answer a hypothetical about an impossibility? And anyway, the answer was really none of Eric's business.

"Of course not," Ramsey said. And that was the end of it. They went back to aligning boards and pounding nails as the sky lightened around them. And when their stage was built and Eric had left, Ramsey went to the garage for his shovel. Might as well get the hard work done while he was already sweaty.

He found a spot away from any large trees and their hard underground roots, and not too close to the stage, and began to dig up the grass in a large circle. He dug the hole about a foot deep with a diameter of four or five feet—a large fire pit—and deposited the soil in the small wooded area at the rear of the fenced-in property. The job only took a half hour, and the result was simple, but a fire pit doesn't need to be complicated. It's just a shallow hole. Some bricks, stacked in pairs, would make an ideal ring around the pit. He'd buy those later this morning at the Home

Depot. As for firewood, that dying dogwood along the back fence no longer needed to be anyone's eyesore.

"Daddy pancakes!"

Meg stood on the back deck. She had on her yellow footie pajamas. "Hi, sweetheart," Ramsey said. "Does Meg want some Daddy pancakes?"

Allie came up behind Meg. "She's telling you that she just *ate* Daddy pancakes." Daddy pancakes were in the shape of Mickey Mouse's head. For a reason only understandable to a toddler, she refused to touch them unless Ramsey manned the spatula.

"I thought only Daddy can make Daddy pancakes," he said to Allie.

His wife shrugged. "The times they are a-changin'."

This stung more than it ought to have. "I'll be in real soon, I promise. I'm just getting some things set out here."

"All right," Allie said. "Come on in, sweetie." She guided Meg back into the house and closed the sliding door.

Ramsey returned to the garage and exchanged the shovel for an axe so he could cut down and section the dogwood. The chain saw would be faster, but a Sandy Oaks resident knows better than to fire up a chain saw on a Sunday morning.

17

David Magruder's front yard had the expertly tended look of someone who farmed out his lawn care. The grass was thriving, with no brown patches. The shrubs running along the front of the house were perfect orbs set in cypress mulch that smelled and looked freshly laid despite it being fall.

The house itself, white with green shutters, looked recently painted. The roof was free of leaves and pine needles, as were the gutters. Ramsey had noticed that the property looked, always, primed and ready, as if a realtor could plant a FOR SALE sign in the yard at a moment's notice. Ramsey appreciated tidiness, but Magruder's property was so immaculate it suggested a flaw in the man's character—not so much arrogance as secrecy.

The Sunday paper lay at the base of the driveway, the single haphazard item on the property. Ramsey picked it up, and as he walked toward Magruder's front door he slid the elastic band from around the paper, unfolded it, and glanced at the front page.

Health Effects of Chernobyl Disaster
a Long-Term Matter

He scanned the first paragraph. In addition to all the radiation sickness and cancers that had cropped up in the last five years, geneticists were now estimating that other maladies might not show up for fifty years or more.

Ramsey refolded the paper and slid the band around it again. It was a little early still to be knocking on someone's door, but there was a lot to do, and he didn't want to miss his chance to catch the weatherman at home.

He rang the bell. A full minute passed before Magruder answered in bare feet, wearing blue jeans and a white T-shirt. He looked different from on TV. Up close, he was smaller and paler—a skinny guy with a weak chin and a concave chest.

"I'm Ramsey Miller," Ramsey said.

"I know," Magruder said.

"I'm hosting a party later today."

"So I've heard."

"That right? Who from?"

"From my mailbox. I got an invitation. Some kind of block party, isn't it?"

Ramsey forced a smile. "That's why I'm here. I'm inviting you to come."

"You inviting everybody?"

"That's the idea of a block party. Everybody's welcome."

"No, I mean are you inviting everyone personally, like this?"

Of all the items on his to-do list, Ramsey had looked forward to this the least. But if he intended to walk the walk—to be magnanimous, or, to use a phrase that Eric and his pal Jesus might prefer, *turn the other cheek*—then he had no choice but to face

Magruder and invite him to his home. "I wanted you to know that you're welcome in my yard."

"Why wouldn't I be?"

Ramsey held Magruder's gaze, letting the weatherman know that his belligerence was noted but wouldn't faze him. "No reason at all." He handed the man his newspaper. "Fact is, I'd be honored if you came to my house. That's all I'm here to say."

Magruder unfolded the paper and glanced down at it.

"Chernobyl back in the news, huh? What a fucking mess."

"So are you gonna come?"

Magruder tossed the paper into his foyer but then had nothing to do with his hands any longer and clasped them together awkwardly. "Ramsey, we've never said a word to each other before now. What's going on here? Why are you so interested in what I do?"

Motherfucker.

In the past, Ramsey might have taken the bait, gotten into some pissing contest. But any pleasure he once took in someone else's insolence, that pure surge of heat, was long gone, and he made himself grin. "Lighten up, Magruder." He reached out and patted the weatherman on the shoulder. "It's just a party. My band's gonna play." And to show his neighbor that he'd made peace with the universe and everyone in it, he added, "I'm sure Allie would love to see you."

The weatherman eyed him a moment, and Ramsey waited to see if Magruder would deny knowing her. But he just looked out past Ramsey at the bright autumn day unfolding—or maybe he was looking in the direction of his lover's house. "What time does your party start?"

"Five," Ramsey said, and then he gave the sky a long look. "You know, you predicted rain for today."

"It still might."

"I don't know—seems to me like it's gonna be a nice one."

Magruder shrugged. "It's the weather. Sometimes I get it wrong."

After that, it was easy. A handful of errands—kegs of beer, ice, the fire pit bricks, a cooler large enough to keep the meat close to the grill—and then he waited at home for others to arrive and set up their own areas of expertise: the sound guy, the petting-zoo woman, the ball-pit guy, everyone jockeying for space in a yard that seemed large until everyone needed parts of it.

Then came the waiting to see who would arrive. And to Ramsey's relief, at a little after five the first neighbors began to show. Ramsey lit the grill, tapped the kegs, and greeted everyone with hearty handshakes and an invitation to eat, drink, and be merry.

At a little before six, beer in hand, Ramsey glanced up at the sky: no signs or celestial winks yet, just late-afternoon sunlight and a deep blue expanse that revealed nothing but the presence of secrets.

"Check," Eric said.

They were on stage. Nothing fancy, but it got them and their gear off the ground and would add some legitimacy to the gig.

Eric said "check" a few more times into the microphone, and then their second-rate soundman was calling up at them, "Hang on a sec!" No juice. Thirty feet in front of the stage, connected to them by a thick snake of cables, Joe Tisdale, assistant manager of Main Street Music, squatted down on his haunches in front of the sound console, turning knobs, pressing buttons, scratching his head as if he had hair there, trying to figure out what was preventing any sound from coming through the main speakers. He was no professional soundman but claimed to understand his gear well enough to set it up and run it. And anyway, Ramsey's three-hundred-dollar tip, up front, promised to make him a quick study.

Behind the drum set, Paul crossed his arms and uncrossed them and then crossed them again. He hunched his shoulders as if the temperature had just plummeted. He'd never been on a stage before.

"You guys have to chill out," Ramsey said. "It's rock and roll."

"I'm chill, man," Paul said.

He wasn't. Paul's tempos were bad enough as it was. Ramsey could hardly imagine the musical crimes that Paul would commit soon if he didn't chill out.

"Get yourself a beer," Ramsey said. That's what Wayne was doing. That's what he wished Eric were doing, too, instead of noodling on his bass guitar, which was plugged into its own amplifier and therefore immune to their soundman's incompetence. Eric was playing the main riff to Led Zeppelin's "Ramble On," which he shouldn't have been doing because it gave the song away. It was unprofessional.

"You're ruining the surprise, man," Ramsey said.

"I'm warming up."

"Well, warm up to something else."

Eric shrugged and started playing some funk riff with lots of slapping and popping, except he didn't have anywhere near the technique for slapping and popping, and it sounded as if a small rodent were caught in the strings.

He was just being nervous, fidgety. And Ramsey had to admit, he was nervous, too. The feeling took him back to his wedding day: suit and tie, spiffy shoes, fear of standing in the wrong place or saying the wrong thing. He was glad that the rent-a-preacher at the Xanadu had kept everything simple. When prompted, Ramsey had said "I will," even though he'd hoped to say "I do" like he'd always seen in movies and on TV.

He looked over now at his wife. She sat with Meg across the yard on a spread-out blanket on the grass amid books and toys. He felt the urge to go to them, send everyone else home, but the urge passed. The reason for this party went beyond proving his own magnanimity and touched on his growing understanding of the connectedness of all people, all living organisms. Each of us was irrelevant in the grander scheme, but our irrelevance was worth celebrating because it was ours and it was temporary.

Still, this wasn't the block party of his imagination. There were fewer people than he'd hoped, only around thirty, not enough to generate the kind of crowd sounds that signaled a party in full swing. For better or worse, though, this was as grand a celebration as Ramsey could summon. It would have to do.

Anyway, his preparations weren't for naught. A half dozen children jumped around the ball pit. A guy and gal, younger than he and Allie, adorned their burgers with sliced tomatoes and onions. The pony was proving to be popular: a small line had formed, mothers and small children, and even the children in line seemed happy enough watching the animal being led around the backyard's perimeter by the Great Dane and, next to the dog, a pretty young woman wearing a yellow sundress.

No one was using the badminton set or the horseshoes, a shame, though a middle-age couple had started rolling the bocce balls. Three older men huddled together along the side fence. Two held loaded-up plates of food, the third a beer. He caught Ramsey's eye and gave him a long-distance toast. Ramsey drank from his own beer, his third of the afternoon, and remembered a long-forgotten truism, how the third beer was always the best. Even today, with plenty of reasons to be anxious, the third beer flowed through him like warm syrup. The challenge was to maintain the sublime quality of the third beer's high when it invariably faded and the only solution was a fourth beer.

He was breaking his one-beer rule, obviously. But after today he'd no longer drink beer or play music or do any other thing. So temperance seemed a little beside the point—even if some part of him suspected that temperance when it no longer mattered was exactly the point. Okay. But facts were facts: In his backyard sat two kegs of beer and, from the looks of his neighbors, not enough drinkers.

A sharp crackling erupted from the speakers—either progress or the opposite of progress. Then an awful, wailing feedback caused everyone in the yard to cover their ears, until a few seconds later the screeching stopped and everyone's hands tentatively lowered again.

"All righty," said the soundman, crouched behind his gear with only his head poking up like a turtle's. "Let's try this again."

The microphones worked now, loud and clear, just as David Magruder came through the fence door and into the backyard. Ramsey was feeling warm now, looser, three cups of syrup loose, plus he had his bandmates with him on stage to back him up. He watched Magruder look around for a familiar face, nod to the bocce couple, glance at his watch, and finally head over to where Allie and Meg sat on the blanket. He crouched down to them.

"Check," said Eric, his voice now crisp through the speakers.

Ramsey stepped up to his own microphone, his mouth already full of the things he wanted to say to Magruder—loud and clear through the P.A. for everyone to hear, things he would have a hard time holding back were he on his fourth beer and not his third.

"Check," he said, watching his family, breathing them in, storing them up—the high five that Meg gave Magruder, the smile that Allie flashed, a smile that Ramsey hadn't seen in ages, a smile that was a promise—a smile that said: *I will.*

"Check one," Ramsey said. "Check two."

18

From her spot on the blanket with her daughter, Allison Miller watched the stage and did her best not to look terrified and torn apart—like a woman whose life wasn't one big sham.

After the band's stupid *check ones* and *check twos*, Ramsey thanked everyone for coming—*from the bottom of my heart,* he actually said, as if this random group of parents, motivated by the simple, desperate desire to occupy their kids on a Sunday afternoon, were his lifelong chums. Then he said an extra thanks to Allie.

"This performance is dedicated to the woman who's always been there for me. My beautiful, faithful wife, Allie. I love you, baby."

Allie matched his smile with her own and replied from her blanket, "I love you, too."

It wasn't so hard—like saying a password when you no longer remembered what it unlocked. So she had little trouble attesting to loving her husband in front of these people. With one notable exception, none of them could be called a friend. Since meeting Ramsey, she had systematically lost touch with everyone: parents, friends, all those people whom the self-help books would call a "support system." No one was at fault. When you're a spouse, you're with your spouse. Add a full-time career, and your energies go there, too. Then you become a mother—a job that devours absolutely everything—and it's little wonder that everyone outside your world's tight nucleus eventually floats away.

Then your husband throws himself an end-of-the-world party.

When she considered it (which she had, constantly, these past three months), she was actually glad that Ramsey had confided in her about his coming apocalypse. There was no dismissing an admission like that, no more pretending everything was okay, that the Millers were just another reasonably happy middle-class family in the neighborhood. No more telling herself that if she only tried a little harder, put on a happier face, cooked healthier meals, straightened the house better, stopped resenting Ramsey for being away when he was merely doing his job, then everything would be hunky-dory. Before his confession, Allie would rationalize her unhappiness in myriad ways. Each day, she'd cycle through them, and what they all had in common was that Allie had herself convinced that she could somehow make it better. If only she were a little more self-reliant, a little more fun, more grateful . . . if only she were a little *more*, then everything would fall into place.

For a long time, years, she'd told herself that if she tried hard enough, she could love her husband the way she once had. *God, I loved him,* she would say to herself aloud. To a twenty-one-year-old college student pissed off with her mother and father, Ramsey was Tom Cruise and Matt Dillon and Bruce Springsteen all rolled into one. He was hot and sharp and smarter than he let on, and he fucking *got* her. He had a scar on his body and a scar inside, too, one that he revealed to her and her alone. His bare apartment with the secondhand furniture, that shiny toaster he was so proud of. She would push down the TOAST button and then she'd go down on Ramsey, try to get him to come before the toast popped up. Her idea. They were creative in that apartment, the two of them. His ideas usually came at night. He'd kiss her neck till it bruised, graze her thigh with his razor stubble and goose bumps would appear. He'd light candles. Nothing was sexier than a tough guy lighting candles, because it meant the toughness didn't reach all the way to the core.

If only we could've stayed that age forever, she would tell herself alone at night, wistful, looking at her face in the mirror. If only she could stay twenty-one, he twenty-eight—the age when they got together, each of them yearning for someone to see their own potential, astonished that they'd found each other. They'd be happy and in love forever, the two of them against the world, *I will I will I will*, till death do they part.

Since June, she'd been rethinking all of this. And by now it seemed little more than romantic drivel, especially since she'd never been honest with Ramsey. For one thing, her parents had offered to pay for her flight to Florida. And when she got there, if she'd patently refused to repent in front of their new congregation, what, really, would they have done? Nothing. Not when push came to shove. Her father and mother were devout and infuriating but not evil the way she'd portrayed them to Ramsey. But now too many years had gone by, and her talk of being estranged from them had come to pass, all so that a hot guy would find her intriguing.

In fact, when she was being the most honest with herself—now, for instance, watching Ramsey and his friends jump around with their instruments on their homemade stage like teenagers trying to impress the neighborhood girls—she wondered if there had ever been that strong a connection between the two of them. Maybe their respective desperations, with their unrelated causes, had simply come into alignment long enough for desperation itself to become its own form of romantic momentum, pushing them forward like a wave through courtship and marriage and pregnancy before receding again.

Which was why Ramsey's confession back in June was as useful as it was alarming. Had he not revealed himself to be fucking delusional, their marriage might have lumbered on forever—Allie looking into the mirror each night and convincing herself that there was no problem, not really, and if there was, then it was her fault. Before his confession, leaving Ramsey had never seriously crossed her mind. As long as no one hit anyone or screamed all the time, there were always more reasons to stay together than to split: because of the child, because you don't want your parents to think they were right all along, because of inertia, because of denial.

Now, at least, denial was out of the picture.

As the band played its first song, a too-fast rendition of "Honkytonk Woman," she clapped Meg's hands with her own, presenting to her neighbors the image of an adoring wife sitting on a blanket under the late-day sun, enjoying her husband's music. She wasn't in denial. She was pretending. But she saw everything now for what it was: The music, shit. This day, shit. Her marriage, shit.

"David," she said. He couldn't hear her over the music. "David!" He turned to face her. He was standing alone, not far from the blanket, wearing his pressed blue jeans and NY Giants T-shirt that was too large on him, holding a beer, looking as uncomfortable as a freshman at a homecoming dance. When he crouched down to hear her, she said, "You didn't have to do this."

"Are you kidding? It's a party," he said. "Anyway, I love these guys." When she raised an eyebrow at him, he grinned. "I own all their albums."

She smiled. "Well, thank you."

He stood up again, making some distance between them. Awkwardly, he tapped his foot and watched the stage. A good man.

She hadn't ever mentioned David around Ramsey, because you do things like that for your spouse. You make their life a little easier. Ramsey was jealous at heart—she'd always known that—and he wouldn't understand why Allie might have a friendship with a man who wasn't her husband. Especially with a man who was on TV. A man who was going places. Anyway, she hadn't set out to deceive Ramsey. For a long time, she and David weren't friends, only neighbors. But Allie was fairly compulsive about walking Meg around the block after dinner, and David was one of those slow-and-steady joggers, and when they passed on the street, they would smile and sometimes say hello—

Can't you do something about all this wind?

I don't make the weather. I only predict it.

—and gradually they began to chat, and over time the chats became longer and more substantive . . . and by the time they were what might possibly be called friends, it was too late to say anything to Ramsey. He would think she'd been hiding something all along.

But over the last half year or so, she and David had become closer. Their relationship was like none she'd ever had before—it was wonderful, frankly—even if from time to time she found herself wondering, *What if?*

The first time they made plans to meet up for breakfast at a diner, rather than waiting for their walking/running schedules to coincide, Allie felt her face become hot as she said, "I want to be clear with you that I have no romantic intentions."

He laughed at her formality, but when he spoke his voice became serious. "First of all, you know I'm also married. Second of all, TV people are horrible. I work in an terrible industry, and I don't make friends at work. I miss having friends. I think we can be friends. I think we already are."

"I think we are, too," Allie said.

"Anyway," he said, "I don't think you're all that good-looking."

He could make this joke because she was obviously beautiful and he was obviously not. Still, he cringed until her own expression let him know that his joke had been received okay.

She hadn't realized how much she'd been needing a friend until she had one. Where before there was nobody, now there was somebody with whom, for instance, she could talk about her job. Such a simple thing. Yet Ramsey seemed to think that her job selling pharmaceuticals consisted of dolling herself up and shaking her ass like a cocktail waitress. Whenever she'd get into the details, he'd smile as if he knew the real story. But David understood how it was to work in a competitive environment, having to look your best and act professional at all times. He was actually interested in the complexities of her career: how she had to be a veritable chameleon in dealing with the various physicians and nurses and office administrators, an expert in persuasion one minute, an expert in fibromyalgia the next.

She found herself, over time, letting her guard down in a way she never could with Ramsey—about how hard and frustrating the daily grind was when working full time and raising a child more-or-less singlehandedly. Or how sometimes the thought of spending her life married to a trucker, living in this quiet neighborhood, nothing ever changing, was enough to make her want to run naked through the street.

And he would tell her that, yes, parenting must be frustrating at times, but look at Meg: a happy kid, thriving, well adjusted. Or when David had no words of wisdom, then that was okay, too. Sometimes the unburdening was enough. And David unburdened himself, too, talking about being picked on as a kid, and how his too-thin body still embarrassed him. His balding head, his weak chin. How his wife, a Wharton MBA and news producer in New York, still intimidated the hell out of him after two years of marriage.

Not that she and David saw each other all the time—sometimes three times in a week, other times not at all for two or three weeks at a stretch. But now, even when the TV news came on, a simple weather report was like a friend speaking directly to her. *Any lingering rain will be moving out to sea overnight. And tomorrow? Well, I think you're in for a treat.*

She was so lost in thought, she didn't notice that the band had stopped playing and that her husband was speaking into the microphone again. The word "weatherman" snapped her back to the yard.

". . . our resident celebrity over there"—he was pointing at David—"said it would rain today. Rain, rain, rain, he said. But look!" He looked up at the sky. "Barely a cloud. Soft air. A perfect day for a block party." He forced an easy laugh. "A weatherman must be the only job in the world where you get paid for being wrong half the time. Ain't that right, Magruder?" Another laugh, but the sound was tinged with meanness. Ramsey's face was red and pinched. "But I'm honored you came. Welcome, welcome— glad you found the time to slum it a little." Ramsey toasted him with his beer. How many was that?

That's when Allie realized: drunk.

In all their years together, she'd never seen him with more than one drink in him.

She looked up at David, who was looking back at her. He shrugged. "I think I'll go now," he said.

"This is . . . wait here, Meg." She deposited her daughter on the blanket beside her and stood up. "This is absurd." People were watching her, watching the two of them. "David, you don't have to—"

"It's fine," he said. "Really. I'm just going to go." He set the half-empty cup of beer on the grass, gave the briefest of waves/ smiles to the small crowd gathered in the yard, walked to the side fence, and let himself out.

On stage, the band watched him leave. From across the yard, Allie saw the change come over Ramsey's face, as if he'd put on a mask, or maybe taken one off. She watched him, and he glared back at her with an expression she'd never seen on him before. There was no word for it other than *hate*, and it took her breath away.

As he held her gaze for two or three interminable seconds, she realized that at some level, she'd convinced herself that her husband was a faker—that all his end-of-the-world talk was some weird play for attention, a midlife crisis, maybe, or a more manly way to be depressed than curling up in bed. Until this moment, she wasn't aware of the extent to which she'd convinced herself these past three months that Ramsey's behavior was ultimately rooted in immaturity, rather than in something far scarier.

He finally broke their gaze and, his face relaxing again to a smile, he turned around to the band. "Okay, fellas," he said, "let's hit it." Paul clicked his sticks four times, and they launched into the Ramones' "I Wanna Be Sedated."

Sedation sounded like a damn good idea right now, and she poured herself a beer. Then she and Meg got food and returned to the blanket. She'd felt bad earlier about not circulating more, playing the hostess or at least the host's wife. But fuck the neighbors, she was thinking now. She owed them nothing. She and Meg would have their own picnic right here, the blanket their own island, their entire world. Allie knew now. Even when she thought she was no longer in denial, she still had been. But not any longer. This was real. This party: real. Her husband, on stage, losing it? Real. She didn't know what she was going to do about it, but she could no longer do nothing.

Meg wouldn't try the hamburger but loved the potato salad and especially the pickle, which made her pucker.

"That's a funny face," Allie said.

"Then laugh, Mommy."

It wasn't easy convincing Meg to leave the party and come inside to get ready for bed, and Allie was in no shape emotionally to deal with a full-on tantrum or to summon the energy that went into preventing one. For a while, there'd been a strategy. Allie had found it in some parenting book several months back, when the tantrums had become unbearable—frightening, really—and Allie and Ramsey were desperate for guidance. The idea was to teach your kid the words for their emotions, get them to say it at the moment they were feeling angry, sad, whatever. A kid who could name her emotions, according to the book, was halfway there.

Meg herself had turned it into a game. One morning at breakfast, she smiled at Allie, who said, "Are you happy?" And Meg said, "Little happy." Then she widened the grin and said, "Big happy!"

They'd practiced that morning over their frozen waffles, mother and father and daughter: They made sad faces—"little sad"—and really, really sad faces—"big sad." Ramsey asked Meg what "little mad" looked like, and Meg scrunched her face into a scowl. Then, unprompted, she whacked the tabletop with her open palm and shouted, delighted, "Big mad!"

They played this game at random times in the day. And sure enough, before long Meg's tantrums started becoming less frequent and less violent. When she'd start to show signs of a meltdown, Allie or Ramsey would ask, "Are you mad right now?" and even if Meg admitted to being "big mad," the naming itself, the awareness, nearly always had the effect of letting some steam out of the pressure cooker.

Ramsey seemed to take special pride in this particular act of parenting. But as with everything else, the solution was only temporary, and Meg's temper these days was as unpredictable as ever. Thankfully, though, after several high fives with strangers, a trip to the stage between songs, where she insisted on precisely three hugs with Daddy, and a fruitless search for the moon, Meg finally looked up at her mother and asked the magic question—"Where are the stories?"—which required the proper answer—"On your bookshelf"—which meant that Meg would now deign to be led up the porch steps toward the back door and into the house.

Allie welcomed the routine activities of Meg's approaching bedtime. It was already past 7:30, so she skipped the bath, but she gave her daughter's face a good scrubbing with a washcloth, helped her brush her teeth, and changed her diaper. A flash of guilt jabbed Allie. She should have started the toilet training by now. There was a girl Meg's age down the street who . . . But this was a project that Allie needed to gear up for, and . . . Okay, she promised herself. Next week.

Pajamas on, stuffed animals properly arranged in the crib (Shouldn't Meg be sleeping in a real bed by now? Another guilt-jab), stand-up fan turned on for white noise. The fan somewhat drowned out the music in the backyard. With any luck, all the excitement would tire Meg out. A last sip of water (from an actual cup—at least Meg no longer relied on sippy cups), and then mother and daughter sat side by side on the wide rocker and read two books. Then one more.

Sure enough, with the last book, Meg was leaning her head against Allie, her eyes heavy. When the book was done, Allie stood up with Meg in her arms and, as always, quietly narrated the day. *We played with puzzles, we watched the beginning of* The Little Mermaid, *we ate special cheese with apples for lunch, we played at the park, we rode around the block in our stroller, we played in the yard, we had a picnic and listened to Daddy's band play music. We had a good day, my beautiful girl. And now it's time for bed.*

Allie shut off the bedroom light. Then one last kiss, and—*sweet dreams, baby*—she gently lowered Meg into the crib. Meg immediately rolled onto her side, a good sign, and didn't make a peep as Allie eased the door shut, keeping the knob turned so that when it latched, there would be no click.

Most nights, Allison would sit in the hallway outside Meg's door and listen to her daughter talk to herself for five or ten minutes before dropping off to sleep. It was one of Allie's favorite times of the day, listening to her daughter's intricate monologue of stories real and imagined, sometimes with bits of songs mixed in.

Tonight, the only sound was the fan's gentle hush, so she walked down the hallway to her own bedroom and lay down fully clothed on the bedspread. Her body instantly relaxed, and she felt her eyelids getting heavy. Then she noticed that everything had become quiet. For a moment she thought that she'd been asleep for hours and that the party had ended. She looked over at the clock—8:20 p.m. She'd slept for only a few minutes. The band must have gone on its set break.

She lay there for another minute, then rose, used the bathroom, splashed water on her face, and went back downstairs and outside to the yard. Fewer than twenty people remained. A few of them were sitting with their cups of beer on the grass around the fire pit, which now blazed, sending smoke across the yard. The smell sent her back to being a young girl, camping with her parents and members of the church. She'd loved the woods, loved cooking hot dogs and s'mores over the fire, but she knew that sooner or later the marshmallows and chocolate would be put away and her parents and their friends would begin their stern talk of Satan's treachery. There would be hours of prayer and public repentance. Yet even that she found herself missing, at this moment.

She collected a few abandoned cups from the grass, a few plates and napkins, and put them into the trash bag by the grill. No one seemed to notice her. Ramsey stood with Eric near the stage, talking and periodically glancing upward. Now that the sun had set, the sky was quickly darkening to purple.

She had to leave him. The hows and whens could be sorted out later, but theirs was not a marriage with a future. When she awoke from her brief sleep, she did so with a clear picture of how this would all play out. Ramsey would wake up tomorrow, shocked that his superconjunction was all a bunch of nonsense. He'd find some excuse to get back on the road sooner rather than later. While he was gone, Allie would get down to logistics: hire a lawyer, find a place where she and Meg could stay if Ramsey refused to move out of the house . . . whatever the details were, she'd tend to them. It would be hard, but her life with Ramsey on the road all the time had only been half a marriage anyway. How could they not grow apart when their home was merely Ramsey's mailing address? When he didn't know the names of any of Allie's coworkers or what Meg had tried eating for the first time or some new thing that she'd said? When he had no clue what it meant to work a full day and then be on all night with a baby, a toddler, day after day after day? When he didn't understand what her promotion to Assistant Director of Sales, Mid-Atlantic Region meant to her because he hadn't bothered to ask? Or that maybe she didn't necessarily want to have sex with him the minute he came home from a week on the road, because she was exhausted from having been a single parent all week and needed some time to reconnect with Ramsey, to remind herself that this was her husband and not just some acquaintance with a key to the front door.

Not that *that* had been an issue lately. Since June, in a relationship in which any emotional or intellectual connection had long since dissolved, the last vestige of their nominal marriage—the occasional late-night screw—had vanished as well. But that wasn't a reason to stay. It was a reason to go.

Superconjunction. Give me a break.

Yes—when he was off on his next cross-country haul, she'd end the sham.

And while she was at it, she'd end a second sham, too.

19

If Allie needed confirmation that her decision was the right one, she didn't have to wait long. Just a few minutes later, the band returned to the stage, and Ramsey walked up to the microphone.

"I want to thank you all again for taking the time to be here on this beautiful and important evening." Another glance up at the sky. "The beautiful part I think is clear enough. But why 'important,' you ask?"

Good lord, she thought. She knew what was coming, because she'd heard the same lecture back in June.

"No, Ramsey." She came forward, right up to the front of the stage, cutting him off. He looked down at her, and she lowered her voice so that only he could hear. "Nobody wants to hear that. They came for a party. For good music. That's what they're here for."

Chastising while also placating—something she did with Meg. But Ramsey wasn't a toddler, and come tomorrow he would have to carry on with his life. Even if Allie were to leave him, he'd still have a daughter and a job. So it was important that he keep it together, or at least keep up the appearance of keeping it together—for his own sake, and also for hers. She could do without the Miller house being a topic of juicy neighborhood gossip.

Ramsey seemed to weigh her words. "Allie, these people have a right—"

"No, they don't." Because he was standing a few feet above her, the closest approximation to an intimate gesture she could manage was to lay a hand on his shoe. "And what does it matter, really? You wanted to throw a party to make everyone happy, right? Then do that." She kept her voice barely above a whisper. "Play your music. Make them happy—don't freak them out."

He looked up at the sky for longer this time, but not for dramatic effect, Allie could tell. Out of concern. She couldn't tell, however, if the concern was because of what he believed was going to happen or because it wasn't happening yet.

He stepped back to the microphone.

"In simple terms," he said, glancing again at the sky, "the real show tonight won't be coming from the stage."

She rushed across the yard, headed for the side gate and the freedom beyond, her eyes blurry with tears.

"Now, we can't do a thing to prevent it," she heard as the gate clanked shut behind her. "But that's okay."

She stood on David Magruder's front stoop, wishing she had a mirror to see how awful she looked. Maybe better not to know. Her eyes burned from crying and from the fire pit smoke.

The music in her backyard had started up again on her walk over, so Ramsey couldn't have spoken for long. Long enough, though. Jesus. She rang the doorbell and waited. An outdoor light came on, and then the door opened, and seeing David in his T-shirt and those starched jeans, an expression of immediate concern on his face, made her well up all over again. She stepped into his house and embraced him, fighting the urge to full-out bawl. She clung to him tightly, breathing in his scent, feeling grateful to him for simply letting this moment linger while mosquitos and moths and humid air rushed into the house. When she released her grip, he took a half step back, looked her over, and said, "Tough day?"

Her response was a half laugh, half sob, and a split-second decision to end the second sham first. She moved forward again, into him, and kissed David on the mouth. Unlike their kiss of twelve weeks earlier, this one was for real, close and lingering, and when they separated again, the look of surprise in David's eyes was comical and lovely.

"I think you'd better come in," he said, looking somewhat dazed.

He shut the front door and turned on a hallway light. Despite how close they'd become, she'd never set foot inside David's house before. His wife wouldn't be home tonight. Allie knew that. She was counting on it. When David and Jessica married, she maintained her Greenwich Village apartment, where she stayed when she worked late at the network. Every Sunday night she slept there to get an early jump on the week.

Allie knew this and many other things about David's life because they were close. They were confidantes. Everything, really, but lovers. She knew, for instance, that he'd been second-guessing his marriage almost since the wedding. *She isn't a warm person*, he once told Allie. *Not like you are.*

He'd been a little drunk the morning he said it, but being drunk didn't make you lie—if anything, it encouraged truth-telling.

They met for breakfast sometimes, when Allie had a gap between dropping Meg at day care and her first appointment with a physician's office. Jessica was usually out of the house at dawn to get to Manhattan, and Allie was pretty sure that David's wife knew as little about these breakfasts as Ramsey did. But that was David's concern, not hers. And anyway, there was nothing to hide.

On that morning, Allie had argued with Ramsey over which level of day care to put Meg into. He wanted her to stay in the younger group, the Ladybugs, but for no good reason, and this tiff—it was hardly more than that—made her seethe. He wasn't home enough to have the right to weigh in. He was dealing in abstractions about *what's best*, while she was dealing with their daughter. Anyway, at one point she said, *Fuck you, Ramsey*—something she'd never said to him before. There were worse offenses between husbands and wives, she knew, but they had both grown up in hostile households, and civility was something they had long ago promised each other. She was immediately sorry, but Ramsey's response—to get up from the table and leave for a week without so much as a good-bye—refueled her fury, which battled her guilt to the point where no way could she meet with that dermatology group in Wall Township at 9 a.m. No way could she put on a tight business suit and act bubbly and informative while overstating benefit A and downplaying side-effect B. Their new, hot product was an "exciting new treatment" for psoriasis called D-Derma. In the trunk of Allie's car were D-Derma mugs, pens, and mouse pads. On none of this swag did it mention that the cream could, in some instances, cause liver damage.

No, the dermatologists could wait. She canceled her appointment, phoned David, and made breakfast plans.

Something in her voice (even she could hear it) made him add, "I'll pick you up." In the past, they always drove separately, despite living in the same neighborhood.

On the ride to the diner, she told him about her argument with

Ramsey. The moment they were seated at the diner, David ordered two Bloody Marys. When their food arrived, Allie backed off ordering a second drink—the first was potent enough, and there were afternoon appointments to be awake for. But David ordered another.

"This breakfast is actually a celebration," he said.

"It is?"

"Indeed." Then he told her his good news: He'd been promoted at the station. Now, in addition to weather, he'd be reporting select news stories on air.

"David!" She smiled. One of his hands was resting on the table. Instinctively, she reached across and took it in hers. "That's amazing."

Though trained as a meteorologist, he'd always wanted to do more than report the weather. He saw himself, someday, somehow, anchoring or producing one of the New York network newscasts.

"I wouldn't call it *amazing*," he said, grinning.

"You know it is," she said, and ordered a second drink for herself.

After breakfast, he drove her home, and she honestly didn't think anything of it when he said, "I'll walk you to the door." They were both a little tipsy. And how they got on to the topic of David's wife, she couldn't remember. But that was when David made his comment about Allie being a warm person. Which made her smile, because at the moment he said it, with the start of summer evident in the growing shrubs and trees and grass all around them, the azaleas blooming pink, the yellow coreopsis, the potted petunias and zinnias framing the front door, she *felt* like a warm person, and then David put his hands on her shoulders as if he were steadying himself.

He's going to kiss me.

She knew it immediately. But when it came, it was a kiss at war with itself, coming only after resting his forehead against her own for what seemed like an eternity. In fact, the head-touching was almost more intimate than the kiss itself. He put his lips to hers and repositioned his arms around her back, and she felt one of his hands dip a little lower, and none of it lasted more than a few seconds.

A drunk kiss—she'd been the giver and receiver of them before and felt no need to pull away. She wasn't even particularly annoyed at David. He'd kissed her because of her warmth. Because they were both tipsy. Because his promotion was making him feel invincible, and because they had become close, these past few months.

He wasn't much to look at. He was married. She was married. This was going nowhere. So she let herself be flattered and amused, and she decided that David's transgression was a forgivable offense. And just as she knew would happen, the moment that the kiss was over, his face got red and he made an "oops" expression, and with a pat on his cheek and a single line—"Not the best idea, probably"—she dispelled the moment's potential severity with a rejection that was its own flirtation. She did it effortlessly, like tossing dust that happened to be magical into the air.

And because David's friendship was important to her, she made sure to call him the next day and invite him to walk around the block, which gave him a chance to apologize, and gave her a chance to assure him that it was no big deal, honestly—the matter was already forgotten—and allowed for the situation to be put to bed before it ever became a situation at all.

But she knew. He desired her.

She followed him now into the living room. His home, like his yard, was tidy and uncluttered, the sofas all leather, the tables all sharp angles—a home with no children. A peaceful home, which she was making less so with her presence. On the coffee table lay two Sunday newspapers, neatly aligned, and several books.

"Do you have anything to drink?" she asked. "I could really use—"

He put up a hand, silencing her, and went over to the bar (in the corner, with a sink, something she'd never seen in a living room other than on TV), poured her a small glass of Scotch, and delivered it. The first sip was like a full-body massage, and she sank a little deeper into the couch.

He poured himself a drink and, to her disappointment, sat across the coffee table from her. But his smile was warm. "So it seems that you, too, have fled the event of the century."

From inside David's house, she could hear traces of music coming from her backyard. In a quiet suburb, sound traveled at night. "I can't do it any longer," she said. "My marriage is over. It's been over for so long." Lying alone at night, she came up with various metaphors, all having to do with movement: ships adrift, birds flying in two directions, or one flying and the other staying still, which, given enough time, still created a chasm. But she spared David the metaphors. "Ramsey and I—we have nothing. Not any longer. Please"—she patted the sofa beside her—"sit here. I need you right here."

David rose, moved around the coffee table, and sat beside Allie. She placed a hand on his knee and looked at him. "You and I are good for each other, aren't we?"

"We are," he said, and hearing this, she released a breath she wasn't even aware of holding. "I'm grateful for what we have."

"You are, huh?" She said it with a sideways glance. She knew what she was doing. The flirtation and the Scotch made her face hot. It'd been a while, this feeling. She missed it. He wasn't much to look at, but he was a good man, and he was intelligent and going places. And their connection wasn't some long-ago remembrance that might not ever have been real. It was happening now, in Allie's adult life, with its experience and its complications, its logistics and uncertainties. An adult connection. It could be love.

She moved her hand up the leg of his pants, just slightly.

"Allie."

She moved her hand up a little more.

He placed his hand on top of hers, stopping its movement. "Allie—listen. This can't happen."

But he was wrong. It could and should. This past year proved it. His kiss proved it. Their easy conversations and their candor and his obvious attraction to her proved it. She wanted to explain all this to him, but when she spoke she was horrified to hear that her voice sounded drunken and pleading and shrill. *"Why not?"*

"It's complicated," he said.

"No, it isn't. Nothing is simpler." Her words came faster. "I'm getting a divorce. And I know you aren't in love with Jessica, not really. So you can get a divorce, too. You don't even have kids. It isn't complicated at all."

"Allie, I can't leave Jess."

She refused to be fazed by his use of his wife's nickname. "You deserve to be happy. So do I. Do you know what a superconjunction is?"

He frowned. "You mean the planetary alignment thing?"

"Ramsey thinks the one tonight is going to end the world."

He raised an eyebrow. "Yeah, that won't happen."

"He's delusional," Allie said. "I can't live with it any longer."

"Then you shouldn't. You deserve better."

"You need to leave Jessica, too."

He sighed. "You don't understand."

"Then explain it to me."

He released her hand, stood up, and went to pour himself another drink, leaving Allie to endure the distant but relentless thumping of drums and bass coming from her backyard. David didn't speak again until he was back on the sofa beside Allie, though not as close as before. "There's a spot opening up on ABC news. New York network. *Jessica's* network. They've narrowed their search to two people, and I'm one of them." He nodded as he spoke. "She's opened this amazing door for me, and I'm *this close.*" He must have seen the tears in Allie's eyes, because his voice raised in pitch, became a little more desperate. "Allie, this is it—the chance you wait your whole career for. God knows I've paid my dues for so long, and now Jessica's opening doors that . . . well, these are doors that open maybe once in a career. It's all I've ever wanted."

She let the words sink in. "Do you love her?"

He looked away. "It's complicated."

"You fucking coward."

"*Allie* . . ."

"Do you love me?" He didn't answer. "Coward."

She ran her hands roughly through her hair, pulling at the roots.

"I'm not a coward, Allie," he said.

"Yes, you fucking are. When you use people to get ahead and ignore the chance to be with your soul mate? What do you think it makes you?"

"We aren't soul mates, Allie. You're only saying that now because . . ." He shook his head. "Look, we're two people who meet for breakfast a few times a month. I keep you company sometimes when you're alone with Meg, because—"

"Because I'm so desperate, is that it?"

"No. But I do think you're lonely."

I don't want to hear this, she thought. He was twisting what the two of them had. Making himself feel better. He was being cold because that was easier than dealing with the truth.

"We're neighbors," he concluded, and the words were like a knife.

"We're a lot more than that, and you know it," she seethed. But were they? She considered, in horror, that maybe she had it all wrong. What she saw as friendship, as intimacy, maybe he saw as nothing more than a charity case. And now she was here, and her daughter was alone back in the house with no adults to hear her if she was crying for something.

Allie thought that nothing David could say could possibly be worse than what he'd already said. "Listen, Al, I'm not going to leave my wife. That just can't happen." He took a breath. "But if you have . . . what's the right way to say this?—*needs* that aren't being met . . ." He looked away. "We'd have to be very discreet."

It took a moment for his words to make sense. When they did, she shot up from the couch and rushed to the door, sobbing.

"Okay, forget I ever said it. I'm sorry. Allie? Come on, Allie. Come back."

But she was already out the door.

The Sandy Oaks section of town was almost completely residential, though one bar, Jackrabbits, was only a couple of blocks away. It probably predated the neighborhood itself. It had a decent jukebox, and when she and Ramsey first moved into the house, they went there sometimes for a beer and a few games of pool. She considered going there now, she could walk it, but her head was already swimmy from the beer and the Scotch, and she didn't want anyone, even in a dark bar, seeing her like this. So with nowhere to go, she went home, walking the too-bright streets of her neighborhood. So many damn light posts. Safety, safety. How about a little darkness at night? Why must a person always be on display?

At least the music had stopped, though she wasn't sure why. When she crested the small hill on her street, her own house became visible. Two police cars were parked out front.

She quickened her pace, and by the time she reached her driveway she was breathing heavier. She went around to the side yard and through the gate in the privacy fence.

A dozen or so guests lingered. The fire pit coughed up smoke, and picked-over food sat out on tables. Near the stage, the band huddled with two police officers. When she approached, Ramsey glanced up at her and, taking little notice, continued talking to the officers. "What does ten p.m. even mean if we can't play till ten p.m.? I mean, you tell me." She could tell she'd walked into a conversation that'd been going on like this awhile.

"Can't allow it," the officer said. "Not with the complaints we've gotten."

"Who's complaining?" Ramsey asked. "Everyone was *here*. It's for them."

"What about two more songs?" Eric asked, looking at his watch. "We'll be done by nine thirty."

"Two songs, nothing," Ramsey said. "I know the ordinance, and it's ten p.m."

"Can't allow it," the larger officer said. "This is a quiet—"

"Yeah, a quiet neighborhood. I get it," Ramsey said. "That doesn't change the goddamn ordinance."

"*Sir* . . ."

"Oh, don't 'sir' me."

"*Ramsey*," Allie said, before either of the officers had a chance to reply, before this escalated further.

"Why, yes, Allie, what is it?" He spoke slowly, his tone mocking and loud, intended for all to hear. "Has my wife returned from one last roll in the hay with the great weatherman to offer us her words of wisdom?"

"*What?*" She glanced around. "How dare you . . . that's not what I . . ."

He leaned in closer and fake-whispered: "So how was his lightning rod?"

She glared at him. "You fucking—"

"Cool it, Ramsey!" Paul moved between the couple, the first responder springing to action. "Whatever's going on, you need to calm it down."

The air was oppressive. Allie's head spun. She thought she might become sick.

"Your friend is right," said the officer. "You need to calm it way down. Because I'll haul you in for drunk and disorderly. I'll be glad to do it. So take a deep breath and count to ten. Because this party's over. And you can either be cool about it, or you can come with us. And I'm this close to making that decision for you. Am I being clear?"

"Officer," Eric began, but his younger brother laid a hand on his shoulder, silencing him.

"Yeah," Ramsey said through gritted teeth. "You're clear."

"That's right—I am." The officer stood almost a head taller than Ramsey and stared him down another few seconds. "I know it's been a while since you've seen the inside of our drunk tank, Mr. Miller. But I promise it's ready and waiting."

Ramsey's face took on a wounded look. "Man, why'd you have to go and say that?"

The officer's expression stayed rock hard. "Why? Because I've been a police officer long enough to know that some things never change."

"That's not true," Ramsey muttered under his breath, like a child protesting to himself on the way to the principal's office.

"We won't have to come back here, will we?" asked the officer.

Ramsey shook his head, still looking deflated. "Nah. It's like you said. The party's over."

Halfway to the gate, the younger, shorter officer turned around. "Since you're so concerned about ordinances, you should know your fire pit's too large and too close to the trees. We could ticket you for that."

They left, shutting the gate behind them.

"I want you all out of here," Allie said, loud enough for everyone in the yard to hear. "Get out of here this second."

"There's all this gear," Paul said apologetically. "It all has to be—"

"Fine. Pack up your gear and leave."

"Allie," said Eric, who stood beside Ramsey, "maybe the three of us should—"

"I really don't want to hear it, Eric. I want you and everyone else gone." She walked toward the house. "You, too, Ramsey," she said without bothering to turn around.

20

September 28, 2006

Such a strange mix of assertiveness and nervousness, Melanie thought while fishing through her purse for change in the Sandpiper's lobby. All of David's fake charm masking his actual charm. And such a large and lonely house. Or maybe she was merely detecting her own loneliness now that the evening's excitement was over.

She perused the vending machine's sad offerings and wondered if she could have a pizza delivered to her room.

She missed Aunt Kendra's garlic cheese toast. She missed Uncle Wayne's Western omelets, which usually ended up being scrambled eggs after the flip had failed. It'd been three days since leaving home. She missed Phillip. How comforting, that lone night spent in his bed. Alone in her hotel room with the too-large bed and the smell of industrial cleaning products, it was easy to feel lost and hopeless.

She was exhausted, and pizza would take too long, so she settled for a bag of corn chips and a Snickers bar.

Back in her room, she opened the chips, which were stale. It felt like a personal insult. She dropped the bag into the trash can, and before allowing herself any time for second-guessing, she picked up the phone in her room and dialed Phillip's cell. She didn't know if he'd pick up, seeing the unfamiliar number, but he did.

"It's me," she said nervously. "Melanie." He might not want to talk to her, she now realized. She'd walked out on him, hadn't she?

"Melanie—where are you? Are you all right?"

"Yes, of course. I'm fine," she said, because now she was.

She told him the truth: She'd returned to Silver Bay to find her father. She refused to live in hiding any longer, and she absolutely refused to raise a child in hiding.

She told some half-truths: She was gathering leads, making progress.

She told an outright lie: No, I don't want you coming here. I want to do this alone.

They talked for thirty minutes—about what? She had no idea. The point was to hear his voice, bridge the distance. Before hanging up, she demanded that he keep her whereabouts a secret, and after a brief debate (*Your aunt and uncle, Melanie. They must be going crazy*) he relented.

She had lied and half-lied to Phillip, but she couldn't lie to herself, and when she hung up the phone (both of them having said *I miss you* but lacking the guts to say any more) she felt lonelier than before. What was she actually accomplishing, being here? David had agreed to help find her father, but what did that mean, exactly? How would he go about it? And how assertively, given how little he wanted to be reminded of the past?

But these were tomorrow's problems. She still hadn't eaten. She should have ordered the damn pizza. She ate the Snickers bar, brushed her teeth, and went to sleep.

She'd forgotten to draw the hotel room's heavy shades before going to bed and woke up at 6:30 a.m. to soft natural light and the awareness that her anxieties had eased overnight. Phillip had been relieved, even happy, to hear from her. And David knowing her secret, even that felt okay. Pretty good, actually. Melanie felt lighter. Someone else just knowing she was alive made her feel more alive. Not only someone else—a man with connections. A man who could get things done, if he had a mind to.

Anyway, there was no choice now but to trust him.

Her plan for the morning was to visit Arthur, see about Eric's statement that he knew why her father had thrown the party. Maybe look into why Eric no longer worked outdoors as a lineman—whether it was his health or his proselytizing or something else. Also, she wanted to learn what Arthur knew about the Monmouth Truck Lot. That was where her father had sold his truck just two days before the murder. She found that fact especially chilling. No one had been able to make a connection between the truck sale on Friday and the murder on Sunday, but surely it meant that he knew he wouldn't be returning to work. She wanted to see if anyone from the truck lot was still around. If they remembered her father. After a good night's sleep, she was feeling more optimistic. She was feeling more sleuth-y. More Nancy Drew-y.

But before any of that, before Arthur or the truck lot, she'd have an actual breakfast. She wanted bacon and eggs. (Why all the bacon suddenly? she wondered. Pregnancy was weird.) And if they had them, grits. A tall glass of orange juice. And she was willing to brave the smell of coffee to get it.

And that's what was on her mind—bacon, eggs—when she walked out of her room a few minutes after 7 a.m. and pulled the door closed. It had just clicked shut when she felt herself being grabbed from behind and mashed against the door, hard enough for her head to thud loudly and for the wind to get knocked out of her.

"*Not a fucking word,*" came a man's voice behind her, low and breathy.

Her wrists were suddenly clamped in his hands, and his body— it was definitely a he—pressed against her from behind, crushing her against the door, against the sharp doorknob. She couldn't move and didn't dare to, couldn't see anything besides the white door in front of her.

She tried to catch her breath but could only gasp.

"Drop all this." So softly, his voice, lips grazing her ear. "Go away and never come back—or you're so fucking dead." He pressed her even harder into the door—forcing a grunt from her. "Now count to fifty before turning around. And *don't* rush it."

She felt her wrists being released. The weight against her body removed. She wanted to drop down to the carpet but willed her legs to keep supporting her. She heard the man running toward the end of the building, toward the exit.

Pain in her stomach, from the doorknob.

Bruised, for sure. She wasn't counting to fifty. She was thinking: *My baby.* And as the man neared the exit, she turned her head. She had to. It might be the only time she ever saw her father.

There wasn't much to see. Long gray coat with the collar turned up and a baseball cap. From behind, he could have been any tall man at all who kept his black shoes freshly polished.

In the hotel bathroom's mirror, shirt lifted, she was horrified by the wide purple bruise from the doorknob. She touched several spots on her side and abdomen, wincing.

Then she was in her car, driving fast.

Then she was in the elevator, then hurrying to Arthur Good-ale's room, a nurse she didn't recognize trailing her, saying, "You can't just . . . excuse me, you have to let me . . ."

His door was open, and she barged in. The room was empty.

When she spun around, the nurse was right behind her.

"Where is he?" Melanie heard the panic in her own voice. She already knew the answer. "Where's Arthur?"

"Miss, are you all right?" The nurse went to take Melanie's arm, but Melanie yanked it away.

"Tell me where he is!" But she knew.

"Let's just calm down a minute. Catch your breath, and tell me who you are."

"I'm Arthur's friend," Melanie said, "and I want to know where the hell he is."

The nurse sighed and pursed her narrow lips, as if Melanie's directness were the problem.

"Downstairs," the nurse said.

"No," Melanie said. "I'm not going anywhere until—"

"Mr. Goodale is downstairs. He didn't need to be in critical care any longer. You can check with the front desk for his room number. But your head is contused—what happened?"

"You mean he's okay?"

"Mr. Goodale? Yeah, he's okay."

And then Melanie ignored some words the nurse had to say about her needing medical attention. She hurried back to the elevator, which couldn't arrive fast enough.

More concern in the face of the woman working the hospital front desk, but she gave Melanie Arthur's room and instructions for finding it. Melanie rushed down the hallway, nearly slipping once. The door to Arthur's door was partly open. She rushed in

275

and, seeing him there, felt such relief that she wanted to throw her arms around him.

"Alice!" He looked up from a magazine and smiled as if they were old friends reunited. Then: "My God, what happened?"

Seeing his face and hearing the worry in his voice made her start to cry. The room was larger than the one upstairs, or maybe it only looked that way because there was less equipment filling it up. Outside the window was blue sky, rather than a brick wall, but the sunlight streaming into the room felt oppressive and blinding. She spotted the chair near his bed and slumped into it.

"Alice," he said, "your head . . ."

Why was everyone carrying on about her head? In the hotel mirror, she'd looked nowhere but her stomach. Why in the world would she look anywhere but her stomach? She touched her forehead now and winced at the sting and by the size of the lump. The room started to spin around her. She gripped the chair's arms for support.

"Alice?"

Her heart raced. The room spun harder: the window, the walls, the ceiling, the bed. She sought and found Arthur's eyes, and stayed locked on them.

"Alice, please—"

The churning in her gut frightened her—it wasn't morning sickness, she felt sure of it—and she remained focused on Arthur's blue eyes as she blurted out, "David Magruder's driver attacked me, and my baby might be dead, and my boyfriend doesn't know about any of it, and I miss my aunt and uncle, and I want to go home, and I'm Meg Miller."

She had never enjoyed food as much as she was enjoying the sandwich that had been delivered on a green plastic tray, placed on a table that rolled right up to her hospital bed. Chicken salad, fresh romaine lettuce, slices of summer tomato, not too much mayonnaise, soft potato bread.

"You need to eat better," the doctor told Melanie when all the scans and tests were done, and she had heard a sampling of Melanie's meals over the past week. The doctor, a middle-aged woman wearing green scrubs, no-nonsense glasses, and a stethoscope around her neck like a scarf, sat on a stool beside Melanie's raised hospital bed while Melanie felt vaguely annoyed at the doctor for pestering her with questions when there was this amazing sandwich to be eaten. "I'm talking about actual meals, not junk from vending machines. The way you've been eating, you easily could have ended up here even if you hadn't been attacked."

"Yes, ma'am," Melanie said, and took another bite.

"Before you're discharged, we'll give you some pamphlets about nutrition for pregnant women."

"But the baby is okay?"

"Yes—but you have to take care of yourself. Just because you're young doesn't mean you're invincible." She kept looking at Melanie for a moment, letting the words settle. "Speaking of which, a police officer will be coming by your room shortly."

She imagined her statement: *I got shoved up against a door by a man who might have been David Magruder's driver.* It would lead to nothing and only make her presence in this town more public. The police have never been helpful, she reminded herself.

"I don't want to talk to any police."

The doctor sighed. "Why not take a few minutes to think about it."

"I don't need a few minutes."

The doctor shook her head. "This is very frustrating—it happens too often."

"Ma'am?"

"A young woman gets beaten up and feels she has to defend her attacker. Especially when it's a boyfriend or a—"

"It wasn't my boyfriend."

"Are you sure about that?"

"My boyfriend is a gentleman."

The doctor nodded. "You can refuse to make a statement to the officer if you must. But then I'd like a social worker to speak with you before you're discharged."

"Why?"

"She can give you important information about available resources: counseling, prenatal guidance . . ." She lowered her voice. "Safe houses."

"What's that?"

"Places where women can go and live for a while to get away from . . . whoever it is they fear." The doctor eyed Melanie as if they both understood. "The woman can feel safe, knowing she can't be found. It's all very tightly run—even I don't know where the safe houses are located." The doctor smiled as if Melanie would find the idea of disappearing relieving, even wonderful.

Why is the answer always to hide the girl? she wondered.

"On second thought," Melanie said, "I'll talk to the cop."

Don't be afraid, said the doctor before leaving her—but she was afraid, and insisted she meet with the police officer in Arthur's room.

Poor Arthur. *I'm Meg Miller*, she had said to him, exploding his fifteen-year certainty. And all he could do was buzz for a nurse to rush Melanie away to the ER. Then two hours of tests and scans to see if the bruise to her stomach might have caused any damage to the fetus (unlikely) and to see if she had a concussion (she did, though it was minor). They took her blood to check for some other stuff the nurse had rattled off—and all the while, Arthur waited, because he had no choice.

So now she would speak with an officer, but Arthur would get to hear it all.

The officer was a stocky man with thick arms and almost no neck. She imagined he could be tough if he had to. They formed a triangle—she and Officer Bauer on chairs, and Arthur in his bed, raised almost to a sitting position. Sometime in the past two hours, he had put on a blue golf shirt and combed his white hair.

"I want to be sure I have this right," said the officer, after Melanie had laid out the basic and amazing facts of her whereabouts these past fifteen years. "You're telling me that you're Meg Miller, daughter of Ramsey and Allison."

The officer had made her nervous at first, but that word the doctor had used—*safe house*—had made her stomach burn. She was through with hiding. She wanted the opposite of hiding.

"Yes, sir."

"And that since 1991 you've been living in West Virginia with your aunt and uncle."

"Yes."

"As part of the witness protection program."

"Yes, sir."

"My, my," Arthur murmured, and the officer shot him a look. "Sorry."

"And now you've come back to Silver Bay to try and find your father," the officer said.

"That's right."

Officer Bauer jotted a few notes into his notebook. "Why?"

"I'm pregnant," she said, "and I don't want my baby to grow up afraid."

The officer glanced down at Melanie's body, then back at her face. "Tell me what happened this morning."

So she told him about leaving the hotel room, getting slammed up against the door, the breathy voice in her ear, the man's fast exit.

"Do you know who it was?" he asked.

"At first I assumed it was my father. But I'm pretty sure it was David Magruder's driver."

"Wait—David Magruder?"

"Yes."

"How do you two know each other?"

"We only met twice. I thought he might know something about my mother's murder."

He frowned. "And what makes you think David Magruder's driver is the one who attacked you?"

"He told me not to look at him, but when he was leaving the hotel I looked anyway. His black shoes were shiny. I think he wore the same pair as the man who drove me to David's house yesterday."

"Do you know the man's name?"

"No."

"Do you remember the kind of car he drove?"

"A black Lincoln Town Car. But I think David owns it."

"How are you so sure about the make of the car?"

"I notice cars. My uncle works on them for a living. And I like them."

"You don't by any chance remember the plate number?"

"No. But—I think his name was Bob. I think David called him that. No—*Bill*. That's what he called him."

"Did you get a last name?"

"No."

"Did you see the Town Car today at any point?"

"No—only yesterday."

"And are the shoes the only reason you think it was this man?"

"He was tall."

"How tall?"

"Like maybe six two?"

"And besides his shiny black shoes, what else was he wearing?"

She told him about the coat, the cap. How she couldn't see his face because of the upturned collar.

"And why do you think this man would have assaulted you?"

"I think David made him."

"Why would—" He shook his head. "Let's back up a little. You said you went to Mr. Magruder's house yesterday."

"Yes."

"Why?"

"Well, I tried to interview him on Wednesday—"

"Interview him? What for?"

"I thought he might"—she looked over at Arthur—"I thought he might tell me something useful about the day my mother died. Something that might help me find my father."

"Why did you think that David Magruder would know anything about the death of Allison Miller?"

She didn't want to get Arthur in trouble. "I just thought he might."

"It was my suggestion," Arthur said from the bed. "I'd told her about Magruder's multiple interviews with the police following the murders. Sorry—the murder."

Officer Bauer watched him a moment. "So did anything come of the interview?"

"No. He acted really rude and then made me leave."

"Why did he make you leave?"

"He didn't want me asking about his past."

"So if he was so rude to you on Wednesday, why would you get into the car with his driver on Thursday?"

Good question. She tried to remember. Her head throbbed, and she knew her thinking wasn't as clear as it should be.

"David summoned me to his house," she said.

"Summoned? Why would he do that?"

It was either his tone or her deeply ingrained distrust of the police, but she thought she heard doubt in his voice and didn't like it. He wasn't so young. He'd probably forgotten how his uniform made a person feel guilty and afraid. She tried to answer accurately. "I think he felt bad about how he treated me the day before."

"So he wasn't rude, when you went to his home?"

"No. He was nice. He even promised to help me find my father."

"You mean he knew who you really were?"

"He sort of figured it out. But then he must have changed his mind about helping me and made his driver . . . do this." She remembered what David had said about his driver the night before. *He isn't on twenty-four-hour call, Melanie.*

"The man who attacked you—he also told you to leave town?"

"Yes, sir."

"And it's your belief that this message, this threat, came from David Magruder?"

"Yes, I do."

"Why would he want you to leave town?"

"He told me he had no alibi for the time of my mother's murder."

"David Magruder told you that." The officer raised an eyebrow. "Officer?"

Officer Bauer turned to face Arthur.

"Please remember," Arthur said, "that you're speaking to a traumatized young woman who's doing her best to answer your questions."

The officer kept his gaze on Arthur a beat too long, but when he spoke again to Melanie his voice was gentler. "Ms. Denison, why do you think Mr. Magruder would tell you that?"

"I think he was so surprised to see me alive that he started spilling his guts. Also, I'm pretty sure he was drunk."

"Why do you think that?"

"He drank most of a bottle of champagne while I was there. And some Scotch, I think."

"So are you suggesting that he had you assaulted because he regretted telling you about lacking an alibi for the night of your mother's murder?"

"I guess so, sir. And he told me he knew my mother really well, which is something he'd lied to the police about."

The officer made a face like a bug had just flown into his eye. "That's—surprising, frankly. We'll have to go back to the file on that. Are you sure you have it right? That Mr. Magruder said he had lied to the police about his relationship with Allison Miller?"

"Yes, sir. I'm positive."

The officer clicked the stop button on his tape recorder. "I know you've been through a lot already, but I'll need you to speak with a detective."

"*Why?*" Her voice sounded panicky even to herself. A cop, now detectives . . . she wasn't supposed to be in this town—ever. Those were the terms. Why was she doing this to herself? To her aunt and uncle? "I don't want to talk to more people."

"Ms. Miller—"

"Denison, please," she said.

"Ms. Denison, someone obviously doesn't want you in this town, digging up the past. He's pissed off enough to hurt you, maybe worse, and whether it's David Magruder or someone else, a detective can move fast on this. I can't. My part ends here. I file the report, and the detective takes it from there. So please—will you talk to her?"

And maybe because of the "her" at the end of his sentence, and maybe because Arthur didn't indicate that she shouldn't, she reluctantly said okay, she'd speak with the detective.

The officer was barely out the door before Arthur Goodale, finally privy to it all, began silently to weep.

21

In a town with little crime, the law moves fast when it must. A nurse led Melanie downstairs for a few more tests, a little more poking and prodding, and then into a small room outfitted with a hospital bed and a chair, a TV mounted from the ceiling, and two paintings of birds hanging crookedly on one wall. A woman standing in the room identified herself as Detective Isaacson. She waited while the nurse helped Melanie into the bed and then left the room, shutting the door behind her.

The detective was tiny and fit, like she could probably run a marathon today and another one tomorrow. Except for her hands, which gave away her age, she could have been in college. Her skin looked flawless, but that made it hard to read her face.

"Ms. Denison," she said after shutting the door, "you told Officer Bauer that you're actually Meg Miller. Is that right?"

"Yes, ma'am," Melanie said.

The detective watched her a moment. "It's an astounding statement. That case—that was my rookie year. I remember it really well. So if you're telling the truth, if Meg Miller is alive . . ."

"She is. I am."

"But you go by Melanie?"

"Yes, ma'am."

The detective nodded. "So where've you been, Melanie?"

She repeated for the detective where she'd been all these years, and how she was nearly eighteen now and pregnant, and how she'd driven north because she was tired of being hidden and afraid. She repeated the events of that morning, but it all felt like so much wasted time, going over the same story again.

When she'd finished, the detective spent another minute writing notes into a small spiral notebook. "May I sit down?" she asked.

"Yes, ma'am."

The detective pulled the chair close and sat. "Tell me a little more about being in the witness protection program. How did that come about?"

Her instincts still said *Don't talk. Not a word.* But she had already said more words than she could ever take back.

"The night my mother was killed, everyone was afraid that my father would kill me, too, so the witness protection people hid me away. And my Aunt Kendra and Uncle Wayne agreed to go with me and raise me."

"And they took you to West Virginia?"

"Yes, ma'am."

"What town?"

Melanie hesitated. Then: "Fredonia."

"Why there?"

"It's where they're from. Not that town, exactly. But nearby, in West Virginia."

The detective wrote down a few notes. "And that's where you still live?"

"Yes, ma'am."

"And who did you say arranged all this?"

"The U.S. Marshals. And a local judge."

"Do you know the name of the judge?"

"No, ma'am."

"But it was a judge from here in Silver Bay?"

"I think so. But it was definitely a judge and the U.S. Marshals. They did it in the middle of the night and no one else knew about it."

Detective Isaacson was looking over Melanie's shoulder, deep in thought. She put the pen down. "I have a problem with this."

And suddenly the small, plain room, the two chairs—it all felt like a trap. "What do you mean?"

"Were you ever involved in criminal activity?"

"No, of course not."

"Were your aunt or uncle."

"No, ma'am."

"Because that's how witness protection works. It's for people who have been involved in criminal activity. So they'll be safe to testify in court."

"Then they made an exception for me."

The detective shook her head. "And they never relocate people to somewhere they once lived. It's always somewhere brand-new." She tilted her head. "You're sure it was witness protection and not some other program, maybe?"

"Yes. I'm sure."

"Not the FBI? Some other organization?"

Melanie was getting angry with the detective for doubting her. "Yes—I'm sure." Why was *she* suddenly under fire? What had she done wrong?

"Tell me about your aunt and uncle. How are they related to you?"

"Ma'am?"

Every question felt like a trap. The detective's small stature—even that felt like a ploy to gain Melanie's trust.

"You said 'aunt and uncle.' Which side of the family are they on?"

"Uncle Wayne was friends with my father. Aunt Kendra . . . I'm not sure. They've been married a long time."

"So they aren't blood relatives?"

"No, ma'am."

The detective gave her a long, hard look. "I'm told you need to stay here a while, make sure you're stable enough to go home. In the meantime, I need to get in touch with the U.S. Marshals. Tell me something—are there any gaps in your past, or in your aunt and uncle's, that they don't talk about?"

Rule: We do not discuss the past.

Melanie didn't answer.

"All right," said Detective Isaacson. "We'll get to the bottom of it. Tell you what. I'm going to see about having a conversation with David Magruder's driver. But I'll be in touch soon." She smiled. "Did Officer Bauer give you his card?"

"Yes."

"Well, don't use it. You need anything, you call me." She handed Melanie a card with her name and phone number.

As soon as the detective was out the door, a nurse came into the room wheeling in a blood pressure machine. After checking Melanie's blood pressure, she said, "We'll keep you here a couple more hours for observation. You can sleep unless you're feeling nauseous. Are you feeling nauseous?"

"A little." But whether it was from the assault, the interviews, or the baby, she couldn't say.

"Then you should try to stay awake," the nurse said.

Beside her, on a small table, was a telephone. "Does this phone make long-distance calls?" Melanie asked.

"You have to dial nine first." The nurse turned on the TV and left.

Melanie called Phillip's cell. He would be at school now, probably lunchtime.

"I'm sorry," she said when he answered on the second ring. "I thought I could do this alone, but I can't." She told him she was in the hospital, and why. She told him she needed him there with her. "Do you think you can come here soon?"

"I can come there now," he said.

"I'm so, so sorry," she said.

"For what?"

For being such a child, she thought. "I miss you," she said.

"I love you, too, Melanie."

She didn't think she wanted to watch TV, but she was wrong. Leonardo DiCaprio and Kate Winslet were on the screen looking beautiful in the sunlight, and she allowed herself a much-needed break from everything other than that amazing, unsinkable ship.

Three hours later, Detective Isaacson was back and escorting Melanie from the hospital. Melanie had been advised not to drive for the rest of the day, so the detective would be taking her back to her hotel. In the hospital lobby, Melanie said, "If you don't mind, I'd like to stop in there."

The flower shop just off the hospital's main entrance was cool and fragrant—peaceful. She ordered a vase of fresh flowers to be delivered to Arthur's room. She signed the note, "Your friend, Melanie."

"Are you hungry?" the detective asked once she'd left the shop.

Melanie nodded. "Extremely."

"Me, too. Let's eat."

While she drove, Detective Isaacson talked about herself, how she was the youngest of six children—runt of the litter, she called herself. How she was the first in her family to go into law enforcement. Her stories sounded prepackaged—like she'd used this exact same small talk to try to bond with previous victims—but Melanie felt grateful not to be asked any more questions.

They went to the diner by Melanie's hotel—she was beginning to feel like a regular—and Melanie followed her doctor's advice and ordered an actual meal: cheeseburger (no bacon—the thought of bacon suddenly nauseated her), French fries, side salad. While they waited for their food, Detective Isaacson's small talk began to worry Melanie. There was no way the detective would spend this kind of time with her unless she had something meaningful to say. "I got the address of David Magruder's driver and hope to speak with him later this afternoon," she said. But that didn't warrant this kind of personal service, did it? "Mr. Magruder is in New York today, working, but I'll pay him a visit at his home later, depending on what his driver has to say."

"Okay," Melanie said, sensing more.

But the detective waited until the food had come and Melanie's burger was nearly finished before saying, "I need to tell you something."

And Melanie knew she wouldn't be eating any more of her lunch.

"My chief," said the detective. "He spoke with the U.S. Marshal in Newark, and *he* made some more calls." It was 3:30 in the afternoon, and the diner was nearly empty. Still, she kept her voice quiet and steady, watching Melanie closely. "After you and I spoke, I got the strong sense that your aunt and uncle have withheld the details of their protection from you. Maybe for your sake, or maybe for theirs. Because like I said, the witness protection program is just that—it's for *witnesses* who have committed a crime but are exonerated in exchange for testifying. The program doesn't just . . . well, the point is, I was wrong, but I was on the right track." She lowered her voice still further. "We think your aunt and uncle have been lying to you, Melanie. The U.S. Marshals Service—they have no knowledge of you, or of your aunt and uncle."

"I'm not lying to you."

She nodded. "I know. You told me what you believed to be true, what your aunt and uncle told you was true. But what I'm saying is, we think they made it all up." And in case there was any misunderstanding: "I don't understand why yet, but I think that on the night of September 22, 1991, you were kidnapped."

22

September 22, 1991

All the party guests were gone.

Ramsey was helping the soundman wrap cables. The repetitive motion was good for him. He snuck peeks at Allie, who sat on the back porch steps. Anger coursed through her like blood, he could tell. He would wait to speak with her until they had both calmed a little. When she stood up and slipped back inside the house, he didn't follow her. Soon—but not now.

The guys said little to one another as they packed their gear. A few words about which songs had gone best, which chords and lyrics they'd screwed up. Before long, the soundman's cables were looped, his microphone stands folded, and his sound console back in its crate. The guys helped him load the speakers. They all shook hands. No one would look Ramsey in the eye.

Why does everything always have to end badly? Ramsey wondered. Those cops had treated him as if he were still some young punk. All his years of good behavior had amounted to nothing.

Some things don't change, the officer had said.

"We're headed to Jackrabbits for a drink," Eric said to him. "You should come along."

Come along to watch Eric sip club soda while everyone avoided Ramsey's gaze some more and the jukebox blasted the Cure and Depeche Mode and every other whiny pop crap?

"No," Ramsey said. "I'm gonna stay here."

Paul frowned. "I think you should do what your wife says and clear out for a while."

"She didn't mean it."

"I think she did," Wayne said.

So now fucking *Wayne* was weighing in? "Well, it's my house, too," Ramsey replied, but his words sounded petulant even to himself, so he tried again. "I just want to talk to her," he said to the three of them. "And then if she really wants me gone, I'll go." The fire pit crackled as a piece of wood shifted and settled. "Heck, I'll even meet up with you guys and endure that horrible fucking jukebox."

Allie must have been watching from inside the darkened living room, because the moment that the other men had left and Ramsey was alone, the door to the back porch slid open and she stepped outside. She looked smaller, shrunken, as if she'd been sick and lost weight. She sat on the top porch step and wrapped her arms around her knees. Ramsey glanced up at the sky and went over to her. He sat down on the lowest step. Looked up at the sky again. As a boy he had known the constellations, but even then the light-filled Jersey sky never let you see many stars. Over the years, he'd forgotten nearly every mythical man and beast who lorded over the earth. He remembered the Big Dipper. *Ursa*

Major. Tonight it was half hidden behind the trees. Cassiopeia was overhead. The other stars were just nameless points on a map. But when the earth was no more, those stars would remain in the sky, unfazed.

Not a word from Allie, who just sat there, breathing deeply.

"Some party," he said, and attempted a weak smile.

She sat up. "What the hell's the matter with you, huh? I mean, you can't keep this up."

"Keep what up?" he said, and she screamed in frustration, high and piercing and long.

"Hey!" he said.

"What—are you worried about the neighbors? You're a little late for that." She shook her head. "And forget about *me*—you have a daughter. If you cared about her even a little, you wouldn't be antagonizing the police, practically begging them to arrest you."

"I *do* care—"

"No. All you care about is your superconjunction, which you have to know isn't real and is nothing and is a fucking joke."

He looked up at the sky. "Al—"

"No, you're going to listen to me now. You're on the road too much. You get these ideas in your head, and there's no one around to tell you you're wrong. Well, I'm telling you now. You're wrong. You're so fucking wrong about everything." She was crying. "I want a divorce."

"How could you sleep with that man?"

"Oh, my God—didn't you just hear me? I'm leaving you."

The words he heard, of course, but they didn't square with the facts. They were married, he and Allie. "You're my wife."

"No—I don't love you anymore." She might as well be taking an axe to him. "Maybe I once did, but I don't now."

He looked at his wife. "You have no right, saying that. Not when you're having the affair."

"*I'm not having an affair!* For God's sake, get it through your head—you're so . . . David and I are . . . nothing. We're nothing. We're less than nothing."

He heard Eric's words in his head as clearly as the day he'd said them.

They were still kissing when I drove past.
A real kiss?
You don't want the answer to that.

"I don't believe you," Ramsey said. He couldn't unsee the image of their kiss, or the images he created in the kiss's after-math, images perfected after three months of seeing them. "You're lying to me."

She stared at him. "Well, then to hell with you." She opened the sliding door, rushed inside, and slammed the door home.

Ramsey sat there a minute on the step. "You're a liar, Allie," he said to the used-up yard with all its trash.

He wanted to go inside. His anger and sense of injustice were such that he wanted to continue this, escalate it. He wanted to lose control. He wanted to break through.

That ain't you anymore, he told himself under his breath, but the words rang false. He said them again anyway, and then a third time, but he wasn't able to convince himself.

I could hurt you, he said.

And these words shimmered with truth.

He went out the side gate to his car and pressed the automatic door opener for the garage. In the garage, he got the empty five-gallon gas can and returned to his car. He started the engine and backed out of the driveway. He'd had more to drink tonight than he had in many years, but not nearly enough. He could still see straight. Could still drive. Could still think—which was why he had to escape from here, fast, before he let his thinking go too far and he acted on those thoughts. He passed Jackrabbits and headed east. Stopped at the Sunoco station that was attached to a mart and liquor store. Filled the gas can, put it back into the trunk, then went into the mart and bought a fifth of Jack Daniel's. Returned to the car and drove toward the bay.

This town, this town. Thirty-four years, and what? One store became another, a diner went out of business and a month later opened under a new name. Same flooding every few years when a nor'easter came through—houses damaged, houses repaired. Same yellow school buses. Same schools. Same firehouse. Everything a little faded, a little dingier after three decades—but not fundamentally any different.

Some things don't change.

The road took him over marshes toward the bay, which at night was dark in the middle but shimmering along the edges from the streetlights and porch lights. He passed two marinas, then followed the road as it curved into a quieter area of larger, spread-out homes with views across the bay. This was a part of town he never visited when he was younger, where the real money was. It was dark enough here to miss the entrance to the boatyard's narrow lot, but Ramsey made the turn—a little too fast—and crunched along the gravel. Some of the boats were dry-docked for the season, but many were still in their slips. Beyond the hedges and trees stood houses to either side.

Ramsey only ever took his motorboat into the bay three or four times a summer. But when he'd bought the boat from the yard's manager five years earlier, the man had quoted Ramsey a next-to-nothing docking fee (the *Sea Nymph* was only twelve feet long), and he hadn't upped the fee since.

The boat was the epitome of simple—aluminum, flat bottom—and ideal for puttering around the bay on the occasional summer morning to fish for fluke. For an hour or two he'd float with the tide and jig his rod and feel the morning air on his skin. Whatever fish he caught he'd take home and cook. If he caught nothing, the outing was no worse.

Tonight the tide was high, the ramp down to the floating dock not steep at all, which made carrying the gas can easier. The bay was absolutely still tonight, but Ramsey knew he wasn't sober, so he stepped carefully into the boat, cradling the gas can and then, once in the boat, setting it down gently at his feet. He opened the cap on the outboard and poured some gas in until it seemed like enough. Capped the engine, capped the gas can. The eight-horsepower engine started on the first pull—a rarity, as if it'd been waiting for him. He untied the line from the clamps at port and starboard, dropped them onto the dock, and idled into the bay. His boat was so small it left no wake, so once he was twenty or thirty yards away from the dock he turned the throttle, and the outboard motor's pitch raised (an almost comical whine compared to the truck's 560-horsepower engine), and the boat moved slowly but steadily away from the lights and into the mouth of the bay.

This was not a boat made for the ocean. But tonight it cut through the calm water like a blade, and with all these houses and condos in sight even from the middle of the bay, he couldn't find the solitude he sought. So he motored out toward the tip of Coral Hook, and even there, a place where the ocean meeting bay usually created strong currents, his small boat glided on. There was an outgoing tide, helping him along, and in no time at all (thirty minutes? forty-five?) he was around the tip of the hook, with the Verrazano Bridge and New York skyline to his north, the ocean to the east and south. He headed southeast, where ahead of him was more water, more water, then glorious nothing, where he would have a front-row seat to the end of all things. In the storage compartment underneath the seat was a flashlight, he was pretty sure, but the whole point was to escape the light. If another boat slammed into him, then so be it. The odds were slim.

He opened the bottle of whiskey and drank. The air was still warm and humid, unusually so, with barely any sea breeze at all. For a while he kept checking the sky, but eventually he stopped doing that and simply piloted his boat. Kept heading southeast, steady and true, and tried to free his mind of everything but the small engine's hum. The shoreline was always in sight but receding. The New York City skyline faded to a brownish-orange smear over the northernmost part of the sky.

For maybe another hour he puttered along. By then, Ramsey's eyes were fully adjusted to the dark, and when he took another drink and leaned back in his seat, he almost got knocked out by what he saw.

Stars everywhere. So many more than he ever could have imagined as a boy sitting high in a tree. Even when he used to imagine mountaintops, he never imagined this: so many stars, they ruined constellations. So bright they were screaming. He couldn't have been more than five or six miles offshore. Unbelievable, that his whole life he was so close to this view and never knew it. He cut the engine. The only sounds were his own breathing and water lapping the side of the boat. Finally a breeze kicked up, warm and comforting.

He slid down to the floor of the boat and lay back, resting his head against the plank seat. He drank some more, capped the bottle, and cradled it under an arm. Looked up at the unobstructed heavens.

Other than the moment when he saw Allie stepping out of the hospital elevator for the first time, this night sky was the most beautiful sight of his life.

"My marriage is ending," he said aloud.

The wide, white-gray splotch running across the sky. That was the Milky Way. He was seeing the entire galaxy from his small boat.

"My marriage is ending, but the world is not ending."

To his ear, the sentence was a paradox. Black was white. High was low. So he tried again. "My marriage, and not the world, is ending."

The boat softly drifted. There was more fuel in the gas can. He could douse the boat with the spare fuel and set it alight. One last grand gesture. But at the moment, grand gestures had lost their appeal. He thought about having sold his truck for a song, and let out a sad laugh. Only one of many problems for tomorrow.

There would be a tomorrow. He had believed in the supercon-junction, just as he had believed that he was nothing without Allie, who had saved his life. But maybe everything he believed, he believed a little too hard.

Some things don't change.

But I did, Ramsey thought.

He knew he was right, and that the cop back at the house was jaded and wrong. Yet he understood how the cop could have made that mistake, understood how fucking tempting it was to cling to easy beliefs and call them truths.

He never should have thrown the party. Never should have stormed out on Allie back in June. Never should have spent so many days and nights away from her and from Meg, who wasn't even remotely a baby anymore, and who seemed, tragically, to be replaced by someone new every time he went away and came home again. God damn, he wished he knew his kid better. His list of never-should-haves was long, and his head, full of whiskey, wasn't up to reviewing all of it. But he knew that even if Allie were to leave him, even if she didn't love him anymore, there would be a tomorrow.

I will never, ever hurt you, Allie.

He added this vow to the one he made seven years earlier. They were vows he'd keep even if they divorced. He would honor her and obey her and protect her and love her till death do they part.

He imagined his wife kissing David Magruder. His hand on her ass.

"But I'm big mad at you, Allie!" he shouted into the darkness, and choked out a pitiful laugh. "I'm big, big mad!"

To the west, over land, a flash of heat lightning punctuated his words.

He lay back and drank some more. Looked up at the canopy of stars and silently mourned the end of this part of his life as the boat drifted and rocked and drifted.

23

September 29, 2006

Detective Isaacson received a call on her cell. She didn't say what it was about. "I'll be right there," she said into the phone, and then offered to drive Melanie the couple of blocks back to her hotel.

Melanie didn't want to spend a minute longer in the company of Detective Isaacson. "No, I'd rather walk," she said.

After the detective left, Melanie remained in the booth and picked absently at her French fries. She had been attacked almost ten hours ago. Since then she'd been scanned, poked and prodded, stuck with needles, interrogated. Her injuries had been photographed for evidence. And now this detective was asking her to accept that her whole life was a lie.

Melanie found herself resenting Detective Isaacson—no, hating her—for laying all this on her. She had known the detective for less than a day. She had known Wayne and Kendra for fifteen years. It was too much, too fast. She sat in the booth a while longer and then walked numbly from the diner to her hotel. She felt tired but didn't want to be alone in her hotel room, and her legs carried her toward the beach. It wasn't a terribly long walk—she had driven it in only a few minutes—but she got winded easily these days, so she took it slowly.

We do not discuss the past.

She'd convinced herself that the reason was so simple, the pain and memory of loss, the sadness that threatened, always, to bubble over. We don't discuss the past because that's our way of dealing with the past. It's how we cope with the present.

But what about Melanie's lack of curiosity over so many years? What accounted for her easy acceptance of her aunt and uncle's explanations? She had wondered about her mother, but never about herself. What if, at some deep level, she knew that if she ever probed too much into the puzzle of exactly how she and Wayne and Kendra had ended up hidden together in that remote West Virginia town, the pieces might not fit together so well? What if she knew she lacked the stomach for the truth? Might she not have been complicit, all these years, in her own ignorance— contributing right along with her aunt and uncle to the myth-making? Ramsey Miller, bogeyman, always about to get her. A terrible way to live—but far better than the possibility that you were being raised by your kidnappers.

But what about the letters from the U.S. Marshal's office? Forged, she supposed. But if the detective was right about her aunt and uncle, then of course there was the most basic question of all: Why had they done it?

Her walk was on its way to becoming a substantial hike when she reached the ocean block. She hadn't noticed the first time she'd been here that the houses were in states of decay. Hadn't paid much attention to the trash on the boardwalk and the beach. Still, seeing the ocean made her wish she'd been seeing it all her life. She wished she'd grown up here. How dare her aunt and uncle convince her that Silver Bay was someplace to fear? She sat on a bench and watched the waves, putting off the return walk as long as possible. When the wind suddenly shifted, cooling the air, she told herself to get a move on.

The walk home left her sweaty and short of breath. She finally crossed the parking lot and was close to the hotel when she heard: "We sacrificed *everything* to keep you safe, and this is how you repay us?"

She turned toward the voice and scrambled to make sense of what she saw: her uncle leaning against the cement ledge near the front entrance.

"How did you—"

"You know you shouldn't be here," he said, and lowered his voice. "My god, Melanie, the one place on this earth you can't be." He squinted in the sunlight. "What happened to your head?"

"I got beat up. It doesn't matter. How'd you find me?" But she knew.

"Of course it matters. You look—"

"Tell me how."

"The young man you've been seeing had the decency to—"

"He had no right." Melanie was already backing away. "And I have nothing to say to you." She rushed away from him, into the hotel lobby.

He followed her inside before the automatic doors slid closed. Followed her right out the back sliding doors to the swimming area, which was deserted and consisted of several dirty chaise lounges around a small pool filled with murky water. Melanie sat on one of the chairs and put her head in her hands. Wayne sat on the lounge chair nearest her.

"Who hurt you?" he asked.

"I don't know," she said. "I just got mugged, is all."

"Figures—this place is a fucking nightmare." His voice was harsh but whisper-quiet. "We were scared to death. I'm very angry with you."

"I told you in my note not to worry."

"Well, we did worry. We worried a lot. We thought *he'd* gotten to you."

"Oh, stop it already!" She glared at him.

"Stop what?"

That damn detective. Melanie didn't want to believe her. "Stop lying to me."

"Honey, I'm not—"

"You kidnapped me, Uncle Wayne."

"What? No. Keep it down. What are you talking about?"

"The witness protection program—I know you made it up."

"That's not true. Why would you think—"

"The police checked it all out. They spoke with the U.S. Marshals. It's just not true."

"The police? You went to the—" He shook his head. "Honey, the police are idiots. You know that. They obviously made a mistake. It's been a long time and the files get . . ." He took a breath. "You shouldn't be talking to law enforcement. You shouldn't be here. It's too risky. We're not even allowed here. It's like I always said . . ." She remained quiet, watching his mouth form words that were increasingly losing any meaning. "It's like I said—we have to . . ."

With every fumbling word from her uncle's mouth, Melanie became more certain. He had taken her and lied to her about it, inventing the sort of lies that made her afraid, lies that kept her within the tight perimeter of their trailer. "Why?" she said. "Why would you do that?"

He watched the pool for a few seconds. Large leaves floated in the water. "Growing up without parents, Melanie . . . the Hope Home for Children—you can't imagine. The beatings, the daily humiliations . . . it didn't matter how well you behaved." He was looking at the leaves in the pool but seeing into his past. "The noise that never stopped—the crying and screaming and moaning. Older kids hurting the younger ones at night with rocks, with handmade knives. The smell of sickness. The stink of it. Vomit and piss and shit." He looked at Melanie now. "At night I'd lie in bed and pray to die in my sleep. And then one day the place closed, and the people that took me—I knew it had to be better. But it wasn't. She locked us in closets with no lights. She put out her cigarettes on my arms. And *him*. He was worse." She had never seen tears in his eyes before. "No way was I going to let you live that way."

"This is crazy," she said. "I don't want to hear this."

"You're the one who came here for answers, Melanie. So now you're going to get them." He took a breath. "The night your mother died, me and Eric and Paul—we went to a bar near the house, but we were worried about her. None of us grew up protected like you did. We had all seen the sort of things that people did to people. And Ramsey—your father—he was acting crazy that day. The look in his eyes—we'd all seen it before in other men. So when we left the bar, I drove back to check on them."

"Eric Pace told me you were drunk and drove straight home."

"You talked to Eric?" His eyes widened. "Well, sure, Mel—that's what I told him. I had to keep the truth from *everyone*, even him. To keep you safe. Damn, Melanie, you know I don't like talking about this . . ." He took a breath. "So we all left the bar together and got in our cars, but then I went back into the bar and had one more drink. I was afraid, you know? I didn't want to go, didn't want to face Ramsey. But I felt like I had to. So I stayed and drank one more beer, and then I got in my car and went over there. It was so much worse than I ever thought . . ." He swallowed. "I saw her in the fire, Mel. And I knew that Ramsey would go to prison, probably forever, and you'd become a ward of the state. I'll admit, it all happened fast. I was practically a kid myself and didn't have time to think any of it through. It was instinct, you know?" He looked distraught, remembering back. "I knew I had to keep you. I'd take care of you. Raise you in a good home. Give you what I never had. And when I found out that Ramsey was on the loose, it only proved I'd made the right decision to protect you. I knew that's why I was put on this earth."

"And Aunt Kendra—she knew all this?"

"She knew we could all be a family," Wayne said. "She knew we could have a peaceful home where we look out for one another, which is all she's ever wanted."

"That's not what I'm asking."

"Then no—she doesn't know everything. She thinks everything is legal. I did her that favor."

Of course: the letters. They were never meant for Melanie.

Every meal together as a family. Every night, going to bed and believing you knew the raw data of your own existence.

"My whole life, you've lied to me," Melanie said. "Everything's a lie."

"No—that's not true." His eyes were begging her. "Your aunt loves you. And so do I. We're a family."

"Don't say that."

"You know we are."

She wanted to get up and plunge into the water, cleanse herself of everything she was hearing. But even the pool was dirty.

Her skull throbbed. "I need to take some Tylenol." She got up and walked toward her room. She let Wayne follow her. In the room, she took two pills and lay on the covers of her bed while Wayne paced the small carpeted area.

"Forget what I said about working in the garage," he said. "You can pick up where you left off at the college. Take any course you want." More pacing. "If you want to be on that newspaper . . . well, I guess that's okay, too."

The school newspaper? Did he not understand anything she was saying?

When he tore open the complimentary packet of coffee grounds, Melanie's stomach seized. "Please don't make coffee." He frowned at her. "My headache is making everything smell bad." He shrugged and dropped the opened packet into the trash.

"You're almost eighteen," he said, taking a seat at the table by the window. "I know we have to start treating you like an adult. I mean, I get that," he said. "But we can make it work. Everything's on the table."

Nothing was simple. Wayne had lied to her for years, but not about sacrificing everything for her safety. And she felt safer around him, still—even now, protected in a way that was familiar and seductive. She could almost chalk this whole trip up to some failed Nancy Drew sleuthing, the stunt of an impulsive teenager, and head home to Fredonia. But she also understood exactly why she felt so tempted: As long as she was with her aunt and uncle, she'd never have to be responsible for herself or anybody else.

"No," she said. "I'm never going back there."

"Honey—"

"I can't live this way anymore. I won't. I'm going to find my father."

"You won't find him," he said. "Not if the police and F.B.I. can't."

"Well, I'm trying, anyway. You might as well go home. Phillip's on his way—he'll take care of me."

"Him? I find that hard to believe," Wayne said, and they both watched through the window as a police cruiser pulled into the lot.

"That's probably for me," she said. "Because of this." She touched her forehead.

"Melanie, this is a bad place."

"Okay. But I should go out there. I doubt either one of us of wants an officer coming to the room."

When she got out of bed, he reached out and touched her arm. "You never should have come to Silver Bay," he said.

She wondered if she would ever feel his touch again. "Go home, Uncle Wayne." And in case he needed to hear it: "Don't worry—I'm not going to turn you in."

It was Officer Bauer, who'd come to take Melanie to the station.

"Why?" she asked.

"Detective Isaacson wants you there."

"Why?"

"I suppose she wants to talk to you."

"Can I make a call first?" Melanie asked.

"Can it wait until we get there?"

"Not really."

She had to borrow the officer's cell phone. Phillip picked right up.

"I'm in Trenton!" he announced as brightly as if he had just entered Emerald City.

She was furious at Phillip for telling Wayne where she'd gone, but there was nothing she could say with the officer standing right there. All she could tell him was to meet her at the Silver Bay police station, not the hotel. She handed the phone back to the officer, who pocketed it and opened the back door for Melanie. "Watch your head," he said.

For nearly an hour, Melanie sat on the hard wooden bench in the station's cramped lobby, her headache not helped any by the fluorescent lights buzzing overhead. Only a few people came and went, taking no notice of her. At some point she heard rain on the roof. Finally, Detective Isaacson hurried into the room from somewhere within the station's depths. "Sorry to keep you waiting," she said, "but if we didn't pick you up at the hotel, there'd be no other way to reach you." She shook Melanie's hand. "You might think about getting a cell phone. Thanks for coming. Coffee?"

"No."

"All right. Let's go somewhere we can talk."

Melanie's body tensed. Every time they talked, Melanie learned something she didn't want to know. The alternative was to choose not-knowing over knowing, and that option was starting to have its appeal. Nonetheless, she followed the detective down a narrow corridor with an uneven floor. On the wood-paneled walls hung framed photographs of police academy graduating classes—trim officers with proud postures and eyes that seemed to follow her accusingly.

The detective led her to a small room with a desk and a few mismatched chairs. She shut the door and motioned for Melanie to sit. The detective sat beside her and opened the file folder. "I had your statements from this morning transcribed off the tape. I'd like you to read them and let me know if you have any corrections. Then sign them."

Melanie glanced at the papers; it was odd seeing her own words in print.

"You were right, by the way, about the man who assaulted you. Bill Suddoth has had trouble with the law before. Misdemeanors: a couple of drunk and disorderlies. He was very cooperative with me when I went to his apartment this afternoon and told him I was investigating an assault committed by a man of exactly his size, wearing the same shoes he was currently wearing. And you were also right about his shoes. I kind of wish he'd polish mine.

Anyway, he immediately blamed Magruder, said his boss wanted you dead and threatened to fire him unless he took care of it."

Melanie looked up from the papers she was holding. Despite her bruises and aches, she had trouble believing this. "David wanted to kill me?"

"That's what Bill Suddoth claims. He also claims he decided all on his own to convince you to leave town—you know, talk to you instead of doing something a lot worse. He claims he never meant to hurt you." Detective Isaacson held Melanie's gaze. "I think it's complete bullshit."

"Which part?"

"All of it. Magruder, with all his money and connections, would never rely on a man like Bill Suddoth to commit a murder for him. He'd pay top dollar for a professional hit man. So here's what I think. I think that driving Magruder's fancy cars is the best job Bill Suddoth has ever had, and he'd do a lot to keep it. Not murder, but a lot. Now, if Magruder was surprised to see you alive yesterday—I think you even used the word 'happy'— then I doubt very much he'd want you dead today. But after sobering up last night he must have become very anxious about something, and decided it was best if you left town and never came back."

"Anxious about what?"

"Well, we don't know for sure. But I'm going to try like hell to find out when I interview him. That's why I want to make sure your statement is totally accurate."

"When are you going to interview him?"

"Now."

"You mean he's *here*?"

"Yes, but he doesn't know he's a person of interest. We told him we've arrested Bill Suddoth for an assault, made it sound like an open-and-shut case. The moment he feels threatened, he's going to demand his lawyer. So I figure we have one good shot at catching him off guard."

Melanie glanced at her statement. All the facts were there, but something didn't add up. "You're doing all this—messing with a famous person—because his driver shoved me?"

The detective sighed. "David Magruder committed a serious crime today, orchestrating your assault, and he did it stupidly, getting Bill Suddoth involved. Why do you think he would take a risk like that?"

"I guess he panicked," Melanie said.

"Exactly. And why did he panic? Because of you." Then the detective did the most surprising thing. She took Melanie's hand. "Honey, I think it's possible—actually, more than possible—that David Magruder is responsible for your mother's death."

"My father killed my mother," Melanie said automatically, pulling her hand away. It was true because it had to be true. It was the one true thing left.

"Melanie, I went back and read the file from 1991. You were right. Magruder had no alibi for the time of the murder. And he lied to us on tape about having a relationship with the victim."

"So what?"

"So in my opinion, the police went far too easy on him back in ninety-one. The lead investigator at the time, Esposito—our careers overlapped by a few years. He was a sweet man who threw great holiday parties. But as a detective?" She shook her head. "All I'm saying is, the fact that he interviewed Magruder more than once is actually pretty astonishing. But he never would have pursued Magruder as a suspect. Not without hard evidence screaming at him. Not when Magruder was already a local celebrity who denied knowing the victim, and especially not with an obvious suspect in your father, whom a dozen people had witnessed acting angry and unbalanced—unhinged—on the night of the murder."

"He's the obvious suspect because he did it," Melanie said. Needing this to be true, she repeated it like a mantra. "My father killed my mother."

"Honey—"

"Please don't call me that." After a full day of being bossed around by doctors and cops, everyone believing they knew best, it felt good, even pleasurable, to stand up to the detective. "I'm not a child. And no matter what David might have done, or why he did it, I know that my father killed my mother. I know it." She stood up.

"Melanie, I agree that your father's disappearance is a mystery. But not everyone who vanishes is a murderer. And I think it's possible that David Magruder killed your mother and fled, and sometime later that night or early the next morning Wayne Denison came upon the crime scene, panicked, and took you away where he thought you'd be safe."

"That's not right."

"It makes sense, your uncle jumping to the same conclusion as everybody else. He thought he was protecting you from your father. I mean, it was a reasonable thought to have. But holding you for all those years." She exhaled. "I can't begin to imagine."

Melanie had been working hard this afternoon to hate her uncle—*he isn't even your uncle!* she kept reminding herself—but she couldn't make herself do it. "He wasn't 'holding me,' detective. He was raising me. He did what he thought he had to."

"But he *didn't* have to. He never should have taken the matter into his own hands." The detective softened her voice. "We'll be coordinating with authorities in West Virginia to pick up Mr. and Mrs. Denison. I hope you understand we have no choice."

Melanie's legs were weak. She sat back down. In her head, she was trying out a new sentence: *David Magruder killed my mother.*

"Given all of this," Detective Isaacson said, "I'd like you to remain at the station while I interview Mr. Magruder. Like I said, I'll have one shot at this before he sees what we're up to and he starts spreading his money around on lawyers, at which point he'll become a far more difficult suspect. So in case he says something I need to verify, or that contradicts something you've said, I need to be able to ask you right away. He'll never know you're here."

My father did not kill my mother.

"We don't have nearly enough evidence for a murder charge yet," Isaacson was saying. "I'm hoping this interview will let me start building a case."

Evidence. Building a case. Meaningless words. My father killed my mother. My father did not kill my mother. Her vision became swirly. She wasn't listening to the detective. She was thinking about every mysterious sound she'd ever heard over the years, all the times she felt as if she were being watched or followed. None of it was real. The tens of thousands of hours fearing that the smallest mistake would mean her death. Being terrified that her father was always just beyond the hedges, always around the next corner.

"Melanie?"

Her attention returned to the police station, to this detective who in a single day had shaken every belief she'd ever had. It wasn't the detective's fault, yet Melanie knew she would never forgive her.

"I want to hear all of it," Melanie said.

"Hear what—the interview? No, I'm afraid I can't do that."

But Melanie was done enduring everyone else's explanations and theories and justifications. She was done learning about everything after the fact. If Magruder was guilty, she wanted to hear it firsthand. If he wasn't, she wanted to hear that, too, from his own lips.

"Sure, you can," Melanie said. "Through one of those one-way mirrors or whatever."

"We don't have any of those."

"Then a microphone. Or a video camera. You've got to have some way of—"

"We use a webcam—but Melanie, I'm afraid the answer is no. We have a way of doing things to preserve the integrity of the evidence."

"Is that so?" Melanie was infuriated by her own powerlessness, and she felt the childish urge to hit something. "Then I'm leaving."

"Melanie . . ."

"I take back my whole story. I won't sign this." She shut the file folder and slammed it on the table. "My father killed my mother. You can't change that. And my boyfriend will be coming soon, and as soon as he gets here I want to go."

"We simply can't do what you're asking," the detective said, struggling not very successfully to control her own frustration. "I wish I could."

"You wish you could?"

"Of course I do."

Melanie looked right into the detective's eyes and said, "I fell down the stairs. I hit my head at the bottom of it. And my stomach."

"Melanie, don't do this."

"It was stupid of me," she continued, "but that's what happened. I fell down the stairs and that's the last thing I'll ever say about it, and I refuse to sign this statement. I don't know why I ever said those lies. Probably because of the concussion. But you can charge me with stuff if you want—for wasting your time or telling lies or whatever. But I want to make a new statement that I fell down the stairs. I'll swear to it and sign it."

In the ensuing silence, the detective looked at the closed file folder, and Melanie could see her weighing the risks.

"You can watch one of the computer terminals." The detective sounded displeased, but she was saying the right words. "Officer Bauer will sit with you. But I'm telling you now, you can't utter one word about what you hear to anyone. You could jeopardize your own case. You could jeopardize your mother's. Am I being clear?"

Melanie was so stunned, having gotten what she'd demanded, that all she could do was nod.

24

If David Magruder had been taken to a formal interview room—
which was as inviting as a jail cell and meant to arouse a person's
anxiety—he would have known instantly that he was under suspicion, and that Detective Isaacson's request that he "help them
deal quietly with a delicate situation regarding his employee" was
at best a half-truth. This was why, Officer Bauer explained to Melanie, the detective had arranged to speak with Magruder in the
station's "swing room"—typically the site of brief officer meetings and coffee breaks.

There were two vending machines, soda and snacks, humming
against one wall, and four chairs surrounding a circular table on
which sat a small vase of plastic flowers. There was also a small webcam, its lens one-sixteenth of an inch in diameter and nearly invisible,
taped to the top of the door frame, recording everything in the room.
A cork board was attached to the wall, and pinned to it were newspaper comic strips of police officers. Magruder, wearing a suit with

the tie loosened, sat beside a uniformed officer, chatting. At one point, the officer laid a hand on David's arm and they both smiled about something. Either the setup was having the intended effect or Magruder faked being relaxed amazingly well, especially for a man who'd just worked a long day after drinking too much the night before.

"This won't work," Melanie said to Officer Bauer, suddenly certain of it. Bauer sat in a creaky chair in front of the monitor. Melanie sat beside him. Watching David on the monitor was like watching him on TV, where he was in total control, always. "David does interviews for a living," she said. "He's a master at this."

Bauer raised the volume on the monitor. "So is the detective," he said.

Together they watched Detective Isaacson enter the swing room and shake Magruder's hand. She was intentionally short of breath and acting distracted, sitting down and flipping through a file folder.

"Thanks again for coming in, Mr. Magruder," she said.

"You can call me David."

She smiled. "I will, David." She turned to the other officer. "We're all good here. Thanks for keeping David company."

He smiled, and shook Magruder's hand. "A real pleasure, sir. I like your show."

Magruder nodded.

When the officer left, he swung the door casually behind him so that it closed most, but not all, of the way. Nobody was being held here against his will. It was all strictly voluntary, a matter of mutual respect.

Detective Isaacson sat on the chair beside Magruder. "Like I said in the car, you have no idea how helpful this is, wrapping everything up quickly. I'm afraid that Bill Suddoth—" She frowned. "Do you want coffee? Soda? Anything? I should've asked."

"Nothing, please." He crossed his legs.

"All right." Another friendly smile. "But if you change your mind. So Bill Suddoth assaulted a young woman this morning. I told you that in the car. Forgive me. Anyway, she got pretty banged up—bruises, contusions, concussion."

"I'm very sorry to hear that."

"Thank you. Well, fortunately, she—Alice Adams is her name—she was able to identify Mr. Suddoth shortly after the attack. When I spoke with her this morning, she could only figure that Mr. Suddoth must have become obsessed with her yesterday while driving her around. She said she'd found him a little odd at the time. I think she used the word creepy. And this morning—well, like I said, he beat her up. We don't believe it was an attempted sexual assault, but we're looking into the possibility."

"That's terrible."

"Have you ever known Mr. Suddoth to be unstable?"

"I wouldn't hire someone who I thought—"

"No, of course not. I'm not suggesting you could have known he might do something like this. But he has a prior record."

"He does?"

"No felonies, but he's no boy scout, either. I'm sure you didn't know that when you hired him."

"No. Absolutely not."

"In the future, you can always check with us." Detective Isaacson got out her wallet and removed a business card. Slid it across the table. "Check with me—I'll personally run the search." She smiled. "One of the benefits of living in a small town."

"Thank you." Magruder glanced at the card and put it in his shirt pocket.

"Oh, I'm happy to. We're living in really litigious times, and you want to be extremely careful."

Magruder nodded. "You know, I hadn't thought of it until just now, but Bill has been acting somewhat erratic. In fact—"

"Just so I have my notes correct, Bill Suddoth drove Ms. Adams to your house last evening around what time?"

David Magruder looked momentarily bothered. He wasn't used to being cut off. Then: "I'd say around six o'clock."

She jotted it down in her notes. "Okay, and Ms. Adams said that she'd come over to interview you for a school assignment. That you'd talked for a while, and that you dropped her off later that night at her hotel. So it was during the initial drive to your house that Mr. Suddoth must have become obsessed with her. Would you say that's the only time he'd have been with her? I'm just trying to get the chronology right."

"That sounds right," he said, and leaned forward. "Just out of curiousity—what did he say about all this? Or is that confidential?"

The detective let out a laugh. "Bill Suddoth knows he could be facing jail time, so I don't take anything he says very seriously." She coughed into a closed fist. "Pardon me. Can you think of any other reason why he might have wanted to hurt her, other than some kind of sexual obsession? Could she have said something to him to make him angry?"

"I really have no idea. But I doubt it. He's just a driver."

Detective Isaacson nodded. "I honestly think this is a pretty straightforward case of a young, attractive girl being in the wrong place at the wrong time." She smiled knowingly.

"What is it?" Magruder asked.

"Nothing, it's just—well, you asked what Mr. Suddoth said. Would you believe he said *you* put him up to it?"

"What?" Magruder uncrossed his legs and sat up straight. "Why the hell would he—"

"Because Bill Suddoth is basically a thug in nice shoes, and he did a bad thing, and now he's trying to blame the bigger fish

322

because he has a prior record and is worried about jail time." She shrugged. "Like I said, I don't take him too seriously. Anyway, you shouldn't let it worry you—it's what guys like him always say. Would you believe he said you ordered him to kill her, and that he decided to warn her instead to leave town?"

"My god!"

"I know—welcome to the police force. We deal with guys like him all the time. 'The president made me do it.' 'The pope made me do it.'"

Magruder risked a tentative smile. "'Jesus and Buddha conspired . . .'"

"Exactly!" Detective Isaacson returned the smile. "Tell me something. What *did* you and Ms. Adams talk about at your home?"

A nearly imperceptible tightening of his face. "Well, like you said. She interviewed me. About my job and my life."

"I never said she interviewed you."

He tilted his head. "Yeah, you did."

"I said she went to your house in order to interview you. According to her, you quickly identified her as Meg Miller, presumed to be dead. Needless to say, that trumped a school interview, am I right?"

Through the computer monitor, Melanie watched Magruder's body stiffen. For maybe ten seconds—an eternity—nothing got said. Magruder glanced around, as if for the first time realizing where he was.

"I'm not following," he said.

"It's okay," the detective said. "I know she asked you to keep her identity a secret. That's why I'm letting you know that *I* know. She told us, too. It's remarkable that she's been alive all these years, isn't it?"

He nodded. "Yes. It absolutely is."

"Amazing coincidence, though, wouldn't you say?" said the detective.

Melanie could tell that David didn't want to take the bait. But he couldn't not. "What coincidence?"

"Well, think about it: A woman is murdered, and her daughter disappears. Fifteen years later, the daughter returns to town and within a couple of days gets violently assaulted herself. I mean, that family has some really bad luck."

"I hadn't thought about it like that," Magruder said.

"Because there's no way those two things could be connected, is there?"

Magruder stared at the detective for a few seconds. Then he smiled broadly, his excellent white teeth gleaming. "Detective Isaacson, what is this?"

"What is what?"

He shook his head. "You're interrogating me, aren't you? *This*"—he motioned toward the vending machines, the partly opened door—"this is all show."

"Absolutely not. I'm completely confident that Mr. Suddoth is at fault here. That's why he's the one who's under arrest. But he insisted it came from you—"

"Which it didn't—"

"Which it didn't. Obviously. But Melanie—that's what Meg likes being called these days, though I guess you know that—anyway, Melanie says that when she was assaulted this morning, Suddoth told her to, quote, 'leave town.'"

"Okay . . ."

"Well, that's a strange thing for him to come up with on his own, isn't it? I mean, why would someone obsessed with a girl order her to leave town?"

Magruder sighed deeply. "I haven't a clue. He's obviously a nut. Obviously, I never should have hired him."

The detective waved the statement away. "Oh, we all make mistakes. Live and learn, right? But okay. I'm sure that when this is all said and done, Bill Suddoth will be charged and either plead guilty or be found guilty. But what—and this is just a hypothetical —but what if you did want Melanie to leave town? Why would that be?"

"Detective, I *don't* want—"

"I know—that's why I said it's a hypothetical. Just let me finish. Why would he want Melanie Denison to leave town? I asked myself. And then I remembered—actually, I didn't remember. I checked the file—but okay. I checked the file and saw that you didn't have an alibi for the time of Allison Miller's murder—"

"Stop." David Magruder had his palm out like he was directing traffic. "We're done here."

"Please, Mr. Magruder," said the detective. "I'm not accusing you of anything. I'm trying to help you."

"Now detective, you know that's a load of—"

"I really am. Hear me out. I'm seeing this through the eyes of a thousand newspapers and TV stations—if they were to learn a couple of simple facts. Now, I don't want to give Bill Suddoth's story credence, because I don't want you to become fodder for . . . well, for journalists. You know how they can be." When Magruder said nothing, she continued. "It just seems a little weird to me that Bill Suddoth's story—that he told her to leave town—actually matches what the victim herself told us." She paused again. "Is it possible that maybe you asked Bill Suddoth to *talk* to Ms. Denison? That maybe you told him specifically *not* to hurt her, but just to make this helpful suggestion that she was better off somewhere other than Silver Bay?"

"What you're saying is all very ridiculous, detective. Still, I'll have my lawyer present before this goes any further."

"Mr. Magruder, of course you can have your lawyer here. Of course you know that anything you say can be used against you in a court of law. But you aren't under arrest or even a suspect. What

I'm doing is just trying to wrap this up fast, get you out of here before anyone in the media knows you're here. See, if I knew that you
had directed your driver to politely ask Ms. Denison to return to
wherever it was she came from, for whatever reason you might
have had—that's not my business—and if *he*—all on his own—took
things too far and became physical, then I should have all I need. It
would explain why he talked to her about her leaving town. And her
injuries certainly prove that he took things too far. We could get this
wrapped up and no one will ever have to know you were here. Because it's certainly no crime for you simply to ask your employee to
speak with Ms. Denison. So is that maybe what happened?" When
he didn't answer, she added, "Because otherwise, I'm going to have
to look into the ridiculous claim that you ordered Ms. Denison to be
killed, and I really don't want to start investigating the wild claims of
unreliable thugs. Especially when it threatens to put a man like yourself in the spotlight—in the news, online—where it will undoubtedly damage your career. That isn't right."

"And I don't want to start investigating a corrupt and incompetent small-town police department. But I will if I have to, and I
have more resources than you do."

"You don't have any evidence of that, Mr. Magruder."

"And neither do you," he said.

"I have the sworn testimony of the victim and the accused,"
she said calmly, "plus the business card of every journalist who's
ever shaken my hand over the past seventeen years. We both
know this is a juicy news story, Mr. Magruder. It's your call."

Magruder stared down the detective for maybe five seconds—
five seconds of fast calculations and cost-benefits and, quite possibly, an awakening to the notion that his invincibility was neither
inevitable nor everlasting—and then he broke eye contact and his
posture sagged. He looked down at the table until he had collected himself somewhat. "I made him promise to treat her

nicely—I *specifically* told him not to hurt her or even threaten her. Just to speak to her nicely. I'd have talked to her myself, but I had to get to New York early this morning."

"See? That's what I figured." The detective sounded almost cheerful as she wrote a few fast notes in her pad. "So help me to understand just one more thing, will you?"

"I'll try," Magruder said. He still sounded extremely wary. He was in uncharted waters, and he knew it, and he knew that the detective knew it.

"You were happy to learn that Ms. Denison—who you once knew as Meg Miller—was alive, is that fair to say?"

"Of course. I was very glad to learn that her father had spared her life."

"That's what I'd assume. So then why did you want her out of town so quickly?"

"Why did I . . ." He bit his lip. "Well, I didn't really want her to—"

"You did. I mean, you just admitted to that."

"*Detective.*"

He took a breath as if he were going to chastise her, and the detective even gave him time to put his words together. But when no words came, the detective said, "Mr. Magruder, did you kill Allison Miller back in 1991?"

"What!" He snapped bolt upright in his chair.

"Because I think you did," she continued. "She was a beautiful woman, and you were in love with her."

"What are you—"

"And on the night of September 22, 1991, when everyone had left the Miller house, you went there, and she rejected you, and so you killed her."

"That's a lie!"

"You strangled her and threw her into the fire pit and let Ramsey Miller take the blame. But it was you."

"I want my lawyer here right now!"

"Fine. I'll get you a phone," the detective said. "But know that I'm seconds away from reaching for those business cards. Every slimy journalist—their numbers are all in a drawer. And I know you understand exactly what will happen to your career when the world learns that David Magruder is suspected of killing Allison Miller and now, fifteen years later, of trying to murder her daughter."

"I didn't—"

"And this will drag on a long time. I personally guarantee it. We'll start tonight with a warrant to search your home. A dozen police cars will park out front with their lights flashing. It won't take long for the news helicopters to start circling. And I'll take as much time as I need to build my case, and eventually I'll have enough evidence for a homicide charge. By then, the David Magruder brand will be long defunct."

"Why are you doing this?" David looked wounded, a child unfairly punished by his teacher.

"Because you murdered a woman," Detective Isaacson said. "And now the daughter returns, and it makes you have to remember —it makes you feel that woman's throat in your hands all over again. It makes you smell her burning flesh."

"Stop it."

"You killed Allison Miller, Mr. Magruder. Admit it."

"I didn't," Magruder said. "I swear it."

"You swear it?" The detective lowered her voice. "Did you order Bill Suddoth to assault and threaten Melanie Denison?" When he didn't answer, she said, "Either you tell me the whole truth about this morning or else the world finds out in the next hour that you're the prime suspect in the murder of Allison Miller." She lowered her voice. "That's how it has to be. If you admit to ordering the assault, we're probably talking probation and a fine. If you didn't murder Allison Miller, then tell me the complete truth about the assault. Prove to me you can say something truthful. Now. Not later."

"I only asked Bill to convince her to leave town."

"What—specifically—did you ask him to do?"

"I didn't say," he said. "I didn't say, 'hurt her.' I didn't even tell him to threaten her. I left it vague."

She nodded. "But you knew he might not be very diplomatic."

"Yeah. I guess I knew that."

"Because you knew he had a criminal record."

David looked at the detective. His shrug was barely detectable.

"So you were lying when you said you didn't know about that." When he didn't respond, she asked, "Why did you want her to leave town so badly, David?"

Silence.

"What were you so worried about that you were willing to jeopardize your precious career over it? And why in the world would you put your fate in the hands of a man like Bill Suddoth?"

More silence.

"You panicked, I get that. But why?" The detective waited a long moment before apparently reaching her limit with David's irritating silence. "I'm giving you ten seconds," she said. "Then I'm out the door and you'll have your lawyer and I'll have your face on the ten o'clock news on every TV in America."

She stared him down, and Melanie was certain that more than ten seconds passed. When David finally spoke, his voice was soft, almost meek. "Can I tell you something off the record?"

"Off the record?" She shook her head as if in pity and closed her file folder. She stood up. "I'm a cop, pal, not a journalist."

She was almost to the door when he said, "What if I saw a crime happen and didn't report it? How bad is that?"

Detective Isaacson closed the door all the way and returned to her seat at the table. "How about you start talking and we let the D.A. decide."

25

Barely able to breathe, eyes glued to the small computer monitor, Melanie listened to David Magruder tell the detective about the night of September 22, 1991, when a distraught Allison Miller came to his house, suggesting that they leave their spouses and give their friendship a chance to become something more. How he'd rejected her—rudely, cruelly—because his wife was about to give him a shot at the big time. He spoke slowly, his tone flat, and Melanie recognized his frequent pauses as attempts to control himself and fight back waves of emotion and probably nausea.

Allison Miller left his house. He called after her, but she kept walking home. An hour or so later, he was sitting on his front stoop, brooding, when Ramsey Miller's car drove by on its way out of the neighborhood. At that time, David decided to walk over to the Millers' house.

"She'd been so angry," he said to the police station wall. "I never saw her like that before. I wasn't going to change my decision, but I had been a bastard and I wanted to apologize."

He went around back—for all he knew, the party was still going on—but everything was dark outside and quiet, lit only by the smoldering fire pit. The gate was ajar, and through it he saw movement near the rear of the property. When his eyes began to adjust, he spotted Allie, kissing someone.

"My first thought was that she and her husband had made up, and I'd been mistaken about it being Ramsey's car. But . . . no. It wasn't right."

"What wasn't right?" asked the detective—gently nudging him along but otherwise staying out of the way.

"How they moved." He was looking beyond her, describing his past as if watching a movie. "Their bodies. It wasn't an embrace. It was something else."

"Did you witness the murder of Allison Miller, Mr. Magruder?" But he wasn't listening to her. He was seeing into the past, fifteen years. "Mr. Magruder?"

"Yes," he said.

"You did nothing to intervene?"

"I got there too late to stop it."

"Are you sure? Was she already dead when you arrived?"

"No, just that . . . it was too late. I knew I couldn't have . . ."

"All right. You did nothing afterward, either. You could have called the police at any time."

"I was afraid."

"Afraid of what, David?" When he didn't answer, she said, "Do you mean physically afraid?"

"Yes," he said. Then: "No."

"Which is it?"

"I know how people are," he said. "If it got out that I was at the scene of a murder, it would've been too much."

"Too much? I don't understand?"

He kept looking at the wall. "It would've been too much. They'd have chosen the other guy."

"What other guy?"

"It was down to the two of us—me and another guy, some former jock out of California. One of us was going to get the job. It was the New York market. I had to get it. That was the only thing that mattered. It was never going to come around again."

"And that's what you were thinking about while you watched your friend get murdered? It's the New York market?" When he didn't answer, she said, "So then what did you do?"

"I went home."

"What did you do when you got home?"

"*Planet of the Apes* was on TV. I watched it."

"Mr. Magruder, who killed Allison Miller?"

He squeezed his eyes shut as if zooming in on the picture in his mind, then opened them again. "That's just it—it was hard to see in the backyard, and my night vision was never any good. But Ramsey Miller, he was a smallish man. The man in the backyard with Allie, he was big."

"Do you mean obese?"

It was Eric, Melanie thought. Eric returned to the house and—

"No," Magruder said, "not that kind of big. Tall, I guess. Broad. You know. Big."

"Who do you think it was?" the detective asked.

Melanie's teeth chattered. Her hands trembled.

"I'm not positive," Magruder said, "but I think it was one of the musicians on stage. The young one on guitar."

333

26

September 22, 1991

Allison paced the house, muttering to herself. Oscillating between humiliation and self-righteousness.

If you have needs that aren't being met.

How dare he. Balding weatherman for a two-bit local station. Well, she'd been dead wrong about him. God, and she would have done anything for him—stripped right there in his living room, screwed him on his leather sofa, on the carpet. She was his. All he had to do was admit what he felt. Admit the connection between them. That it all meant something. So either she'd been wrong about the connection or wrong when she thought he might have a little courage.

But all that was over now, leaving her with a marriage that was also over. Her whole body hurt, thinking about it. Better not to.

She went to the kitchen for trash bags, stepped outside to the backyard, and began picking things up—paper plates, balled-up napkins, plastic ware—from the grass, the tables, the porch railing, the bushes. People were slobs. She emptied beer from plastic cups into the grass and threw the cups away. Same with the soda cans.

She took her time. At one point she poured herself a beer from the keg, drank it a little too fast, and threw the empty cup into the trash. The yard was quiet at last. Peaceful. The air was warm with a gentle breeze. The only light came through the kitchen window. She kept cleaning up. Twice, she almost stepped in pony shit, but otherwise she was glad to be outside. She felt exhausted, worn through, but knew she wouldn't be able to fall asleep, and cleaning gave her something to do.

In the fire pit, a few last chunks of wood smoldered. She would have to throw dirt over it before going in for the night.

She was carrying a full trash bag across the yard toward the garage when she heard: "Hi, there." She started and turned toward the side gate.

Wayne was tall, over six feet, but the way he stood—hands in his pockets, bad posture—he looked smaller. And embarrassed, as if he'd caught her doing something shameful.

"What'd you forget?" she asked, more rudely than she meant. Not his fault that he was good enough on the guitar that shitty musicians latched on to him.

"Ma'am?" He glanced around, like maybe she knew something he didn't. "No—I just came by to see . . ."—he made a pained expression—". . . how things are."

"*Things*? Things couldn't be better."

"Oh, that's good," he said. "Where's Ramsey at?" He looked around, as if Ramsey might've been hiding behind a tree.

"Your guess is as good as mine."

"Oh." He picked up a plastic cup in the grass that she'd missed. She opened the bag, and he tossed it in. "Need some help?"

"Actually, I could use some help moving these chairs." Before the party, Ramsey had carried rented folding chairs into the yard as well as several chairs from inside the house. Together, Wayne and Allie moved them all into the garage. Wayne carried four at a time. When they were done, back in the yard, Allie looked around. "One more favor?"

"Sure thing, Mrs. Miller."

"Will you cut the Mrs. Miller shit and just call me Allie?"

He said nothing. Too dark to see his face turn red.

"All this extra wood," she said, nodding toward the fire pit. "You mind helping me move it all back to the tree line? If we don't do it now, I know it'll still be here in a year."

"Okay, Allie," he said.

Several trips back and forth between the pit and the back edge of the yard, where the tall trees were.

"You're not much of a talker, are you?" Allie asked him after their fifth or sixth trip.

Wayne shrugged. "I don't always know what to say."

"Since when has that stopped anyone from talking?" she asked.

He smiled. No—definitely not a talker.

It was sweet, him checking up on her, but Wayne obviously wasn't the brains behind this particular operation. "So why didn't Eric come himself?" she asked.

He stacked some of the wood so it wasn't so haphazard. "Him and me and Paul were over at Jackrabbits, and I said I'd do it. I don't know. I guess I'm trying to be better."

She looked at him in the dark. "Better at what?"

He seemed to consider the question. "Just better. Like what Ramsey did."

"What are you talking about?"

337

"Used to be, he was a sonofabitch, the way he tells it. But he made himself better. Got himself a nice house and a family. He got you." Wayne shrugged. "I want what he has."

In the dark, she couldn't see where his own gaze fell. "Well, it was a decent thing to do," she said, "coming by. And you can assure all interested parties that I'm fine." Then she told herself to drop the phoniness. "Really, Wayne." She forced a smile. "I'm okay."

Wayne picked up another load of wood, and in the rear of the yard he dumped the logs onto the stack.

"You know, I skipped rehearsal on Friday because of you," he said.

"What do you mean?"

"I get nervous when I'm here. I think about you, and . . ." He paused, as if choosing his words carefully. "You're in my heart, Allie." He coughed. "That sounded so dumb. Listen, can I ask you something?"

You're in my heart. Her whole life, men had said things like that to her. And Wayne was right—it *was* dumb. But it was she who'd invited talk. And undoubtedly, this day had been strange for him, too—between Ramsey yammering on about the apocalypse and the police showing up and then him having to return to the house to make sure Ramsey hadn't beaten Allie senseless or drunk himself into a coma.

"All right, Wayne," she said. "What do you want to know?"

He sniffed once and nodded toward the stage. "What song do you think we played best?"

She laughed. "I thought they all sounded pretty good," she said.

"For real? Do you think?"

Typical man—why settle for one compliment when you can hear it repeated?

338

"I think you're a guitarist with a future," she said, and he looked away, embarrassed. "I think you've got big things ahead of you." She stepped closer, slowly—she had his attention now. He was youthful and very handsome, and *Just do it, Allie, for God's sake*, she said to herself, and put her arms around him.

The sensation of holding on to him nearly took her breath away. Wayne was not only tall, he was deceptively muscular in the shoulders and back, a surfer's body, and holding him was a wonderful, thrilling experience. He smelled like the outdoors, and he was boyish—not a kid, but a young man, and, yes, he reminded her a little of how it was with Ramsey when they were both so much younger and everything was full of possibility. She hugged him tightly, and it felt like exactly the right thing to do.

So did kissing him. She searched for his face in the dark and found this beautiful, youthful mouth, and he might've been naïve but he wasn't without experience, she discovered, because he kissed her back forcefully and without shame, his one hand on her cheek, her neck, then his arms around her back, a hand on her ass. She pressed into him, and he pressed back hard enough that she was pushed backward a step into one of the big oak trees, which provided support for her shaky legs. He lowered his head and bit her neck, and a soft moan escaped her.

Wayne stopped cold.

"This ain't right," he said.

"What? No—" Her face was hot. Her whole body. "Keep going." She stepped forward to kiss him again.

He stepped back.

"Wayne." Her breathing was labored. "Listen to me." Her eyes had adjusted to the dark by now, and she focused on his face. "This night has torn me apart. I can't handle another rejection right now. Can you understand that?"

Conveniently, he was back to being wordless.

"Listen," she said, "I guarantee I need you more than he does."

He backed up more. "I'm sorry, Mrs. Miller."

That's when she shoved him with all her might. He barely flinched.

"*Mrs. Miller!*" he said—same words, different tone.

The fucking nerve of this one. Innocent only when convenient.

"I said don't call me that!" She went to shove him again, but he was ready and blocked her hands. And she knew it was just him being nervous, but he smirked and laughed a little, and Allie could have killed him for it. She tried to punch him—anywhere: face, side, gut—but he was far too strong to be bothered and easily held his ground, and now with tears of shame her fury mounted, because it was so clear that she could neither hurt nor move him.

The longer her rage lasted, the more pitiful it became, until finally Wayne pushed her away. To him, it must have felt like nothing at all—flicking away a bug—but the shove sent her backward, off balance, knocking the back of her head into the hard trunk of the oak tree.

For a moment she was stunned. She worked to stay on her feet and make sense of what had just happened.

"Mrs. Miller, I didn't mean to."

She felt the back of her head: already, a large lump. "You son of a—" She blinked. Something wasn't right with her vision. The outlines of everything were off. She felt frightened, but less of Wayne than of what she realized Ramsey would do when he came home and found her injured. "Ramsey's going to kill you."

"No, he isn't," Wayne said. "Don't say that to me."

"So help me God, he is." This wasn't a threat, so much as fact. Despite everything that had happened tonight, she knew that Ramsey would protect her, always—and with as little nuance as he did everything else. Her fists had inspired no fear, but her words, her words . . . "He's going to make you pay."

"Shut up, Mrs. Miller. I mean it."

Despite her blurry vision, she saw the change come over him, his own terror mounting, then mutating. Hardening.

"Now, Wayne, you get out of—"

The second shove happened completely outside of time. One moment the two of them were standing several feet apart, and the next she was on her knees at the base of the tree. She wanted to move a hand to her head again, but for some reason she couldn't. The only sound was a low, low hum, as if the earth itself were shifting and cracking beneath her. Something was badly wrong. Wrecked. She tried to stand but couldn't. She would have cried out, screamed, wailed, but her voice was already beyond reach.

Wayne came toward her again, crouching low, and like before his hands moved toward her face, and like before his hands were on her throat, and like before their bodies were pressed so closely together they could have been dancing or making love.

27

September 29, 2006

Melanie was pleading with Officer Bauer to get Detective Isaacson. She struggled to catch a breath while the officer left the room and pried the detective away from David Magruder. The moment the detective entered the office, Melanie blurted out, "He's talking about my uncle Wayne. He was here at the hotel."

"Wayne is in Silver Bay?"

"I should have said something." Her whole body was shaking. "But I didn't know—" *The young one on guitar.* Magruder's words were blackening out everything else. "I thought—"

"Okay, try to relax." The detective put a hand on Melanie's arm. "What kind of car does he drive?"

"A black Ford Escort."

"Plate number?"

"I don't know."

"Did he go into your hotel room?"

She nodded. "That's where he was when I left to come here."

"What room number?"

She gave the number and handed her room key to the detective, who hurried away. But Melanie knew there was no need to rush. Wayne was long gone. She had left him at the hotel almost three hours earlier and practically dared him to run. By now, he'd be halfway across Pennsylvania. Or in Maryland. Or Connecticut. New York. Delaware. For someone whose whole life was centered around hiding, a three-hour head start was an eternity.

In the video monitor, David Magruder sat perfectly still in his chair, hunched over the table, head in hands.

Officer Bauer, perhaps feeling the need to fill the silence, began talking about procedure: "Officers will head to the hotel," he was saying. "If the suspect is still there, hopefully he'll surrender peacefully. Usually, people do. If he's not there, they'll put out a bulletin with the information about his car. More than likely, highway patrol will spot him heading back to West Virginia. Especially if he doesn't know he's being—"

"I need a bathroom," Melanie said. The image that Magruder had painted in her mind of Wayne strangling her mother overtook everything. "I'm going to throw up."

Officer Bauer led her quickly down the hallway, toward the station lobby. "I'll wait out here," he said, and Melanie barely made it into the stall before vomiting. She sat on the bathroom floor until the nausea subsided. Her throat screamed, and her headache had returned full force. When she felt steady enough on her feet, she went to the sink and splashed cold water on her face and cried and splashed more water. When she left the bathroom, the officer was waiting for her, and from the lobby she heard her name being called.

Phillip looked bedraggled and anxious. "What's going on?" he asked. "Are you okay?"

She was so completely not okay that she went to him and for a full minute all she could do was keep holding on, unable to speak. When she finally found her voice, she disregarded Detective Isaacson's directive to say nothing by saying everything.

No one seemed to care. One of the officers, a young woman, offered Melanie a bottle of water and joined the chorus of reassurance. The truth was finally out, everyone was telling her (word traveling quickly around the station), and Melanie could take solace in the knowledge that she was finally safe, finally free, and that the guilty would soon be brought to justice.

So well meaning, all of them, and so naïve.

Wayne had murdered her mother and let her father take the blame, and his disturbed version of atonement, apparently, was to kidnap Melanie and raise her. Yes, the truth was finally out, but where was the solace in a truth like that? And the worst part, she thought, sitting beside Phillip now on the wooden bench in the lobby and looking out the windows at the dark street, is that it had worked. All these years, Melanie had grown up feeling indebted to her mother's killer. All these years, she had felt loved, and she had felt love.

"Where's my father?" she said to Phillip.

"I don't know," he said.

"If he didn't . . ." She choked back a sob. "Where has he *been* all this time?"

He put an arm around her. "I don't know."

They sat there together saying little else, while across town a team of officers surrounded, then entered her hotel room. And when they finally radioed in, Officer Bauer knelt down and told Melanie what she already knew.

"Don't worry, though—we'll find him," he added, his words sounding so scripted that Melanie could only shake her head.

In the meantime, she wasn't allowed to return to her hotel room. Everything there was now evidence. "We can check you into another hotel," Officer Bauer said. "We aren't expecting it to be long, but I'm sure you could use some rest."

If she weren't exhausted and hurt in every way, she would have laughed at the officer's optimism.

Officer Bauer called ahead and reserved a room for Melanie and Phillip at the oceanfront Atlantic Hotel. After giving them directions, he wrote down Phillip's cell number and promised to be in touch the moment there was any word.

"And you should feel free to call the station anytime," he told the two of them.

"Okay," Melanie said.

"And check in with either me or Detective Isaacson in the morning, regardless."

What the hell for? Melanie thought. Despite everything that had happened and everything she had learned, her mother's killer was out there, same as before. Nothing had changed. Or rather, it was so much worse now. Ramsey Miller at least had the courtesy of being a bogeyman. But Uncle Wayne had handcrafted a puppet theater for her, a birthday present when she'd turned six, with shiny gold curtains that opened and closed when you pulled a string. He made the puppets himself, too, out of foam and felt and yarn—a pig and a frog. He watched her endless performances. When she asked, he would play the frog. Or the pig. His pig voice made her laugh. For some reason it had a British accent. Later, for other presents in other years, he added to the menagerie. A horse. A wolf.

"Melanie? Will you do that?"

"Sorry?" Melanie asked.

"Will you call one of us in the morning?"

"Oh," she said. "Sure. Whatever."

★   ★   ★

The police station sat on a lonely side street between a tire store and a plasma donation center. Everything was closed at this hour, and only a handful of cars were parked along the curb.

Melanie walked beside Phillip toward his car, her arms crossed for warmth. It had stopped raining but remained dreary. The sidewalk and street were wet. They had passed the tire store when Melanie's peripheral vision caught movement near one of the parked cars—someone coming their way. By the time she turned around, Wayne had a hand on her arm and was saying, "Come on—let's go."

She yanked herself free. "Get away from me!"

"Mr. Denison." Phillip approached Wayne. "Leave her alone."

"You?" Wayne dismissed him with a head shake. "Melanie, I waited for you, but there's no time now. Please—you have to trust me."

When he reached out to take her arm again she tried to pull away, but his grip was firm. Phillip grabbed her body and got her away from Wayne, and then stood in front of her, creating a barrier, protecting her body with his own.

"Now listen, don't you come one step—" Phillip started to say, but he never finished the sentence, because Wayne smashed his face with a lightning-fast punch and he stumbled backward into Melanie.

A second punch caught Phillip in the gut when he was already teetering, and then he was thrown to the ground—where he was headed, anyway. He hit the wet pavement with a thud and curled into himself.

"Damn it, we don't have time for this," Wayne said, and motioned to his car. "Now *please*, honey, let's go—we have to get out of this town."

Melanie was on her haunches, a hand on Phillip's face, trying to get a look at him without taking her eyes off Wayne, whose face was full of anguish. He should have been long gone by now, and she couldn't understand why he would have stayed behind. How could he think she'd go with him? Of course—he had no idea that Melanie knew the whole truth. And where the hell were the cops? For God's sake, the station was *right there*.

"If you scream," Wayne said, reading her mind, "I swear to God I'll bust his head in."

"I know you will," she said, terrified but enraged, too. Because that's what he did. He killed the people who loved her. *"Murderer."*

"What?" He shook his head. "No. No—don't say that. It's not—"

"Someone saw you."

He froze for a moment. "You don't know anything about it. Who? Who said he—"

"David Magruder. He saw you in the backyard, choking her. He saw you kill her."

"You're gonna believe *that* guy?" A police siren wailed in the distance, someone else's tragedy. "No, your mind's been poisoned, honey—it's this goddamn town."

"No. It's you. You did it." She wasn't even trying to make him believe her. She was saying it because it was true. And yet she wanted him to deny it again. The longer he denied it, the longer a tiny part of her could deny it, too.

"It was . . . I was just a kid." His gaze shifted, and it seemed to Melanie that he was no longer seeing her or this street. "I never meant to."

Hearing Wayne's admission made all the breath escape her body as if she'd been the one he'd stomach-punched.

"You killed my mother," she said, unsteadily, trying out the words. They seemed to bring Wayne back to the present, to this cold wet night.

"I gave you a home," he said. "I raised you right."

"You didn't."

"Of course I did!" He looked deeply hurt. He must have been repeating that refrain to himself for years. *I'm giving her a home. I'm raising her right.* Maybe that was how he slept at night. "I loved you like—"

"Don't you use that word."

"It's true. And look at you now—so beautiful and smart."

"I fucking hate you," Melanie said.

"You don't. Don't say that."

Phillip let out a groan. When Melanie glanced down at him, he said, "I think I'm okay." But he wasn't. Blood pooled under him.

"Come with me," Wayne said. "You know you're not staying here with him." Wayne could have left town the minute she got into that police car back at the hotel. He must have known that the longer he stayed, the greater the risk. By now he could have been hundreds of miles away. Yet he had stayed for her. Did he really expect her to go home with him again? Return to Fredonia? Live under his roof? Or did he think the two of them would escape into the night, find some new place to disappear? It was terrifying to think he might be that deluded, but even scarier was the possibility that he didn't know *what* he wanted from her, just that he had to have her because she'd always been his.

"I'm staying with Phillip," she said.

He shook his head sadly. "Oh, Mel—this isn't the good-bye I wanted." For an instant she felt positive he was about to reach for her throat, do to her what he'd done to her mother. Instead, he backed up a step toward his car. "You're going to let me go, and when I'm gone you're going to help your boyfriend get to his car. You'll leave with him. You'll both leave town tonight and won't come back. Not ever. You'll do that for me, Melanie."

"I won't do anything for you." Another glance toward the front of the police station, where absolutely no fucking officers were coming or going.

"Don't be a brat, Melanie," he said, voice rising. Then it softened again. "If the cops find out from you that I stuck around, I'll still get away. You know I will. You know I can hide. But I'll come looking for you both."

"You love me, but you would—" He caught her eye, and she stopped talking because she could see that yes, he did, and yes, he would. She shivered.

"This isn't hard," he said. "If you ever loved me even a little, you'll let me drive away. Let me go, and you're free. It's the freedom you always wanted." Three more steps toward his car. "Now promise you'll let me go."

She held his gaze for a couple of long seconds.

"Go," she said.

"*Melanie*," Phillip said.

"Good girl," Wayne said. Five more steps. He'd almost reached the car. "Melanie?"

"What."

"Tell me you love me."

She almost screamed right then, and biting her lower lip hard enough to draw blood probably saved Phillip's life. She gritted her teeth and, still looking at Wayne, forced the words out. "I love you, Uncle Wayne," she said.

For an instant, his face softened.

Then he got into his car. It started right up. His cars always did.

She watched him drive away, and then she was alone with Phillip on the wet street.

"Can I leave you here a minute?" she asked.

"Melanie, how could you let him—"

"It'll only be a minute. Is that okay?"

A raspy breath. "Where do you think I'm gonna go?"

In the station, she hurried through the lobby, past the dispatcher, and shouted for help. When Officer Bauer appeared, she said, "Wayne was just out front, and he drove away in a tan Honda Accord with New Jersey plates—BZM-18A. He turned left on the far side of that bar. And Phillip is hurt outside. He needs help, and something to stop the bleeding—a rag or paper towels. I'll be out there with him."

She said it all with the calm efficiency of a pro. And then she left the station.

When she woke up, the room was dark but a door was cracked open to a lit hallway. Then she remembered. Hospital. She lay on a narrow folding cot beside Phillip's bed. Half his face was bandaged. The one exposed eye was shut. She listened for his breathing, and when she heard it she reached out and found his hand under his sheet and gently squeezed. No response. So he was either asleep or heavily sedated. Those two punches had done a job on him, the doctor told her. Broken eye socket. Ruptured spleen.

It had taken the police just minutes to spot Wayne's car and arrest him. So in that way, Wayne had been right—for the first time, she was free. Yet lying there in the dark, with all the strength she'd demonstrated in the police station now gone, all the adrenaline depleted, she felt sad and guilty and overwhelmed—homesick, but with no home to root the emotion to. She held on to Phillip's hand, and that made it better, though it wasn't enough. Maybe someday it would be. But right now she was seventeen years old and she wanted her mother. And for the first time, she wanted her father, too.

28

September 23, 1991

Ramsey Miller awoke in panic, heart racing: *I fell asleep while driving!*

But no. The boom he'd heard—felt—was no head-on collision, but thunder. The deep sway was no deadly truck roll at 80 m.p.h., but a wave moving his boat. And boats were made to roll.

As he assessed his actual situation—*on my boat, in the ocean*—another wave blasted the boat, sending it rolling again. Lightning splintered overhead like shards of a giant windshield, giving Ramsey a couple of seconds to take in the whipping ocean, to notice the absence of stars, and to understand the magnitude of the storm that had moved in while he slept. Understanding came just seconds before the rain began—almost as if his understanding had caused the rain to start.

The fucking weatherman. Though still shaking off sleep, Ramsey could see the comedy in it: The fucking weatherman had it right all along.

The narrow band of man-made light—land—was clear enough to the east, but he had no idea how far his boat might have drifted. He wasn't even sure how long he'd been asleep, though the sharp pain in his neck from lying against the seat suggested hours, not minutes. He didn't like the idea of being in a metal boat during a storm, but that fact was nonnegotiable, so he put electrocution out of his mind and leaned over the engine to pull the starter. Not easy, given the boat's swaying, but on the third try the little engine revved to life.

The rain fell in torrents, carried by gale-force winds. Lightning and thunder intensified into the sort of storm that made you say "Holy shit" even from inside your house. But the waves were his concern. The flat-bottom boat wasn't made for this. He'd turn into the waves if he could tell where they were coming from, but they seemed to come from everywhere. So he headed east, toward shore. Too far away to recognize any landmarks, but he'd deal with his position once he got closer. The main thing was to get moving.

The wave that knocked him overboard came out of nowhere, a huge roller that sent the boat onto its side. Ramsey hit the water and forced his head to the surface so he'd keep sight of the dark boat in the dark water. At first he couldn't spot it. Then, as he rose on a wave, he saw it bobbing in the water fifteen feet away: to the west, he thought, but couldn't be sure. The fall into the ocean had sent him spinning, and with only his head above water now, he could no longer see the shoreline. He could see nothing at all except the wave in front of him.

He swam toward the boat, but when he rose again he was dismayed to see that the boat's position had shifted. He should swim east, to shore. But which way was east? He had a sense. Yet he *might* be able to catch the boat, which, without his hand on the throttle, seemed to move in a wide arc. If he swam toward where the boat might end up—

Another wave pounded him, and when he surfaced he could no longer find the boat. He turned in a circle. Which way was east? His waterlogged clothes pulled at him. He tried to kick off his shoes but ended up with another mouthful of water and a frantic race back to the surface. He needed to find east. The boat would keep moving but the shore would not. Swim to shore. Which way was the shore?

Ramsey was a strong swimmer. The water wasn't cold. The storm would let up.

Another wave knocked him under. Which way was up?

He surfaced again but no air came, only a hack, and more rain, and he vomited something sour, and when his mouth dipped below the surface again, that's when the first full intake of sea-water came, and that's when the first full moment of understanding came.

And although he was drowning horribly in the pitch dark, surrounded by nothing and no one, anyone watching would have been proud to know Ramsey Miller, who did not give up.

29

Alive and Wrong

*December 26, 2006 * by Arthur Goodale * in Uncategorized*

"That's how we know we're alive: we're wrong."

So wrote the novelist Philip Roth in his Pulitzer Prize–winning novel *American Pastoral*, which I read when it was published a decade ago. I remember that sentence striking me as surprising and provocative when I first read it, and over the years it has stuck with me. But only recently have I come to appreciate its insight. We spend our lives trying to understand the hearts of those around us and the actions those hearts inspire, and we get it wrong, wrong, wrong.

Because let me say this now: I was wrong about everything.

I knew—absolutely *knew*—that Ramsey Miller had killed his wife.

I knew that Meg Miller was dead.

I knew that the Miller case, my self-declared white whale, would remain open, at least during my lifetime.

And on a more personal note: I knew, twelve weeks ago, that I was dying, my bad habits finally overtaking my acceptable genetics.

Every bit of it, wrong.

As you've probably noticed, this is the first post since my macabre musings of September 22. I'd have thought that recent events would motivate me to write a flurry of posts about the Miller case as well as my own road to recovery. Not so. (Wrong again, self!) In fact, I haven't felt the urge to write at all. More to the point—after this entry, I plan to abandon the blog altogether. If I decide to resume it someday, then so be it. But I don't think I will, now that the blog's purpose has been fulfilled.

For three years I believed I was casting my private musings into a vast and swirling world, when in fact I was reaching out to Meg.

I just didn't know it.

Nonetheless, my blog did attract 75 of you along the way, and I owe you some facts:

1. I did not die. :)

   (Until this very moment, I have never in my life used an emoticon. Let that, my loyal readers, tell you something about the vicissitudes of old age.)

   More precisely, if I was dying that weekend in September, I'm not dying anymore. The doctors demanded that I change my lifestyle, and that's what I've done. You should see me eating oatmeal. You should see me eating fish. Also, after two-thirds of a century, I finally quit cigarettes back in October. Cold turkey. Boy, has that been a horror show. I've become an irritable SOB—but an SOB who walks the boardwalk five mornings a week and who no longer becomes winded climbing the stairs.

2. Wayne Denison pled guilty to the second-degree murder of Allison Miller and the first-degree kidnapping of Meg Miller.

   Details from his confession can be found in any number of newspaper accounts. But a friend on the Silver Bay police force who shall remain anonymous did me the favor of showing me the actual document. After killing Allison Miller, Wayne Denison evidently abducted young Meg and drove her straight to West Virginia, where he convinced his girlfriend to look after her, and returned immediately—that same night—to New Jersey in order to feign surprise around plenty of witnesses when Allison's body was found the next morning.

   Quite a different story from what he told police fifteen years ago—that he left Jackrabbits bar at 10:45 and drove straight home to his apartment. His earlier story was corroborated by his downstairs neighbor, who swore he saw Wayne entering the apartment—an alibi that we now know was purchased for the price of three marijuana cigarettes. In the days leading up to Allison's funeral, Wayne dropped hints at work that he'd become disillusioned—after all, Ramsey, a man he'd looked up to, had apparently murdered his own family in cold blood. When Wayne quit his job and left town shortly after Allie's funeral, nobody thought much of it. He returned to West Virginia, reunited with Kendra and Meg, and the three of them disappeared together, this new family that would remain in hiding for the next fifteen years.

In exchange for his guilty plea, Wayne was spared a first-degree murder charge. He is now serving forty years with no chance of parole in the U.S. penitentiary in Allenwood, PA. Kendra Denison claimed that she had been duped by Wayne all these years into believing that she was lawfully protecting Meg (who has grown up using the name Melanie). Prosecutors found Kendra's story hard to believe but reduced the charge to second-degree kidnapping in exchange for testifying against her husband. She was sentenced to ten years in a federal correctional institution. She is currently serving her term in Cumberland, MD, and will be eligible for parole in five years.

3. Regarding the many news stories praising David Magruder's investigative prowess as instrumental in cracking the long-cold case and leading the police to the proper suspect, I have only this to say: Don't believe everything you read.

4. Ramsey Miller's whereabouts remain unknown.

Yesterday, I ate Christmas dinner with Melanie and Phillip Connor. Like every time Melanie has invited me into their home, I felt uncomfortable and intrusive on the drive over, until the moment their front door opened and I realized there was nowhere I'd rather be. This time there was another guest as well, Eric Pace, whom I failed to recognize from our few conversations years earlier. He was physically larger than I'd remembered, yet somehow diminished. We had nothing in common save our mutual affection for our hosts, but that was enough.

Eric hadn't yet seen Phillip's scar, a fact that Phillip remedied by lifting up his shirt at the dinner table and recounting what happened on the sidewalk outside the police station on the night of September 29. He used phrases like *My body was her shield* and *In a fair fight, I'd have. . . .* Having now heard the story on a few separate occasions, I will note only that Phillip's role in the narrative seems to increase in drama and heroism with each telling.

"Your face was highly effective against his fist," Melanie added.

Good for them, I found myself thinking, for tinting a tragic moment with comedy in the retelling so they can move beyond it.

It would be impossible for me to gush properly about the Connors or for me to enumerate all the reasons why I tear up so easily in their presence—especially now that Melanie is well into her pregnancy and visibly showing. Suffice it to say that I ate too much last night, stayed too late, and went to bed feeling immensely grateful and lucky.

After sleeping late this morning, something I rarely do anymore, I awoke with that line from Roth's novel in my head and went to my bookshelf to discover that it's actually part of a much longer passage that includes the following:

That's how we know we're alive: we're wrong. Maybe the best thing would be to forget being right or wrong about people and just go along for the ride. But if you can do that—well, lucky you.

I'd like to say that from now on I'll live my life that way—content with being along for the ride. Trouble is, I've had an entire lifetime to practice being wrong. I don't know if I can stop this late in the game. So let me close out this post, and this blog, by saying the following:

Melanie Connor—formerly Melanie Denison, formerly Meg Miller—rose from the dead, sought me out, and became my friend. That will always be one of the great joys of my life.

About that, I know I'm not wrong.

Posted by Old Man with Typewriter at 12/26/2006 5:42 PM | Comments are enabled.

30

June 17, 2009

Eight a.m. and already a scorcher. Soon the slides will all be too hot to ride.

Melanie sits on the park bench while her daughter climbs and slides, climbs and slides, and monologues a nonstop jumble of songs and stories that Melanie can only half follow.

The two of them are alone in the park. All the other young children in town are either later sleepers or their mothers are less desperate than Melanie to start burning off excess energy.

Phillip is at the high school administering final exams to restless seniors. If the weather holds, the three of them might head to the beach in the afternoon.

"One more, sweetie," Melanie calls to Brianna, who turned three in April. They named her Brianna—Brianna Allison Connor —because the name is trendy and other girls have it. Melanie wants her daughter to have many things in common with other children.

"Two more!" Brianna shouts back.

In not so long, Brianna will have a sister, or brother. Melanie peed on the stick this morning, and plans to tell Phillip tonight after Brianna goes to bed. If Melanie can hold on to the secret that long. She's out of practice keeping secrets.

"Okay—two more," Melanie says. "And then we'll feed the turtles."

There are newer, better parks in town, but this one has Turtle Pond. Melanie always enjoys coming here with her daughter, knowing that she used to come here with her mother. And with her father, who is out there somewhere.

After Wayne and Kendra were arrested and briefly made national news, Melanie kept waiting for her father to return. She would scan the faces of men she saw in town, hoping for that flicker of recognition. At night she dreamt that she was still living with Wayne and Kendra in Fredonia, imprisoned in their trailer, and Ramsey would find her there and set her free.

Her home phone number was listed. Her address was listed. Her information was there for the taking. He could have found her if he wanted. But as the weeks and months passed and the media moved on to other stories, Melanie began to accept that her father had chosen to remain hidden. He had been a fugitive for fifteen years, and it must have been agonizing for him, knowing he was innocent but that everyone had already convicted him. By now he must have started a new life somewhere and decided that, all things considered, the best choice was to keep living it.

Still, Melanie wishes he'd return. There will always be a light on for him. But that's his decision.

She has decisions to make, too. She is enrolled part time at the community college but is still too many credits away from graduating. Her major—journalism—is a dying field, she's coming to find. Or at least it's shifting too quickly for her academic courses to adjust. Lately, she's been thinking of something completely different: enrolling in the police academy. At first it was only a fleeting thought, but she's warming to the idea. When she floated it to Phillip a couple of months ago, he shrugged and said, "Well, you're tough enough."

She agrees with him—she *is* tough, but not tough enough to join the force while she's pregnant or has a newborn. She can wait a couple of years, she supposes.

"Okay, kiddo," she says to Brianna. "Last one."

"Then the turtles!"

"That's right."

Silver Bay is hers now. She hasn't returned to Fredonia and knows she never will. She visited Kendra, once, in prison in Maryland early on in her sentence. There were things Melanie wanted to know.

I was so young, Kendra said into the phone receiver on the opposite side of the thick glass divider, *and I loved him so much. He kept me safe when we were in foster care and made sure I didn't get it too bad. When he left for New Jersey, I fell apart. I spent two months crying. Three years, he was away—I saw him a few times, but he seemed older. He was tougher. Then he came back all of a sudden. And he needed me so badly.*

Kendra sobbed into the telephone the whole time she spoke.

But all those years, Melanie said. *My whole life—you were never suspicious?*

He had those letters from the Marshal's office. And why would I doubt him? Why would I try to wreck our family?

Almost immediately, Melanie realized it was foolish to have driven the three hours expecting an honest look into Kendra's heart when Kendra herself was unwilling to look there. A full minute passed without either of them saying anything.

Melanie tried again: *But how could you never even wonder?*

Anger flashed in Kendra's eyes. *I could ask you the same thing,* she said. Then she began to weep again.

The visit was scheduled to last a half hour, but after twenty awkward minutes, Melanie stood up to leave, and Kendra said, pleadingly, *When are you going to visit me again? You have to tell me when.* Her eyes were shot through with red. Melanie left the prison knowing little more than she knew before coming, and with no better sense of in what proportion to feel hatred or pity for the woman who had raised her.

It doesn't matter, Melanie told herself then and has continued to remind herself. I'm home now. This is my home.

The beach, the bay, the roads, the neighborhoods, the shops and restaurants. The schools and cemeteries. At some point this week she'll visit the cemetery off Cedar Lane, where her mother is buried and where Melanie does her best thinking. Should she try to become a police officer? she'll ask her mother. Then she'll ask Arthur Goodale, who is buried there, too. She'll leave flowers by both graves. She tries to make a point of doing that regularly, though she often goes too long between visits. With a young child, everything is hard.

How hard it must have been for her mother, she often thinks, with her father away so much of the time. Phillip goes to Atlantic City for the New Jersey teachers' convention just two nights each fall, and she always dreads it.

But it must have been hard for her father, too, being away, knowing he was missing all those small moments that transform a child every day, it seems. She wishes that Ramsey could meet his granddaughter, get to know her. But if he were going to reach out, he'd have done it by now. She knows that. She also knows that her father might not be alive. Yet she chooses to believe Eric's assessment. Since her return to Silver Bay, Eric has introduced her to a side of her father that was unavailable in any newspaper, the side of him that explained why he once had friends and a wife who loved him and a daughter who did, too. So she chooses to believe, as Eric does, that Ramsey Miller is too stubborn to die, and is still out there somewhere.

Of the several scenarios that she imagines for her father—he has a new, adoring family; he works as a mechanic in the mountains, maybe Colorado; he drives a big rig under an alias—here is what she always comes back to.

Somewhere outside of the United States, maybe in Panama or Costa Rica, a quiet man with a slight limp rents out his small fishing boat for day trips. He has a kind face and is the most mild-mannered man anyone has ever met, and although he's only in his fifties, he seems much older. He never misses a day of work unless the ocean is very rough. Each night, he returns home to his cabin in the woods, away from everyone and everything. He pours himself a single drink, looks up at the stars, and thinks about his wife and daughter with nothing but fondness and light.

To Melanie's surprise, after going down the slide one more time, Brianna comes right over and takes her hand.

"Did you remember the bread?" Brianna asks. (Three weeks ago, Melanie forgot the bread, an oversight that caused a full-on tantrum.)

Melanie removes the zip-lock bag from her purse. "Right here."

Brianna drops Melanie's hand and runs toward the footbridge, stopping at the center. Melanie follows her, and when they're together on the wooden bridge they both look over the railing.

"There's one!" Brianna says. A small turtle is sunning on a branch sticking out of the shallow water. Moments later, a second turtle swims their way. The turtles know. For years, decades, people have been feeding them from this footbridge. Now, all you have to do is stand on the bridge and the turtles begin to gather.

Melanie removes the slice of bread from the zip-lock bag and hands it to Brianna, saying, "Remember—small pieces."

Brianna breaks off a corner and tosses it over the railing and into the water.

The second turtle swims closer, jerks its head forward, and grabs the bread. Brianna breaks off a few more pieces and throws them into the water as more turtles gather. As always, the turtles multiply, until there are fifteen, twenty, thirty, of every size. The largest are probably forty pounds and almost certainly swam this pond before Melanie was born.

By now the turtles are churning up the water only a few feet below. It's a little unnerving, all those prehistoric creatures jockeying for bits of stale bread, furiously snapping and climbing over one another. But Brianna isn't afraid.

She feeds the turtles one small piece of bread at a time. And when a third of the slice is left, the massive head of one of the largest, oldest snapping turtles rises above the surface.

"Look, Brianna!" Melanie points. "Over there."

There are probably only three or four turtles this large and old in the whole pond. They're so heavy that usually only their heads rise out of the murk. But something about the sunlight this morning, the early hour, makes more of the shell visible—faded green and splotched with moss. The animal is easily sixty pounds and as many years old.

"Look at it!" Brianna beams. She knows this is a rare sight. All the locals know it.

"Why don't you give him the whole piece," Melanie says.

"*All* of it?" asks Brianna.

Melanie nods. So Brianna holds what remains of the bread over the railing—tentatively, with beautiful anticipation—before letting it fall down to the water. A perfect drop, it lands inches from the turtle's head, which shoots forward and back again like a cobra's strike, the bread vanishing in its jaws, and then the old animal drops beneath the surface and is gone.

Acknowledgments

I couldn't imagine a better team than agent Jody Kahn and editor Otto Penzler; I am incredibly grateful to them and routinely amazed. My sincere thanks to those who read the novel in manuscript form and helped to make it better: Catherine Pierce (a.k.a. Katie), Felice Kardos, Michael Piafsky, Christopher Coake, and Sarah Reeder. Thanks to Captain Ron Albence (Ret.) and Sergeant Laura Hines Roberson for their help with police procedure, and to Julie Kardos, Stephen Kardos, and Tracey McKinnon for guiding me through hospital logistics. Any mistakes are mine, though any mistakes will invariably be dismissed with a coy smile and an utterance about artistic license. I am thankful for the marvelous support and camaraderie of the faculty, students, and administrators at Mississippi State University. Thanks to Carl Pierce for his immense generosity in allowing his town of Rehoboth, Delaware—where much of this book was written—to become ours, and thanks to John and Judy Rioux for my table at Gallery Espresso. Finally, one more thanks to Katie, whom I couldn't have done this without and wouldn't have wanted to.

BOOKS BY DAVID PLANTE

THE CATHOLIC

THE
CATHOLIC

DAVID PLANTE

ATHENEUM

NEW YORK

1986

Library of Congress Cataloging-in-Publication Data

Plante, David.
   The catholic.

   I. Title.
PS3566.L257C3 1986   813'.54   85-48284
ISBN 0-689-11788-4

PREFACE

———————— • ————————

A young nun told us one morning during catechism class how missionaries from France had been captured and tortured by the Indians in America. The Indians stripped the missionaries naked, tied them to stakes, then pressed red hot tomahawks to their flesh. This was done to them because they were Catholic and loved God. The nun's face, in her fluted wimpel, was flushed. My knees were shaking.

When I left, imagining I was following a narrow path through the dark woods to my home, I felt I was in danger of being stopped by Indians, who would wrap a blanket around me and bundle me off to a clearing where they would undress me.

My family was part Indian from my father's side. Though he and some of my brothers had straight, black hair, black eyes, strong cheekbones, large noses, I did not look at all Indian, but had my mother's blue eyes. If I were captured, I would say, "I am an Indian, too," but they wouldn't believe I was one of them.

I was seven years old and had attained, according to the Church, the age of reason, so was about to make my First Communion, which was the subject of my catechism lessons. The Indians had appeared unexpectedly, as they had a way of appearing, during the last lesson.

At the supper table, I asked my father if he knew any Indian words.

"No."

My mother said, "I know a story about Indians."

"Does it have Indian words in it?" I asked.

My mother, who shared French ancestry with my father, had translated, for the son of Irish neighbors – he was studying French in college and not doing well in it – a small part of Chateaubriand's *Atala*, a class assignment, and kept a copy of the translation. She read it to me. My father listened, too.

This was the story, told by Chactas to René, a young Frenchman in America, in the year 1725.

Many years before, Chactas, a Natchez, fell in love with Atala, a Muscogules. Their tribes were at war. Chactas, when captured, was saved from torture and death by Atala, the daughter of the chief, Simaghan. Atala was Christian, and wore a gold crucifix on her breast. Chactas and Atala escaped into the Allegheny Mountains, where, in a dark forest, they had to stop because of a storm. Chactas protected Atala from the thunder and lightning and wind, and Atala told Chactas her story. Suddenly, they heard a dog barking.

I became, at this point, wary of what was to appear from the forest.

"An old missionary, carrying a lantern, came upon us."

He struck me as strange, this missionary with a lantern in the forest.

"Atala was at his feet in an instant, telling him she was Christian."

I thought: She must have spoken the missionary's language.

The missionary, who might, I had a feeling, have done something bad to them, took the young Indians to his grotto. He said he would instruct Chactas in the Catholic faith. The missionary and Chactas made up a soft bed for Atala to repose on and the men went off to the Mission, where Chactas would get his instruction.

"We started out and soon we arrived and stopped at the foot of a large cross. It was here that the missionary celebrated the mysteries of his religion."

I vividly recall an odd sense from this: the mysteries of my religion celebrated in an Indian forest.

When Chactas and the missionary, named Father Aubry, returned to the grotto, they found Atala ill, and about to die.

"Atala's voice grew weaker and her suffering was intense. She seemed to be waiting for something and, when I told her I would embrace the Christian religion, she uttered, 'It is time to call God here.' I fell on my knees at the foot of the bed, and saw Father Aubry open the chalice and take between his two fingers the host, white as snow, that he placed on Atala's tongue. Then he took some cotton, dipped it in some holy oil and rubbed her temples. 'Father,' I cried, 'will that medicine give her life?' 'Yes, my son,' he replied, 'eternal life.' Atala had expired."

The rest of the translation I heard with a kind of awe.

"That night, we transported her precious remains to the opening of the grotto. Father Aubry rolled her in a piece of linen, woven by his mother. Atala was resting on a bed of mimosa and in her hair was a flower from the magnolia tree. The missionary prayed all night. I sat in silence at her head. The next day, I carried Atala, and with Father Aubry preceding us we marched to her final resting place. We dug her grave and when it was finished I placed her there and picked up a handful of earth and, taking one last look at my beloved, I sprinkled some over her face until her features disappeared."

I felt everything give way in me.

"Upon leaving, I fell on my knees at her grave and cried, 'Sleep in peace, in the strange land.' That is my story, René, and many years later I, feeling very old, am looking forward to a reunion in Heaven with my Atala."

The evening before my *première communion*, in the bathtub with my younger brother, both of us jumped up and down in the shallow water as if it were a stream and splashed one another. No one came into the bathroom to tell us to stop. Our thin, hairless bodies fell against one another. When we drew back we stood looking at one another. My brother and I concentrated, with bright halos of attention, on one anothers' prepubescent members, and I said, suddenly, "Ainque les Peaux Rouges ont cela." ("Only Red Skins have this.") My little brother didn't deny it. We were different from anyone else.

THE CATHOLIC

1

————— • —————

I often thought, in my teens, that I would like to distance myself so far from myself that I would see the dark, angular-faced, blue-eyed person I was as someone apart from me, and I would try to account for someone altogether different. Though I would use the first person, I would be thinking always in terms of the third person, so "I" would think "he" and he would have nothing to do with me.

I believed that a person shouldn't think about himself. I thought about myself all the time. Other people thought about themselves a lot, and did so with pleasure. I imagined this was because of what they had to think about in themselves. What I was helplessly drawn to thinking about in myself gave me great displeasure. If only I were able to consider myself as someone different from myself, he would maybe give me something else to think about.

This someone became my college room-mate.

Sitting at my desk in our room, I heard shouting from the shower room, and I went in. Charlie was in one of a line of occupied cubicles, the plastic curtains drawn back, and he and other dorm-mates showering were shouting and laughing. I associated this image of Charlie, not in retrospect but at the moment it occurred, with everything that was outside me. Though we were both male, I imagined I was so different from Charlie that we didn't share a sex. I had often seen Charlie naked, sometimes with a vague sense of disgust at his white skin and pink nipples, but when I saw him now it was as if he appeared

I

before me for the first time. His body gleamed from the hot water, which flattened his crew cut, ran in rivulets down his face, neck, shoulders, arms, chest, thighs, groin, and sprayed off his cock; a fine line of hair ran, like a dark rivulet, from his navel to his streaming pubic hair. I knew Charlie, but, suddenly, I didn't know him.

His popularity – and he was very popular, elected President of the Freshman Class – was, I later imagined when I saw him on the campus talking to a group, the popularity of his body, which was not covered but suggested by his shirt, chinos, buckskin shoes. This body shocked me, but I did not know what it meant. It was as if I became aware that, unlike some time in the indefinite past, I was now living among people who had taken over where I'd lived, had chopped down the woods and built houses and criss-crossing roads. They took it for granted that everyone had the same kind of body as they. I must take my place among them, must, in a way, become converted to their ways. Charlie's active body was that of someone from the outside world.

I tried to disassociate Charlie's body from him to make it a body in itself. I liked it that he was irresponsible, and quickly became unpopular as the Class President because he never appeared at meetings. This should have made his body, too, irresponsible, but, despite Charlie, it retained its vast associations; relevant to a world I didn't know, it was free in that world to do everything. I loved Charlie and admired him for being Class President, but I was a little pleased when he was impeached and someone else took his place.

We had conversations from our beds in our dark room.

I told him I was making a very great effort not to think about myself, but it was difficult.

Why shouldn't I think about myself? he asked.

It was wrong, I said.

Wrong?

Well, I said, I didn't like it.

He asked me if I'd read Walt Whitman, who thought about himself all the time, but who obviously liked it.

I said I couldn't read Whitman, he was on the Vatican's Index

2

of Forbidden Books.

"The Vatican?" Charlie asked. "You let yourself be determined by the Vatican?"

"I do, yes."

"That's quaint," he said. "You're a quaint person, Dan."

"I resent it," I said. "Of course I resent being told what to do."

I thought he either fell asleep or didn't want to hear about my resentments.

In a bookshop below the campus, I decided – in the way one decides to do what one knows one shouldn't and therefore taking full culpability – to buy the poems of Whitman. I went with the book back up to the campus, and in the front row of seats in the auditorium in the library where I often went during breaks between classes to study or sleep, I opened it. I read:

Oh my body!

This startled me.

> I dare not desert the likes of you in other men and women
>   nor the likes of the parts of you,
> I believe the likes of you are to stand or fall with the likes of
>   the soul, (and that they are the soul,)
> I believe the likes of you shall stand or fall with my poems,
>   and that they are my poems,
> Man's, woman's, child's, youth's, wife's, husband's,
>   mother's, father's, young man's, young woman's
>   poems,
> Head, neck, hair, ears, drop and tympan of ears,
> Eyes, eye fringes, iris of the eye, eyebrows, and the waking
>   and sleeping of the lids,
> Mouth, tongue, lips, teeth, roof of the mouth, jaws, and the
>   jaw-hinges,
> Nose, nostrils of the nose, and the partition,
> Cheeks, temples, forehead, chin, throat, back of the neck,
>   neck-slue,
> Strong shoulders, manly beard, scapula, hind-shoulders,

and the ample side-round of the chest,
Upper arm, armpit, elbow socket, lower arm, arm-sinews,
    arm-bones,
Wrist and wrist-joints, hand, palm, knuckles, thumb,
    forefinger, finger-joints, finger-nails,
Broad breast-front, curling hair of the breast, breast-bone,
    breast side,
Ribs, belly, backbone, joints of the backbone,
Hips, hip-sockets, hip-strength, inward and outward
    round, man-balls, man-root,
Strong set of thighs, well carrying the trunk above,
Leg fibres, knee, knee-pan, upper leg, under-leg,
Ankles, instep, foot-ball, toes, toe-joints, the heel –

The body, which was Charlie's body, took over my entire attention. His body was a country with its own special gravity, where I believed I would get everything I wanted. I was not sure what I wanted, but the moment I got to that other country I knew that what I wanted would both be revealed and realized.

To go into that country and live there and have everything, I made love to Charlie. During an early spring break he and I went alone to the lake home where I used to spend summers with my family. The house was cold from being shut up all winter. I forcibly imposed my body on Charlie's.

In the morning, I woke to find he had gone. I searched the cold room. Dead insects lay on the wooden floors. I dressed and went out to find him. The trees were dry and brown, and through the bare branches I could see the lake, on which the ice was breaking up. I walked now in one direction, now in another. For a while I stared at a leafless bush covered with red berries. The woods were silent. Then I went along the rutted dirt road out of the woods, thinking he might have decided to walk to the nearest town on the other side of the lake, get a bus into the city and a train to Boston. When I saw him coming along the road, I stopped and waited for him. He smiled.

"Hi," I said.

"I went out for a walk," he said, and smiled more.

4

We never mentioned the night before.

The transformation in me, I imagined, was total. Of course it wasn't, but I felt it was.

To be free of myself was to be free of my religion. But that I couldn't, according to the Vatican, love Charlie's body and love Christ's at the same time was not really the reason for my sacrificing my love of Christ. What made me decide that I loved Charlie and didn't love Christ was that Christ made me think about my sinful self, whereas Charlie removed me from my world to one where there was no thinking about yourself and therefore there were no sins.

On a Sunday morning in my parents' house, awake and waiting for my father to come into my bedroom and tell me to get up and get ready for Mass, it occurred to me that God did not exist. I lay in my bed, filled with joy. I was a little late for Mass.

The image of Charlie's body relieved me from all my past thoughts and feelings. My soul came alive in me, and I honestly imagined I was starting a new life. What was promised was that my new life would be made by going away, which was to go into the world around me, inhabited by people whose relations with one another were free.

2

————— • —————

Walt Whitman's poetry never appeared in the house I grew up in. The fine trembling that had spread over me as I'd read him for the first time wasn't only sexual, but was the wonder at how Whitman had given me the sense, from so many particulars, of his whole body, amazing in its wholeness. It was as if he had looked in a mirror and described what he saw. I could never see my body whole. I saw only ears, navel, toes, etc.

My wonder at this wonder came from a course in epistemology I was obliged to take at the Jesuit college I attended.

I tried to understand how Whitman had managed to give me a pleasurable sense of the whole body. My excitement in his pleasure expanded into a sense of everything, everything all together, and from this sense rose the idea that I could, in a body, have everything, all together. This could occur to me, not in mine, but in the body of another. And I wanted to know how it did occur.

The image of a man's body, but not a woman's, was to me the image of everything.

Whitman had written about his love of women: "Fast anchor'd eternal O Love! O woman I love!" But he wrote differently about his love of man: "I ascend, I float in the regions of your love O man!"

Of course, I knew I could not have everything. Everything easily broke down into particulars, too many to take in. There was no way of experiencing directly that wholeness. Yet, I wanted to experience it. I wanted everything.

Making love with my room-mate, whom I loved, promised it but did not give it to me. Afterwards we went separately to our homes. When I saw him again in our room at college, less than a week later, he said, "We should cut classes this afternoon and meet at the Fine Arts Museum."

I liked it that Charlie was irresponsible towards the outside world, but I did not like it when he was irresponsible towards me. I waited for two hours on the steps of the museum. It was bright out, and once or twice I thought I saw him come up the steps in the brightness.

Inside the museum, I wandered from room to room. I stopped when I came to the Attic statue of a boy's torso. From time to time I looked beyond the small, headless, armless, legless, sexless body and out the large windows to the spring trees. Each time I looked back at the statue it appeared to me, on its supporting rod, to hold itself more tensely still, and I thought how strange it was that I should feel in the torso an intentional stillness. I looked round to make sure I was alone in the room; I got near the statue and delicately touched a finger to its thigh, then quickly withdrew it.

I wanted the inaccessible body.

It came to me that that torso, in the warm spring light, was more naked than any body I had ever seen. Because it was stone and I couldn't really attribute to it the nakedness of skin I raised my hand towards it with the temptation of what was deeper than skin. I wondered where the sense of its completeness resided in it – in the same way Descartes wondered where the soul resided in the body, and decided: the pineal gland – because the statue was so shattered. Again I put out a hand, not simply to touch, but to push the statue over; above the fragments its nakedness would hover in the light. Someone came into the room and I stood back.

Just as it was impossible to see everything together, it was impossible, I thought, to see the body. You never saw the body. You saw toes, etc. Yet you were aware, as an apprehension, of the whole body. How?

In my scholastic philosophy, our instructions in dogmatic

7

logic led us above logic, for the irony of such dogma was that, remaining in itself strictly logical, it should attempt to prove what could not be proven by logic. It gave us every reason for rising above logic to apprehend the idea of God in faith, which came, in a flash of grace, from God. Logical thinking was, in the end, made infinitely vague, because infinitely inaccessible to reason, by its ultimate purpose, the existence of God.

I was, I thought, being vastly ironical. I did not believe in God.

I thought impressionistically because I was not good at reasoning. Was an idea what preceded an argument, or was it the conclusion to an argument? I didn't know. But I did know that to have an idea was not, in itself, to reason. An idea was, in a way, like an image, the image of the body and the idea of everything being similar in that they *occurred*. An idea was a bright sense of something being centered. The great mystery was why the vague bright idea should occur.

The idea could only occur in the same way God occurred, with grace. Without that grace, I would not even be able to see a body.

I went around to the back of the statue. Its buttocks were chipped, and there was a scar-crack diagonally across its back. I saw it against the light from the window, and it appeared black.

Outside the museum, small blossoms from the trees streamed through the air. I walked down Huntington Avenue to Symphony Hall, then slowly down Massachusetts Avenue, and more slowly down Commonwealth Avenue. The whole body beyond the shattered body could exist everywhere, at a street corner, in a passing car, in a window, and you looked for it. And sometimes you saw it. In someone you stood by at a corner waiting to cross the street, you saw the image of the body glorified and immortalized by grace.

The windows of the brownstone houses were open, and students were sitting on the sills or leaning out to talk to others on the sidewalk, and others were lounging on the stone steps. Sometimes they touched one another on the elbow, the shoulder, the cheek.

8

3

———— • ————

Outside a fraternity house, the door and all the windows open wide, a girl, wearing a sweat shirt and shorts, was talking to some men. She leaned in towards them, a hand out, and as I passed her, the men, five of them, closed round her.

At the end of the avenue, I stopped and looked across into the Boston Public Garden, where the light was green.

Entering the Garden, I pulled off my sweater; with my sweater I pulled out my shirt tails, and, as I was tucking them in, I thought, No, and I let them hang out. Inside the Garden, I unbuttoned my shirt and felt the air against my chest.

Off a curve of the path was a bank of grass, and I stopped on it. I practiced, in my mind, sitting in the least awkward way, as if I thought everyone was watching me to see how I would do it. I was not sure how I did it. The others on the bank of grass, which swelled up behind me and sank away into a hollow, were lying flat, and no one looked at me. I, too, lay flat. The grass was humid. When I sat up quickly, I was dizzy.

A group of three young women were sitting on a bank of grass on the other side of the path. One had her back to me. Her back was bare, and tanned, and when she leaned more towards the others the curved edge of the red dress came away and revealed the white skin of her body. The other two girls were listening to her talk. I saw her hands move. Her arms dropped and she turned her head away from the others, so I saw her in profile, frowning a little, as if she were thinking. One of the other girls was now talking, moving her hands. Perhaps the one in the red dress was

9

thinking about what she said, or what she was hearing, or both. Then the third girl spoke.

They seemed to be in big business, and were discussing that, and the business was complex and required a lot of talk. I felt that if any one of them had been left waiting by someone for hours, she wouldn't assume it was her fault and accept it in that way, but would think out, even discuss with others, why that person hadn't shown up, and decide if she'd ever see him again. What these young women were seriously discussing was the rights of a person who made a date and broke it. I believed that person had the right to do whatever he wanted, but they didn't, and I wished I could hear, in the same way I wanted to hear how a big business was run, what they said about him.

The girl with the red dress turned towards the others and spoke, her hands raised. One of the other two, facing me, started to plait her long hair loosely at the side of her neck, listening all the while. When she saw me looking at her, she flicked her loose plait over a shoulder and said something to her friends, so they all turned quickly towards me, then as quickly to one another, and they closed in.

After a while, I rolled over and lay looking at the sky. Then I sat up.

The girl who had braided her hair was combing it out with her fingers. She drew the strands out and up to the top of her head with one hand and held it piled on top with the other. She pulled up the long strands at her nape. When she placed both hands on her hair it hung in thick loops under her fingers. She smiled at me, lifted her hands, and her hair fell.

She scratched the side of her nose and rose a little, and for a moment I thought that she was going to come over to me. But she shifted her weight and looked away from me and continued to scratch her nose.

When she lounged back to listen to the girl in the red dress, the third girl, in a white dress, shifted to the side to give her room.

Though I couldn't see her mouth move, I saw the hands of the girl in the red dress move, more and more, as though she were stating her final decision.

The girl in the white dress unstrapped her sandals and took them off and pressed her toes into the grass. Her neck was smooth, her chin rounded, and her nose was round and smooth. The straps of her sleeveless dress were tied at her shoulders, and the thin white cloth hung away from her body.

I studied the details: her lower lip, the small, inward curve of her jaw into her earlobe, the shine high on her cheek, her temple, the downward curve of an eyebrow.

She appeared to be outside the talk of her friends, thinking of something that had nothing to do with them. Then, wincing, she looked up at the girl in the red dress and spoke briefly, after which they were all silent.

The other girl sat up and drew her fingers through her hair.

While the girl in the red dress talked again, the one in the white slowly ran the tips of her fingers along the top of her bodice, inserted her hand under, and held a breast.

As if the meeting had been called by the girl in the red dress, she ended it. She was tall, and her black hair was pinned up on her head. She talked down to the other two, who looked up at her.

I heard her say, "Well, then to hell – "

The two got up and, the girl in the white dress carrying her sandals, they all left.

I sat for a while, and got up and walked.

I rambled deeper into the Garden, towards the pond and the bridge, and on the bridge I stopped at the rail. Below me, one duck swam, its wake gurgling. I leaned my elbows on the stone rail to study the duck, which beat its wings against the water and flew off.

I crossed the bridge, then went down stone steps to the edge of the pond, and I crouched at the water's edge. The layers of light and water appeared to separate, and a fine layer of water, I thought, floated over a deep layer of light. From behind me someone threw something into the pond, and, startling me, the water and the light rose up in one bright spurt.

As I walked along a path I saw, alone in the middle of a green bench, the girl in the white dress. Some people passed between us, but once they passed she and I looked at one another.

This had to be thought out. It was like asking a girl at a hop if she wanted to dance. I always wished that the girls had to ask the boys to dance. Within three steps, however slow, I didn't have much time to think. People going past me walked in a speeded up way. I thought I had to talk to her because she expected me to. At least, I had to turn round to her and make a gesture – hunch my shoulders and raise my hands – to let her know that I'd like to stop but I had to go on and there was nothing I could do about it, and that way I wouldn't hurt her. I felt, suddenly, free to do anything I wanted. She wasn't looking at me. Standing in the middle of the path, I pushed my shirt tails under my belt, and as I was buttoning my shirt she did look at me. I went quickly to the empty bench across from her and sat.

Go on, I said to myself; do it.

I got up from the bench and stepped onto the path, out in front of a pedestrian who bumped into me. The girl on the bench laughed. I let the pedestrian pass, then I went straight to the girl and sat, without looking at her, at the end of the bench.

She leaned back and said, "You did that pretty well."

"Not very well."

She smiled. "Pretty well."

Though I didn't know what her business was, I knew it determined people's lives, and she couldn't have been over five years older than I. I was nineteen.

"Maybe we could take a walk," I said.

I let her lead the way, back towards the pond, over the bridge, and through the Garden to the gates on Charles Street. We were silent. I could not imagine what she was thinking. Across Charles Street, we sauntered onto the Common, our bodies, side by side, sometimes bumping at our hips.

At the side of the cement footpath was a black man on a bench, bent far over and placing cards, face down, on the cracked cement. In front of him another black man was standing looking now down at the cards, now along the path. The man setting out the cards was saying, "Choose a card, any card." The standing man, just as we were passing, pointed to the top of the seated man's head and said, "That one." The man with the cards turned

12

one over and announced in a loud voice, "You got it, you won ten dollars," and held up a bill. The girl stopped, and when she did the seated man lowered the hand with the ten dollar bill.

She asked him, "How do you play this game?"

The winner, who hadn't been given his ten dollars, folded his arms.

She said to him, "I know you're the con man."

The seated black man gave her a demonstration. They were all laughing.

When she looked round to see where I was, I went to her.

She asked the men, "Do you guys know of some place where we can play pinball?"

"Not any place you can get in," the dealer said.

"You don't know me," she said.

He laughed. The other man didn't laugh, but winced.

She said to me, "Come on. We'll go find a place."

She set the slow pace. We crossed Beacon Street, and I followed her up Bowdoin Street.

"Maybe we'll find some joint around here," she said.

She turned left, up the street behind the State House. Policemen were at the back entrance to the State House.

"In there, maybe," I said.

"For sure."

I was playing, and I wanted to, but I felt that I was playing against a sense of desertion, as of something general having gone out of the world, leaving only details, and all that could be done with the details was to play with them.

She told me her name was Jessica.

Mine, I said, was Dan.

I studied her blond hair swinging against her bare shoulders, her arms, the clavicle above her white, ruffled bodice.

Her silence made me think I must talk, must show her that I was interested in her. When I asked her about herself – "Are you from Boston?" – she talked about all the building being done in Boston. I wondered if she was trying to impress me with what she knew.

We turned into Louisberg Square.

13

I said, "There won't be a pinball arcade here."

She squinted at the windows. Then she asked me, "So what would you like to do?"

"Anything."

I led her down Beacon Hill, and on the way we sometimes separated to get round the garbage cans on the sidewalk. At the bottom, on Cambridge Street, we paused to look, beyond fences made of long sheets of plywood, at a vast building site. Around stark cement towers bulldozers were digging. There was water in the holes, and there were heaps of black earth by the holes. I asked her what was being built, and she told me. Maybe, I thought, she was working for the city. She was interested. She put everything together, as if all the millions of atoms of which the building scheme was composed were held together by her in the shape of a chair, or a shoe, or a milk bottle. She did this easily.

She kept talking as we went along Cambridge Street, past narrow restaurants with dirty windows, shops which sold automobile parts, and bars where, I thought, we would find pinball machines.

She was leading me. We turned to our left, back up Beacon Hill, along the brick sidewalk. Towards the top of Joy Street she stopped at a wooden house, painted lead grey, its steps worn down to the wood.

"This is where I live," she said.

I thought she was waiting for me to say I'd like to see her place.

When she went up the steps, I followed her. Through the small panes of the wide living room window was a magnolia tree in blossom. The room was warm. I thought she was crossing the room to open the window. A step from me, she seemed to have forgotten where she was going. She placed a hand on the side of my neck, then she went to the window, unlocked it and opened it.

I asked, "What do you talk about when you're with your girl friends?"

"Why do you want to know?"

"Because I wondered."

"Men," she said.

14

She raised a foot and slipped off one sandal, then the other, and threw them under the wing chair, which she sat on. Her dress rucked under her.

I sat in the middle of the velvet-upholstered sofa, silent. After a minute, I stretched out on the cushions, my head resting on one bulging arm, my shoes hanging over the other. I turned my head to the side and smiled at her, slouched in the wing chair. She drew her fingers through her hair. She looked me over, from head to shoes, one corner of her mouth lifted.

If I were in her arms, everything would be all right. But so much had to be thought out before that could happen. To make love with her would be to enter into some kind of business with her, and the agreement required careful attention. To put my arms around her, to kiss her, to insert my hand into her bodice might take all the consideration of committing my life to her. It would take a very long time for me to say, "I love you." She didn't move when I got up from the sofa.

After I dressed and kissed her and said good bye, I asked, "Can I see you again?"

She answered, "No, you can't."

I drew back. She was smiling.

"I think we'll make this a once upon a time deal," she said.

I left relieved that she didn't want to see me again.

4

————— • —————

I remained close to Charlie after we graduated from college and both of us, for a short time, lived in Boston. We met often to have lunch or supper in delis, or to go to bars.

He liked to show me the drawings he was doing at life class at the Boston Museum of Fine Arts. These were of large, nude women, done in conté crayon with thick, black strokes. They impressed me. I would have liked one of the drawings, as much for the big women who stood naked before Charlie, as for the drawing. He didn't offer one to me, however.

Then he showed me a series of drawings of a young woman, slender and yet full at the same time, both dressed and undressed. Charlie gave me one of these drawings. Nude, the model was lying on a bed.

I recognized her from the drawings as soon as I saw her. She was at a table with Charlie in the small upstairs restaurant where he'd asked me to meet him for supper. Charlie was pleased to introduce me to Roberta.

I could understand a man making love with a woman, but I could not understand a woman making love with a man. A man could easily hurt a woman by making love with her, even if it was only to chafe the skin of her face with his beard. I thought that women must find men, if not dangerous, painful. Charlie's blond beard was stubbled about his chin, and at the table I noticed Roberta look at it, look at his ears, eyes, nose, as he talked. I could not grasp her attraction to him. Surely, Charlie was, to her, too big, too rough. Surely, she didn't want to make love with him. And yet she did, I saw, because of what was most unfeminine about him: the hair curling over the neck of his undershirt, his veiny hands.

All the while Charlie talked, he gestured. He pressed the tips of the fingers of one hand together as if holding out an atom, too small for anyone to see, yet elemental; and his talk revolved and revolved around that atom, or I imagined it revolved around it because, as I couldn't see the atom, I didn't really see the point of Charlie's talk. He opened his fingers and raised his hand higher and higher, and, as he did, his voice also rose, to make his appeal heard by the world. I was embarrassed for him. I thought Roberta would suspect him of being a phony. I wanted to pull him away to be alone with him so I could listen to him talk without the worry that others would think his talk was nonsense. It was filled with his sense, as expansive as his smell. (Living with him I'd become familiar with his smell.) But Roberta enjoyed him.

His open palm held over his head, he was saying, "Now, my idea is – "

His body gave his talk subtlety, or whatever subtlety there was in it. That was Charlie's secret: he was able to infuse his words with the beauty of his body, and while you listened to him you sensed the warmth of his skin in words which would otherwise have been dead. Was it because of this that Roberta indulged him, I thought. But my sense of Charlie was mine, not hers; hers had to be different. For me, if it hadn't been for his body, Charlie would have been a fake, would have been as embarrassing to me when we were alone as when we were among people who frowned after the first five minutes of his talk. By the way she laughed sometimes, with a hard edge, I imagined Roberta might easily be seeing Charlie was a fake.

She and I ate and Charlie, gesturing with his fork, talked, and I wondered what I would do if she suddenly decided she didn't like him. I felt that it was my responsibility that she should. She must have liked him or she wouldn't have been with him, but I had the feeling she could, at any moment, change her mind, and I didn't want her to change her mind. If she decided she didn't like him, she wouldn't like me either.

17

Laughing, she said, "You're so funny, Charlie."

Though she didn't say much herself, she could, I knew, have taken over the conversation and talked Charlie into silence with a sentence. But she kept him talking by asking him questions, laughing. Her narrow, ironical questions sent Charlie off into wider, unironical airs. Or maybe he was more ironical than I thought. She must have been making fun of him, I thought, by asking him the questions she did, and he, smiling at her before he took them up, must have seen that she was; but he seemed to respond to her irony as if it were affection. I always treated Charlie seriously; maybe he didn't want to be treated seriously. She seemed to see ironies in Charlie I hadn't ever seen, not until now.

She was wearing a sweater, and a gold chain round her neck, and her heavy blond hair appeared almost wet when it swung as she leaned forward. The V at her neck showed soft skin; the fine chain was stuck to the side of her neck. I imagined that her covered arms, the sleeves pushed a little way up her wrists, and her covered breasts were bare.

I was unsure about the differences between sexes, and could only distinguish them by the feelings they aroused in me; and I noted, as I'd noted in the presence of many women, that Roberta's body was, to me, fixed solidly in her personality, which, being a unique personality, made her body unique, so it was as if she, as each woman, had her own sex. There was not a female sex.

To me, all men belonged to the same sex, and men did not have fixed personalities, nor fixed bodies.

Worried by the way Roberta would react to Charlie, because her reactions, being that of a woman, were unpredictable to me, I watched her more than I did him. To understand her meant studying the details of her body, all of which were, I thought, details of her self. As I felt I already knew her well enough to see that her personality was in her control, I felt that her body was in her control, and she could make it do whatever she wanted it to: she could decide she was sexually attracted to, say, dwarves. I imagined she was capable of peculiar sexual attractions. I never thought men's sexual attractions could be peculiar, because they did not depend, as they did in Roberta's case, on a choice, but on not being able to help their attractions, which were always larger than themselves. Roberta determined her attractions, and if she decided she wanted to make love with a dwarf, she did, and if she decided she didn't, she didn't. But there was no way of knowing – no way of my knowing – what made her make her decisions, and what might make her, suddenly, change her mind. She liked Charlie now. I wanted her to like him, and not only because in liking him she would like me; I wanted to because, in liking him, she became a little more general than she was, and I was not so worried by her.

All at once, she placed her fork on her plate and she sat away from her chair-back with her hands in her lap and her shoulders slumped. Her lids were half lowered as she looked at Charlie in a way she hadn't before, and he stopped talking.

Charlie brought some food to his lips, chewed a little, and, his mouth full, started to talk again, and to smile. He talked to no one but her. If I'd been talking, I would have tried to say what I thought she wanted to hear, though I'd always be unsure what that was. He talked as if he knew what he was doing. He knew she was listening to him.

I saw her lean slowly backwards till her shoulders rested on the chair-back. When she said, "You really are funny," her voice was low.

And here I remarked another difference between men and, from my point of view, a woman: that men were "visionaries", and she, Roberta, was – Charlie laughed, loud – "political." I almost wished Roberta wouldn't indulge Charlie, but reprimand him for being stupid. I should have reacted by saying, Charlie, you really can be stupid. But Roberta didn't, and I didn't.

A glow rose to his face, and with the glow a wide, wide smile, and he himself became, for a moment, an inhabitant of his bright world.

Blood rose to the surface of my skin, and I felt my penis turn.

Roberta reached across the table and touched Charlie's cheek. He was startled and laughed. She laughed.

19

Afterwards, Roberta told Charlie she wanted to walk with me alone and talk a little. Charlie put his hands on our shoulders he left us on the sidewalk to go in the opposite direction. I thought that Roberta would talk about Charlie, but she didn't. As she talked about Boston, we walked more and more slowly, and sometimes we stopped in the middle of the sidewalk.

Roberta's body drew me close to her for the warm smell that came off her.

Outside the house where she lived, I held her for a moment before saying good night. She might have thought I did it to let her know I was, in my way, happy about her relationship with Charlie. I was happy because with her I felt that the world was without ghosts, that objects – stones and trees and water – were not haunted by presences, that people were not lost souls.

5

————— • —————

After I left Boston, I lived in different cities, some abroad, for five years, and then I returned to Boston. At twenty-four, I was beginning to know a little what I felt towards men and women.

To me, men were like the inhabitants of a city, all characterized, as New Yorkers or Londoners or Parisians or Romans were, by their city.

A woman was incomprehensible to me for her individuality, and I was more interested in her as a person than in any one man; I was not interested in men as individuals, but I wanted to live in their city.

I had a job teaching foreign students English in a private school.

On Friday and Saturday evenings, I went to a bar (near the bus station) where only men went. During a holiday week in the early summer, I went to the bar often, when the sun was still high. After the glare, I could not see the walls or floor or ceiling, but red bulbs fixed at crazy distances from one another in the darkness. The hot bar smelled of cigarette smoke, beer, damp cement, and sudden whiffs of cologne. As soon as I had bought my bottle of beer and stood at the bar, swigging, I looked at the barman.

His long arms bare to the shoulders, reaching in all directions as though at once, he opened bottles, poured out drinks, placed them on the wet bar. His sweaty neck and face gleamed in the red light. A kind of official, he knew the laws of the place, because here there were no written laws but laws by precedent. He was young, but he knew everything. Listening to someone describe a broken affair, he smiled and wiped his hands on a towel. Watching him, I drank down the bottle of beer and then ordered another. Whenever I asked for a beer from him, I felt that I was serving him.

The bottle held out, I turned to face the room. In turning, I exposed myself, as if I became naked. I held the bottle of beer up higher. I caught myself making many small adjustments to my body; leaning on the bar and bending one knee then unbending it, putting one foot before the other then moving it back, drawing in my stomach to let my belt sling further down my hips. I tried to make myself stand still.

Among the red lights, three men, not far from me, stood leaning together, talking. Whereas everyone else seemed to walk about as if not quite sure where they were going, these three stood at a center, turned away from the rest. They didn't notice me. I raised my bottle to my eyes to see how much beer was left in it. I didn't belong to any country, really, so they could not make me feel, if it ever occurred to them to want to, that I was excluded.

Thrusting myself away from the bar, I swung my bottle up, drank, and walked about the room swinging my bottle. I wanted everyone to think I was there by some momentary choice, and as soon as my beer was finished I would leave.

I was, myself, my own country, different from and above any other.

At the back of the room, in a corner, was a wide metal door with an illuminated EXIT sign above. The sheet metal was dented, and around the edges were cracks of light from the summer evening outside. If I pressed the bar, the door would open, and I would find myself in an alley.

Nothing should come of the possibilities aroused by people of the same sex being drawn together, and yet some promise, as elliptical as a body smell, held me. All together, but not singly, these men possessed a sex which was different from my own.

Turning away from the door, I drew back when the three young men passed me to go to stand by a pinball machine in a corner of the bar. They wore white dress-shirts, the collars unbuttoned, the sleeves folded back on their forearms. One gave his bottle to another and rolled his sleeves further up his arms, and the other two watched him; he took his bottle again and drank, and the other two continued to watch him. He talked and the others listened.

I studied them all as if from a great distance. A shock came over me when I saw the one with the rolled-up sleeves look towards me, then at me, and I felt that distance contract, and they were all suddenly near. I stood away from the wall as he and I looked at one another. When he turned to the others, I thought it was because he'd been asked a question. As he turned back to me, I stepped forward, not quite sure of my footing, and he, seeing me come forward, turned altogether away from me. I saw his hair, his ears, his nape, the stiff collar, the neat seams of his shirt, his belt, the back pockets of his chinos, the creases, the heels of his loafers.

One of the others was standing sideways to this first one. He was taller, his cheekbones and jaw sharp. He had a more intelligent body, if there was such a thing, than the first, whose body was, after all, dumb. I wondered if the first one said something about me, because the thin one glanced towards me. Our eyes met and I thought: him. But he glanced away.

The third one wasn't that attractive, and yet I looked at him with my expectation aroused, and the more I did, the more I saw he was, really, the most attractive of the three. He didn't look round at me, but the fact that he didn't made me sure that he knew I was there and that he wanted to look. He laughed too much, running a hand through his hair, when one of his friends said something.

For a moment, I felt I was making a choice from among hundreds, maybe thousands of possibilities, and I was completely free. In the next moment, however, that free choice would stop being a choice, and become a need. I would suddenly become possessed by this young man, if I dared myself to think: him. I didn't want him, didn't want what one man had.

He pushed his sleeves up his arms, and they fell back; he undid

23

and did up the buttons of his shirt. His clothes appeared a little damp at the shoulders, arms, curves of his chest, his buttocks, his thighs. His clothes would have taken in the warm moisture of his skin, its smell, and, perhaps, its sensitivity, because the clothes themselves seemed alive. Whereas the clothes of the others stiffly encased them, his shirt and trousers moved with him.

I wanted him. He must have known that I did, because he reacted. When he looked round at me, it was not to reassure himself that I was there looking at him, but to let me know he had his body and I didn't have any, and he almost smiled. He looked away and did smile. In its awareness of itself his body became the most beautiful I had ever seen in my life. He stretched out an arm as if reaching for something, then ran a hand up and down it so the sleeve was raised high. He reached behind a shoulder to scratch, I imagined, the itching cloth at the shoulder and yanked it so his shirt was pulled a little from his trousers. Again he turned towards me and, as he did, he undid the top button and slid his hand inside to touch his chest, and he did it to tell me: this is mine.

By my lowered look I told him: no, it's mine.

I felt our views of one another were controlled by movements of our heads, so that when I pulled, he looked away, and when I looked away, too, just at the moment he looked again at me, he pulled me back. Our faces were impassive. I was almost able to pull him towards me, in little jerks. He said something to his friends. The tall one said something, and they all laughed. They all turned away and leaned in towards one another.

Though I kept my eyes on him for a while longer, he didn't look back.

I walked away and stood in another spot, against a wall.

I caught my body making odd movements.

Then I saw a young man standing along the wall to my right, who, raising his bottle to his lips, lowered it without drinking when he saw I had my eyes on him. He thrust his jaw forward and stuck out his lower lip. First I studied the empty bottle, then the ceiling, then the floor, and then I turned to look towards my left. Someone down the wall on my left was looking at me. I was amused to be between the two, and I glanced back at the first, who was leaning sideways against the wall to stare at me, and again at the second, who was standing away from the wall to face me squarely. Given there was no difference I could make out between them, I asked myself what should make me choose one instead of the other. With only a slight sense of daring, because I didn't care much, I stepped towards the first, holding my empty bottle out to him, but before I spoke he pushed himself away from the wall and left. Quickly, I went to the bar, bought another beer and returned to the wall to stand closer to the second but, as I was taking a gulp of beer, he left.

I thought I should go, and I swigged down my beer to empty the bottle. The door opened and I noticed it was dark outside. The red neon sign on the front of the bar room reflected in cars parked by the kerb. I was sweating.

The toilet was behind the bar. The door was open, and a black man was standing at the bowl. The stream of his pee splashed so much, I imagined it would splash over the edge. I wanted to see him pee, and got a little closer. I imagined that here he wouldn't mind, but he kicked the door shut with the heel of a shoe to finish. I didn't look at him when he came out.

I left the door open when I used the toilet.

When I came out I saw at the bar, alone, the young man I had wanted. His presence startled me, because he had ceased to exist and all I'd retained of him was a recollection. I stopped at the end of the bar, imagining the room was empty except for him. I stepped to the bar and put my hand on it, and, as I did so, he looked up at me, then looked down. It occurred to me: maybe he had been following me around after freeing himself of the others. The bartender came to me and I politely ordered another bottle of beer. He smiled when he gave me the dripping bottle. As I drank, I looked down the bottle at the young man and saw he was looking at me. I lowered my bottle and returned his look as if from a height. I was taking a great risk. He might decide I was playing a game with him, which was worse than my simply not being interested. With his elbows on the edge of the bar and his shoulders hunched so his head lolled, he glanced to right and left,

25

VISTA

but he kept looking back at me.

I recognized what happened to me when I became possessed. I could hardly take in that young man, except in details: not an ear, but the lobe of an ear; not his neck and chin, but the curve of his jaw under the earlobe; not his hair, but a fine curl behind his ear. And even these details gave way to greater details, details of points of light against darkness. I knew what was happening. It had happened before. Of course, I knew the horrors, but the horrors came later, and what came now was that sense, that deepeningly amazed sense, of something happening for which you will give up everything. This happened to me only with men, and only with men I didn't know. Among them, I didn't have to do anything, didn't even have to move, and it happened.

My pulse pumping, I kept telling myself: You must do something.

But I didn't want to do anything. I thought: It'll happen, and you'll have him.

No, I thought, it won't happen unless you go to him.

He pushed himself up from the bar, walked along it and came round the corner. He stood in front of me, his face stern.

A total self-possession came over me.

He had a low, resonant voice. His name was Henry. He was Bostonian.

None of this mattered. What mattered was his body, so near me I could have reached out and touched it. From the exposed parts – his hands, his wrists, his forearms, his neck, the glimpse of his clavicle under his open collar – I tried to imagine all of it.

I wanted to be modest and say things that would interest him, not about myself – because I didn't think that would interest him – but about Boston.

When he leaned towards me to hear better in the roar, I thought I sensed the warmth of his moist body. I leaned very close to his flushed ear to speak.

For a locked moment, we leaned towards one another.

He drew away and said something and I answered, eagerly, "I know just what you mean. I'm like that, too."

His brow lowered as if I had said something, if not wrong, at

26

least out of place, and he wasn't going to answer me. He said, "Excuse me," and he walked away, across the room to someone, and they talked.

I tipped the bottle up to drink more, but there was no more in it. Rolling the bottle between my palms, I stared at the bartender.

What I'd done wrong was to talk about myself.

The bartender came over when I raised my hand. I asked him for another beer.

When I looked across the bar room again, the two were gone.

I wandered around with my beer.

You shouldn't be able to bear yourself for the embarrassment you cause yourself, I thought.

I knew these moments, too. They were more familiar to me than any other kinds of moments, and they could turn me, if I didn't turn against them, into someone I would despise: someone who tried to live in the strict terms of his false self. I had met many who did. Perhaps I didn't have enough style to assume a fine edged cynicism which allowed me extravagances of emotion and reasoning. With that cynicism, you could do anything and you remained irreproachable, to yourself even more than to anyone else. You would never embarrass yourself. It might have been that I had not embarrassed myself enough, as I was sure some men I'd met had, when they'd been as young as I: embarrassed themselves so deeply, so often that all that could save them was cynicism in a grand style. In some, much older men, the style had terrified me, not only for its cynicism but for its grandness. I understood these men. I had met some, and respected some, but, really, I could not be one because of my sense of risk. They could not take what to me was the greatest risk: the risk of embarrassing myself by pretentions so vast I was a fool to risk them.

Someone tapped me on the shoulder.

6

—————•—————

The warm, clear night was high and wide. Walking beside him, I didn't ask him where we were going.

He talked about Boston.

We entered the Public Garden. The darkness there expanded under the dark trees.

He too had, I thought, the sense that we were going anywhere, to do anything. And we knew that whatever we did, it needed no consideration.

We climbed Beacon Hill, then down the other side, where he lived in a narrow, brick building.

As he opened the door to his apartment, I wished, suddenly, I were back in the bar. I didn't want one person, didn't want someone who lived in a particular apartment in a particular building on a particular street. I followed Henry into the small entrance hall, where he turned on an overhead light which made his hair shine.

Without thinking I grabbed his head and he tried to draw it away. I yanked it back, closer, to kiss his eyes, nose, his mouth. He held my hair, turning my head at angles to kiss it all, to wet it with his saliva. He pulled my shirt out of my trousers as I pulled his out, and, still pressing together and kissing, our noses and chins knocking into one another, we wedged our hands between our chests to undo one another's buttons and pull our shirts off. As I pressed, writhing a little, against his exposed chest, more revealing of him than anything else I could know about him, I felt rise in me the sudden impulse to say, I love you.

I licked his cheek, his ear. He dug his fingers into my back to press me closer to him, so close I felt that if he let go we would spring away from one another, and, keeping me so tensely close, he sucked at the side of my neck. Again I wanted to say, I love you.

When we drew away from one another it was only long enough to kick off our shoes and pull off our socks before we drew in together again, with a force that had us pressing as though to hold each other, kiss one another, more deeply than our arms and lips could. I forced my tongue into his mouth, his nostrils, his ears, and his eyes; his face was slippery with my saliva. While I kissed him, he drew his thighs away, undid my belt, unzipped my fly, and shoved my underpants down with my trousers. My erection got caught in my underpants, and I released it with a finger; then I slid off my trousers and underpants and, as he looked down and watched me, I unbuckled and unzipped him and pushed his trousers and underpants down to his feet and he stepped out of them. We remained separate, looking at one another. It seemed to me I had expected him to have another sex, one different from mine, different from any I'd known. He looked up at me and smiled.

As he stepped towards me, I stepped away, out of the light, so he wouldn't see my body.

I had not made love often. The first contact with another's body was still, to me, the most amazing sense the world allowed.

Our arms around one another, we went into his living room. We didn't get as far as his bedroom. As if he couldn't go further, he pulled me down onto the sofa, where, on the cushions, we thrashed and bounced, locking together and unlocking our arms and legs. One of the cushions slid from beneath us, another flipped up. From a point of view above us, which I took from time to time, we were fighting, not trying to break one another down into one position, but trying to break one another into many positions. Over him, on my knees, his legs between mine, I clenched him in my arms and lifted while he tried, his arms clenched about me, to pull me down. With a wrenching motion, he turned us over and our bodies fell apart, but we hung on to one another, he about my neck, I about his shoulders, and he twisted a leg around one of mine. I tried to turn him over, and we dropped off the edge of the sofa. I fell on him, and he immediately locked both his legs around mine and held my arms so I couldn't move, all the while kissing me. When I tried to kiss him, he drew his head back; I strained my neck forward to reach him with my mouth, but couldn't, so rocked up and down to try to kiss him, and when I did he bit my lips. On the floor, we rolled over and over, and each time we did, as with a spasm, we unlocked our arms and legs and locked them again in another position. Sometimes, my face pressed into the side of his neck, or his shoulder, or a buttock, we strained our holds on one another so our muscles and tendons stood out and we remained motionless, until, again spasmodically, one of us let go, and we rolled into another position. We were sweating and our bodies slid against one another. I licked his armpit, his navel, and sucked at his erection. I felt his body convulse as he shouted, and that convulsion and that shout made me shout, too. We remained on the floor, holding one another. When he fell away, our sperm drew out between our stomachs. He lay back loosely on the floor, his arms extended over his head, his eyes closed, and I lay sideways by him.

He rolled his head towards me and asked me, hoarsely, if I would spend the night.

"If you want me to," I said.

"I want you to."

I felt everything in me give way to him.

His body was wet and his hair was thick with sweat. He raised himself heavily, as I did, then I followed him down a passage way into the bedroom, where the bed was unmade. Dun light came in from down the passage way. Tangled in the top sheet was a towel; he pulled it out, wiped his stomach, and gave the towel to me. It was stiff with dry sperm and it scratched. I threw it on the floor and lay down on the bed beside him. He lay on his back, his arms folded under his head. The wrinkled sheets smelled of body odor. The room was hot. As if it occurred to him all at once that I was beside him, he turned his eyes to me; he looked at me for a moment, his face stark, then raised himself and leaned over to kiss me. His eyes closed, he fell onto his back again, his arms by his sides, his legs stretched out and separated, his cock lying backwards on his pubic patch.

Propped on an elbow, I scanned his body, and my sense of it was of there being too much of it to see, to touch. And while trying to take it in, fixing on the details – the little fold of flesh at the arm pit – you knew you were missing what gave the real shape. You never saw what counted, but what distracted you. You thought the exposed details didn't count, but something else did, which was not invisible, but visible if only you could see it. Finally, you knew that the details seemed to distract because you saw them as parts, not all together, and it was only in seeing them all together that you'd know what drew you with the concentration of someone possessed. But there were too many details to take in, to take in and remember. Presented with an infinity of cells, how could you bring them together so that the cells disappeared and a body appeared?

The apparition of the body was your own doing, and you had to strain your attention to make it appear from such a mass.

He might have been asleep, his breathing light, and I didn't want to wake him, but wanted to touch him. Instead, I pulled at the sheet.

I wondered how many people he had made love with on this sheet. It was penetrated with the presences of how many lovers, their sweat and saliva and whatever sperm hadn't been wiped away by the towel? I smoothed out the wrinkles between our bodies and was reminded of the sheets I used to see in the college dormitory pulled from the beds by women every Monday morning and thrown into piles in the corridors. As I passed them I used to imagine they retained the impressions of all the bodies that had slept in them, had jerked off and maybe made love with others in them, and I wanted to fall into one of the piles. I recalled going down a flight of stairs and turning to see a bundle of sheets tumbling towards me, thrown down by a cleaning woman at the top, and I stood and let the bundle, unloosening, tangle about my legs, then I reached down and bundled it together in my arms and

31

dropped it on the landing. Out of his sheets rose the bodies Henry had made love with. They engorged my possessiveness of him.

He had a watch on, and I wondered why I hadn't noticed it before. The watch seemed to cover him, so he was not exposed as I wanted him to be. It attached him to a country of constraints, and his body, for me to make love with it, had to be a country of total freedom, where we had the right to make love with everyone. I had to take that watch off his wrist. On my knees, I leaned close, slipping my fingers under the band to undo it as carefully as I could. When I got it off, I rose and found Henry staring at me. I placed the watch on the bedside table then, still kneeling, turned back to him. He was now completely naked, the completeness like something beyond one's understanding.

He kept his eyes on mine. He was frowning, and I wondered what he was thinking. When I glanced down to his groin, I saw he had an erection lying back on his stomach. It seemed to me that this could have nothing to do with me. Perhaps I didn't want it to have anything to do with me. I wanted it to have to do with all the lovers rising from the sheets. I looked into his eyes again, filled with thought. He could not, however, have been thinking about me.

What kept us apart was the desire, closely considered, of all the possible ways of making love, and the desire, when we were in each other's arms, to hold all those possibilities open. There was something deeply thoughtful in the way we moved towards each other, he rising as I lowered myself. I was thrown off balance as much by my thinking as by the awkward way I shifted my position. Carefully considering what we were doing, we inserted fingers in one another's mouths, into one another's anuses.

We sat cross-legged before one another, our knees pressing; we ran our hands over each other's heads, shoulders, abdomens, and sometimes one of us leaned in close as the other got to his knees to take the wet head of his cock into his mouth, saliva bubbling and drooling about his lips.

I put my hand on his chest and thought that what I most wanted from him was that he should be different from me, but that he wasn't, he was like me.

For him to be not one man, but many, a countless number, was to promise that one of these many men was different at least in having done what I hadn't yet done. But that meant doing what was beyond arms and legs, cocks and mouths and assholes to do. No multiplicity of men, however great, was any more capable of doing more than one man could do to realize the truly unimaginable. An orgy of men was reduced, finally, to what was familiar. A multiplicity of men suggested involvement with something shared among them, and the more men, the more shared the involvement among them, the more abstract that something was, and the more abstract, the higher above my imagination it went, towards something so different it was not even humanly conceivable. To keep myself aroused by him, I would have to see him as not one of many, but many, too many for love making.

Maybe it was a hairy mole, to the side of a nipple, that reduced Henry's body to a low fact and made it no different from mine.

And, after all, no man's body was really different from mine. All my strained attempts to see the relationship of two bodies of the same sex, not as an image of one body contemplating itself, but of two bodies contemplating one another for the differences that made each appear to the other to be more than a body, were attempts to give spirit to a body that had no spirit. And that was what I did, had always done: started with the spirit and tried to give it body, started with the vague idea and tried to make it a fact, always more interested in the spirit and the idea, because to me they appeared to promise everything. Everything was in the spirit of another's body, and not my own. My own body was without spirit. But so, now, was his.

I knew that no amount of passionate exploration would lead me to discover that he had, in the essential way I wanted, a sex as yet unknown to me.

It wasn't that I wanted him to be a woman.

I wanted him, in his body, to be altogether similar to me and altogether different. The potency of the difference should be great in inverse proportion to the similarity. The more like mine

33

his body was, the more different I needed to believe it was.

I didn't want him to be a woman because a woman's body could not be abstracted from her.

My longing for him to be spirit, and utterly sensual as spirit, was so great it couldn't be reduced to detail. The details of his body couldn't account for what his body did to me in rousing such a longing for something more than those touchable details. He, slouching and loose-limbed, closed his eyes as if he were meditating, and I raised my hand again and placed it on the side of his neck. He hefted his shoulder and lowered his jaw against my hand and smiled a little. The body I was really attracted to, the body I wanted to be aware of at its fullest, was larger than any false idea I might have of it, and it was this that must take me over. Perhaps the difference between us was that he had a spirit in my longing for him to have a spirit, and I had no longing for one in myself.

My hand caught between his shoulder and jaw, he fell backwards, so I fell forward onto him, and we continued to explore one another's bodies.

I wanted to do to him something I had never done before with anyone else. Because my sexual encounters hadn't been frequent, after each one I'd thought it out carefully, not so much to go over what I had done as to figure out what, next time, I'd do that I hadn't yet done. I'd tell myself: remember to run your tongue along the gums under the lips, to run a finger along that puckered ridge between the asshole and the scrotum. In meditative pauses, tracing his outlines with a finger, I wondered what I could do for the first time.

My tongue exuding spit, I licked him, as he lay still, from a big toe, up to a knee, up the inside of his leg, up under a hanging ball, around the pubic patch, at an angle up the groove in his groin to his hip, from his hip to his navel, up the softly undulating space between his abdominal and pectoral muscles to the hollow at the base of his throat, up under the stubble-rough chin and to his lips, which were open. I didn't kiss him, but collected more saliva and spat into his mouth, and he moved his tongue in the saliva before he swallowed. And then I kissed him.

At the same time I felt a small disgust, I felt the need to say, I love you.

Whatever we were doing to one another, we were in control, a delicate control sustained by the desire to experiment.

He rolled me over to do something I, even without knowing what it was, would have to submit to. I lay on my stomach, head to foot on the bed, the sheet rucked up under me. I felt his tongue slithering between my buttocks. I felt disgust and love together. I knew what the Biblical "a stirring in the bowels" meant, and writhed as his wet tongue went in. My bowels loose, I could, just then, have shit in his face. I thought: How could anything that so fills me with disgust fill me, too, with a love almost unbearable? And what more disgusting things might make me feel even more unbearable love, so unbearable the only expression equal to it, the only expression that could make it bearable, would be to shit on him?

Then something happened between us. It came over us to go as far as we dared, even if our experiments might go too far and destroy the very freedom which inspired them.

I lay so limply, he rolled me over with difficulty; I lay intentionally passive, arms and legs akimbo. He was kneeling over me.

What he'd done a moment before expressed, for the very intimacy the disgust inwardly suggested, some strangely moving love; now his just touching me on the arm, with an outward suggestiveness of no more than light intimacy, left me cold.

When he grabbed my erect cock in his two hands and jerked it, he said, "Fuck."

I yanked his head down by his hair.

Embarrassment being an awareness of oneself as false, we were attempting to assume, in the falseness, attitudes which would shock. We could have invented entire personalities for ourselves in our expansive falseness, and it was in this, more than anything else, that we could devise acts no one before us had performed.

On his knees, he kept pulling at my erection. He said with a

35

high voice, "Tell me about the people you've fucked with."

"No."

"Tell me."

My voice, too, was high. "Tell me if you've ever asked anyone that."

"No."

"I think you're lying. Are you lying?"

"Yes."

When he said that, I felt a sudden rush up into my erection. "Stop," I said, "I'll come."

"I won't stop."

"I'll come."

"No, you won't. You can control it. Tell me," he said.

My voice went shrill. "I can tell you about the first time I fucked with my room-mate." I laughed. "I don't want to tell."

"Tell me."

I rose up and grabbed his cock and sucked it, my saliva splattering, and when I pulled back I looked at the wet, red, swollen head.

"He had a more beautiful cock than even you have," I said.

He hit me on the cheek with his cock. "No, he didn't."

"He did. Every time I jerk off, I think of it. I'll always think of it. It's a picture I carry around with me that I pray to."

"Are you a fucking Catholic?"

"Yes."

The cold I felt exuded a fine sweat.

"Aren't you ashamed, a Catholic fucking like this?"

"No."

"Tell me about fucking your room-mate."

He hit me again on the face with his cock. I laughed. He hit me again.

"Tell me," he said.

I could make up a pornographic story that had nothing to do with what had happened, like the stories men told one another about the men they'd fucked. As he tapped my cheek, sometimes my lips, with his cock, I said, stopping often to swallow my saliva, "We were spending the weekend at the lake. He said we

36

should play strip poker, so we sat on the floor and played the game. He was the first one naked."

"Did he have a hard-on?"

"No. I said there was a rule to the game, that after a person was naked, if he lost again, he had to be given a hard-on."

"Did he lose again?"

"He didn't lose again until I was naked, then he lost. I sucked his cock. When he had a hard-on, we went on with the game."

"You should be a writer," Henry said. He nudged his cock into my face.

"I said there should be another rule. Whoever lost after being given a hard-on had to be fucked. He said he didn't want to go on, but I said he had to play the game. With his streak of bad luck, Charlie lost again. I grabbed him before he was able to get out of the room and pulled him to the sofa – " I was shivering with the cold sweat, which coated me like thin slime. Henry's cock was sticking up before me, nudging my cheek just under my right eye. I looked up at his face. "I don't want to go on," I said.

He frowned a little.

I laughed. "This is silly."

"Is it?"

"Yes."

The frown went from his face and he sat back on his legs, his hands on his knees. "All right," he said.

As soon as he said this I felt something given up I didn't want to give up but to hold. My blood began to drain out of me. Not sure what I would do, I crawled on all fours up to him, where, on my knees, I reached for one of his nipples and pinched it, then twisted it. He winced a little, looking down at what I was doing, but he didn't say anything. His shiny red erection, sticking up from between his legs, looked ridiculous. I wanted him to think he was a fool for it. My blood rose up again in me when I leaned forward and closed my teeth about his nipple.

We pulled the sheet up from the mattress when he or I grabbed it to hold onto something, apart from one another to steady ourselves, and temptations came over me. They were like inspirations which had no real object; inspired to make love, I

37

couldn't think of anything equal to the inspiration. The temptations were everything, and they surrounded me as if pulling me in different directions to realize them. The moment I went in one direction I would feel myself pulled in another. Not able to act – and, somehow, not wanting to – I nevertheless felt the impulse to act, an impulse that urged, Do it, do it. But I didn't know how to, couldn't, do it. The more we made love, the stronger the temptations became. Sometimes I felt so pulled to one side I thought I must give in, still without knowing what I would be giving in to. When it did verge, suddenly, towards one direction – my chafing the stubble of my beard hard against his jaw for what seemed hours – it would flash in my mind that what we were doing no longer had anything to do with making love. My own body was tingling from being chafed hard. And when he held me, on my stomach with my arms locked behind my back so I couldn't move, as he chafed my nape, it flashed again that we had gone far from sex.

I couldn't believe that he felt what I felt, or, even, that I could arouse feelings in him. If his feelings were in any way like mine at the moment I experienced them, their arousal was caused by what had to do only with him, as if he were at a distance from me and no connections could be made between our feelings. And yet, when he turned me over and straddled my thighs and looked down at me, I recognized in his eyes and the set of his jaw my own sense of wanting to press our love making, or whatever it was we were doing, outside our bodies. It was as if I could hear him thinking, It isn't enough, it isn't enough just driving my cock up his ass, there must be something else.

Whatever he did would be incidental to his need. That need frightened me. He smiled, his wet hair stuck out. As he lowered his face slowly towards mine, I said, with a deep, unfamiliar voice:

"You look crazy."

I stopped him from doing what he was about to do. The moment I saw the uncertainty in his eyes, I grabbed his shoulders and pulled him off balance, so he fell. I clinched my arms tightly about him.

38

I believed I could do anything. The danger inherent in imagining I could do anything was not in what I would do; the danger was in what I could do.

If I asked myself the question, Could I draw blood? the answer had to be, Yes. Not only was I capable of what was human, I was, too, of what was inhuman. A potent smell emanated from our sweating bodies as I fucked him, he lying submissively, his face crushed sideways into a bare part of the mattress. But fucking him wasn't enough to control everything I was determined to control. I thrust my erection more and more roughly into his asshole. His eyes closed, he grunted. I clenched my teeth, wanting to say something more than "Fuck", some word strong enough to express my desires.

My cock, as I pulled back to thrust in more forcefully, slipped out. I took it in my hand. It was gleaming red, dripping with fluid.

If I used my imagination, really put it to use to invent experiments meant for shocking discoveries, not even the most original imaginings would, finally, appear to me original enough. I was capable of imaginings, I knew I was. I also knew that I would never believe I had come upon the one shocking discovery that all my experimenting was meant for, the one shocking discovery that would reveal all. And because my imagination would keep trying and trying for greater and greater originality, it might try to make of me an original – that is, a grotesque.

Perhaps the great fear was just that of being like anybody else.

But that was backed up always with the fear of what you would do to be extraordinary. The mattress seemed to shift. I knew this sensation of a short, abrupt movement outside me came from the impulse to do the most extreme I was capable of. That wouldn't be a sustained action, but a spontaneous act. I could have – I wouldn't have, but I was positive I could have – cut off his cock, or, more likely, mine, and to do it for no other reason but that it was possible.

Frowning, he raised himself and looked round at me, wondering what I was doing.

My erect cock in my hand, I wanted to make a joke. I laughed before knowing what I was going to say. I said, "What a fool's tool."

I saw his frown deepen, and, as I laughed, he lunged at me and threw me backwards onto the mattress. My head hit the headboard, then slid down, so my neck bent and my chin pressed into my chest. My limbs twisted under me, I was unable to move because he pinned me down, and he tried to pin me down more by continuing to lunge at me with his chest, all the while punching my shoulders. My joints, my neck, seemed to lock. All I could do was force myself to laugh in a way to let him know I thought he was just fooling.

He said, "Stop it."

My laughter was false.

He slapped my face. "Stop it."

Perhaps he was just fooling, because I saw him smile, his face so close to mine it blurred. With a wrenching movement, I threw him off me, and was only able to rise before he lunged at me again and pinned me down again, this time sprawled crosswise on the bed. He grabbed one of my arms and was just about to try to turn me over and twist the other arm up my back when I yanked myself free. He tried again to grab one of my arms as I flailed them and, when I unintentionally hit him in the face with a hand, he fell forward onto me so my breath shot out. He slid his arms under my arms, and with one hand dug into a shoulder and with the other held my chin and the lower part of my face and twisted my head to the side. I could have got out of the hold by hunching my slippery shoulders, but I knew he was fighting me, and I remained still. When I tried to turn my head to look at him, his fingernails cut into my cheek; but I was able to roll my eyes towards him enough to see his face, red and running with sweat. His anger couldn't have been caused just by me, nor his desperation. Feelings blew up and separated themselves from us to billow like huge, sweat-wet, windy sheets around us. He snorted. Then he let me go, slid sideways off my body and turned his back to me, his dishevelled head on an extended arm.

His body appeared huge in the still room.

I sat up, breathing heavily. I raised my knees, rested my elbows on them, and looked at Henry.

In a small voice, I asked, "What's wrong?"

He didn't move, and I didn't expect him to. When I felt a stickiness run down my thigh I glanced down to see my drained penis, fluid pouring from it like transparent blood. I was the person to say, Everything is wrong. I looked at his back, his head, his buttocks, his arm, his legs.

I was terrified of everything, as I was terrified of the unknown.

I longed to hold Henry's body.

If I touched him, though, he'd pull away, or push me away.

Frightened, I put a hand on his shoulder, and he immediately dropped onto his back, as though thrown from a height; his head to the side, and his eyes, like his head, rolling a little, he smiled. I leaned over, and, with my unbalanced body falling forward, I clasped him. He, too, had lost his erection. We remained still.

When he kissed me, I felt my body stir in response, and I kissed him. If our kisses were embarrassing to us, we admitted our embarrassment. Not speaking, we were in our speechless embraces and kisses nevertheless close to admitting everything, all the moles, pimples, scars on our bodies.

There was in our love making, somehow, an awareness of the vanity of it, and admitting the vanity was admitting everything. There was nothing beyond the love making, however violent it was.

A great pity for Henry came over me. The pity was entirely for him, and I made love to him as if to commiserate with him for the very fatality of his living skin and muscles and blood. I brushed his hair away from his forehead and kissed it, and then I stroked the sides of his face with both hands.

I did not know if it was my sex which attracted me to death and artifice, but I knew that the easiest fantasy for me, one that occurred of itself, was this: of the pale body at its most beautiful, dead. My imagination, isolated in my skull, engendered images of the body submerged in water, or floating in air, the limbs softly rising and falling in the currents. These images were as easy for me to conjure as metaphors and similes, and I had come

41

to recognize them as products of a mind which tried to make them relevant by believing they suggested more than what they were. The more removed they were, the more I attempted to see in them greater and greater relevance, and that, finally, was the relevance death had. The fact that I should think the relevance could only be made in the image came from the belief that, against death, the image had to survive in itself. I could so easily see the body surviving its death in the holy picture of a dead body, which roused all one's pity.

What made me relevant was what extended me beyond myself. All I could extend myself into, however, was the possibility, as illusive as metaphor and simile, that there was an outside. My overwhelming longing for possibility, in which I looked for salvation, exposed my isolation.

Shifting his weight, he turned me over and lay on me. He held me and kissed my face.

I felt a strange numbness around my erection.

Our love making had to have a meaning, and I would give it meaning.

He tightened his arms around me and held me while he licked my eyes, temples, ears. I turned my face from side to side, not so he wouldn't be able to reach it, but so that he would just be able to reach it, and that slight tension of his reaching out and my drawing back, or my reaching and his drawing back, went throughout our bodies.

I made a crazy act of faith: in the certain knowledge that our love making had no meaning, I nevertheless believed that it did.

Our longings existed as our bodies existed.

All, all of the outside was in Henry's body.

We fell down together as we held one another.

We were two ridiculous young men holding one another.

Our crossed arms rubbed. Henry spit into his hand for lubrication, then kept his little finger out and crooked. It was taking a long time. My wrist was aching. Sometimes, Henry stopped, threw his head back and said, "Ah," and I moved my hand frantically, but nothing more happened, and he started again.

42

Just when I took my hand from Henry's erection he grabbed my nape and went rigid. I continued. His thighs rose. He shook his head so the sweat switched from it, all the while his chest going in and out with deep inhalations and exhalations. He shut his eyes to wrinkles. I covered the head of his erection with my hand, and I saw the sperm ooze out between my fingers. He fell, the back of his head knocking heavily against my shoulder, and he turned to press his face hard into my shoulder.

I slid my hand, coated with his sperm, up and down my erection as I held onto Henry with my other hand.

I thought, I am a fool, I am a fool, and I ejaculated into the air.

A kind of wail came from me, which surprised me as much as it seemed to surprise Henry. I felt the tension of his hold slowly release, and I, too, released my hold. But we didn't fall asleep.

We lay for a long time, our arms loose about one another, our eyes open but not looking at one another. We shifted a little when he or I felt an arm going to sleep, but we remained awake. His eyelids kept blinking. To pull him towards me and kiss him, as I wanted to do, would have taken energy I found difficult to believe I'd ever had. It seemed a very long time that we lay as we were. At moments, his eyes glanced as if at something outside the bed. When he pulled himself closer to me, I had the feeling he did because he was frightened of what was around us, and when he effortfully lifted his body and lay alongside mine, I felt it was to get away from what he had seen. He lay motionless against me. The movement I felt around us was extended, I imagined, from our breathing, our pulses, whatever moved involuntarily in us under our skins. He was as attentive to it as I was, and we lay against one another waiting for it to rise or fall. Something around us moved like the movements of air about heavily moving, big bodies. It became imperceptible, and then it came back so strongly that, changing all our motions to involuntary motions, it began to move us on one another, to lift and lower our limbs, our heads, to roll us over together. It engaged us in a sixth sense, the most passionate, which controlled us and took us over. At first moving us slowly, heavily, then quickly, lightly, so the impetus made us make wild gestures, and we felt as

43

though we might, at moments, rise from the bed when one of us pulled the other up. Under us, about us, above us, movements struggled with one another, and we had to give in to them. Sometimes Henry seemed to be pressing me down to a level from which I had to force myself up for breath. I had never before found myself making love as though I were being forced to.

We took positions because we seemed to be made to. Henry and I stood up on the bed a little away from one another; his forearm rested on one of my shoulders, the hand of his other arm was on my hip, my arms were by my sides, and our inclined heads touched. We stood like this for a long time. What caused my awe was the recognition that, at this level of love, which should have disallowed all but the most elliptical demonstrations, the demonstrations were at their most affected. We should have been too embarrassed to do anything.

In my religious fervor, I did this: knelt beside him, reached my arms under his shoulders and knees and, hefting him, slid him onto my naked lap, and I held him, loose limbed, as closely as possible. Some low sound rose from my throat.

The greatest possibility in our love making opened up beyond the vanity of our love making, beyond everything we felt, or could feel, towards one another. I couldn't know how it had happened, but we were taken up by large presences about us, so different from us we would, had we been able to see them, have been terrified. They were trying to make us give in. It was only the rank smells of our armpits and groins and our breaths that kept us in our bodies. We were so close to giving in, but didn't, not quite, because we were anticipating the moment when we didn't have a choice. We were thrown at one another, and the impacts of our lunging bodies burned. It was as if we were promised that enough kissing, enough sucking, would turn our bodies inside out, and we would become invisible. The most extravagant temptations shook about us, and our struggle, if it was a struggle, was against the temptation of giving in, which was like the almost irresistible impulse to fall into space.

I was on my back and he was lying on me. I held him about the waist, my face wedged between his legs, sucking at the soft sides of his testicles. Then I drew back a little to look at them swinging between his open legs. His cock was against my chest. On top of me, licking my thighs with sharp licks, he began to shake himself, so his balls knocked against my cheeks and lips. Nothing could make this ridiculous. I felt his warm, wet mouth about my erection as he thrust. I thrust upwards. As I sensed all my senses rush inward and outward, he sucked more and more deeply, so I ejaculated, and he, while I was ejaculating, pulled his mouth away and arched his back and screamed.

We remained loose limbed in that crazy position. When he drew away his sperm fell in a gob on my chest. I rubbed it over my skin.

While we stood on either side of the bed, pulling and tucking the bottom sheet into place and drawing up the top one, our penises contracted. We wiped our thighs with the towel before we got back into bed. Though our bodies were still hot and sweating, we lay in one another's arms.

Henry fell asleep. I couldn't, and lay awake. He kept moving, trying to fit himself against me comfortably. I pulled away, because our bodies, wherever they touched, seemed to melt with heat. Asleep, he moved close again. His face and his neck were wet, and gleamed in the dim light that came from outside the room. He licked his lips and opened and shut his mouth, then he pressed his lips to my shoulder. His breath burned on my skin.

I couldn't sleep for watching him. The dim light smoothed out his skin, his features, and made him pale. It was as if it were only at this moment that his great beauty could be exposed.

I would make blessed objects of his bare shoulder, his arm, his hand, his eyelids, his nose, his mouth.

But I couldn't bear the heat of our bodies. It made him move again, listlessly, licking his lips. As I was at the edge of the bed, there was no margin to move away, and I didn't want to push him away. Sweat trickled over me. I didn't want to lose contact with him, no matter how unbearable, but finally I had to.

Out of bed, I found, down the passage way, the bathroom, where I splashed water onto my face and gulped water from my

45

cupped palms. To cool off, I walked around the small apartment, into the living room, the kitchen, examining the objects of his life.

By the telephone was a pad with names and numbers. They were the names of people of a society which excluded me.

In the entry hall, where our clothes were on the floor, I looked at a framed photograph on a table of a family, a mother and a father and, between them, a boy, Henry, all of them staring out and smiling.

I shut off the overhead light and walked back to the bedroom in the light from a street lamp outside the living room windows.

Henry was lying on what had been my side of the bed, so I went round to the other side and got under the sheet. It was soft, and settled coolly over me. He was asleep on his stomach, his head turned away from me on the pillow.

I still couldn't sleep, and I didn't want him to, both because his sleeping took him away from me and because it opened him to experiences I couldn't share with him. Propped up on my elbow, my head in my hand, I continued to study him, resentful that I had been left behind as he walked through some high, or deep world, which was unfamiliar to me. I had no idea what world his body referred to in any of its social duties. Our love making had nothing to do with daily life, which he reverted to when he stopped making love, leaving me wondering where he'd gone. He'd gone home to his apartment.

Lying flat on my back, I thought I should leave and go to my own apartment. Maybe I would be able to sleep if I were in my bed.

Being in his bed, in his apartment, kept me awake.

And then I began to think of all the embarrassing moments in my life – or I felt that all of them were coming back to me and making me think about them. I thought of the time, in Paris, when I'd said to a young Frenchwoman that I wasn't American, but Canadian. In London, I said to a priest I met in a Catholic church that I was a practicing Catholic, though I hadn't practiced in years. While I was going through a museum in Rome, an American girl started to talk to me, and I gave her a tutorial on early Italian painting, about which I knew no more than what was in the guide book in her hand. Once, in a bar in New York, I told a man I was married and had a daughter. No doubt no one had believed me, and this made it easier for me to support my pretentions now; if I thought they had believed me, the support would be difficult.

The night, like a dream, seemed to go through a cycle.

Yet, I couldn't sleep. I reached across Henry's body for the watch I'd put on the side table and tried to see the dial, holding the face at different angles. I put the watch down.

Instead of lying back, I turned on my side and, again, looked at the body next to me. It appeared so much outside me that it might never have had anything to do with me, not even to have been engaged with my body in sex.

I rose up close by him, then pressed my forehead and my face into his nude back, between his shoulder blades, leaning my weight on him. With a start, he woke, but he didn't move for a time. I drew my head away and he turned over. His face was calm. Half asleep, he reached up and put his hands around my neck and pulled me down to him to fit my head into the space at the side of his neck. All his body felt calm, dry and cool. Perhaps he was more asleep than awake because he went still again and his breathing wheezed a little. My nose and mouth were pressed into his cheek. I began to kiss his face, my lips swollen huge by being chafed, and with each kiss on his growing beard my lips swelled more. I imagined my hands enlarged, too, and my feet, and my entire body. Slowly, as if in his sleep, he began to kiss me in return. I felt his body also become enormous, not solid, but a smooth, thin surface.

His body became very small, as did mine. Our arms and legs minute, we clasped one another on a vast bed, and fell asleep.

I fell into a dream cycle, involving me more in movement than in scenes as it swung me, slowly, downwards, and, going down, sideways, too. Then I began to rise, always, as I did, turning at odd angles. Sometimes I was both rising and falling at the same time.

I woke and didn't know where I was. I sat up, trying to focus my eyes in the almost dark room, not sure how I related to the walls, which appeared distorted, or even to the bed, which also seemed distorted. When I saw a body half covered by a sheet at my side, I didn't know, though I thought I should, who it was. For a second, it came to me that it was my younger brother and that we were in bed together in our bedroom. But this couldn't have been my brother. Lying back, I fell asleep, but woke again and again, never sure in what room, in what bed, or with what person.

Sometimes when I woke I was frightened by what might happen.

Asleep, I dreamed again, and this time, as I was being swung, in a wide curve, downward, someone woke me by touching my shoulder.

I didn't start. In a way, I'd expected to be woken, though I didn't know by whom. It didn't matter that I didn't know who he was. He leaned close to my face and made a gesture which I understood to mean I must be still, mustn't make any noise, because people were standing in the darkness of the room watching us, and we had to escape. He placed a finger on my lips to keep me silent.

Or perhaps he was waking me, not to warn me against those others, but to draw my attention to them as people who wanted something of us, who wanted to take us somewhere and show us something outside. When he clasped my hand, I imagined it was to lead me up from the bed and out, following those others, and there, in the dark outside, he put his arms around me and kissed me.

I didn't understand. Sometimes I was aware of making love with someone, sometimes I wasn't, and yet, all the time, I had the sense of making love, of moving, swung downwards and then, abruptly, upwards, in those great arcs which were the extensions of the motions of love making.

That love which moved us now, so much greater than any intentions we might once have had, made us innocents, in awe of making love. We had never before made love.

7

—————— • ——————

In the early morning stillness, I got out of bed, leaving him
asleep, and went into the bathroom. In the shower, my nerves
felt exposed after the gush washed away the outer layer, like a
shrunken skin, of all the bodily fluids, his and mine, which had
dried on me. It was as though I were alone in the apartment.
Even using his towel, I didn't feel close to him; my feeling was of
being at an airport hotel, getting ready for a flight abroad. I
picked up my clothes from the floor in the entrance hall and
dressed.

I thought I would just leave. If I went back to him he might
wake up, and then he might think he had to get up and prepare
breakfast for me. I didn't want that. I wanted to go, to start on
my trip, to be at the airport early and wander around the
terminal. But then I thought I'd have a last look at him.

He lay on his back, the sheet rumpled under him. Sunlight
crossed his chest.

As soon as I was outside, I felt I had arrived in a foreign city. It
was a good time to be there: Sunday morning. None of the few
people I passed in the street knew what a long distance I'd
travelled. I had all that sense of possibility you have on arrival.
Crossing the Common, then the Public Garden, it struck me as
odd that people were doing ordinary things when I felt that
everything was extraordinary and that everything I would do in
this city would be extraordinary.

In the Public Garden, I sat for a while on a bench in the
sunlight.

My apartment was on Marlborough Street, in Back Bay. I ate, then corrected the essays of my students, Panamanian, Israeli, Venezuelan, Belgian, Japanese, Senegalese students who wrote in English. When I finished, it was only ten o'clock. I cleaned my apartment.

About twelve o'clock, still feeling there was so much I could do, and wanted to do, I telephoned Charlie and Roberta. They were married and had a baby son. I telephoned them whenever I felt I wanted to do something and didn't really know what. Roberta answered and invited me for Sunday lunch.

What I felt now was completely separated from what I'd felt during the long night. All my movements seemed light, so light they required no effort. I could have done anything, but this lightness might have come to me. Sitting on the streetcar, I thought suddenly, You're all right, and my happiness seemed to arrive at that moment.

It was as if the person I'd made love with was back in the city I'd left. I realized I hadn't left him my address or telephone number.

On a table spread with a towel, the baby was kicking while Charlie changed its diaper. "Will you hold him?" Charlie asked, "so I can get rid of this?" He unfolded the disposable diaper to show me the shit in it. The baby laughed. Charlie left and I tickled the naked belly of the baby, whose penis flopped up and down as he kicked and laughed. When his father came back and raised his legs to wipe between his buttocks, the baby went stiff, then continued to kick and laugh when his father released him.

In another room, Roberta was talking on the telephone.

"We'll let him go naked for a while," Charlie said. "He likes it."

A blanket was on the floor in a bay formed by three windows, and Charlie put the baby on the blanket and lay on his back by him, so the baby crawled onto his chest. Standing, I watched them play. Charlie pressed his face into his son's stomach, then softly bit the flesh with his lips, then kissed it. I wondered if Charlie was putting on a show for me, was demonstrating to me what privileges a father has with his infant son. When Charlie

50

began to lick his son's belly, so the baby hiccupped with laughter, I was sure Charlie was putting on a show. Whether he had any intention to exclude me or not, the sight of my friend playing with his baby became an icon that had nothing to do with what he intended; this icon existed for me in itself, and I was moved, not by my old friend and his infant, but by a young father and his son. That ability to see someone referring outwardly to the world rather than inwardly to me, I took as a manifestation of my happiness.

Roberta came in and stood by me to watch the show, and after a while she smiled at me to let me know that she saw Charlie was putting it on for me. I always imagined Roberta understood all the complex reasons why a person did something, and I felt she credited me with the same understanding. She assumed that I was more intelligent than I was – more, anyway, than Charlie – and that she and I could communicate as she and Charlie couldn't. We both saw that Charlie was acting, was doing what fathers did before old friends, particularly an old friend who had loved him. Because we understood him more than he did himself, we could indulge him, we could even find him charming. What she perhaps didn't know about me was that, though I had a vivid awareness of the complexities of the human act, I did not have the intelligence to study and sort out those complexities; I was drawn to the image that suggested all the complexities and more. Yet I wanted Roberta to think I was with her, and that my appreciation of what Charlie was doing was, like hers, scientific and large. I very much liked her believing that I was more intelligent than Charlie and saw him more clearly than he saw himself.

"Let's sit down," she said to me, and took me to an old sofa in the middle of the room. She seemed to be saying, We've indulged Charlie enough. When we sat, Charlie stopped playing with the baby and put a clean diaper on him.

Roberta said to me, "I was talking to one of my Indian women."

"About what?"

"They call me up to ask me if I can help when their sons get

51

into trouble with the police."

"Do you?"

"I try. The problem for me is I don't know how far I should go. I tell myself it doesn't matter, as long as I'm studying them."

"Because otherwise it might be painful?"

She laughed. "No. Otherwise it would be boring. My God, it sometimes takes a lot of looking to make a culture interesting."

I wanted to talk about being a Catholic with her, as if she could explain to me, a little, why I gestured and dressed and spoke and ate and shit and made love and slept and dreamt as I did. But she never seemed to want to talk about me. She would talk to me about Charlie, sometimes for hours when we were alone, and she'd question me about his life before she knew him. And she would indulge Charlie when he talked about himself, looking at him closely and listening to him, but never me. I wondered if she did this because she believed I was as interested in Charlie as she was, maybe more interested, and also because she thought that I, who was supposed to be intelligent, would never indulge myself with talk about myself.

She told me a story about the Indians she was studying. She said they had lost nearly all their identity as a tribe, and hardly anyone knew anything about them; they had almost disappeared into the city.

Charlie came over to the sofa with Jerry, the baby.

"Can I hold him?" I asked.

He handed him to me. I held him with his head against my shoulder, his face turned toward my neck. He fell asleep. He felt solid and warm.

I would have liked to ask Charlie what he thought about my holding his son so closely to me.

Charlie and Roberta sat on either side.

"What I keep wondering," I said, "is what impressions he's getting. In thirty years' time, if he wants to explain his life, he'll only be able to if he can remember this moment, which he won't be able to remember, because at this most important moment he's asleep."

Charlie said, "You should keep a record of it to show him in

52

thirty years."

"I'd like to keep a record of every single one of his impressions," I said.

This started Charlie off. He said he understood exactly what I meant – remembering your impressions was very important, not, though, to explain yourself, but as moments you live in terms of. He said he believed the Sacraments of the Church were important because they were vivid moments and you could always, later, look at those moments like fixed points, a constellation in the firmament of your life, and know you have had a life, all on a scale that surprised you, because you thought your life was unmemorable. The average person thought that. He, as an average person, certainly thought it about his life, until he remembered, say, his confirmation when the Bishop hit him on the cheek to startle him into the realities of the world.

Roberta said that was an argument for people to be baptized when they were old enough to remember it.

I said, "But surely Jerry wasn't baptized."

"We never considered the possibility," Charlie said.

"All of a sudden it seems odd to me," I said, "that our parents wouldn't ever have considered the possibility of our not being."

Charlie said it was amazing when you stopped and thought that Jerry's generation, brought up without religion, would find the iconography we were familiar with as foreign as that of oriental cults. Jerry would wonder what in God's name was going on in the pictures he'd see in museums and books: what was that person with wings saying to the young woman kneeling, and what was the radiating dove doing over her head? But he saw Roberta's point in not inculcating him with the imagery of a religion they no longer had faith in, imagery which, at best, would have abstract values, but no values for concrete life. Also, he thought, to bring up Jerry without the iconography of religion, leaving him, from Charlie's traditional Catholic point of view, with no imagery, would be an experiment; because if men needed images, Jerry would find them, would create them, and, if he had to create them, it would be interesting to see what they would be. But perhaps Jerry would show that they weren't necessary, no more necessary, as Charlie himself had discovered, than belief in God, which his mother had thought essential to live. Charlie had proved his mother wrong, and maybe his son would prove him wrong, even though Charlie, as an artist, believed in the necessity of imagery. (He was now teaching drawing at a Catholic preparatory school.) Charlie related his life to images, and the strongest, he felt, were sacramental. But he had to admit it was possible that someone else, of another tradition, could lead a happy life without once revering even a photograph of his father. Anything was possible, which was what made the prospects of Jerry's future so exciting.

Jerry sighed, and moved a little in my arms.

Roberta listened to Charlie with more attention than I did, and it came to me, suddenly, that maybe she didn't think he was banal, but original, and if this were so, it was because she was, after all, less intelligent than he. Then I thought she made out in his talk original relationships of words and ideas I couldn't make out.

She said, "You're so funny, Charlie."

Among this family, I thought of my own family, my father and mother and their children, and I thought about the religious images of the Holy Family by which my family was assigned to certain ways of living. Everywhere in our small house images confronted us with the signs that, unless we lived in their terms, we were damned to have no relationships that would work. For us to have been a family fulfilled in the way a family was divinely meant to be fulfilled, my mother would have had to be a virgin, yet impregnated, not directly by the father of her son, but by a go-between, and that father not her husband; he, her husband, would have had to be the foster father of his wife's son, and to accept that, though his wife gave birth to a child, she remained a virgin, and he would have had to respect, throughout all their marriage, her virginity. And as for the son –

For those who believed, divine grace was so powerful it could transform a dead human body into a resurrected and glorified body that would exist forever in a world more real than this, but I wanted my life to be free of images that were fantasy. I insisted that the image of the risen Christ, his shroud a sheet flung from a body rising from the bed, must be expunged from the center of my thoughts and feelings.

Whenever I thought of those images in my family house, I thought of the house as a small cabin, and through the open windows and door of the cabin I looked out into woods, where, though I couldn't see them, I knew dark natives were moving about, looking towards the house through bushes and tangled vines.

While Roberta prepared a late lunch, I, sitting silently by Charlie with Jerry still in my arms, felt a restlessness beginning to take shape in me.

Jerry woke up, stared at me for a long time, wide-eyed, then his lower lip stretched over his gums, his eyes closed, and he cried. Saliva drooled down his chin. I tried to quieten him by bouncing him in my arms and saying "Gna, gna, gna," but he cried louder, and I had to give him to his father.

I thought, I could be a better father to him than Charlie.

"You'll just have to come more often," Charlie said, holding Jerry, now quiet, with one arm, and reaching out with the other to touch my shoulder.

Charlie's fatherhood made him sexless to me.

"Maybe I should come and live here," I said.

"That'd be great! That'd really be great!" He called out to Roberta, "Dan's going to come live with us!"

"Now that'd be interesting," she called back.

"I honestly do wish we could all live together," Charlie said.

With one hand, Roberta fed Jerry, on her lap, then fed herself, while she and I listened to Charlie talk about Jerry's future.

My restlessness deepened.

Charlie would interrupt himself often to say, "This is really good cooking, Roberta."

Suddenly, I thought I would have to get up from the table and walk around the room.

And just as suddenly, I felt that I was very heavy and couldn't move.

Roberta asked me, "Are you okay?"

55

I said, "I think I'm tired."

"All at once?"

My eyes flickered around her, but didn't fix on her. "I didn't sleep last night."

"What were you doing?" Charlie asked.

I looked at him and smiled. Roberta laughed first, then he did. They laughed, I thought, too much. Frightened, the baby began to cry. My eyes closed, I felt I could, sitting at the table, fall asleep. My eyes opened, I said, "I should go home."

"Don't go," Charlie said. "If you want to sleep, go lie on our bed."

"I've got to get back to my bed, because once I let go I'll probably be out for the night."

"Sleep here tonight."

Holding the baby over her shoulder and patting his back, Roberta waited for me to answer.

"It's been a joy to be here," I said, "a real joy, but now it's time to go because I can't take in any more joy or anything else. My senses have closed down for the day."

I kissed the top of the baby's head, then Roberta's cheek, and hugged Charlie before I left.

"You're really going back to your apartment?" Roberta asked.

"Sure," I said. "Why?"

"Well, you know you don't need to make excuses to us if you want to go somewhere else to see someone."

I kissed her again. "There's no one I want to see more than you," I said.

I leaned against the window of the streetcar. The vibrating glass shocked my skull. I sensed come over me, like sleep, the old, old possession of Charlie, and the old, old desire to possess that possession. Roberta possessed him.

Half asleep as I was, when I got out of the subway station, I thought I'd go, for five minutes, to the bar I'd been to the night before. The sun had set, but the air was light. Just for five minutes, I told myself.

There were not many people in the bar. I looked around at them, and stared, briefly, at one. Even if he had responded to me,

I wouldn't have been up to going out with him. I hadn't come to pick up anyone. It occurred to me why I'd come, why I came here again and again: to look, to keep renewing images. Maybe that was all I ever wanted here. I left after I finished my bottle of beer.

On my way to my room, through the deepening evening, a sense came over me that something had happened that had so changed me I'd always be different from what I'd been. But I didn't know what had changed me, or what the difference was.

I went to bed. I realized I'd forgotten what the person I'd spent the previous night with looked like, and I fell asleep trying to remember.

8

————— • —————

One morning, when I stopped in the office to pick up my class forms, the proprietress, Mrs. Hart, gave me a letter which had been sent to me care of the school. I kept it unopened till the end of the day of lessons. The envelope didn't have the sender's address on it. After my last lesson, alone in the empty classroom, I opened the letter. It was from Henry, asking me to telephone him at home or at work.

He was at work. His voice was lower than I remembered it, low and steady. I expected him to be surprised that I called, but he wasn't. He said, "I won't be free until Saturday."

"All right," I said, and waited.

"Suppose you call me Saturday morning," he said.

"No," I said, "you call me, around ten, if you want."

He said he would, and hung up.

I told myself that he'd been brusque, but maybe that was because he was at work and couldn't talk. In my room, I read his letter once more, and thought, the fact was he was a brusque person, and the terseness of his writing had more to do with him in himself than the way he wanted to appear to me.

I felt powerful; and this sense of power over him disposed me to be warm towards him. The more I thought about it, the more warmly disposed I was towards him for having got in touch, and the more strongly my desire to impose myself upon him was replaced by the desire for him to impose on me.

He telephoned at ten o'clock.

It was a bright, hot morning.

"You come here, then we'll decide what we'll do," he said.

"Anything you want," I said.

Henry came to the door with a book closed over a finger. He was wearing chinos and a dress shirt, unbuttoned and out of his trousers, and he was barefoot. Holding out his free hand, he smiled; I took his hand and leaned towards him to kiss him, but I felt his arm was rigid, and I stood back.

He said, "Come on in."

He'd been reading in an armchair. On the floor around the chair were notebooks, looseleaf papers, pencils, eyeglasses. The living room smelled of dust. He sat back in the armchair and rested the book on a knee, his finger still inserted between the pages, as if, after a pause, he was going to resume reading.

I sat on the sofa, a little angry, as if all my affection towards him had been turned back on me.

He asked, "What would you like to do?"

I laughed.

He laughed also and closed the book and threw it on the floor, then leaned into the armchair.

I had to leave it to him.

He said, "I had an idea that we might go to L Street."

"L Street?"

"It's the old Boston beach."

"I'm sorry," I said, "I don't know it."

I didn't want to go to the beach. Maybe, I thought, I hadn't been forward enough in saying what I wanted to do, and he'd thought he shouldn't be more forward than I. So, neither of us wanting to, we were going to a beach. This seemed a waste of time.

In the car, I thought that maybe it was against Henry's way of doing things to make love during the middle of the day. I wanted, at any time, to make love as we had, but he, whose life was regulated by a different sense of right and wrong than mine, was only happy making love at night, or, perhaps, in the late afternoon. He was probably a person of many proprieties, none of which I knew. But this didn't mean that he was incapable of spontaneity. I thought that I knew everything there was to know about his spontaneous feelings and thoughts, as he knew everything about mine. We had gone so far in our world, no other could matter.

Sitting side by side in the front seat of the little car, we began to talk about books. Henry was better read than I was, or he'd thought more about what he'd read. But I never felt at a loss to make a comment after he'd made one, and he took my comments more seriously than I gave them. I thought I was being mildly ironical. I hadn't often met someone who loved books, which was as embarrassing, in its way, as admitting you loved sex with men. I thought you had to be a little ironical about both. Not, I thought, that Henry could have been embarrassed about reading or liking sex with men, because his direct manner would always have made him say, without apology to anyone, I read books, I fuck men. He was not a person who had to justify himself. I was. With others, I had to justify my reading, and I had to justify my sex. With Henry, however, I didn't. He would have been considered by my home parish as affected, affected in his language as much as in his interests, but I realized he was, in fact, totally unaffected. He was able to express himself with total confidence, without once using a slangy word or phrase or changing his tone to one of even slight self-mockery. I liked it when he said, in his deep voice, "I'm of the opinion that – " He had the authority to do this, and his authority was sustained as much by his voice as by his face, which no one would have taken to be that of a weirdo reader of books.

We were now undressing in the locker room of the L Street clubhouse. Still talking about books, we went out onto the beach. I had a towel over my shoulders. Walking ahead of him, I pulled off the towel, and as I turned to him to respond to something he'd said, I saw him look at my body, then look away.

The sky, the ocean, the beach, even the buildings backing the beach made me feel more naked than I'd ever been, and the air around me, too, seemed to magnify my nakedness, as I walked across the sand behind Henry to a spot not far from the changing room. We spread towels and lay on them. We were among other

60

naked men lying on the sand. Henry turned over on his stomach and closed his eyes, as if he had come here to sleep. I, propped on my elbows, looked around.

A group of boys were throwing a medicine ball to one another. They jumped about in the sunlight. Perhaps they were a familiar sight to Henry, but to me they represented a culture I knew nothing about. I had never, before I'd met Henry, known an authentic New Englander, though I was born and brought up in New England. My childhood friends, my high school and college friends, had all been Irish, Italian, Polish, all Catholic.

Oddly, I did not sense an air of rank sex among so many men naked together. Unlike me, a Catholic brought up to hide his body and to believe the naked body was always the occasion of sin, these people were brought up to believe that the naked body was nothing to be ashamed of: it was God-given, I thought. And what was mine? The naked body did not, for them, reflect sensuality, but health. I understood that this club had been instituted for the athletic body, which was chaste. If sensuality came upon it, the body should withdraw from public; but the body in itself was pure. Henry, here, seemed to have no awareness that he was among men who, simply by being naked, were in a state which couldn't be taken for granted, but had to astound. He slept.

I looked at his glistening body. Sand adhered to his calf and thigh. He came here often enough to be completely tanned. Perhaps he'd come as a boy, brought by his father, and he and his father had thrown a medicine ball to one another. As I always saw people in terms of their cultures I saw Henry now as an Old New Englander, and everything he said and did I'd interpret as an expression of that. Maybe because I'd never known any Yankees, I had strong preconceptions of what they were really like, and I was already attributing to Henry characteristics which he probably didn't have. He was supposed to be exclusive. He had asked me to come here. I wondered if he'd ever ask me into more private places. I was sure the Yankees had to lead lives unlike the one I'd led in New England, and unlike, too, those I'd assumed they led.

After a short time, he woke up and turned over onto his back.

61

He lay with his eyes open. All the fine hairs on his arms, nape, buttocks, legs were brilliant, and glowed about his body.

I asked, "Do you come here a lot?"

"Yes," he answered.

He didn't seem to want to talk now. He was so terse I wondered if I'd said or done something that had offended him. But I couldn't think what, and I decided he was just being himself, though I didn't know him in himself.

I thought he had to be aware that we were lovers.

Forget it, I said to myself. If he's not interested in you, you're not, after all, that interested in him.

Henry's Yankee body appeared perfect to me. That was what made it New England: it was perfect. There was not one detail, not a toe or a ball or a nipple or an eyebrow that was not ideal. His skin was clear, his limbs, his thighs, his chest, his shoulders, his head were finely proportioned, and I imagined his bones and muscles and blood and bowels as specimens of the body at its peak. And though someone might have said this body was characterless for not having one small disfigurement, it was just that characterlessness I liked about it: the body itself was the perfect outer personality of someone who perhaps didn't have a personality, or whose personality didn't matter. I knew I was making all this up. His body was not perfect.

I wondered what I looked like to him. He never seemed to look at me. Maybe, when I momentarily turned away, he did, but I never caught him.

In front of me, leaning against a brick wall, was a middle-aged man talking to an old man. The old, wrinkled man wore a cache-sexe. The middle-aged man had a large, powerful body, and his dark genitals hung heavily. I caught Henry looking at him at the same time I did, and he turned away. Immediately, I tried to dissemble my embarrassment by being ironical in a way I thought he would like.

I said, "I wonder what Walt Whitman would make of this beach."

Henry said, "Most every time I come here, I think of Whitman." He smiled at me. "How peculiar that you mentioned

62

him."

He was serious, and this moved me.

I thought no one else on the beach knew that we, two comrades, had made love. That was our secret among men, who were not supposed to make love. And the secret made us a couple. But perhaps everyone could see that we were a couple, that we had gone so far in our love making that the secrets which had been revealed to us had turned us into more than blood brothers. We were blessed as loving comrades by the blessing of our nation's greatest poet.

While Henry was talking, I wondered if my love for him was derived from some precedent he might be able to explain to me. I myself knew no precedent, and in my ignorance assumed my love was not derived from anything but the immediate body of Henry. And yet, as he talked about Whitman, I became nostalgic about the poetry I had not read at any length since my freshman year in college, nostalgic for what Whitman himself was so drawn to creating images of: the naked, perfect body.

His image of it was so fantastic, I wondered if he had ever made love with anyone.

Reading him, I had sometimes stopped with the sudden suspicion that he was an old faker. He was the greatest fantasy poet ever.

The miracle of Walt Whitman was that the self-consciousness, which he had to such a depth and height that it extended into the whole universe and beyond, did not condemn him and the universe, but made him exult in himself and the universes outside his universe. It was not out of some lack of un-self-consciousness that he was able to express the perfect body, the pure and natural body, with such passion, but because his self-consciousness went so far, went so high and so deep. It was what survived his self-consciousness, what he couldn't talk about, what he knew was pure and natural because he couldn't talk about it, that made him passionate.

The beach I was on was derived from Walt Whitman, and on it I felt, for a moment, love for all men, for all men and for all women, for everyone.

Whitman had written about himself and his poetry as he'd walked along a beach by the ocean:

O baffl'd, balk'd, bent to the very earth,
Oppress'd with myself that I have dared to open my mouth,
Aware now that amid all that blab whose echoes recoil upon
    me I have not once had the least idea who or what I am,
But that before all my arrogant poems the real Me stands
    yet untouch'd, untold, altogether unreach'd,
Withdrawn far, mocking me with mock-congratulatory
    signs and bows,
With peals of distant ironical laughter at every word I have
    written,
Pointing in silence to these songs, and then to the sand
    beneath.

I understood what Whitman meant when he wrote, " . . . it is not for what I have put into it that I have written this book." What saved him, and what, at that moment on the beach, saved me, saved our entire country from thinking mockingly about ourselves, was his and my and our belief that there was something beyond the most extreme self-consciousness. "The words of my book nothing, the drift of it everything." He believed that everything appeared of itself in the vastness of his work, a vastness that was vaster even than his self-contradicting ego. It had so little to do with what he could intend, this everything he loved, that he thought it might come to him only with death.

I imagined that if I, lying by Henry in the sunlight, had died of my love for him, I would have had everything.

I did not, with Henry, feel that I was a fool.

Those images I saw about me – because I saw images of men rather than the men themselves – of men with sheer waists and massive arms, sunburnt, glistening with wet, little streams passing all over their bodies, men floating on their backs in the green water with their white bellies bulging to the sun, young men sousing one another with spray, struck me as if I had, just

64

then, seen what no one else had ever seen before, not even Walt Whitman.

I avoided looking at the physical deformities of the men, but if my attention fixed, for some reason, on a birth mark or a twisted leg, I thought: These, too, are natural, and in their way pure. There was no good and no bad. There was simply everything.

At the same time I was vaguely considering all this, I was thinking that, in fact, I was not in any kind of special place, and that I'd have preferred to be alone, back in my room, to do what I wanted to do, though I didn't know what that was.

I did not really like to be out in athletic America, but always wished I were in my small Catholic room, which was quiet.

I was made a little restless by Henry's talk.

I wanted to kiss his shoulder.

Our love making had given me certain rights of possession over him that he couldn't deny me. He was beautiful, and we were, together, beautiful. His having been in bed with me made me as beautiful as he was, because he wouldn't have gone to bed with anyone less beautiful than himself. Lying close to one another on the beach, we were more beautiful together than we were singly, and what drew us together was sex. So our sex, according to some syllogistic rule I'd long lost grasp of (all A is B, all B is C, therefore –), was beautiful. Henry had to be impressed, as I was, that because we had made love together once, we would make love again and again.

I turned more to face him, but he got up and said, "I'm going in for a swim." It was as if I wasn't allowed to go with him.

He didn't come back for a long while, and I went to where the grey waves broke into foam. Unable to see him, I went in deeper and swam up and down. When I returned to our towels, he was drying himself.

"I think we should go now," he said.

9

————— • —————

As we drove into Back Bay, our talk about the nude kept open the promised sex between us. But Henry could see the nude denuded of sex, as, say, an object of history. He was deeply interested in history (I wasn't really) and he talked mostly of poems, plays, novels from the point of view of the periods in which they were written (I regarded them as transcending all periods). I couldn't deny that his approach was probably better, because less sentimental, as a valid appreciation of literature; my approach left literature inexplicable, which was not an intelligent appreciation, but an ecstatic one. With him, I was absolutely sure that my approach was wrong and implied defective intelligence, while his approach, filled with intelligence, was right. But while I admired him, I wished he were able to detach himself, just a little, from his sense of serious study, which was, to him, work, and take me up for trying to be funny about it – especially now, when I wanted to bring it all down from the sky into our laps, to resolve it into fucking. But maybe Henry was ashamed to talk about sex.

Then I thought: he doesn't allow himself to say anything, to do anything, that is in any way self-conscious.

I reached out and grabbed his thigh and squeezed it, digging my fingers into it.

"Be careful," he said quietly, "or we'll have an accident."

I took my hand away.

Everything is going to be all right, I said to myself, you'll see, everything is going to be fine.

I let my body go loose, tilted my head back, and closed my eyes. My skin was tingling with sunburn and dried sea salt. If, for now, I couldn't touch him because it was dangerous, I could, in anticipation of touching him later, touch myself, and I slipped my hand under my tee-shirt.

You'll get everything you want, I thought.

Then this event took place: I felt myself thrown off-center and pulled to the side, and when I opened my eyes, I saw the maple trees along the street, lawns, porches all pass as the car, with a long screech, swung round. I went rigid, and even when the car stopped, facing the opposite way, I felt some continuing momentum would make the car inevitably crash, and I waited for the impact. I knew what it would be like. I felt that it was about to occur, and I reached out to hold Henry. My arms went round the motionless body leaning slumped against the steering wheel. Henry's eyes were open and staring.

I tried to pull him towards me. He turned only his head to look at me, though he seemed, too, to look through me. I said, "Henry." He asked in a low voice, "Yes?" "Are you all right?" "Yes," he went on in the same low, still voice, "I'm all right." There was no traffic in the sunlit street. We sat for a while longer, then Henry turned around and continued.

In silence, we drove into Back Bay. Students were lounging on the stoops and stairs of the brownstone houses. Henry stopped in front of the house where I lived.

Before I could say anything, he said, "I've been thinking I should go back to my apartment and work."

"Right," I said. But I didn't move, half thinking: this isn't everything. I opened the car door. "Thanks," I said.

He nodded.

I got out of the car and held the door open, then shut it when he went into gear.

I was twenty-four years old and I had studied myself in different circumstances enough to recognize the outward signs of my reactions to happenings. On the sidewalk, I saw in the many details – a crack in the cement, a popsicle stick – that what was happening inside me had happened before. I didn't want it to happen again. The details held me for a while. I shook my head and looked into the distance, where the heavy sunlight blurred. Then I went up to my room. I stared at the map of Boston tacked to a wall.

What happened? I asked myself.

Look, I told myself sternly, whatever happened was entirely to do with him and had nothing to do with you. You said nothing, did nothing to make him leave you standing alone on the sidewalk the way he did. Nothing. And yet I kept asking myself, What happened?

Put it out of your mind, I thought. Without too much difficulty, you can put it out of your mind. Put what? Never mind what. Just stop thinking about it. About what? Stop it, now. Stop it? Yes, now.

I decided I'd be active. Lying on my bed, I thought a lot about being active.

The sunlight was flashing through a tree outside my window and into my room.

I got up and had a shower, then, drying myself with a towel, I wandered around my room thinking, You've got to go out and do something. You can't stay in.

Then I thought I wanted to be with Roberta. Not with Charlie, too. With her alone. I knew so little about her experience in the world, but I felt she would be able to tell me what to do because she seemed to be a person of greater experience than I.

I telephoned her, but there was no answer.

In clean clothes, I went out. I went to the Charles River Esplanade and walked along it, sometimes stopping to study the sailing boats in the bay.

When I found myself staring at a boy lying on the grass, I realized I had been staring at him with no sense of why I was, as if I could have no reason.

Although it seemed to me I was out for hours, not even an hour went by before I returned to my room. And there I would, after a short time, want to go out again.

This time Charlie answered the phone.

"I thought we might get together," I said.

"I'm taking care of Jerry while Roberta's out working in the library," he said. "Come on over. We can fool around with Jerry on the lawn in the back yard."

In the back yard, we sat and drank beer while Jerry crawled on the grass.

The fact was, I didn't want to be with Charlie.

He talked and, from time to time, got up to stop Jerry putting grass blades or sticks or pebbles into his mouth. I tried to pay attention to Charlie. I even asked questions, though I wasn't sure if they related to what he was saying. I drank a lot of beer, thinking that would give me some control. As often as I said to myself, you can't let it happen, you've got to do something so it won't happen, something like the round rim of my beer can would assert that it was happening and there was nothing I could do about it. All that would be left of me would be some thin, peripheral perception of details.

The father picked up his son and jogged around the yard with him. I would soon imagine that there was nothing in their relationship, that, at best, Charlie was pretending to be a father (which was a suspicion I always had anyway) and that Jerry, in his infantile way, was pretending to act as a laughing son (an entirely new suspicion). Soon, it would seem to me that nothing ever happened between them that could make any difference to one or the other. That was not true, of course. Everything they did to one another made a difference to them. But in a while I wouldn't think it did. I looked at a little black and blue mark on Jerry's forehead, and a similar mark on Charlie's neck, and these seemed to me of more interest than their playing together. Their playing together not only bored me, I began to be irritated by it, by its pretentiousness. Charlie really was a phony. He always had been, and he always would be. Even as a father, he was a phony.

"Haven't you played enough with him?" I asked.

"You're jealous," he said. "You wish I were playing with you like this."

He went on playing. I got up and went into the apartment and walked around.

I wished I could go back to Charlie and say, Look, something terrible is happening, and you've got to help me stop it.

Roberta came in and found me walking up and down the living room.

"Where're Charlie and Jerry?" she asked.

"Outside."

"Is anything wrong?"

"Why should anything be wrong?"

"What're you doing in here while they're out there?"

I shrugged.

Charlie came into the living room carrying Jerry. He said to Roberta, "Dan telephoned and told me he was restless, so I told him he should come on over to us. Isn't it great that he telephoned us when he was restless and wanted to see people?"

She asked me, "What's making you restless?"

"I don't know," I answered. "It just comes over me."

I was frightened to be on my own, but, while we were eating supper, I realized I had no less reason for being frightened among this family. They were not going to stop what was going to happen; they couldn't. I began to imagine it was more dangerous for me to be among them than to be alone, because they were a family, and as a family all their relationships were fixed and everything they said and did was predictable. I sensed that among them nothing could be different.

I thought, looking at Charlie: I could show you a time you've never even dreamed of.

I said, trying to laugh, "Don't you two ever get bored being a family?"

"Bored?" Charlie asked.

Roberta said, "Of course we get bored." As I'd seen her do over and over, she was feeding the baby from a bowl next to her plate. She dipped the spoon into the mush, then scraped it against the rim of the bowl.

An edge came into my voice. "I'm sure I'd end up killing the baby."

Charlie said, "Oh, come on."

"Sometimes," I said, "I think they're aware of what ego-

70

monsters they are, aware that they can get away with demanding everything just because we believe they're helplessly unaware."

Charlie said to me, "Dan, we look forward to the day when he's grown up and we can give you the same attention."

I came away thinking I had to sustain my sense of possibilities by going to the bar by the bus station.

It seemed to me that Henry had, after leaving me, disappeared and could not have any presence anywhere. When I saw him at the back of the bar I wondered who this person was. He was talking with another man. I didn't know if he saw me or not. I turned away.

It annoyed me, even angered me, that he existed, because he should have been so dependent on my imagining him that he could only exist because I did imagine him. He could exist only if I allowed him to, and if, suddenly, I decided I didn't want him to, he would disappear. I was especially angry to see him wearing a foulard tucked into his open collar, which I would never have imagined him wearing and therefore never allowed him to wear. He should have asked my permission to dress as he did, to eat what he did, to shit, to sleep, to say what he said. He didn't. He did what he wanted.

I went to a wall and leaned against it and drank my beer.

He came to me. "I thought I'd take a little break from work," he said.

"You don't have to excuse yourself to me."

"No."

"It was a nice afternoon," I said.

He held out his hand, and I shook it. He left the bar and I finished my beer, then left.

In my room, as I stood by my bed, I imagined there appeared over my head a halo, not of gold, but of black iron.

I undressed.

I found myself thinking there was something I should be considering, but it was not anything that could come from thinking.

It came to me: the image of Henry lying on his bed, asleep. This image took possession of me.

71

10

————•————

What happened to me could only be explained, I thought, by my being a Catholic. There was no way I could tell Henry this. He would find my explanation ridiculous. And so it was.

As a Catholic, I felt my childhood had, in a way that seemed simultaneously concrete and elusive, been like that night I'd spent with Henry: there was no explaining it, there was only experiencing it, like some strange conversion, to have any sense of it. I was born and brought up in the Mystical Body. This was as real a body of flesh and blood, I, taking off from dogma, imagined, as the body of someone I loved. The Church I was a part of lay on the earth, its arms and legs wide, its head thrown back, and Christ loved this body. Every time people made love, they re-enacted in their love act the mystical love of Christ for his Church. At the end of the world, this body would rise, glorified and immortal, made of the millions of bodies of the glorified and immortal members of the corporeal Church, and Christ and this gigantic body would be, forever, lovers. In my Church, to deny your body was to deny your soul.

No one could take this seriously.

I didn't take it seriously. But I understood, and I was suspicious that I was using my religion to explain my ridiculous obsession by a body denied me. I was using, or trying to use, my religion not only to explain, but to excuse the sense of my ridiculousness. Of course, of course, my obsession was ridiculous. So was my religion.

Henry knew how ridiculous it was.

What bewildered, what angered me most was that he had got in touch with me, not I with him. What had he expected?

And what had made him turn away from me? He didn't know me, as I didn't know him. Whatever it was that had turned him against me couldn't have had to do with my personality. What was wrong with my body that he had seen it, naked in the sunlight, as repellent to him? If he had denied me his body, I, in my body, had repelled him, had made him deny me. It was all the fault of my body.

While I taught my students, I imagined that we weren't dealing with the real subject of the lessons. In every composition I read, not the absence, but the presence of the absence of Henry.

A young South American student, my first for the day, gave me his composition.

My problems in English
I have seven day of live in Boston city. This has for object
to correct my problems and to desire very much outcomes.
The End

I thought, I will never be able to correct his language any more than I'll be able to put right what I did wrong. And yet, there was no question but that I had to.

As I thought out, with effort, explanations for the simplest and yet most complicated mistakes, I tried, at that level deeper than the compositions, to explain what it was about me that made Henry not want to see me.

I told myself there was nothing shocking about Henry's not wanting to make love with me again. He had not been powerfully moved by it, as I had. To him, it was no more important, maybe less important, than a casual conversation about, say, Boston. He would have been puzzled, angered too, to know how important it had been to me. The more I considered the image of him, however, the more important the image became, meaning everything I wanted and couldn't have. I was no one for not being able to have what it promised. I was shocked by his denial of me.

73

As I sat at the classroom table during a short break, there came to me, as if I had for a fraction been distracted, the sudden suspicion that I was not looking at his image. I closed my eyes. I saw, not a whole body, but an ankle, an elbow, a featureless face. I saw, as hard as I tried, nothing whole. And yet, the sense was of something utterly whole. But what did this sense rely on?

I could have gone through the class hours haphazardly, or I could have gone down to Mrs. Hart and said I wasn't well and had to leave for the rest of the day, but I never thought to.

In the end, the strain I felt was like having to correct, all over again, what I still believed was impossible to correct, though I'd done it. In the waning afternoon, as I sat alone in the classroom after I'd filled out the register, I thought that I must correct not only what made me wrong according to Henry but what made me wrong on earth.

Drawing circles, squares, triangles on a sheet of paper I asked myself, what *is* wrong with me? My mind stopped.

In the next room, I heard a lesson going on. The teacher was saying, "No, not snows. It snows."

"It?"

"Yes, it snows."

"What is it that snows?"

"What is it?"

"Yes." There was a silence, and after a while the teacher said, "It. You don't understand?"

I thought: I don't understand –

I stopped.

What sin I committed –

You know, you know, a voice said. You wanted everything. You only thought of yourself. That's what's wrong with you. You only ever think of yourself, and you know that's a sin. You are in a constant state of sin. You are, in the very fact that you are yourself, embodied sin. Your body is a sin. Your –

Don't be stupid, I said. I don't believe in sin.

The voice laughed. And what else don't you believe in? it asked.

I concentrated on the geometrical figures I was drawing to try

74

to think of nothing else, and I wished these figures were all I ever thought.

I don't believe in anything, I said.

The high, thin voice said, It doesn't matter now if you believe or not, your beliefs are with you whether you want them or not. You believe you are a sin.

I don't, I said, and pressed my pencil to make a heavy line.

The voice said, You do.

Maybe, I thought, I'm not possessed. Maybe I only imagine I am, and, with the smallest effort of will, I could dispossess myself. I should do this, should exert this smallest effort of will.

I drew a circle.

The voice said, But maybe you need to feel you are possessed. Maybe your need is such that even if you have to invent the possession, you'll do it to imagine you're possessed. Maybe it's only when you feel you are possessed that you're in a state of –

I drew a square.

The voice: Grace. A state of grace. That's what possession is for you.

I: But I don't want to be possessed. I want to get rid of my possession.

The voice: You don't.

I: I do.

The voice: You don't. You want the possession.

I said, For Christ's sake, if you had any religious training, you'd know you can't be possessed by grace and in a state of sin at the same time.

The voice, high and thin, said, Don't tell me I don't know religion. Of course you're in a state of sin. You'll always be in a state of sin. But your possession is the longing to be in the state of grace. And I suspect that's the closest you'll ever come to grace.

I put my hand up to my forehead and closed my eyes to try to see in my mind simple squares, circles, triangles.

I am possessed by him, I thought, I am possessed by him, I am possessed –

Another voice, low and thick, said, No, you're not.

I am, I said. I haven't invented the possession. I am possessed.

No, the voice said. You could stop it, with the slightest act of will. But you don't want to.

I can't stop it. I can't.

You want to remain in a state of sin.

I opened my eyes and stared at the geometrical figures on the piece of paper. I said, All right, I'll stop the possession, I'll make the act of will, I'll – I tried to think of only the asymmetrically drawn figures.

The lesson in the next room finished. The teacher and the student went out and the building sounded empty when I heard a door downstairs shut.

A third voice, that of a young woman, almost a girl, asked: But why are you possessed by something that has been taken away from you?

What? I asked.

She said, I can understand being possessed by something you're given, but not by something taken away. Why are you possessed by what is denied to you?

I have to think, I said.

You're not very good at thinking, she said.

Let me think.

The thin, high voice said, Maybe you can only ever be possessed by what you can't have.

The girl asked, But why?

Because he can only ever want, never have.

The heavy, low voice asked, But why?

The girl said, That's what I want to know. Why?

I said, I don't want to listen to this talk about me. I don't want to hear about myself, don't want to think about myself.

I hit my forehead.

The voice of an old man whispered, What do you want?

Lowering my head to the table top, I said, I want not to think about what I want. I want not to think about myself. Help me not to think about what I want, about myself and my wants. Help me do that.

We can't, the old man said.

Can't you talk about something else? I asked. Can't you try?

76

The old man's voice: You wouldn't be interested in anything else.

I sat up. I said, I'm not possessed. I'm imagining I am. I can stop it at any moment.

The girl's voice: Then stop it.

I'll stop it.

We're waiting, the old man said.

Instead of talking about me, I said, why don't we talk about the outside world? There's a lot going on in the outside world, a lot that's very interesting. There must be a war going on somewhere. We could talk about that. Or a famine. Or unemployment. Or, if you want, we could talk about other people. Other people are interesting.

You're not interested, the old man said.

I am.

You're not, the girl said.

I am. I am.

The high and low voices said, together: You can only think about yourself.

Fuck off, I said. Out loud, I said, "Fuck off."

I threw the paper with the geometrical drawings into the wastepaper basket, then went out.

In the office downstairs, Mrs. Hart asked me about the Panamanian student.

"I wonder," I said, "if he's hopeless."

"You can't have that attitude and teach," she said. "No one can ever be hopeless."

She had no sense of humor.

All right, I thought as I walked through Back Bay. Someone wants to ask me a question.

I heard the girl's voice say, Are you prepared?

Ask it.

Listen carefully.

I'm listening.

There was a pause. I've forgotten it, she said.

I'm waiting impatiently.

I'm trying to think of it.

77

Come on.

Your impatience is making it difficult for me to concentrate.

Come on.

Here it is. Now listen. I'll say it slowly.

Come on.

What is it you want from him that he won't give you?

That's a question I can't answer.

You should be able to answer any question.

Should be?

Well, why not? If you did a little more thinking, real thinking, you'd probably be able to answer. But I know you. You don't like thinking, not like I do. All questions can be answered if you think hard enough.

Maybe I should ask you a question or two, I said, as you think so hard.

It may take me time to answer, and you're impatient.

I'll give you the time.

Then ask me a question, any question.

What do I want from him that he won't give me?

She laughed.

I said, I don't want anything from him. Nothing.

But you do, the old man said. You want his –

Stop it, I said, stop it.

He laughed.

I said, You're right to laugh. You're all right to laugh.

The girl said, You want his –

Laughing more, the old man said, His heart.

All I want, I said, is to stop this.

The woman said, Oh, his big, bleeding heart–

Stop it, I said.

Oh, his thorn-tangled heart, dripping with blood, the old man said.

If you won't stop it, I said, go on, go on. Make it a joke. That's fine with me.

Oh, the girl said, his scourged, nailed, speared heart–

Go on, I said. Exaggerate.

His bleeding heart, that would bless you with grace if only he would give it to you–

Exaggerate more, I said. Exaggerate.

I heard another voice, that of a woman and a man combined. It said, No, we're going to take you very seriously.

Shocked by this voice, I thought, I am going to think this out on my own, and, once it's thought out, I'll be able to see it, like a geometrical figure. I'm going to be logical. My premise is: A) that I want to be dispossessed of him. B) If I want to be dispossessed of him, I don't want anything from him. C) If I don't want anything from him, I have no reason to think about him. D) If I think about him without having a reason to, I think about him unreasonably. E) Unreasonable thinking is not true thinking. F) I do not think about him. G) If I do not really think about him, he doesn't truly exist for me. H) If he doesn't truly exist for me, I can't want him. I) I don't want him –

I unlocked the street door to the house and climbed the wooden stairs. I locked the door to my room behind me. I threw school papers onto my desk. Sweating, I pulled off my clothes and went into the bathroom. As I stepped into the old, claw-footed tub to draw the shower curtain around it, I caught sight of my body in the mirror on the back of the bathroom door.

I thought it was an attractive body.

I said to myself, If I knew what is wrong with me that keeps him from wanting to see me, and if I put that wrong right, he'd want to see me.

You can't make what's wrong right, someone said. It's not possible by thinking about yourself.

What's wrong about you can be made right only by thinking of someone else, another voice said. You've got to think of someone else.

But I only think of someone else, I shouted.

No –

Yes. And I will devote my life to thinking about him. I will make him want me. I will think of nothing else, devising ways, with all the subtlety of someone devising strange meetings and relationships, to get him to long for me. I can do it. I'm French. And not just long for me. Long for me to fuck him – in the mouth, the nose, the ears, and oh up the ass, again and again up the ass – all the while saying, More. He had to want me, he had to want to make love with me again. How, after our love making, could he not want to? I would make him long for my sinful body.

He'll want me, I thought, and I'll have him, and then I won't ever want him again.

The semen on my fingers gummed in the hot water and I had to scrape it off with my nails.

I dried myself and sat in an old arm chair, the towel wrapped about my waist, and tried to read a student's composition.

I heard another voice. It was the voice of a terrifying queen. He said, You!

I sat still.

His voice rose to a screech when he said, Pay attention to me.

I lowered the composition, then remained still again.

We want to examine you, he said.

There was faint laughter.

He said, Everything about you is wrong. Everything.

The laughter became louder.

No wonder he doesn't want you, the queen said.

Fuck off, I said.

The voice trilled as it screeched. Fuck off? it exclaimed. Fuck off?

Yes.

I listened.

I'm not going to think about what I want, I said. I'm not going to.

I listened again.

I don't long for anything, I shouted.

I stood in the silence, and swung my arms.

What do I want? I said. What do I want? For Christ's sake, can't everyone see? It's not grace. No, no. It's nothing as high as that. All I want is his low body.

I went to a wall and leaned my forehead against it and pushed with my weight.

His body was mine, and it was taken away from me. Why, now, was I possessed by what was taken away from me?

80

I hit the wall.

I am going to make him want to make love. I am going to make him long for it, as with a longing for salvation. I'm going to make him wish he had never met me.

11

———— • ————

It seemed to me the day had been a night, and I had been asleep, and now that it was night, I sat at my desk and woke up.

I wanted to be – and I was amazed when the word came to me in my appeal for a word – free. I would not be able to love anyone, not know anyone, unless I was free, and to be free was to apprehend the world as it was, to apprehend even objects – a shoe, a sock, underpants on the floor – as they were.

To be free, I told myself, was to be without intentions. To be free was to be large and open, to be universally accepting, and, in the midst of such large openness, to allow objects in themselves to occur to you without trying to make them what they weren't. I must learn, I thought, I must learn not to impose myself on things. I have always tried to impose myself on things, on people, on whole countries. I think I have tried to impose myself on the universe. I have imposed all my thinking and feeling on Henry to make him mine, something that should be mine, something I fantasized as mine and even as being myself. I must not do this, though it may mean that I must stop thinking and feeling altogether. That was what I really wanted: to stop thinking and feeling altogether.

In my hatred, I imagined that if I hit my thigh and the side of my chest against an edge, his perfect body would fly out from me and disappear. All fantasy was impure, was sinful, I thought, and it was because it had nothing to do with the world. All my thoughts and feelings, fixed in fantasy, had nothing to do with the world.

And yet, how I was pulled with amazed wonder to the photograph, in a pornographic magazine, of a young man and a young woman making love.

What was the most hateful fantasy? It was of a body, but not anyone's body. It was of the ideal body. We all loved it for its wholeness which we didn't have. It did nothing, but it existed, and we referred our small particulars to it, or we would have if we could have found, by some process of collective intuition, its center. We wanted to believe the general could exist in itself, without the particular, if it had a center; for some reason we wanted to believe this, wanted to believe we could have, without having any one thing, everything in itself. We wanted the body at its most abstract, at its most whole, which was a secret kept from us by that brilliant body. This was the worst fantasy.

I told myself I must see someone I had no image of. I knew I wouldn't be able to sleep. Before it got too late, I thought I would call Roberta.

Charlie answered. "What are you up to?" he asked.

Suddenly, as I'd known would happen, I wondered why I had called. "Nothing. I was missing you."

"How about going out?" he asked. "I'll pick you up in my car."

"It's not too late?"

"I know some places where you and I can spend the night drinking if we want."

"I mean, for the family."

He held the receiver away from his face, but I heard him talking, I presumed, to Roberta.

She came on the line.

"You are family," she said.

When Charlie came back on the line, I said to him, almost as if it rose out of me like a pain, "I've got to talk to you," and immediately I laughed.

I was on the curb when he drove up, and he leaned over the passenger seat to open the door.

We went to a bar down by the wharves and sat in a booth and ordered bottles of beer. Charlie liked going to rough places. He thought of himself, in some ways, as being rough, as having, he sometimes said, the soul of a truck driver.

He was waiting for me to tell him what I had to tell him, but Charlie wouldn't press. His way of not imposing on me was to talk himself, hardly with any expectation of my listening. Nodding, I hardly listened.

Smiling, he held his bottle of beer up to me and said, "You're not interested in what I have to say, but you wouldn't tell me that for the life of you."

"I like listening to you."

"You don't."

"I like listening to you talk, but it doesn't matter at all what you're talking about."

He laughed loud.

If I didn't tell him what I had to say, he'd feel that I was holding something back from him, and I didn't want him to feel that. But to tell him would be to exaggerate what I had no reason to think was important. In the unpainted wooden booth with him, drinking beer, I felt close to him. Though it would sound like an exaggeration, I'd still have to tell Charlie, because he was waiting. I couldn't remember ever having telephoned to tell him I had to talk to him. Across the table from me, he put his head against the high, straight back of his seat.

I said, "I've fallen in love."

"Who with?"

"It doesn't matter who with, because I'm the only one who's in love."

He drank beer and put the bottle down, then crossed his arms.

"I want you to tell me how I can get over it," I said. "I don't want to exaggerate. I'm not in any kind of desperate state. Don't think that. You know I'm not the kind of person who exaggerates. And you know I'm not the kind of person who imposes. I don't because, really, I never have any reason for imposing, not any reason important enough. This isn't important. You mustn't give it any importance."

He said, "If it isn't that important, you shouldn't have any trouble getting over it."

84

"It isn't important," I said, "but I can't get over it. It isn't greatly interesting to you, or Roberta, or anyone, not even to me, but there it is, and I can't get over it."

"Look," he said, "You come and spend the night with us."

"I can't impose."

"I'm going to impose on you."

"I'll pay for the beers," I said.

In the car, Charlie talked without stopping. I couldn't talk.

The apartment was dark.

I whispered to Charlie in the entrance hall. "I should go back to my room."

"You're staying here."

He switched on a light in the living room, and told me to wait while he went into his and Roberta's bedroom. I could hear them talk, her voice low. He came out with a blanket and a pillow.

"Roberta said she went to bed because she thought we'd be out late."

I used the bathroom after him, then undressed to my underpants, switched off the lamp, and lay on the sofa.

From their room, I heard Charlie and Roberta talking. They stopped.

The ceiling in the living room of the old tenement apartment was high.

I must sleep, I thought. I have to sleep.

But I couldn't, and I finally got up from the sofa to walk around the room.

I said, "What am I going to do?"

I was angry, but it took me a while, walking around the room, to figure out why. It was because Charlie and Roberta were asleep and I was awake. Half-intentionally, I stumbled and stomped hard with a foot. In their bedroom, the baby cried, and I heard Charlie and Roberta speak. One of them got out of bed to quiet the baby in his crib. I listened. After a long silence, I walked around the room again, hitting the floor with the heels of my feet. When I heard voices again from the bedroom, I lay on the sofa and covered myself with a blanket.

In the living room, Roberta said, "Dan?"

85

"Yes," I answered.

"Are you all right?"

"I'm sorry. I can't sleep."

She came to the sofa in her nightgown and sat at my feet. "Charlie told me what happened," she said. "I hope you don't mind that."

"No," I said. "I'm glad he told you. I wanted him to tell you." I folded my arms behind my head and could smell my own odor. "But I don't know what more to say."

"Maybe you feel you have too much to say."

"There's that."

"Who is he?"

"It's as if it doesn't matter who he is."

"You fell in love with him, and not just anyone. It does matter who he is."

"I fell in love with him because he wouldn't fall in love with me, no other reason."

"I see."

"No," I said, "there are other reasons. You're right. I fell in love with him and not just anyone, and that's because when he –" I stopped.

"What?"

"Nothing."

She said, after a moment, "I'll tell you what you should do."

"Oh?"

"Bring him here."

"Why?"

"Just so you'll be able to see him from the outside and recognize he's not as ideal as you think."

"From a scientifically analytical point of view," I said, "it's interesting, isn't it, that when you are in love with someone you go into a state of finding him ideal. It's a very distinct state of awareness."

I could see Roberta in the dimness smiling at me.

"You see," I said, "I'm not completely without awareness."

"I never thought you were," she said.

It seemed to me that, given the time, I could explain

everything to Roberta by making subtle connections among the flashing ideas in my head, so they would be resolved into a whole. She expected me to be very clear-headed. I said, "I sometimes believe the sense of wonder implies a state of mind as distinct as the most logical conclusion to a syllogism."

Her smile widened. I wondered if she was going to say, "You're funny – "

"At moments, while you're making love, and, all at once, you see your lover's face, you feel – "

"But – " she began.

I couldn't allow her to break in on my connections. "Suspicious as I always am of wonder, that moment of wonder, I allow myself to – " The connections were breaking. I spoke quickly. "I have to allow that, as a distant state, it has – That if it, in itself, survives my suspicions that it is false, is corrupt, what remains of it – " I stopped. "It's all broken down."

"You haven't told me a word about him."

"I can't."

"Try."

"He has a nice apartment. He works in a library, where he can't earn much, but maybe he doesn't have to earn much."

She grunted.

I said, "Why am I not at all, but not at all, interested in his life?"

"It'd help if you were."

"I see that. But, still, why aren't I interested?"

"You're asking an impossible question."

"Has anyone ever made a study on lapsed Catholics?" I asked.

Roberta yawned. "You think it's as a lapsed Catholic that you've reacted to this guy?"

"You're very good at being interested."

"I have to be whether I want to or not."

I said, "My getting in touch with Henry to invite him here would be false, because I would be doing it for some selfish intention. If he, however, telephoned me and asked me if he could come, I would believe that wasn't false, because that would have nothing to do with my intending it. He'd know I was trying to get him to react for my sake, to get something from him. He has to telephone me."

"You telephone him and invite him."

"He won't come."

"Maybe he will."

"I know I'd feel completely false calling him up to invite him."

"Then bear yourself feeling false."

"I do. I do. I do that all the time. I bear my being false, and I do what I have to do. I'm a fake as a teacher, but I do teach, and well, I think. I'm a fake as a reader of books and as a looker at pictures and as a listener to music, but I do these well, too. I'm pretty sure I'm a fake being a friend, but I hope I'm good at it. And I will not allow myself to become cynical. Mildly ironical, maybe, but not cynical."

"You'll be very good at calling him up and asking him to come here."

"It's as though you were imposing some terrible responsibility on me."

"That's exactly what I want to do."

"I don't want to do it, Roberta."

"You do it."

I said, "You know, I have a very strong sense of responsibility. I really do. I keep telling myself, You're strong willed. It's odd, but I sometimes think it's this strong will that would make it possible for me to have a strong relationship with a woman. Yet, all the while, self-consciously, I keep wishing I could relinquish all my responsibility and make that simple act of faith by which I would be taken over by a will stronger than mine, and that would be a man's will."

"He's not going to call you," Roberta said, "if that's what you're praying for. You're going to call him."

"I can't. As a lapsed Catholic, I can't. I don't have the faith."

"Keep telling yourself, Tomorrow, I'm going to call him, tomorrow I'm going to speak to him, and you'll be all right, at least until you call him."

"The comfort of taking on responsibility – "

"It is a comfort," she said.

From the bedroom, Charlie called, "Roberta."

With a note of mockery that, in some way, pleased me, she said, "My husband's calling me," but she didn't move.

I said, "Here's a subject for a study: the Holy Family as a paradigm for the human family."

"Roberta," Charlie called.

12

———— • ————

Every time the image of Henry appeared to me in my sleep, I woke up.

A friend who was a psychologist once said to me that I could not possibly have the dream images I insisted that I did have, and still be able to sleep: I told him I had dreamt I'd made love with my mother and that my father cut off my balls with a straight razor. Such images, he said, would never be allowed to pass whatever it is in the mind that censors unbearable images. But they did come to me without my waking up, and I remembered them vividly. After what my friend told me, I imagined that I hadn't been so disturbed by the images that I woke shouting, because such images are so common we are not disturbed by them. I thought: either the very notions that arouse such images were themselves so exposed that we accepted them as a matter of course, or the most frank images of those notions had become irrelevant to the notions themselves.

I did not know what the image of Henry referred to, when it came to me in my sleep and woke me, but it frightened me.

I knew I'd be all right if I could sleep and really dream. That always helped me if I got into a distracted state. There had been a time in my life when I slept for fifteen hours a day, for day after day, and, afterwards I was all right.

But just asleep, suddenly free in the spacious freedom from thought, I would think, Shouldn't you be thinking about something? And just as I'd tell myself, No, no, don't think, I would, with the sensation of being joltingly caught up short, be brought back to the image.

I thought that I should try to think what the image of Henry meant to me that it kept me awake. Perhaps I could explain my obsession away. But this was like attempting to explain why the images that occurred of making love with your mother and being castrated by your father did not frighten you. The difficulty was not that my explanations of the frightening possession by the image of Henry were too complex, it was that they were too simple. Every meaning I came up with seemed in the end too simple.

What about Mère Ste Epiphane, in the parochial grammar school, saying that Christ's greatest suffering was not the flagellation, not the crowning of thorns, the carrying of the cross, the crucifixion, but his having to hang on the cross naked, his body entirely exposed to everyone?

My religion did not allow meanings outside itself, and in itself all its meanings were obvious.

I went through all the images, all the fantasies of my religion I could think of. They all struck me as irrelevant to anything but the most banal explanations of that image of Henry. In the same way as easy psychology could not be used to explain the most obvious of its images, so my religion could not be used to explain the image that frightened me because it possessed me. The real reasons for my possession and fear of the image surely were deeper than my religion. I believed, too, that they were deeper than the psychology of my particular personality, a personality completely determined by my religion.

In the dawn light, I heard the baby cry. I heard the consoling sounds of Roberta, who went into the kitchen with him. After a while, she returned with him to the bedroom.

I didn't want to speak to anyone. When Charlie came into the living room to say, "Dan," I pretended I was asleep. He came over to the sofa and touched my shoulder. "Dan," he said. I opened my eyes. In his underpants, he was standing over me and looking down at me.

"I thought you'd want to get ready to go to school," he said.

I licked my lips. "Thanks."

"How are you?"

"I'm fine."

Out of the bathroom, where I'd shaved with Charlie's razor, I dressed and folded the blanket on the sofa.

Charlie came in, dressed. "We'll have something to eat," he said, speaking softly. "Then I'll drive you."

"Thanks," I said, "but I'll go now."

"Dan – "

"It's all right. I'm all right. But I want to go now."

While I was waiting for the streetcar, it came to me that my perceptions had changed, that I was not seeing or hearing as I had been the day before. What I saw – the windshields of passing cars reflecting overhead trees, telephone posts and wires, the clear morning sky – was without dimension. It was as if some sense in me had ceased, some sense of dimension which had put me in the same space as what I saw. It took me a long time to figure out that things were visually disconnected from me because I had no visual awareness of space. Without space, objects existed in a baffling way, and perhaps my concentrated wonder about them was how they could exist so assertively, with hard, sharp edges, in no space.

I got on the trolley.

Something else, I knew, had happened which the visual flatness merely indicated: a break had occurred in my very appreciation of objects, so that nothing I thought about them applied. I fixed myself on them to try to make some kind of sense of them, but I couldn't. They kept their meaning to themselves. Never did I think they were without meaning. They were nothing but meaningful in themselves. But I was incapable of appreciating this, as incapable as I was of understanding how objects could exist in no space. They defied me by their own weird state of being, which frightened me.

As I was walking up the steps of the brownstone school I imagined I saw Henry standing still behind the glass in the wooden front door where the school's name appeared in gold letters, and a horror passed over me. I stopped on the steps. The door opened and a colleague came out, but the horror remained.

My colleague held the door open for me to go in.

I was horrified, but I was, at the same time, not at all interested in my horror.

My students' compositions were flat. I had to work against my complete lack of interest in them. Sometimes I wanted to say, Give up, it isn't worth it. And yet, their attempts to get the sentences right, both written and spoken, moved me. Something moved me that maybe had nothing to do with my students.

Often, I thought, you've got to telephone Henry.

In my room, I asked myself how I had got through the day.

You did it, a voice said.

Of course you did it. What happened that was so terrible you couldn't work? You think it's a reason not to work that someone doesn't want to fuck with you? What is this? Not fucking the person you want to fuck is going to change your life? Come off it. What you want isn't important enough to make you even think about not being able to work. Jerking off should take care of what you want. No, if you think you can't work, there has to be another reason. If you can't work, it won't be because of a non-fuck. But let me tell you, no reason is going to be enough to excuse you from working. You'll have to work, correcting your students' talk and writing, day after day, because nothing's going to excuse you. You hear?

Shut up, I said.

I got up and went to my desk and sat at it. The telephone was on a corner, on a book. This was just the moment to telephone Henry. I had to keep reminding myself of it, as if it were the least important thing I had to do that day.

At my desk, I conscientiously tried to devise images that would apply to my state of mind. All my concentration went into this, because I thought I must be able, somehow, to make a connection between a particular and an abstract state. I tried to do this because the split I had noticed that morning between my inward state and the outward world – the outward world being, now, nothing but flat images – had come between me and my image of Henry lying naked on his bed. I knew I would not be able to make contact with what that image inspired.

The telephone rang. "Have you called him?" Roberta asked.

"I tried," I said, "but there was no answer."

"You'll try again, won't you?"

"Sure."

"You won't believe me if I tell you he isn't perfect, because no human being is. You'll say it's because I haven't met him. So let me meet him."

"I don't know if I should," I said, "if your intention is just to make me see his defects. Why should I see his defects?"

She shouted, "You've got to!"

I would have gone through day after day of the heaviest work rather than telephone him.

"All right," I shouted back, "I will."

I would do it after I ate. But even opening a can of soup and heating it on an electric ring seemed to me to require too much concentration, so I went out to a delicatessen and had a sandwich and a beer at a table on which the wipe marks of a rag had dried.

At the next table, I heard this conversation between two old women:

"For crying out loud, I says to him, let's get off the subject."

"And did he?"

"What do you think? Him get off a subject? He never gets off a subject. He jumps up and down on it till it's a patch of blood on the ground."

I drank another beer and felt a little drunk.

When I told myself, Maybe you're crazy, I heard, No, you're not, you're not crazy, you're something else.

I didn't call Henry.

13

———— • ————

I slept for a little while. I knew it was only a little while because I woke to the sounds of people in other rooms preparing to go to bed. I didn't sleep for the rest of the night.

In the morning, it was as if I had forgotten Henry, and nothing remained of his presence but my state of mind, which I didn't necessarily associate with him. With each day, perhaps, I would get further and further away from Henry until, in the end, I would wonder what state I was in. I couldn't now imagine the state would simply vanish with Henry's vanishing.

At the language school, while watching the talking mouth of a student, I wondered why people spoke.

As I watched a student write a sentence, I would wonder, why do people write?

As I went through the lessons, I found myself more and more impressed by my responsibility towards my students. I hated having to do what I did, but I did it, and I did it well. In that day's lessons I taught my Panamanian to speak, in the past, present, and future, and in the negative past, present and future. To do this I stood and took up positions that corresponded to different tenses and in each position I performed an act or did not perform an act: sleeping, eating, walking.

During lunch break, in a local cafeteria with another teacher from the school, I felt I didn't have the power to open my mouth to talk. Yet I did, and I admired myself, in some stark way, for what I would do whether I liked it or not. I imagined I had to move the hands of the clock on the wall to make the seconds of the afternoon class pass. But as I moved them with one hand, I taught with the other, and sometimes I moved them back to explain, once again, that in English you could not use a double negative. Sometimes I imagined I was trying to teach a language to natives, who had no language, to civilize them. The last hour took all my strength to move, at fractions of a second, the hands of the clock, and then the most difficult part of the day was filling out the class register.

Leaning back in my wooden chair, I asked myself: Where does this center of responsibility come from?

Before going to my room, I walked around the Public Garden, and there were long moments, filled with late sunlight, when I forgot I should be thinking about something. When I was reminded what I should be thinking about, it appeared not to bear much attention. I looked at people as though they were walking on the same paths as I was, as though they were in the same park as I was, as if they inhabited the space I inhabited.

I had walked among people on the streets, stood with them in lines at post offices and banks, sat with them in movie houses, without seeing them. My fantasy had been so strong, it could have limited my senses for my entire life, and I would never have recognized that I was limited by fantasy. It would have been very easy for me now to turn against that image, to turn against it and destroy it, rather than draw back from it and simply see it diminish in the outside air. I would have given up everything for even the faintest possibility of its being realized. I would have given up my friendship with Charlie and Roberta. And only I wouldn't have known that I'd given up everything for a banal image that was repeated again and again pornographically. How I hated fantasy. If there were no ways for my sex to enter into life, if my sex fixed me in fantasy, then I must give up my sex. I had enough control to do that.

As I was opening the door to my room, a large third-story room which overlooked a tree-lined alley, the telephone rang.

"Did you call him?" Roberta asked.

"I'm feeling better."

"You won't get over him unless you see him again."

"But I'm feeling better without seeing him."

"It's up to you – "

She put the responsibility on me, and she would be annoyed with me if I didn't fulfill it. I suspected that she wanted me to fulfill it for her sake, which meant she'd be even more annoyed with me if I didn't.

"Come on," she said, "show me you can do it."

"I can do it."

"Show me."

I asked to speak to Charlie, but she said he was out.

"Out where?" I asked.

"He went drinking with some friends from where he teaches."

"Oh," I said.

After I hung up, I looked at the telephone, and as I did I saw it flatten and become merely the image of a telephone. When I reached for the receiver, my hand and arm seemed to detach themselves from me and cease to have anything to do with me, and when I heard my voice say, "Hello," to a voice that said "Hello," it wasn't my voice, or his, I heard.

"It's Dan," I said.

I thought, Now you have risked everything.

After I hung up, I began to tremble. I told myself that my trembling, which made the desk chair creak, was exaggerated. When I tried to stop it, my arms and legs would break the self-restraint I was using, and jerk. Because I knew why I was trembling, I should be able to restrain it, but I couldn't. I yawned more and more as the trembling decreased.

I felt deeply sleepy.

I telephoned Roberta to tell her Henry and I would come round Saturday evening. She said, "Don't you feel better for doing it?"

"No," I said.

But I did.

For the rest of the week, I tried not to anticipate seeing him. Much as I told myself not to expect anything, I knew I expected everything. I would say out loud when I was alone, "You expect everything." But I did keep myself from anticipating what the

97

everything might be.

The only image that dramatized my anticipation came to me as I was standing at a corner waiting for traffic to pass: running. It surprised me that the image expressed my sense of accelerating longing for him. It surprised me and it pleased me. As I walked slowly, my mind ran and ran.

As it ran, I said, as if on a wild thrust forward, to run even faster, "I love him."

All day Saturday my mind ran faster and faster, and in the hour before I was to meet him it ran so fast I thought I wouldn't be able to stop and would burst past him.

He drove up, on time, in his car.

He must have just had a shower, as his hair was wet and his face shone. All at once he looked to me like a boy, not a man. Perhaps I looked the same. We were boys. But he had a man's voice.

"How do we get there?" he asked.

In the car beside him, I thought: I have spent half my life in this car.

Excited by being with him, and intimidated about expressing my excitement, I needed to contain it in some way, so I would contain it and express it in talking about our one permissible subject: books.

I translated his body into his talk about books. When we stopped at a red light and he unbuttoned two buttons on his shirt and ran his finger over the revealed skin, I thought: But my impression that he has no awareness of his sensual body must be wrong, he's very aware of it. In talking about literature, which was meant to de-personalize, he was being entirely personal; he wasn't rising above himself, but raising himself to the level of what he considered most important. I had imagined he was a person with a fine, transparent ego, but he might have had the biggest, most colored ego of anyone I'd ever met. Well, if he did, his ego was his right.

Listening to him, looking at him, I thought: No, you aren't wrong to be in love with him.

Climbing the wooden steps to the porch, I wished I was alone.

After I rang the doorbell and turned to see Henry in the yellow porch light, standing still with no expectations of any kind, I realized I wished I'd come alone because I wasn't sure Charlie and Roberta, who were in a way family to me, were people Henry would be interested to meet. He already knew he wouldn't be interested, and this was why he had no expectations.

I remembered when, in freshman year, I first took Charlie to visit my parents in our house, remembered my worry, as I opened the door into the entry, that our lives were nowhere near the level of his and his family. But Charlie being Charlie, said to my parents, "What a nice house you have." And, being me, I said, "Come on, I'll show you around." With each grim little room I showed him, he said, "This is pretty," and I'd say, "Isn't it?" We both knew what we were doing, and knew that this made us friends. With Henry (not that I wanted to compare him and Charlie) I would have had to say, The rooms are grim, and he would have, of course, agreed. This truthfulness, in a way, precluded our understanding one another and becoming friends. Charlie opened the door.

"Hello," he said, in a loud voice, holding out both hands and smiling.

I thought, How young we are.

Roberta did not make any special efforts with Henry, nor did he with her, but from the moment they met one another they talked, effortlessly, as they talked the whole evening.

He hardly spoke to Charlie, even during the moments he was alone with us when Roberta was in another room. Charlie tried at least to make Henry the center of the evening by saying, "What a pleasure it is to have someone visit for the first time," which Henry, stepping as it were to the side, smiled at a little.

I answered, "Yes."

Then Henry went off to find Roberta, into the bedroom to watch her, he said, take care of Jerry, or into the kitchen as she prepared supper.

I spent most of the evening with Charlie, both of us making efforts to talk to one another.

I said, "I think there's going to be another war."

He said, "Don't say that, Dan."

During the meal, Charlie said again and again, "This is great food, really great," followed immediately by my saying, "Really great." Henry didn't comment. Roberta said, "You two are very funny," then asked Henry, "Aren't they funny?"

He smiled again.

She said to him, "After dinner, they tap-dance on the table and sing."

"Are they good?" he asked.

She laughed. "They're terrible."

He laughed too. I hadn't seen him laugh. I'd thought he had no sense of humor. Charlie, too, was laughing at what Roberta said. I forced myself to.

I saw all the falsity of Charlie, and saw that we were similar. I was certainly more like him than Henry, which indicated, in its way, how little sex had to do with setting the terms of a relationship. I was not sexually attracted to Charlie, except at odd moments when I recalled how I had been, and I was again, for that moment, nostalgically attracted to him. And yet I was closer to him than to anyone else I knew. Roberta was right, we were a kind of comedy act, two loving bums who loved one another and whom no one else loved.

I resented Henry's lack of self-consciousness. His lack of falsity made him, I thought, less of a person. He was born into a state of self-possession. And this was why Charlie and I were not on his level. Charlie wasn't putting Henry at the center so that I would feel Henry was a friend of friends and not someone from the outside. Really, Charlie couldn't help putting Henry at the center. Our reasons for doing this were not dissimilar: if I wanted Henry at the center for his body, it was in his body that his self-possession most showed itself. Charlie and I sounded false in our honoring him, and we were false, because we did not know how else to be. Charlie, drunk, raised his wine glass to Henry and said, "To the hub of our evening," to which I, drunken and raising my glass, said, "To the hub of the hub," as if I were not going to allow Charlie to upstage me. But there was something more than the honor we showed the guest that Charlie and I shared, and we both knew it: our desire to make fun of Henry. We wanted to deride him for being at the center.

Roberta, also a Protestant, had what Henry had. But we didn't deride it in Roberta because she was a woman.

"Will you two ring down the curtain?" she said to Charlie and me.

But Charlie and I continued to talk to each other, assuming that what we said was important for the listening world.

"I do believe there'll be another war," I said.

"Don't," Charlie said.

"What do you mean, don't? Don't what? Don't say what's going to happen?"

"How do you know, Dan? How can you say you know?"

"I know," I insisted.

"You can't."

"I do."

Henry and Roberta talked about Boston.

I got drunk. I hoped Henry would, but he didn't. When I tried to fill his glass, he said, touching the rim with a finger to stop me, "I've got to drive." I refilled my glass. "I should be going," he said.

Charlie said to me, "If you're not going on to anywhere else, stay the night."

I didn't answer, but was angry at him, because I wanted to leave with Henry.

Staring straight at me, Roberta said, like a business woman, "It'd be better if you didn't stay. I've got a big day tomorrow, and –"

I hugged her.

Henry kissed her cheek and shook Charlie's hand with, I noted, a firm grip.

We were silent as he and I sauntered through the warm night to the car.

I was running, really.

He said, "If it isn't too personal, is Charlie the room-mate you were in love with?"

This shocked me. I said, "I don't mind your asking personal

questions," but my shock kept me from saying anything more.

"I'm sorry."

"But I don't mind."

"I wondered only because he is so beautiful."

"Charlie?"

"Yes."

"I guess I know him too well to see it."

"You can take my word for it."

After a moment, I said, "Yes, he is the person I told you about. But it didn't happen the way I said. That was fantasy. You must have known."

"I know it was a fantasy." We stood by the car. Henry asked, "What did happen?"

"Charlie and I have never mentioned it to one another."

I had Henry's interest and I wanted to keep it. "I'd like to say it was the most wonderful experience in our lives," I said.

"I'm sure you would."

I said, "It lasted about five drunken minutes, and I can hardly remember anything about it."

He asked, "And you're no longer attracted to him?"

"I am, at moments, but I don't think I could ever make love to Charlie, even if he wanted to."

"Why?"

"I know him too well."

He said, "I tell myself that the more I know a person the more I should want to make love with him."

I said, "But that's not the way it is."

"It should be."

Then he left me to go around the car and get in the driver's seat.

Driving, he said, "Roberta is interesting."

"She is."

Then he said, "She holds that family together."

I didn't know what he meant.

As he didn't say anything more about Charlie, I presumed he didn't find him interesting.

In my drunken state, I felt great sentimental love for Charlie.

I said, "Charlie's silly, but I love him. I love him for everything we've been through together. There've been some very silly moments."

I was about to go off on a long reminiscence of moments in Charlie's and my lives together in college, but I checked myself.

The silence in the car was Henry's, and it was intentional. He didn't want to speak. I wanted to speak, but didn't dare to, because he wouldn't answer. He was thinking, I imagined, about me, and I had no idea what he was thinking. Or maybe he wasn't at all thinking about me. I wondered how I could make him think about me if he wasn't.

Studying him as he drove, appearing in the sudden light of street lamps, then half disappearing, I imagined I had gotten to know him a little. Roberta was right to have thought that would happen. But she was wrong in thinking I would no longer want him, because I imagined, looking closely at him, that this happened: he, whom I was beginning to know as a person, had a body which existed apart from him, had a body which didn't essentially belong to him and could belong to me as well as to him. Solid as it was, it seemed to me that by reaching out for it with my arms I could remove it from him, and he, in some bodiless form, would continue to drive the car while I held his body against me, ready to jump out with it as soon as he stopped in front of my rooming house.

I wanted to steal his body. I should be able to do it. I thought, if I really put my mind to it, I should be able to get him to give it to me.

Somehow, it should be so easy, since neither of us really owned our bodies, to let them go off together, while I would sit with him and talk about whatever interested him: books. Our free bodies should be able to do what our bound bodies hadn't done when Henry last drove me home – go up to my room and make love. This seemed to me something neither of us could object to, and it would put right what had gone wrong. It was what our bodies instinctively wanted.

He knew he controlled his body and would only rarely give it the freedom it wanted. His free body would want to make love with mine. But he didn't want it to. I needed to break his control over it.

To say, as we were going down Marlborough Street, I'm not very tired, would have been a cheap way of letting him know that I wanted him to say, I'm not tired either. We weren't that cheap. Or at least he wasn't. I had only minutes, seconds, to think of something original that would inspire him to react to me, that would make him give over control to me. He could find anything I said cheap. What I needed to say was one sharp thing to convince him he should let his body go free. Only one sentence was needed. But it had to be a good one. If it wasn't, if it didn't convince him, I would risk everything and lose. He stopped in front of the rooming house and switched off the engine. I could have had him, I knew I could have had him, by saying the right thing. I could have said, Look, I love you and I want to make love with you, which was at that moment the most truthful thing for me to say. He raised his hand for mine. I couldn't take the risk. I held his warm hand only for a second before I got out of the car.

On the landing outside my door I stopped and placed against my face the hand he'd held.

14

———— • ————

I didn't sleep at all during the night, and at some point in the early morning I became aware, with a terrifying attention, of a function of my mind I'd never experienced before. Uncontrollably, my mind released image after image. I was not asleep. I was completely conscious and looking at a scene.

In my mind there appeared a square outside a train station at night, with hundreds of standing people, and soldiers brought a young man into their midst. The soldiers held the young man while doctors, in blood-stained smocks, undressed him, and the people around watched. One doctor looked down his throat, another grabbed his testicles and made him cough, another shouted at him to bend over and spread out his buttocks for a rectal examination. The doctors said, "All right," to the soldiers, who tied the naked young man to an electricity pole, and then the soldiers beat him with lengths of barbed wire. All the while the spectators were laughing. If I, studying the scene, wasn't laughing with them, I thought they were right to laugh at the young man for no other reason but that what he was going through was totally without originality, and therefore to be derided. It was as if the young man deserved what he was getting because he was, himself, unoriginal, and did not have the imagination to make up a more original dramatization of his thoughts and feelings. The jeering crowd had seen it all before, we all knew where.

Among the spectators, some people, turning away from the whipping, amused themselves by farting or seeing who could pee the farthest. I knew that if an equivalent had to be found between some image and what I thought and felt, it'd be among these people, not with the young man. They knew that what I was going through shouldn't be taken seriously. When, from among them, the image came to me of a naked, skinny man balancing on his head a naked, fat man, the one so skinny his cock was as big as a leg and the other so fat he hardly had a cock, I wondered if this was an equivalent: my state was as superficially silly, it really and truly was.

But the scene in the middle kept drawing me to it, as it became more and more violent. I did not want to look at it. This was not because I was upset by it, but because I was embarrassed by it. Perhaps the young man had staged it himself to demonstrate his state. Now, the soldiers were wrapping his body with the barbed wire, while he, dripping with blood, stood motionless, his eyes staring into the cavorting crowd. He wanted to be taken seriously, wanted the crowd to believe his feelings were equal to his pain, when all the crowd knew they weren't.

As I, in the crowd, looked at the young man, an old, toothless woman next to me said, hitting me in the side with her elbow, You feel bad for him.

I said to her, No, I don't.

Yes, you do.

I don't, I repeated.

An old man next to her said, I can see you do.

No, I insisted.

People around me laughed.

Then why aren't you having a good time, joking and laughing with us? the old woman asked.

All right, I said. I will. You'll all see: I'm the silliest person in the world.

He doesn't have it in him, someone said, to joke and laugh.

I do.

You're so serious.

I'm not.

You're so deep.

I'm not.

You have such deep and serious thoughts and feelings.

I don't. I don't.

A bearded transvestite pushed people aside and said to me, harshly, Then show us you can have a good time.

What do you want me to do?

He laughed.

I heard a groan. The soldiers were hefting the stiff, burnt carcass of a war victim onto the shoulders of the young man whose arms and legs were entwined with barbed wire. One soldier pushed him to start him walking. Nausea came over me for what I could only think was the sickening exaggeration of the scene; the very strain of the demonstration to be original belied the violence of it, made it dishonest. The people about me were honest; if they exaggerated, they did it deliberately, and had fun exaggerating. I kept looking at the young man, however, who staggered under the weight of the dead body as he walked towards the train station. I took a step in his direction.

In the crowd I heard a screeching laugh, and, startled, I turned to see, in the crowd but overlooking it, a horned monster, surrounded by the transvestite and the others who had derided me for having no sense of fun. The monster was looking at the young man make his way through the crowd, while the hot night sky was pulsing with the pink light of exploding bombs, and the monster's laughter rose higher than the bomb blasts. This, I knew, was the true metaphor for my state of being, this monster, for whom all metaphors were fake. It turned its head towards me a little and smiled at me with spiky lips, and I knew he knew the truth, knew that all things were vanity, so when, hearing a cry of pain from the young man, I looked round at him, I did so with the sudden terror that all he was suffering was vanity, that all the metaphors from my religion were vain. I hated that young man.

In the grainy, grey, dawn light, I got up from my bed, on which the sheets were twisted, and sat at my desk. I tried to write out, sentence after sentence, the most basic questions, thinking that in this way I was being reasonable, and what I needed to be above all was reasonable.

Be reasonable, I thought. Don't ask yourself, Why is this madness happening to me? because that will only bring you down to the level of the madness. Ask yourself simpler questions that have to do, not with what is happening to you, but with what you can do about it.

Ask yourself: What can you do to stop wanting what you can't have.

I wrote: I do not want to live with him. I do not want a friendship with him. I do not want –

I knew what I wanted, and there was nothing I could do to achieve it. No amount of the most reasonable thinking would realize that want or, by default, explain it away. Any attempt to explain it away brought me down again to the question Why do you want so much what you can't have? This, in turn, brought me down to other questions, each crazier than the last, so that I imagined it was my very attempt to ask reasonable questions, never mind answer them, that produced more fake monsters. They began to hang from the picture rail around the walls.

The room filled with hot sunlight.

When the telephone rang, I felt a moment of real fear.

Roberta asked me how I was.

"I'm all right."

"Are you sure?"

I said, "Look, I honestly don't want to talk about it."

"So it's not all right."

"Let's not exaggerate." I said, "It doesn't matter."

"It matters."

"It doesn't."

"Come over here," she said.

"I don't want to talk about it."

"Fine. We won't talk about it. But come over."

If I don't go, I thought, she'll be annoyed with me, and I can't allow her to be annoyed with me.

All my life, women made me do what I didn't want to do.

We sat in the backyard. Charlie held Jerry in his lap, and we talked for a while about his first tooth, which wasn't giving him any trouble.

Roberta said to me, "You don't want to talk about it, I know, but I wanted to tell you how much better looking than Henry you are. Charlie thought so too."

"You are," Charlie said. He was making an effort.

I laughed.

"I also happen to think you're more intelligent," Roberta said.

"Stop lying," I said.

"I mean it."

"It seemed to me he didn't have much to say," Charlie said.

"He had a lot to say," Roberta said, "but it was limited. He never talked about himself. I don't think he's had much experience to talk about. Did you know that he's never been abroad, for example?"

"No," I said.

"He's hardly ever left New England."

"I didn't know."

She said, "All he said to me that was interesting, I thought, was that at holiday dinners his family passed round genealogies, so relatives could try to figure out just how they were related to one another. That was the only personal thing he said. Otherwise, his talk was all commentary."

"I thought he was good at that," I said.

"Again, limited," she said. "Very limited."

I felt Roberta didn't have the right to be negative about Henry. She should have praised him, as he deserved. I didn't like what she was saying, and I didn't like the pleasure I was getting from it. Any reaction to Henry, whether negative or positive, was a false reaction.

I said, "Anyway – " as a way of changing the subject.

"I know, I know," she said, "you don't want to talk about him."

"Not really."

She said, "Now you should forget him and stop floating around, and get back to earth."

"What?"

She kept her eyes fixed on me, her smile, too, fixed. "You

know."

"I've never lost an hour's work," I said. "Ask Mrs. Hart, ask my students. I've been a good teacher all along."

She shook her head. "I didn't mean your teaching."

"What did you mean?"

Charlie was silent, trying to hold the baby, who punched him in the face and kicked his groin. It was as if he was trying to hold his worry about what was happening between Roberta and me.

"I wish you'd tell me," I said.

"You never want to talk about relationships."

I frowned.

"If you had really wanted a relationship with Henry, you could have tried to work for it. But it was obvious to me, when I saw you together, that you didn't. No doubt you're right, and he's not worthy of you. But I'm pretty sure he'd try to have a relationship with you if you'd only try one with him. I felt that about him, that he knows about family ties, and – "

I said, "I don't want a relationship with him."

"What else do you imagine happens when two people come together, even if for a fuck?"

"It's an experience you have to have had," I said.

"Don't you see that there is no basis, none at all, to loving someone except in a relationship, however complex, however massively complex, it is?"

I wished I could tell her how much I hated the way she spoke, the way she seemed to be trying to impress me with the way she spoke.

"I don't want to live with anyone," I said. "I can only think that to live with someone is to have a family, and I refuse to have a family."

"And friends?"

"And friends, if that means having to listen to them talk about my relationships with them and my responsibilities towards the relationships."

"Dan," Charlie said, bouncing Jerry up and down, "what else is there among people?"

"There's not having relationships," I said.

Roberta's voice rose. "There's taking from them but not giving anything to them."

I turned to her full face.

She said, "You're very good at imposing yourself on others and not good on letting others impose on you."

"I don't impose on others."

"Don't you? Don't you, didn't you, on Charlie?" She paused, and then she said, quickly, "Didn't you impose demands on Charlie that he had to accept, because he knew that otherwise you wouldn't keep him as a friend?"

Charlie got up and went into the house with Jerry.

Roberta said, "You want everything your own way, Dan. I admire you for that, I suppose, because so do I want everything my own way. And I'd no doubt admire you even more if you did get everything your way. But you won't."

I lowered my head and looked at my hands in my lap.

I wanted to say, For Christ's sake, tell a joke.

"The very quality in Charlie that keeps him your friend," she said, "is, I'm sure, the quality you least admire in him, if you've even suspected it in him. That's his sense of duty towards others. You think he's irresponsible, and you like it that he's irresponsible. But you've never noticed, I'll bet, how he tries not to be, and how he works to fulfill his duties. Your old irresponsible room-mate is working to realize his duties as a husband and father and as an art teacher and as an artist. If you considered, for a moment, your sense of duty towards him –" she stopped.

I intertwined my fingers.

She said, "He and I are trying to help you get over what's keeping you irresponsible. I'm not sure our help can do any good."

I squeezed my hands between my knees.

Leaning towards me, she said, "It's up to you," and she put her hands on my hands.

I asked, "Do you mind if I go home now?"

"Why do you think you need my permission?"

"I don't know," I stood. "I'll just go. I won't say goodbye to Charlie."

"He'll be offended."

"I'd offend him more, I think, if I saw him. Maybe I should stay away from Charlie."

"He'll be angry with me for having brought up what I did," Roberta said. "Maybe I shouldn't have."

"Say goodbye to him from me."

"Don't dramatize it too much. It's not as though you were never going to see one another again."

I smiled.

She said, "Listen, what I would do if I were you, which I know I'm not, would be to treat what you're going through as though it were a disease that has taken over your body. Like any disease, it has to be cured, and it can only be cured by people who know about curing."

"I could never make myself go."

She said nothing.

I said, "I'll go into the woods, and come out when I'm cured or I'll die in the woods."

"I wish you'd stay out of those woods," Roberta said.

I left by the gate between the house and the old garage.

The monsters in my room moved silently and swiftly when I wasn't looking; when I was looking, they remained still and invisible, and I knew that, though I could hardly see them, their presences were indicated by thin, horn- and spike-lipped smiles. They never stopped making fun of me. When I went into the bathroom to pee, I imagined they followed me in then followed me out, waddling on thick, squat, scaly legs, nudging one another, pointing at me, and stifling their laughter with wart-covered, knubbly-knuckled hands.

I wanted to turn to them and say, For Christ's sake, can't you be a little more original?

But that would have offended them, and I didn't want to offend them.

They jumped up and ran into the walls when the telephone rang.

Charlie said, "I'm sorry you left like that, without saying anything."

"It seemed the best thing to do at the time."

"I don't know, Dan. Roberta is a truthful person, and what she said she said because she believes the truth is best. She probably went too far, though."

"No," I said. "If anything, she didn't go far enough."

"Can't I see you?"

"I'm not in a very good state, Charlie."

"I know."

"You're the one who should be asking yourself if you want to see me."

"Come on," Charlie said. "We've seen one another through all kinds of strange times. Roberta's too pure, in a way. You've got to be very careful with Roberta. She doesn't understand that two people can have a relationship that's, well, odd according to certain ways of thinking, yet good. I try to tell her she has to take a more oblique view, but she can't. I know I can."

I said, "Let's leave it a while, and then we can get together and talk."

"I don't want to talk," Charlie said. "To tell you the truth, I think she's exaggerated it all. I mean, I don't believe that the way you think about me, or about Roberta either, has any connection with the way you think about this guy."

"Is that what Roberta believes?"

"I can't stand her talking about it any more. She's out now. I told her to go away to visit a friend for a couple of hours. It's become too much."

"I don't understand."

"Neither do I. Roberta's desire to get things right makes her a great person, in a way, but – "

"She wants to get me right?"

"I'll tell you, Dan, that sometimes I get tired listening to her talk on and on about you."

Without saying anything, I delicately lowered the receiver. Then I pressed my nose against a white piece of paper, my eyes staring at it. The telephone rang again. It continued to ring, and wouldn't stop until I answered.

"Dan," Charlie said.

113

"I'll speak to you some time next week," I said.

"I'll get in touch with you if you don't with me."

"I'll get in touch," I said.

"I wish you hadn't hung up on me," he said.

"I'm sorry."

I didn't want Charlie to see me. He should think I was incapable of being unhealthy. I needed to be, to him, perfect.

Then I thought, It is just because you feel this that you should see him, should let him see you.

I had, I'd thought, hidden so much from Charlie. I had hidden all my sins. Or I had tried to.

The sun was still up when I went to the bar, not the bar near the bus station I usually went to. It was dark inside. There I picked up a young man named Karl. The sun had set by the time we left the bar to go, first for something to eat, then to his place. We could walk there, he said. We went into the South End, to a street where all along the sidewalks and gutters were shattered liquor bottles thrown by derelicts from the windows of their rooms. Not even the poor lived in this neighborhood, just derelicts and gypsies and Karl. His room was above an old shop inhabited by gypsies. As we climbed, he told me to be careful of the bottles on the stairs. He didn't apologize. I had the feeling that I had been here before, or, at least, that it was as I had expected. Karl talked non-stop. He, too, seemed familiar to me.

He was young, maybe seventeen. He was effeminate.

I was sure I had heard everything he told me before. He didn't know who his father was and, since leaving his mother a couple of years before, he hadn't seen her. When he stopped going to school at sixteen, he started working. His job was in the kitchen of a hotel restaurant. He lived alone, and he'd done up his room.

Opening the door, he stood to the side to let me go in first. The light was on, and I saw a big brass bed in a small room. On the bed was a royal blue, chenille-like spread, with royal blue bolsters and throw pillows in what looked like pale blue satin cases, and everything was fringed. The draperies on the windows were royal blue, too, and hung in deep velvet folds from beneath a velvet valance, all, again, fringed in gold. The room was painted pale blue. The light, refracted, came from a small chandelier hanging from a cracked but painted ceiling.

Karl stood beside me. I presumed he thought I was so surprised I couldn't speak. He put a hand on my shoulder.

"I saved and saved for the fucking bed," he said. "Then when I got that together I saved for all the materials, and I made all the fucking drapes and the bedspread and everything."

"It's a beautiful room," I said.

"I worked hard enough for it."

"You should be an interior decorator."

"I do it for myself."

Looking around more, I said, "But where do you keep your clothes and things?"

"I put them in boxes under the bed," he said.

In this room, I thought, I won't be able to make love with Karl. His effeminacy had put me off him from when we'd started to talk in the bar. This was because I always felt effeminates were affecting their effeminacy; I found myself wanting to say to them, "Stop acting." This room gave the act its setting. I could not, ever, make love without feeling at some level in the love making that my life depended on it. There was no way life could depend on Karl in his room. I wondered how I could leave without hurting him. As much as I could have hated Karl for being so fake, however, I made myself take his hand from my shoulder and kiss it.

"Wait, wait," he said, and stepped away to pull from under the bed a cardboard box from which he took a negligee. "Turn away," he said, raising a commanding hand. When he commanded, "Now look," I turned back to see him in the negligee. With a hand on a hip, the other at the back of his head, he thrust one knee forward on the edge of the bed so the gown was held parted to reveal his cock and balls.

No, I thought, I can't.

I wanted to get away from him, I realized, not because he was pretending to be a woman, but because he in no way equivocated about it. He wasn't being ironical about his negligee or his room. It didn't occur to him that I might not find the act as wonderful as he did. It did not even occur to him that it was an act.

If I had sensed in him the slightest sadness, I might perhaps have felt sympathy for him. But there was no sadness in him. He was all brightness. He flashed around the bed, swinging the negligee open as he strode to reveal his long, white, slender, and beautiful body. I couldn't stand his spirit. He threw off the gown and, naked, came to me and put his arms around me.

I made myself make love with him with great and delicate affection. I wanted him to believe in my affection. In the rumpled bed, he himself rumpled, his hair messed and pungent smells penetrating his cologne, a moment came when, suddenly apart from him and looking at him, I saw that he was helpless, and the sense of his helplessness was all that was needed for me to make love with him as if his life depended on it. He was startled enough by my intensity to give in to it, and I found myself crouching on the bed with him in my arms, keening and kissing his face. I felt his body stiffen, and I let him go. I turned away from him.

A moment later I asked him where the toilet was.

He didn't know what had happened, but he knew I was using the toilet as an excuse to get away.

"It's on the landing. Put your shoes on, or you'll be crushing roaches with your feet."

When I got back, he looked at me as if expecting me to say I had to go.

"Can I ask you something?" he said.

"What?"

"You're not falling in love with me or anything like that, are you?"

"Why do you want to know?" I asked.

"Because I've got to tell you I'm not dependable." He tickled me under the arm, and as if he had touched the most senstitive spot on me, my body jolted and I began to laugh. He kept tickling. "You're not, are you?"

"Stop it," I shouted.

He held me tightly and continued to tickle me while I writhed with laughter.

"Stop it, stop it."

"Tell me you don't love me."

I howled with laughter. It was as loud as unrestrained screaming. He was strong, and held me tightly while he hardly touched the tips of his fingers to my side.

Gasping, I shouted, "I don't love you."

15

────── • ──────

Though I was not able to sleep in my bed, I felt, each morning, that I wouldn't be able to get out of my bed. I lay and watched the clock on the bedside table, thinking, It'll go past the time when I must get up, and then it will be too late, and then, when it is too late, there will be nothing I can do, so I'll stay in bed. But I did get up in time and went to work.

I saw no one outside the language school.

My Panamanian student, towards whom my feelings were becoming more and more loving the less he was able to learn, brought me this composition:

About of Boquete
In this composition, I have to like in narrate about of a small town from Panama. Boquete is situate on a Volcano.
The End

José was missing his country very much, and as I asked him questions, tears rose to his eyes. Tears then rose to my eyes.

At those moments when I thought I would not be able to do anything, I found myself longing for Henry as if he were an age in which a culture had realized its highest ideals. And now what was left of that civilization was broken statues.

Charlie knocked on my door. He had a bottle of whiskey, which he put on the floor of my room. For a moment, I felt my sinuses begin to fill with tears. But when he stood with his arms out and said, "Let's forget about our responsibilities and have a good time," a rage went through me and burned the tears. It was as if the rage had been in me since the first time I'd seen Charlie, just seen him, when he came into the dormitory room where I was sitting on my assigned bed and wondering who my room-mate would be. He had startled me, clapping his hands and saying, "We're going to have a good time in this room." He gave me now the same smile he gave me then.

I had never been able to get Charlie to admit, not even for a moment, that anything was wrong. In our years as room-mates, some students asked me how I could stand him, he was so irresponsible, but for Charlie everything was fine. And I went along with him, and was even proud of him for insisting that everything was fine. After he did body exercises in our room that kept me from studying, he would say, sweating and leaning over my desk, "Isn't it great being room-mates?" and I would suppress my irritation, thinking his activity was more important than my stillness. Really, I should have been as positive as he was. When I'd gone out with him on dances, I'd tried to be like him, but I resented having to be. I resented him telling me what a good time I'd have, was having, had had. Now, it came to me as never before that he must see there was no way I was going to raise myself and have a good time with him, and I felt in my rage the strength to pull him down with me. We were not going to have a good time. It was exactly about responsibilities that I wanted to talk with him.

I turned away from Charlie and said flatly, "The only good time I can have is dead."

"Come on, Dan," he said.

I turned back to him. I knew that what Charlie found most unbearable was, as he would have said, locking feelings into grand gestures and grand words. His enthusiasms were demon-strated by a lilt in his voice and a clap on the shoulder, and no more. He was pretentious, but his pretentions were, really, modest, as if he thought he could get away with them. He would not allow himself the great pretentions, the great negations. These expressions more than embarrassed him, they frightened him. I wanted to frighten him.

I stared at him and, keeping my voice low, said, "You'd better get out of here before I knock you down, too."

He picked up the bottle and held it towards me. "Come on."

"I'm not going to get drunk."

Twisting off the cap, he said, "I will," and he took a gulp. He sat on the edge of the bed with the bottle between his knees.

I sat at my desk, the chair turned to half face him.

"Roberta sends her love," he said.

"Does she? I thought she finally recognized last time I saw her that I'm too low to be loved."

Charlie laughed and held out the bottle. "I'm not going to leave before you take that back, because you know it's not true."

Leaning far over, I took up the bottle, gulped from it, and held on to it by the neck. Wincing, I stared at Charlie. "You have never known what is true about me."

He reached for the bottle. "Come on, Dan," he said. But I remained motionless and Charlie lowered his arm.

"Give me the bottle, Dan," he said.

After another gulp from it, I gave him the bottle.

I said, "You'll be sorry you're making me drink."

Charlie laughed, but it was a forced laugh. I could see the crooked hairs of my brows above my narrowed eyes. Charlie put the bottle on the floor between us.

I said, "At the same time, I think you do know what's true about me, have known it for years, and you've never been able to admit it."

He laughed again. "Never been able to? I could have admitted it if I'd wanted, but I never wanted to."

I sat back in my chair.

"Let's forget this," Charlie said. "Let's just get drunk together."

I said, "No, I'm not going to forget it."

Charlie picked up the bottle and handed it to me. I stood, drank from it, handed it back to him, and walked up and down the side of the bed where he sat. I stopped in front of him.

"Admit it, then, admit it now."

"Dan –"

"Admit it."

"I was joking."

"You weren't joking."

"You know I'm always joking."

"Admit it."

"Dan, please, I came here to make up for last time. Maybe it was my fault, what happened, as much as Roberta's. I thought Roberta was forcing something, to tell you the truth, as I was – "

"You know it was my fault. You've come with a bottle of whiskey and a generous heart to forgive me my sins, though, in your generosity, you wouldn't want me to think you thought I'd sinned against you, you'd generously want me to think you'd sinned against me. You're so nice, Charlie."

"Dan, don't say anything you'll be sorry for. Once you put your feelings into words, you'll regret them. Don't – "

"I'll say anything I want." I flung up my arms. "I'll do anything I want."

"Dan – "

"The fact is, you want me drunk because you want to hear me say what I want. You like me to do what you can't do, make grand pronouncements, make grand gestures. You can't say what you want, ever. I know you. You want to know what I think about you, what I really think, that you hope I can only admit with the grandest words and gestures." I spread my legs and stretched out my arms wide, and I lifted my head. "Oh, you're so nice, Charlie."

He stood. His closeness to me surprised us both, and we stepped away from one another.

I said, "That's the grandest pronouncement I have to make about you: you're so nice."

"I'm not," he answered.

"You are."

In a low voice, he said, "I'd like you to think I am, I've always wanted you to think I am, but I'm not."

"I know you. You're such a clean cut, all American boy, you help old women and dogs, you say hello to the mailman, you can't think an unkind thought about your neighbor. You wouldn't even turn against someone who was trying to kill you, as I – "

"Dan, you don't know – "

"You don't have it in you to be bad."

He shut himself up, as though he didn't want to say what he was thinking. He drew in his chin and his neck bulged his collar. His eyes were large.

"I'm the bad one," I said, "and you know it. Admit it. Go ahead, admit it. You like being with me to see how un-nice a person can be, to hear someone else say everything you'd never allow yourself to say, because you know that what I'm saying is what you believe and would never admit you believe. You have a responsibility to tell the truth. Friends have a responsibility to tell the truth about their relationships."

Charlie said quietly, "Dan."

"The real reason why you came to see me," I said, "was because you wanted to see how un-nice I am."

His voice went high, like a woman's. "If you continue like this, I'll go. I don't want to leave you in a state like this. But I will."

"Go."

He turned round, as if searching for something, then he sat back on the bed.

I said, "Now admit to me what you've always hated about me."

Looking up at me, he licked his lips.

I leaned over him. "Admit it." I took the bottle from between his knees where he held it, drank, and gave it back to him. I said, "Tell me."

"I've always loved you."

"Tell me what, for years and years, you've found so unbearable about me you've wished I'd die from it."

His eyes, raised to mine, opened so all the blue irises showed.

"Tell me," I said.

"You wouldn't want to hear."

"Come on, come on," I said, "I can already see it in your eyes."

The muscles of his face tightened.

122

"In all the years of demands I've made on you," I said, "demands for more, much more, always more, than you wanted to give, you had to have had bad thoughts about me. When, at the lake, I – "

But I stopped when I saw Charlie's eyes focus now with anger. We had never mentioned what had happened between us at the lake perhaps because to bring it up was embarrassing. It gave significance to what now had little significance, and this, I knew, angered Charlie.

He said, "I hated, and hate, your jealousy."

I stood back.

"You're jealous of me, of me and Roberta, of me and Roberta and Jerry."

"Jealous," I said.

"You were when we were room-mates. You couldn't stand me talking in the shower with some of the guys while you were in our room. You were jealous of me and the guys. You were jealous of the entire college. There were times when I thought you were jealous of the whole city of Boston. There were times when I thought you were jealous of America."

I looked at the floor. After a while, I turned round to my desk and sat at it and looked at a piece of paper.

He got up from the bed and came to the desk, but stood behind me. "Let's not go on."

I looked at him over my sholder. He smiled and held out the bottle. I took it, drank, and handed it back. I was drunk. I stared again at the piece of paper on my desk while Charlie stood behind me.

I said, "Jealousy is the one notion I know I am sincere about."

In his silence, Charlie didn't deny this.

The telephone rang.

Turning to Charlie, I said, "That must be Roberta checking to find out if I've killed you."

"She wouldn't do that."

"You answer."

He picked up the telephone receiver, said, "Well hi, how are you? Yes, fine, really fine," and held out the receiver to me and said, "It's your friend Henry."

16

————— • —————

Henry's voice sounded thin over the telephone. He asked, "How's your work going?"

As I didn't know what he meant by my work, I answered, "All right. And yours?"

"I keep at it," he said.

"That's good."

He said, "I thought I'd take a break. I've been invited to a party tonight. I was told to take anyone I wanted, so I thought I'd ask you if you'd like to come."

I almost said, No, I can't tonight.

The nerves of my body seemed to expand suddenly so I felt myself become enormous, and out of control.

"I'd like to come."

After I hung up, that sense of an expanded self, with only the most delicate points of control within it, stayed with me. I was so little in control, Charlie could have said to me, You can't go to the party, and I would have submitted. I would have, in an almost completely detached way, done anything Charlie asked of me, but I waited for him, and wanted him, to tell me I must go.

Charlie said, "Do you want me to go home?"

"I won't be leaving till later. But I don't think you'll want to wait."

"Not really."

For a long while after he left, I felt lost, and walking around my room I bumped into furniture on my way to I was never quite sure where.

It was not the anticipation of seeing Henry that caused this effect on me, I realized, but my letting Charlie go.

Bumping into a door jamb, I thought, What have I done?

As I changed my clothes I considered carefully what I would wear, then decided I mustn't do this, and put back on the clothes I'd taken off.

I was thinking, What have I done to Charlie? while going downstairs to meet Henry.

I saw him standing by the car and I thought, I love him, as if the thought occurred for the first time, not in my mind, but in my body, and it gave to the body its impulse to make a great gesture. It was in me to make such gestures, and as I walked down the steps to him I imagined I was, inside, throwing myself from the last step to lie on the sidewalk before him. It was only when I felt my knees and elbows and my chin strike the cement that I knew I had given in to the impulse. The blood I tasted rising between my teeth was still more imaginary than real, but it was real enough for me to suck it back and swallow it. I reached for his legs and half wailed, "Ah." He quickly leaned over to put his hands under my arms to raise me, and when I was on my knees, he, too, got down on his knees to support me.

"Are you all right?" he asked again and again.

For a moment I leaned all my weight on him, and he was forced backwards trying to keep me up. My cheek pressed his. He drew his head further back to see me.

"Are you all right?"

I looked into his eyes and I felt that I made another wild gesture with my arms and legs and torso, all projected out through my eyes. His eyes went blank.

Pulling away from him, I said, "I'm all right."

"Are you sure?"

"Yes." I got to my feet. "I slipped."

He stood, too, but kept a hand on me to steady me.

Examining my trousers at the knees and my shirt at the elbows, I said, "They're not even torn."

He let me go and frowned.

"Honestly," I said, "I'm all right."

At the party I knew no one, and Henry didn't introduce me to anyone, not even the host. He stood with me to the side of a large room, half turned away from the crowd of men, and he talked to me. I kept telling myself that I should have been pleased that I was the only one he was attentive to, but I also told myself I was bored by Henry's talk, which was about what he'd been reading. I was pleased that he took me to be up to his talk, saying from time to time, "You'd understand this," but I wondered why he had come to a party to stand so at the edge of it that he was hardly there, and to talk about what had nothing to do with the party.

You would have had a better time if you'd stayed with Charlie, I heard myself say.

And yet Henry was standing next to me within reach. It didn't matter what he said as long as he was standing next to me. He was concerned about me and had decided to stay with me all evening. I stared at his lips as he spoke, and I wondered what he would do if, as I had an urge to do, I kissed him. I couldn't believe he hadn't kissed with those lips and made love with that body over and over again, simply because to do anything else but kiss and make love would have been a waste, would have been to deny the lips and body their nature. What a waste, I thought, what a waste. And then it came over me that Henry's sex did not tolerate his being kissed by, his making love with, men.

As though the awareness had come to him by some extra-visual sense, I saw him, with a quick shift of his eyes to their corners, glance at a young man standing alone and facing the room. I looked at the young man, long enough for Henry to see that I was, and when I looked back at Henry I smiled. He didn't smile.

Standing side by side, I felt I could talk with no sense of consequence, as if we were, say, room-mates at a college dance only interested in one another enough to talk for a while, however intimately, because there was no one else to talk to. For the moment, we could think of nothing to say to one another, and I asked:

"Have you ever had a close relationship with anyone?"

When I spoke, I realized that this was the most important talk we could have.

He said, "I've tried."

"I wonder if that's something you can't try for, but something that has to happen of itself."

"I think it has to be worked on."

"I see."

He looked over my head. "Though maybe you're right and I'm wrong. I like things to happen rather than make them happen."

Rising a little on my toes, I tried to look him in the eyes. I said, "I thought you were like that because of me."

He lowered his eyes to mine. "Why you?"

"Because you've got to be careful with me in case I interpret something you say or do to mean something it doesn't. I'm always interpreting what you say and do."

"Why should you do that?"

He looked over my head again. I left him to go to another part of the room to look for the young man. I couldn't find him, and looked back to see Henry, standing, as if by choice, on his own among people talking to one another. He seemed to be looking to the side at a wall. He put his hands to his face. I thought I was seeing him at a moment of desperation. I went back to him quickly. I wanted to get to him before he lowered his hands, as if what I had been shocked into doing was to help him at this moment. He lowered his hands. His face was set.

I said, "Do you want to go?"

Frowning a little, he said, "Go where?"

Perhaps, I'd seen the desperation in him because I wanted to see it. His set face was calm.

I stood silently beside him and we looked at the people about us.

With a little jerk towards him, I asked, "What moment with someone else do you most remember?"

He stared at me. Quietly, he said, "I was just thinking about that."

My pulse began to beat in my neck. "Were you?"

He continued to stare at me. "I was walking through woods in New Hampshire with a friend. He was playing a harmonica. That was all."

We could have gone on talking, I felt, in the way we were, both a little sad because of circumstances that had nothing to do with one another but which brought us close.

It seemed to me that he had, walking through the woods with his friend playing the harmonica, done more, with more passion, than I could ever do.

I remembered that at the hops I used to go to with Charlie I talked and talked to girls while the band played and others danced. Then, suddenly in a pause, the thought apparently not having come to me before, because our talk was so interesting and neither she nor I would really have wanted to do anything but stand and talk, I asked, "Oh, would you like to dance?" It was only in retrospect that you realized the girl was longing to dance. Now that I had grown up enough to deal with hops, I had no idea if the man next to me wanted to dance with me. Henry, for all his uncompromising sexuality, might repulse any man who got too close to him. And yet I said to him, "Wouldn't you like to dance?"

He smiled and said, "No, thanks."

I had taken a very weak drink, but even so my mind swung out. I told myself I mustn't drink more. My mind would swing very far, yanking me out with it, and, if it let me go, I had no idea what I would do.

A voice said, Let go.

No.

What I did next, I did with what I believed was total control. I thought, All right then, if this is the way I am, I'm going to act out of unforgivable, unrepentant jealousy. It gave me the control to say to Henry, "Then I'm going to go find someone to dance with."

He blinked.

"Do you mind?"

"No, of course not."

I went, to let him know what I could do, to the young man who was now on the other side of the room. His name was Tom. He must have been eighteen or nineteen. Talking a little to one another, I held him loosely in my arms. Then, with a sense of complete control, a control that seemed new to me, I brought the boy to Henry to introduce him. Henry shook his hand.

I said to Henry, "Wouldn't you like to dance with Tom?"

Henry drew his chin in as his eyes widened. It pleased me that he was angry. He couldn't have been angry enough with me.

"Wouldn't you both like drinks?" Henry asked.

"That's good of you," I said.

Henry left and I stood in silence with Tom, to whom I was not attracted. I thought Henry wouldn't come back. When he did, with one drink in one hand and two in the other, I felt my control deepen. He gave a glass to Tom, then one to me, and raised his own halfway between the boy and me before he drank.

He asked Tom, "Are you a student?"

"I'm a college sophomore."

"What are you studying?"

While Henry asked Tom questions which he answered in a disconnected way, I ran my finger round Tom's neck, under his collar, and drank with the other hand. I imagined Henry didn't like, and wouldn't allow himself, these intimacies between men.

You shouldn't be drinking, I told myself.

Henry drank quickly. He went for another, saying he'd be right back. Tom said he wanted to dance again; as much as I didn't want to, we put our glasses on a table and our arms around one another and we danced where we were. I didn't want Henry to come back and not see us holding one another.

Tom asked, "Are you lovers?"

"Henry?"

"I wondered. You look as if you are."

I said, "He's not my lover."

"Then I can say I don't like him," Tom said.

"Why?"

"He has to be as cold in bed as he is out."

"Cold?"

"Isn't he?"

"No," I answered.

I wanted to go to Henry and say, I understand, I know what you feel, and that admission, said with passionate commiseration for what I knew he endured, would have us weeping in one another's arms.

I pressed my nose, my brow, into Tom's cheek, and I felt my tears stream down between our faces. I hoped he would think it was sweat. He didn't. He pulled his head back and looked at me.

"What's wrong?"

"I shouldn't be drinking," I said.

You're losing control, I said to myself, you really are losing control.

I broke away from him and went to Henry.

"Do you want to go home?" I asked.

"Home?"

"I mean," I said, "do you want him?"

"I don't want him if you do."

"If he doesn't want you, I don't want him either." I was wiping my eyes with my palms.

"I don't know what you mean," he said.

He knew.

I said, "I can't ever think of you as being capable of doing anything silly. Maybe I should leave before I do."

"Silly?"

"Before I take home with me the boy you want."

Henry said, "That wouldn't be silly."

His arms akimbo, Tom was waiting for me. I held him around the waist with an arm and drank as we revolved. The more we revolved, the more he laughed. I didn't laugh.

What I will show Henry, I thought, is that I can let go. I will show him that I do, always do, what I want. If I wanted to let go, no one would stop me. All that mattered to me now was that he should be watching me.

I was going to do something I had never done before, and I didn't know what was going to be revealed to me when I did it. I took Tom's glass from him and put it, with mine, on a table, and

130

as we continued to revolve, now in the center of the room, so people had to move out of the way, I began to unbutton his shirt, and he, laughing, unbuckled my belt. We lurched a lot as we undressed one another in a space now made into a circle by people watching. What was revealed to me was this: that my self-consciousness, at what should have been its apogee, left me. As Tom pulled my trousers down, I stepped out of them, then stepped out of the underpants he pulled down. I held up a foot for him to pull off my sock, and almost fell backwards, which had the crowd around us shouting, but I knew that the most embarrassing act I could commit among them would not embarrass me. And what I was doing concerned me as little as our being watched. My only point of reference was Henry. I didn't care if he hated what I was doing. Maybe I even wanted him to hate it. Tom stood, the hand with sperm covered fingers held out, as if to give it to someone. He smeared it over my chest and stomach.

Henry had left. Not even collecting our clothes and dressing made me feel anything except that I'd done something I wanted to do. I had made Henry go. A man, who turned out to be the host, came toward Tom and me carrying two fizzing high-ball glasses which he gave to us, then, slapping us on our backs, he said, "You're all right, you're really all right." I drank, thinking there was nothing else I would do if I got drunker. While I talked to the host, Tom walked away.

17

———•———

Henry had seen my sins. There was no way I could wipe out those sins, because there was no way I could make him not see them. If my sins were those that my romantic agony aspired to – the great sins – I would perhaps have been proud of Henry's seeing them in me. But, instead, they were the sins for which there was no forgiveness because they were not important, not even interesting, enough to be forgiven. What had happened was that Henry had seen my sins and ceased to be interested in me. I had done nothing by my act of jealousy but bring on Henry's condemnation. For two days, then another, I lived under the condemnation.

There were moments when I enjoyed this feeling of unworthiness.

When, kneeling for a long while in the center of my room, my arms hanging by my sides, my head bent, swaying a little, I felt that I was about to be justly punished for being an incompetent, a kind of shocked awareness of my humiliating submission made me get to my feet quickly. I told myself I must never, ever, do that again.

And yet I wanted to live on risk. My life should be made up of risks, one after another, leading me further and further into what I could not imagine, and wanted to imagine.

The greatest risks for me were not the risks of madness or suicide – I knew I was nowhere near going crazy or killing myself, however much I may have fantasized about these – but of pretension and self-indulgence. I knew I must risk these in loving, because without them I couldn't love.

I knew that the greatest risk I had to take was to call Henry and ask him to let me see him. I did not enjoy the humiliation I felt in dialing his number at work. His voice was cold. I tried to keep any supplication out of my own voice.

"I'll meet you anywhere you want. I'll meet you at the library if you'd like, and go along with you on your way home so I won't take up any of your time."

He said, "You'd better come to my home, about 10:30."

"I'll stay only fifteen minutes."

I could make myself telephone Henry, but I couldn't make myself telephone Charlie.

As I walked across the Public Garden, I felt better, and as I was climbing Beacon Hill, I felt so much better I thought that I didn't need to be going to see Henry, that, even without seeing him, I would have got over my love for him.

Following him into his small living room, I thought: The only risk I was taking was of being foolish, and that would be much less foolish than he had already observed me to be. In the hot room he was sweating. Sweating too, I said, "I want to tell you, as a simple statement, that I love you."

He said, "I should have told you when I met you that I was just getting over a bad relationship with someone who used to live here with me. It's weak of me, but I couldn't take on another relationship. There's nothing I admire more than close relationships, but I don't feel I'm up to one."

I sat on the edge of the sofa. "You don't understand. I don't want a close relationship with you. I don't even want to see you." I said, "I've become possessed by an idea of you that I think doesn't have anything to do with you." I put a hand to my head. "And yet, I think it must have everything to do with you."

He said, "I'm sure it doesn't have anything to do with me."

"Don't say that."

"You don't know me, so how can it have anything to do with me?"

"It sometimes seems to me that in carrying around the notion of this most beautiful person – you – I'm carrying around the most perfect and lucid idea a man can have. My mind is a closed room containing this amazing picture. But what should be wonderful isn't. I don't know why it isn't, but it isn't. It's horrible." I dropped my hands.

Wincing a little, he said, "I'll help you break it."

I said, "I don't want that." I got up.

"I can do it."

"I should go. I've been here longer than I said I would."

"You can stay."

When he put his hand on my arm, as if to hold me back, I pulled away. I left quickly.

My students frowned at me when I tried to explain simple points of grammar. Maybe, I thought, I wasn't saying what I thought I was.

Mrs. Hart told me I should go away for the weekend.

Instead, I called Charlie and went to see him and Roberta. None of us mentioned Henry. I studied them to make out the terms of their relationship.

18

———— • ————

I went to different bars in Boston, and one night met Tom O'Neill, who came back to my room with me. In the midst of our love making, I felt my chest seem to expand out towards him with love so sudden it surprised me. I didn't want to feel such love for anyone but Henry, and I tried to hold it in, but it went out to this young man, as if it were reaching out, with a little muscular spasm, for almost anyone. I didn't understand. Tom was in fact more beautiful then Henry. But his naked body appeared to me a pretence, and as a pretence it was ugly. The very shape of the body struck me as ugly, and I wondered how people could be attracted to one another for their bodies. I pretended to fall asleep. He fell asleep before me.

Sunday, we went to the Museum of Fine Arts. He was not interested, however, not even in the statue of the nude torso of the boy I took him to see. Later, we walked through the Fens, looking, as he said he liked to do, at people.

During the weekday evenings, I read novels. I had told my Panamanian student he should read books to improve his English. "What books?" he asked. "Try novels," I said. He looked at me with an expression of high disapproval and answered, "On, no, not novels." To him, novels, if not exactly immoral, did not add to one's moral vision and were a waste of time. For me, to read a novel was to improve one's moral vision, but this attitude was, I realized, unfounded. Novels added, perhaps, to one's understanding, but not to one's faith. José struggled through a few of the *Lives of the Saints*, which he said he had found in a Catholic bookshop. His English, after all my work, was no better at the end of the summer, when he returned to Boquete. I read many novels.

With Tom, on Friday and Saturday nights, I went to movies or to restaurants, then we separated for the night. If he telephoned at the last minute to break a date, I didn't mind. I thought I should start a friendship with Tom which would be based on an understanding that we were free, and that we would come together only at those points on which we agreed. Our relationship would be open to all possibilities because it would be open to everything around us, for no symbolic system would be imposed on it and reduce it to responsibilities towards one another. It seemed to me that two men did not have duties towards one another.

Roberta came to see me. It was as if Henry had never occurred in our relationship. She lay by me on my bed, each of us propped up by a pillow, and we ate sandwiches and drank frappes. She stayed on and on, until she finally said, "Charlie will think I've left him." Then she said, "He gives me reason enough to want to."

I didn't wish to talk about Charlie, but I said, "I can't imagine Charlie doing anything that'd make anyone want to leave him."

"You don't know Charlie."

"Yes, I do."

"Charlie would never show you, or any man, sides of himself that he shows me." After a silence, she said, "But let's not talk about Charlie. Let's not talk about relationships. We were having such an interesting conversation before."

"Yes," I said.

"Anyway, you never want to talk about relationships. To get you to talk of your thoughts and feelings about others is like trying to get Jerry to talk."

After she left, her smell remained about the bed, and on the pillow were strands of her blond hair. I thought I would be able to sleep.

One weekend morning while I was cleaning my room, Roberta telephoned and, in a high voice, asked if she could come see me right away. I was a little worried that she was coming to see me too often. Though I was going to stay in, I wanted to keep my day free, as I wanted, I told myself, to keep my life free.

As I was closing the door behind her, she said, "I've got to leave Charlie. I've got to." She sat at my desk and I on the edge of my bed. A hand raised to her temple, she said, "I can take his irresponsibilities. In a way, I'm even amused by them, but I can't take his fits – "

"Fits?" I asked.

"You don't know? You've never seen Charlie angry?"

"No."

"That's not possible."

"I never have."

She said, "Just last night, he threatened to burn the house down."

"Charlie?"

"I ran out of the house with Jerry, got into the car and drove to Charlie's parents' house and spent the night there."

I stood.

Roberta said, "I'm not sure whether I have a house to go back to, or a pile of charred ruins."

"I don't understand," I said.

"No?"

"Will you call him," Roberta asked, "just to find out if the house is still there?"

She got up from the desk chair to let me sit before the telephone.

Charlie's "Hello" was sullen, but when he heard my voice his changed, and he said, "Hey, hi."

I told him I was getting in touch just to find out how everyone was and I hoped I'd see him soon.

"What about tonight?" he asked. "What about going out and doing something together?"

I couldn't, I said; I had a stack of students' essays to correct.

"You sound all right," he said.

I was, I answered.

"It's always great to hear from you," he said.

"And Roberta and Jerry are well?" I asked.

"Very well," he said with a lilt. "We're all very well."

I hung up.

Roberta was leaning a thigh against the desk. "What do you think?" she asked. "Should I go back to him or not?"

"How can I say?"

She thrust herself away from the desk and walked about the large room. "Every possible reason is against it." As she continued to walk about the room, I watched her. Her hair, in one long blond braid at her nape, was pulled back from her finely angled face. "Tell me what we should do," she said to me.

"I'm not sure I can."

"You have so much influence over Charlie." She stopped in front of me. "You have so much influence over me."

"I do?"

"Over us both," she said. "You won't talk about relationships, I know. That's not what I mean. I mean being with you makes a difference to us."

I asked, "What difference?"

"Come with me now," she said. "Come on now, and we'll see Charlie together. I know you don't want to, but it'd mean a lot to me if you did."

I felt it was wrong that Roberta was asking something of me.

She said, in her car, "I'd like to go off now and, say, play pinball machines in some cheap bar."

As I didn't want to go to her apartment, I said, "Why don't we?"

"Do you know a place where we could play?"

"Yes."

"Where?"

"In the bar I go to, near the bus station."

Roberta laughed. The sunlight through the windscreen made all the hairs that had come loose from her braid shine. She asked, "Have you ever been in love?"

"No," I answered.

She gave me the key and asked me to go into the apartment ahead of her. As I opened the door, I saw Charlie, in an armchair in the living room, drawing on a large sketch-book flat on his knees; he looked up, his expression unlike any I had seen on his face, twisted, but when he saw me his face went blank. Roberta was behind me.

I said to him, "Roberta and I are going to go out to play pinball, and we wondered if you'd like to join us."

"Where's Jerry?" Charlie asked Roberta.

"With your parents."

He looked back at me, waiting for me to say more.

"Well, come on," I said, "let's go."

We went into downtown Boston to a little upstairs restaurant for lunch. We sat at a table by a window which gave on to a big tree. Roberta and Charlie were silent towards one another, so I did all the talking. Often, not knowing what else to talk about, I went on about what was happening in Boston. Finally, we were silent.

I said, "Have you ever wondered about the crazy relationships among the Holy Family?"

"You've brought that up before," Roberta said.

I said, "I'd like to know some reason why their relationships are held up to us as an example."

"I know," Charlie said.

Roberta said to him, "Now you're going to make one of your funny observations."

"I'll try to make it funny. I suppose we need a laugh."

"Tell me," I said to him.

"It makes sense to have over us examples of a world that makes no sense," he said, "so that we don't expect our world to make sense. And yet, however nonsensical all the relationships of the Holy Family are, we know that they have great love for one another, they up there, and they are models for us down here to love one another as greatly as they do. What we learn from them is that love has to be irrational."

Roberta said, "Don't count too much on that."

On the way back to their apartment, we stopped to pick up Jerry.

19

———— • ————

I knew some definite change had turned me around inside when, alone in the museum one free afternoon, I stopped before that torso of a boy on a black plinth which I had studied as a student, and I saw it as standing above the world, beyond anyone's individual and jealous attempt to possess it.

If ever I wrote a novel, I thought, it would have to be saved, if it was in any way worthy of being saved, by something occurring in it which had nothing to do with me. Anything moral in my writing would have nothing to do with me. It is absolutely true, I thought, that the greatest works of art are those created not for men but for God, whose ambition is that humankind should be one in its love for God.

As I was walking through the Fens, I heard a voice say: "Call Henry."

In a telephone booth that smelled of urine, I called his work number at the library and was told that he was at home. I was reluctant to call him there, because I might be disturbing him; but I felt generous, and it was as if I would, by calling him, show him how generous I was.

His not answering made grey feelings come back which I thought had gone.

He answered.

I said, "I hope I'm not disturbing you."

He asked me to come over.

The sunlight was horizontal, and Boston appeared to extend sideways in long, narrow shadows.

Henry answered the door in his bathrobe. He was unshaven, his hair messed, and his skin was moist.

"I've got a fever," he said.

As I followed him into his bedroom, which I had thought I would never enter again, I imagined I was returning after a long trip to a place which amazed me for existing, never mind existing unchanged. I was surprised that the same carpet was by the bed, the same lamp on the bedside table.

Then Henry did this most remarkable thing: he took off his bathrobe and stood naked for a moment before he threw it onto a chair and got into his bed. What struck me about his pale body was how devoid of sex it was. He pulled the sheet over his chest.

As I watched him, I thought that the feelings coming over me couldn't have to do with sex, though with some desire.

Sitting back to watch him more closely in a moment of silence, I felt, with a sudden outbreak of sweat, all my love for Henry come back to me as if it had never gone.

Henry was ill, but he was not going to die. My longing was for him to die, my longing was to lie down by him and hold him dead. My chest heaved for the hopelessness I felt towards such a pleasure, which was the pleasure I imagined of sitting on a fallen pillar in a destroyed city, weeping for such destruction. I must, I thought, accept that the pleasure of destruction was the only pleasure allowed me, and for that pleasure I became an altogether destructive person. The more I wanted to see Henry dead the more I felt my love for him.

His lips parched, he said, "I feel so hot."

"Shouldn't you see a doctor?" I asked.

"I'll be all right. It's just the grippe."

"Is there anything I can do?"

"I wondered if you could go out and get me some aspirin. I don't have any."

"You don't take care of yourself," I said.

On my way to the drugstore, I thought my desire to see Henry dead was a fantasy I had affected because I could only trust myself to love someone dead. I bought the aspirin, and returning up the hill thought my desire for Henry was something else, perhaps worse, than to see him dead. I had not gone as far as was possible in my desire for him.

He'd given me the key and I let myself into his apartment. It was odd that Henry didn't have anyone else in his life but me who would go buy him aspirin.

In the kitchen, I filled a glass with water. I didn't want to go in to him, as if I was worried what feelings he would finally reveal to me there. For the moment, my feeling was that he had used me by sending me for the aspirin. But this feeling was just to block my anticipation of the other feelings that were waiting for me in his room. It was as if not only he, but others were waiting for me, and I couldn't imagine who they were. They had come unexpectedly.

But when I held the aspirin out to him with a glass of water and he swallowed them down with gulps, I felt a kind of pity for him. I sat in a chair by his bed.

He said, "The worst part is that I haven't been able to work."

The work he was so keen on wasn't his library job, I was sure. I didn't know what it was, and I felt I couldn't ask, but only mention it, in all seriousness, as his work. He was probably writing a book, and I wondered if he assumed I was, too, whenever he asked about my work.

He raised a hand. His voice was hoarse. "I'm not sure it matters."

"It matters."

His head raised by two pillows, he looked into the air for a moment, then at me. "What've you been up to?"

I smiled but I didn't say anything.

Then Henry, licking his lips, raised himself on his arms, perhaps to cool himself, and the damp sheets fell away from his chest and thighs, so, again, I saw his body, and I knew that my desire, which, because I must think the worst about myself, I had imagined was the desire to see the end of Henry, was not a desire at all, but a great fear. I was frightened that I would never again see Henry; it was not he who would die in himself, but would die in me. I couldn't let that happen. But, in the presence of his sick body, the fantasy was not strong enough to make him glow with health, so he fell back into his sheets and his body repelled me. If there was any desire in this fear, it was only the desire to leave.

I said, shifting in the chair, "Maybe you want to sleep."

"No," he said.

I couldn't say anything. To see him as he was now was to see, not only his body, but everything promised by his body destroyed. He was a young man not much different from me. I could not accept the revelation.

What was happening to that body, come from outside the world and standing above the world, which the world loved?

When I thought, What could he have meant to me? I got up from my chair.

He wasn't going to hold me, because, I recognized, he never tried to hold anyone against his wishes. But he said, "You just got here."

"I've got to go."

He didn't ask me why I'd called him. If he had, I wouldn't have been able to answer.

20

———— • ————

In my room, I took off my shoes and a sock. One sock on, I walked about the room hitting the edges of the furniture with the other.

I had always, I thought, prayed for a presence to appear to me – a presence so abstract it had no qualities, and all my efforts would be to give it qualities. I had always hoped to bring down spirit into matter. What I knew I couldn't do was to force spirit up from matter. I wanted to start with everything, and work to make something. It wasn't in me to start with something and make it everything, and yet this was what I must do if I was to have what I needed to live.

But everything I created embarrassed me. Against my embarrassment, I would have to contrive something, to make it stand above my embarrassment and, if nothing more, shock. At the risk of being cruel, so as not to make a joke of myself, I must try to imagine a presence which could do anything – which could be, with the darkest intentions, cruel, and never joke, and could incise with a knife the skin of a naked body, then cut deeper into the flesh and open the wounds to the bone, then, to cause the most pain, insert burning thorns into the wounds. I stopped this fantasy, but thought the only real creativity was to create pain, which couldn't be falsified. I shook my head.

I had to believe that what I wanted was not false, and, as only I could give it to myself, how could I make it not false? If what I wanted was belief, how could I have it except by bringing it out of myself?

If what I wanted was faith, I must recognize that the highest abstractions were acts of will, that the most elusive faith had to be worked for, and belief in God came from making oneself believe in God. Then I thought this wasn't true, and what was true was that the highest abstractions of thought simply occurred of themselves, that faith simply occurred, that faith in God simply occurred.

All my contradictory observations seemed uninteresting to me. What was impossible was uninteresting.

I fell on my bed.

I was taken up by a presence that came down to me and picked me up.

Images from my love making with Henry came to me, image after image, of him bright in his amazing beauty. These images came from beyond my inability to create such images. They filled me with joy.

Then I saw in his eyes when he looked at me that he wasn't making love with me, but struggling with me. He hadn't come down to make love with me. He had come to dispossess me of my continuing love for him, to dispossess me of all the images of love making. His eyes were blank. He could do it; he could remove himself entirely from me; he could do anything. But I was not going to let him do this.

Even if he had come down to save me from what we both knew was a meaningless possession, and which it should give me pleasure to see destroyed, I would not let him do it. I would turn the struggle with him into love making, and I would make our love making meaningful. Henry was trying to lift from me the stark image of himself. I restrained him. His forehead furrowed and his eyes filled with tears. He didn't want me to suffer this image. I held on to him, trying to hold his arms as they went through me, trying to kiss his face as it went into mine. I would not let go.

"Let go," he said quietly.

I turned him over and over on the bed, struggling with him.

If what I was struggling for was faith, I had not even reconciled in myself how that faith was to be achieved, through my own will or a vast will-lessness. I would never reconcile these. I was struggling both to overcome and to be overcome, and in doing this I was struggling for the realization of my greatest desire, for belief.

There were meanings, there were meanings, there were. The image of Henry meant, had to mean, for the overwhelmingly simple fact of my being aware of it, more than I could say. I loved it.

How could the very person who revealed faith to me destroy it? That couldn't be. How could he, any less than I, not want everything, because only in everything could we be whole. How could he not want to go with me again as far as we'd gone, again and forever? If he gave in, we would go there, turning and turning about one another, our struggle the struggle to go further. It was only with him that I could have what I needed, and he would not take it from me.

When I forced my mind to concentrate, precisely, on his face, his arm, his thigh, I saw less and less. I saw nothing.

I retained only the sense of everything, without any particular sense, and this was embodied abstractly as nothing but a great need. I needed to have happen again what had happened, and I needed it because it was general, because only the general promised. But that sense was so general, perhaps I would not have it even if I did make love with Henry again, because it no longer had anything to do with our love making. If my senses at their most acute in making love could not give it to me, I could only imagine it existed by an act of faith. I know it did exist, because it had changed me into someone essentially different from the person I had been. That was what I could not believe would never happen again. I had to believe I could be made different, by nothing more than someone touching me or looking at me or saying a word to me. This wouldn't happen. But it would happen. I was not different. But I was different.

I imagined shouting out.

I would not let everything go. Because my love for Henry was irrelevant to the world, it was only by meaning more than the world that it had meaning at all. He meant everything to me, he

146

had to mean everything, and my faith in the idea of such meaning was all the faith I had. Here was the moment for me to make an act of faith, an act that would realize, in a flash, what was so near. And I could make it, it was in me to make it, as it was in me to do everything. I could, I could. I could destroy. I could make. I could now, with faith, do what I had imagined was impossible. I could believe that every thought I had about another person was an expression of universal love.

A total sense of absurdity was my blessing. I would not let myself be destroyed by the absurdity. That would be my act of will; to refuse to give up everything because it is ridiculous. No. But the fact that my desire for faith should be inspired by a neurotic obsession for someone I could not have, made that desire neurotic, too. It did not refer to anything outside itself, and any attempt to make it refer to what was outside only made the desire more ridiculous, more and more ridiculous. No. The desire did have relevance outside itself, it did. It was not ridiculous. But I couldn't give relevance to it myself; someone else must do this for me. I could do it on my own; I could make it happen. I couldn't. It could only happen by being made to happen by another. It could only happen beyond my intention to have it happen. And it wouldn't happen. It would. I would make it happen. I would realize my faith by the strongest act of will. It was in me to be that strong. But then it wasn't, and something stronger than my will had to sustain the faith. No, I would have belief. I could believe, I could, but why would I not allow myself to?

I must get Henry to be aware as I was aware, I must get him to see that our true natures were more than human, that we could have everything, if we believed we could. He must love, as I loved, what we'd known in making love.

He must at least allow me the image of him I carried around with me with so much adoration that I could not sleep, or ever be really awake.

But Henry's most convincing reason for my not loving the image was that it would never perform the miracle I hopelessly expected of it, because it did not refer to anything. For an image

147

to be real, it must reveal a need beyond ours, in which alone our need could be satisfied. It must reveal everything. I must destroy images, all, which came from me as an effort to realize my need.

Henry told me no image was going to come to me, no apparition, from beyond imagination. No images, ever, had come from afar and revealed what was beyond imagination, but came, everywhere, from the selfish imaginations of the people who had created them to realize their human desires. These images were not real because they referred only to such human desires. All images were false, and all images in the world should be destroyed.

My mind, suddenly unable to think, stopped for a moment, and Henry, wrapped in a sheet and holding something in his folded arms, left me.

He left me with a desire for faith that was impossible, one that pulled my skin, my hair, with the demand to be made possible, to be realized immediately. There was nothing I could do but ask myself where such desire came from. Where did such awareness, never to be fulfilled, come from? Why was there such a sense of promise in us, if the promise would never be kept? Why should we so want what we knew we would never get?

My mind searched for something to center on. Irrelevancies came to me, if they were irrelevancies. Maybe they were essentials. I had no more clean socks. It could be that my faith would be revealed to me by attending to my socks.

What survives the most extreme self-consciousness, I wondered? What survives the self-consciousness that makes you say of yourself, even at the highest moment of love making, "Fool, fool," for even presuming for the moment that you could rise above yourself? Does anything survive the derision of such moments? And what is the result of such derision but a hard determination to survive, at least, your self-condemnation as a fool? You think, All right, I'm a fool, and you live by some intention to live, and the intention is not to justify yourself in your own eyes or anyone else's, but simply to bear the condemnation. What adds to the depth of the condemnation is that you know you have exaggerated it, and that it is only a perversion of the self-centeredness you want to have all rights to. Your great exaggeration makes you a fool on a minor scale. So you tell yourself, All right, all right, I've got to stand myself as a minor fool. This takes more determination than if you were a major fool. And how can you not, with such intention, become an artificial person? You listen to the way you speak and, no matter how neutral you try to make your speech, eliminating what strikes you as affected, it still sounds affected, as much to others, you're sure, as to yourself. You want what is unintentional. That is why you long – in ways, passionately – for those states of mind which are undefined and cannot be intended. That sense of intention itself, that abstract and yet distinct state of mind before you contrive the intention – you like to ask yourself what it is. And the more abstract the sense is the more you are drawn to it for occurring unintentionally, as a sudden blessing. But you can't even allow yourself to pray for the blessing, which will make you an altogether different person, because you can't bless yourself. You can't make yourself a different person; you can only make yourself a more artificial person, you can only ever make yourself more of a fool. You want deliverance from yourself, you want those visitations upon yourself when you're made natural. What survives the extremest derision is the passion to be natural, to be pure. What survives is the most acute apprehension of those moments, just before you destroy them, when all your apprehension shifts, and you know it is possible to be other than what you are. You hate what you are, and at the same time you don't hate, because you know that your apprehension of another is wonderful. You will destroy it. Of course you will. You try to sustain some faith in it after it is gone, but you can't. The faith itself becomes an intention, and you know how false your intentions are. What accounts for such visitations, though? You have no idea, except that you have this idea: that they come to you, only for a moment, because you are aware, and you know that they will come to you with greater and greater force the more aware you are, aware of the ocean curving over the horizon, of mountain ranges, of cities at the mouths of rivers, of men farming the flat lands, of women in country shops, of young men wandering in woods, of young women swimming in green ponds, of people in cities walking the pavements and calling to one another across streets, of people in their houses eating, sleeping, making love on sheet-rumpled beds, of rugs, tables and chairs, cups and plates, mirrors, rolls of string, calendars, pencils, vases of flowers, of the world's soul itself from which the world's being is derived. All this happens in a moment. What survives self-consciousness, if anything survives, is the desire for those moments that can't be derided as false. It is a longing for the illuminating idea that precedes all thought, and perhaps all feeling – an idea that we know is the center of all true thinking and feeling. As a totally intentional person, your greatest intention is to keep yourself open to such ideas, to take such risks. Nothing will enter. But it will. Everything will enter.

Though it was after two o'clock in the morning, I dressed and went out. I walked conspicuously along the curb in the light of the street lamps. When I crossed over into the dark Public Garden, I stayed in the light to be seen, as though to let anyone who might be looking know that I was just out for a walk. There couldn't have been anyone else in the still garden to look at me, unless they, in the shadows of the trees, were still.

I wished I had drawn blood from Henry, just a little, then drawn blood from the same part of my body, from our arms or chests, and pressed his blood into mine.

Nothing was left, I thought, of our having made love.

Walking now across the Common, I imagined I saw people standing among a clump of trees.

A moist wind began to blow over the Common. Walking in the wind, I imagined I was in a place that had once been Boston. Natives from outside the city had killed everyone and burned the wooden buildings, so the city was reduced to fields and to dark woods shaking in the sea gusts.

I was following a path through the woods. In them, I expected to be met, to be taken where I had never been, and there I would undergo a conversion, one that would make me so different from what I was that it had to be beyond anything I could intend, anything I could imagine. Did I suddenly make an act of faith that such a conversion was possible? Did I?

Back in my room, I lay on the floor. I thought I lay for a long time, but when I looked at my watch I saw it was minutes. I thought, Well, you can't lie here forever, and I got up and undressed. In my bathroom, I washed socks in the washbasin. I rubbed a sock between my knuckles.

From my bed, I switched off the lamp on the side table. The room seemed large, and I lay as thoughtless as I was motionless. I imagined I heard someone in the room, heard a movement or a voice. A thrill spread over the surface of my skin. I looked out and listened. There was someone in the room, and, if I waited, he would come just close enough to the bed for me to see him in the dark.

DAVID PLANTE was born in Providence, Rhode Island, in 1940. He is the author of several novels—including the Francoeur Trilogy (*The Family, The Country,* and *The Woods*) and *The Foreigner*—and one work of nonfiction, *Difficult Women.* He has been the recipient of a Guggenheim Fellowship and an Award in Literature from the American Academy and Institute of Arts and Letters. David Plante was Writer in Residence at King's College, Cambridge, 1984–85. A regular contributor to *The New Yorker,* he lives in London.